THE ENCHANTER'S REVENGE

Phillip L. Ramsay

THE ENCHANTER'S REVENGE

Fiction4All

DEDICATION

So many people have been kind enough to urge me to publish the sequel to '*The Enchanter's Torment*' that it is impossible to thank them all individually. However, I would like to thank especially the following people: Alex, Lucinda, Marcy, Lisa, Beccs, and Samantha. Especial thanks to my long-suffering wife, Gail, and to Mary, my favouritest Mother-in-Law.

Thanks, too, to everyone else who has helped me. Without all of your help and input, this novel could not have been edited, revised, rewritten and completed.

Phill Ramsay, May 2015.

PROLOGUE

The night was clear and cold. High in the sky the stars twinkled and the moon cast its insipid white light upon the Earth. The temperature had fallen well below zero, ensuring that only those whose journey was an absolute necessity travelled this night.

Three men, seemingly impervious to the cold, approached an impressive office block. In silence, they approached the glass doors fronting the building. Although the entrance was locked, the man leading the trio opened the door with apparent ease. The other two followed their leader into the carpeted reception area. A bored-looking security guard sat behind a desk, reading a magazine.

He didn't look up as the men filed past him, seemed totally unaware of their presence. The men approached the lift, and having entered it, took it to the executive suite.

The lift whined quietly as it carried them past countless floors, before drawing smoothly to a halt and opening its doors.

With the same assurance which they had manifested from the time they had entered the building, the men left the lift. They looked around them, seeing two passages leading off to the left and right.

A second security guard wandered in their direction from the corridor to their right, seemingly more alert than his colleague on the ground floor. He glanced suspiciously at the lift as its doors closed. He looked around to the passage leading to the left. His suspicions obviously aroused, he made his way to a desk opposite the lift and reached for the telephone.

"No," the leader of the trio hissed sharply: "sleep."

The guard wavered on his feet and then crumpled to the floor. The leader motioned to his colleagues. Silently, they interpreted his gesture. They moved forward to the now deeply-sleeping guard and lifted him into a chair situated behind the desk.

"Which way?" queried one, softly.

The leader indicated the corridor from which the guard had

emerged. Their direction decided, they resumed their journey until, at the end of the corridor, they reached a door.

Opening this, they entered a large office with another door leading off it. As they crossed the office and approached this second door, the murmur of muted voices could be heard. The leader raised his hand in a warning gesture. Softly, he hissed, "let us listen for a while, before announcing ourselves."

The other two nodded understanding. Listening carefully, they managed to overhear what was being said in the next room.

"....and so he was able to manipulate Congress into granting the concession which we needed. But this has brought another problem to my attention. The Mafia families are becoming interested in this particular operation. I expect them to attempt a take-over with their usual directness. I have ensured, however, that they will be sorry they ever considered the attempt. We have had problems with them before, but each time, they learn that attempting to move in on us is not possible — and *may* be fatal. Unless you have any further questions, or require clarification on this matter, Superior Brother, I have nothing else to report."

"Your report is satisfactory, Brother," replied a voice with a strong American accent. It continued, "Brother Andrew, what do you have to report to this preliminary gathering?"

There was a pause, presumably whilst the person in question stood. Then a voice with a distinctly Irish accent spoke. "All goes well. I have finalised details with the I.R.A., and we will begin selling shipments of arms and explosives within the next few months. As previously, I urge that I be allowed to proceed at my own pace. The F.B.I. and C.I.A. will be quick to pick up on any loose end. An operation of this magnitude demands caution and meticulous planning, and that takes time. If we proceed carefully we will reap massive benefits. The I.R.A. have contacts in many countries, and we may well be able to utilise them once we have demonstrated that we can deliver what we have promised."

There was another silence whilst this speech was digested. The Superior Brother's voice became audible again, although it had dropped considerably in volume. "I agree, Brother. Take your time — but be sure that you achieve results."

8

"I will, Superior Brother," the Irish voice replied firmly.

The three men grinned at each other. The leader smiled a frigid smile at his two companions; they smiled in return. After six months in America, they felt as though they were coming home.

The leader returned his attention to the voices issuing from behind the door. Apparently, all business of importance had been discussed, and the Superior Brother was speaking.

"It appears that all is well. This same information must be related before all Brothers at our next General meeting, as usual. Before I dissolve this preliminary meeting, as is customary, I ask for any ideas from you all for schemes or anything else which might further our objectives. Anything at all?"

Silence descended. Outside, the three grinned at each other, remembering how similar requests had occasioned just such responses, in days past. The Superior Brother's voice resumed, "No one?" Then, in a more impatient tone, he continued, "Well, in that case, I suggest that you think about your resp...." his voice trailed off, suggesting that his tirade had been interrupted.

"It seems that one person, at least, wishes to present an idea to us. Be good enough to give us your thoughts, Sister."

The leader of the three men made a strangled sound in his throat. He turned furious eyes upon his companions. "Did I hear correctly?" be demanded in a whisper.

Cautiously, his two companions nodded confirmation.

The leader frowned and straightened up. His eyes seemed almost to be ice within their sockets. From within the room, a woman's voice could be heard.

".....and so, it is known to us that the Defence Secretary has certain erm... *unusual* sexual preferences. All I suggest is that it would be relatively simple for us to exploit the knowledge. Some photographs, blackmail, and we could get hold of *very* sensitive information from his Department."

For a few seconds there was silence whilst what she had said was considered.

"Sister Margaret, thank you for the idea. It has lots of potential. I will give some thought to how best to pursue this matter. Would you be willing to undertake this mission yourself, sometime in the future?"

"I would, Superior Brother," she replied.

"Are there any other ideas? Any final matters needing attention?" the Superior Brother queried.

Behind the door, fury radiated from the man with ice-cold eyes. His two companions, recognising the danger signals, exchanged wary glances, each silently warning the other not to get in their leader's way.

"I think," their leader snapped in a frigid whisper, "that *that* was our cue."

Suiting action to word, he motioned towards the door which burst open with a bang, as though violently assaulted, making all within the room jump.

The leader strode in, closely followed by his associates. A long table dominated the conference room which they had entered. Seated around it were approximately thirty people, of whom seven were women. Several had risen to their feet in consternation at the nature of the interruption.

However, the man at the head of the table remained seated, although he glared darkly at the trio. "How did you get in here? How did you get past security? This is a private Board meeting."

The leader of the trio turned his eyes upon the man, who fell silent.

"I will answer your questions," he rasped. "Firstly, through the outer door. Secondly, security didn't see us. Wouldn't you say that this is a rather unorthodox Board meeting?"

The man at the head of the table pondered this statement silently. "So," he said, finally, "a visit from the Mafia. Well, you can tell your superiors this. . ."

"Not the Mafia," replied the leader of the trio, his expression becoming more dangerous as he attempted to bite down his rage at the presence of women.

"Then..." said the Superior Brother, and quickly pointed directly at the man who opposed him. A burst of orange light exploded in the intruders' direction. As it reached them, it dissolved. The Superior Brother opened his mouth in surprise. What had just happened was impossible.

"Kill them quickly," hissed a sharp female voice.

"You may find that easier *said* than *done*," replied the icy voice of the intruder. His colleagues said nothing, simply stood alert for any signal which their leader might give.

The Superior Brother stood slowly. "What do you want?" be demanded. The other smiled his frigid smile. "Everything and nothing. Your deaths — or your lives," he replied enigmatically.

However, what he said struck a chord with the Superior Brother. Eyes narrowing, he considered his options. He resumed his seat. His colleagues followed his lead.

"You are the Superior Brother, I take it?"

Involuntarily, his eyes jerked to those of his interrogator. "I don't know what you are talking about, and I'm calling security."

"No, you will do no such thing."

As the man reached out to pick up a phone, the icy eyes which glared at him seemed to intensify. Abruptly, the Superior Brother pulled his hand away from the phone, sweat breaking out upon his forehead. A mutter of fear and surprise ran along the table, yet none attempted to interfere.

"Who are you?" Superior Brother demanded.

"That should, perhaps, have been your first question," the man replied. Then, slowly, with heavy emphasis upon each word, he said, "I am the *Supreme* Brother."

The statement was greeted with astonished silence. Supreme Brother continued, "and these," he indicated the two men just behind him, "are Brothers Richard and Jerome."

"But," Superior Brother spluttered, realising that his actions had constituted sedition, "we were given no warning..."

"Your manners are somewhat lax, Brother," Supreme Brother cut in. "Do you think that you could find seats for us — and remember that I *do* outrank you?" he added with heavy sarcasm.

Superior Brother needed no reminding that Supreme Brother did, indeed, outrank him. The sarcasm was not lost on him either, and he began to feel intimidated.

"Supreme Brother, please, take my place; make room there for Supreme Brother's companions," he added, indicating the chairs nearest to his own.

Sitting in the comfortable leather chair, Supreme Brother motioned to his companions, inviting them to sit on either side of him. One of the assembly, at a motion from the Superior Brother, took their coats.

Supreme Brother glanced around the table. "As I recall, the position of Superior Brother within the US was created because it was not feasible for the Supreme Brother to devote his full attention to both organisations at the same time."

"That is correct, Supreme Brother," Superior Brother muttered, uneasily.

Supreme Brother smiled slightly, knowing that he had made his point.

"You will all be wondering about my unprecedented appearance here. There is no way to relate what I have to say except by being direct about it.

"I am here to inform you of a most tragic and devastating piece of intelligence. The British Brotherhood has been destroyed."

"But how?" questioned one of the assembled women, incredulously.

Supreme Brother frowned at the reminder that things here were done differently. He pondered the wisdom of making alterations, but decided that for the present, at least, he could live with things as they were.

The woman — Sister Barbara — misunderstood the cause of the frown, and blushed. "I beg your forgiveness, Supreme Brother."

The courtesy of the apology diminished his irritation slightly. "We were attempting the eradication of the Baron lineage once and for all. As you all may know, Brother James came here about eight months ago attempting to trace any relatives of Scott Hobard, the so-called 'last of the American Barons. James succeeded. We found that there were just three descendants of Anton Baron alive in the world, and all were located at the same place. They were protected by a formidable occultist named George Hayter, one of Anton's descendants.

"Eventually, we kidnapped one of them, Margaret Hunter, and tortured her in an attempt to gain information about

Hayter. Finally, fearing that she might die, we summoned our Patrons and commanded them to destroy the last of Baron's descendants."

As he fell silent, Supreme Brother could feel the tension which his recitation had generated. Each person within the room wanted to hear the conclusion, yet none dared to ask him to continue — except one.

"Supreme Brother," Sister Margaret said quietly, "please finish what you have to tell us. If, as you say, our British colleagues have truly been destroyed, then I for one claim *vengeance*. Blood for blood. *Life* for *life*."

Supreme Brother's face darkened as he looked upon the face of the woman who, earlier, had advised that they be killed quickly. But, as she continued, her words brought an intense, burning gaze into his eyes.

"Your desire for vengeance is to your credit, er...Sister," he stated, feeling unusual using that particular form of address. After a moment's thought, he continued.

"All seemed to be going to plan," he resumed. "We were about to sacrifice Margaret Hunter when she became protected.

"We killed George Hayter, but we had not counted on a physical resurrection by Anton Baron himself. Our occult powers were ineffectual against him. He possessed the three Barons — even though one of them was dead — and began the destruction of our Brotherhood.

"I was able to relocate myself and these two Brothers here away to safety. All our Brothers were assembled in the crypt of a ruined church. Anton Baron caused an earthquake. All of our — and your — Brothers were crushed."

"Supreme Brother, I too demand vengeance, but how may we be avenged upon one already dead?" Superior Brother wanted to know.

"By rebuilding the British Society. By eradicating the Baron line, as all here are sworn to do. These are my reasons for being here, and you will assist us in achieving that. All other considerations are secondary."

The Superior Brother took a deep breath. "The Brothers and Sisters you see here represent the equivalent of your Third

Circle. To rebuild on the scale which you imply will take time, effort, and ingenuity. I think, Supreme Brother, that we should begin immediate discussions about how this rebuilding might best be achieved. All here will have suggestions to offer, I am certain."

The cold face with the icy eyes regarded the people sitting around the table. The Supreme Brother smiled. "Though it take years, we *will* succeed. And then, Tony Baron, Margaret Hunter and John Brandon will suffer all the agonies of the damned before they die."

Chapter One: *Deliberations*

The five men sat in casual chairs sipping coffee. Their discussion was intense, yet somehow muted, as though all were depressed by the enormity of their task. Dominating these discussions were two men who radiated authority. It was obvious that these two were used to giving orders, and to having those orders obeyed promptly, without question.

When either of these two spoke, the others listened in obedient silence, before making comments or suggestions.

It was six months since the Supreme Brother had interrupted a meeting of the hierarchy of the American Brotherhood. In those six months, both the American organisation and the Supreme Brother had undergone subtle but unmistakable changes.

Initially, the news that the Supreme Brother and two of his companions had flown to America and taken charge of the American Brotherhood had caused both consternation and anger among members of that organisation.

The general consensus of opinion was that, although — in theory — they recognised Supreme Brother's overall leadership, the Brothers saw this intrusion as a usurpation of their own leader — Superior Brother — and of his position.

Indeed, before the news of the destruction of the British branch of the Brotherhood had been made general knowledge, several Brothers had considered the possibility of assassinating the Supreme Brother — although they would have found that task easier to consider than to achieve.

Expecting this response, the Supreme Brother had acted to conciliate even the most disgruntled of the American Brothers. He had confirmed Superior Brother in his position as leader of the Brotherhood in America, and at the same time made it plain that he had no intention of remaining longer in the States than he had to. Furthermore, he had refrained from issuing any direct orders; rather he had made requests of the Superior Brother regarding the things he wished achieved.

The Superior Brother, understanding that he didn't want to antagonise the Supreme Brother, and that the more quickly he acceded to these requests the sooner his troublesome guests would leave, gave every assistance. He realised that Supreme Brother's last intent was to cause a division among the Brothers, and he appreciated the tact and diplomacy which Supreme Brother had displayed, especially when technically, at least, all Brothers owed loyalty to Supreme Brother before anyone else.

These considerations had, in fact, drawn the two leaders together, and each was mildly surprised when they realised that they could work together without either feeling in any way threatened. Their mutual respect had added another dimension, and the two had become friends. It was an unusual scenario for each of them, since along with the mantle of leadership came an obligation to avoid such friendships, lest they ultimately undermine the leader's position.

But since, in practice, neither would be under the authority of the other — under normal circumstances — each had allowed the friendship to intensify to an extent which could never otherwise have occurred.

Supreme Brother had explained personally to the entire American assembly exactly what had transpired in Britain, and why he had suddenly appeared in America. As he recounted events, a sense of outrage more violent than Supreme Brother had ever experienced exploded from the Brothers. The Brotherhood were united in their response. They called for the deaths of the perpetrators of this atrocity, and demanded that Superior Brother give every possible aid to the Supreme Brother in this endeavour.

Supreme Brother's eyes had become icy at this response, but with rapture. He had smiled to himself as he caught sight of Superior Brother's face. He was stunned. It demonstrated to Supreme Brother more than anything else could have that his American counterpart was as unused to receiving demands from his Brothers as he himself was.

This statement, coupled with the conciliatory gestures which he had already decided upon, had had the desired effect.

No longer was Supreme Brother regarded as a potential usurper, but their overall leader who had been almost overwhelmed by forces beyond his (or anyone else's) control. Their overall leader who needed help to fulfil the basic tenet of their Brotherhood; the eradication of the Baron line. Supreme

Brother was hailed as a hero that he had come so close to killing Margaret Hunter, and fulfilling their Curse.

Most of the Brothers had suggestions to make about how the Supreme Brother might continue. Each was discussed; Supreme Brother hid his impatience with those suggestions which were plainly impractical, or a patent waste of time. He realised that, if he so wished, he could easily have ousted Superior Brother and taken control of the American Brotherhood, but his sense of caution dissuaded him. If, once he returned to Britain, he needed the aid of the American Branch of the Brotherhood, he sensed it would be to his benefit to have acted cautiously, to have made allies, and not enemies.

He had enhanced his sudden popularity by listening to all suggestions, never shouting down or ridiculing any Brother — or *Sister* — who had anything to offer, but by appearing to consider everything, and thanking each individual for their thoughts.

Brothers Jerome and Richard had been surprised by Supreme Brother's duplicity, by the tact which he put up so convincingly that all — with them excepted — thought of Supreme Brother as thoughtful and considerate.

However, in private, Supreme Brother remained the same as ever, aloof, evil, dangerous. He took Jerome and Richard fully into his confidence, explaining exactly what he intended, and how he intended to manipulate the American Brothers into giving their aid freely.

Throughout the time that they remained in America, only those two Brothers fully understood exactly what Supreme Brother was doing and his reasons for doing it. They, in turn, passed on all news from the body of the Brotherhood which Supreme Brother might find of interest. They had taken to attending meetings and mixing with the assembled Brothers, as though they considered themselves subject to Superior Brother, when, in fact, they revelled in the fact that they were loyal to Supreme Brother alone, and could demonstrate this loyalty by spying for him at every opportunity.

Each evening, they discussed what progress they had made, how things could be manipulated more quickly to achieve the desired end. On one point Supreme Brother was adamant. It would be he, with the rebuilt British Brotherhood who would exact the final revenge for the destruction of so many Brothers. The Superior Brother had suggested that his branch of the Brotherhood could take over the pursuit of the Curse whilst Supreme Brother rebuilt the British Society.

Supreme Brother's eyes had become dark and dangerous at that suggestion, a fact not entirely unnoticed by Superior Brother, who had retreated from following up this suggestion.

"No," Supreme Brother had rasped. "The insult was to me and the British Brotherhood. Whilst you are right that either organisation could fulfil the Curse, I cannot and will not allow it. *The insult was to me.* The repayment shall be made by me and my rebuilt Society. I *swear* it."

"But that surely means that the Curse will have to take second place whilst the rebuilding is in progress," Superior Brother observed, quietly.

"*Then so be it*," Supreme Brother snarled in reply. Then, as though he realised that his facade as a reasonable man was slipping, he continued: "I apologise, Superior Brother. Remember, I witnessed the annihilation of my Brothers — close to three hundred of them. My anger at their murder overcomes good manners. I will be there to witness the destruction of the Barons, and Brothers Jerome and Richard will be there with me. Were our roles reversed I am certain that you would feel the same way."

"I suppose you are right," Superior Brother conceded, seriously.

Without further discussion being necessary, Supreme Brother's viewpoint was accepted. It was the first — and only — time Supreme Brother had demanded anything, and the Superior Brother sensed that this was not the best moment to begin arguing.

If Supreme Brother's appearance had startled and unsettled many of the Brothers, he, himself had been startled at how different was the organisation and composition of the American Brotherhood.

For one thing, it was a lot more relaxed than the British version. At general meetings, the Brothers were *not* segregated into the three circles which would give away each Brother's standing within the organisation. Nor did the equivalent of the Third Circle wear the customary robes and ceremonial daggers. It seemed that any Brother, no matter how subordinate, could interrupt Superior Brother at will, and suffer no penalty. Supreme Brother wondered just how the Society could function as a coherent whole under these conditions. It seemed, to his mind, to be a recipe for chaos rather than anything else.

Yet it *did* work.

He realised that this was, in the main, due to the Superior Brother, who guided the Brothers along with consummate skill and confidence.

This was one aspect of the American Brotherhood which Supreme Brother found difficult to stomach. He thought of the strict rules of decorum which he had insisted upon, in Britain. The lack of such discipline, he thought, could seriously undermine the Society in certain circumstances. Further, it implied that they didn't take their Brotherhood seriously enough. Supreme Brother wondered how they behaved when performing the Ritual Sacrifice to their Patron Demons. Obviously, they took *that* part of their Society with appropriate seriousness. If they didn't there was a better than even chance that their Patrons would turn on them.

The thought made him wince, since it forced him to think about the last time he had performed just such a Ceremony. It had been an unmitigated disaster, culminating in the destruction of so many of his Brothers...

There was one thing which had amazed and stupefied Supreme Brother, and that was the inclusion of women in the Brotherhood. Even worse, seven of them belonged to the equivalent of the Third Circle.

Scandalised, but impotent within his own scheming, Supreme Brother had questioned Superior Brother about the wisdom of allowing females to join what was, after all, a highly secret male-oriented Society.

Superior Brother had smiled, mistaking Supreme Brother's frown as one of confusion rather than carefully hidden, but impotent, fury.

"Yes, I must admit that I thought about it long and hard.

Initially, I was not in favour of it. But Brothers argued that times had changed, and that there were certain tasks which might be more easily accomplished by a woman, rather than a man. I had to agree with that reasoning, but I was *very* unsure of our Patrons' response to such an innovative action. After all, it would have accomplished nothing to have admitted women just for our Patrons to destroy them."

"And?" Supreme Brother prompted, a curious edge to his voice.

"And I checked all relevant statutes within our Pact. I was amazed to find that there was no statute which actually debarred women from active participation within our Society. If there had been, I would have left it at that, or at most referred the matter to you for adjudication. As it was, there was nothing to stop women being admitted, except for the reaction of our Patrons. As you know, they can, at times, be erm... unpredictable. I confess that I was curious, but not so much so that I would initiate one and then call upon our Patrons and watch their reaction."

"So, you summoned our Patrons and put the question to them," Supreme Brother murmured.

"Yes. I knew that there were risks involved. Our Patrons could have demanded some alteration in the terms of our Pact in return for allowing the inclusion of women; had they done so, that would *again* have been the end of the matter. Only the Supreme Brother could sanction such an alteration."

Supreme Brother smiled mirthlessly. "That is so; but I deduce, from the obvious fact that females have been allowed into the Brotherhood, that our Patrons made no excessive demands."

"Virtually no demands at all. When I posed the question there was a few seconds' hesitation, almost as though they couldn't believe what I was asking. And then they agreed, with two provisos."

"Which were?"

Superior Brother smiled a trifle nervously, as though what he were about to relate he'd rather leave unsaid. He shrugged before continuing.

"The first was that no woman should be allowed to

20

progress to a position of leadership over either organisation. That they could not attain a position equal to that of mine — or yours. Further, that they might not attain a position of deputy leadership. I found the idea of a female leader of either branch of the Society so repulsive that I agreed before I had had a chance to realise the ramifications of what I was doing. It was a decision which, rightfully, only *you* could have made. Indeed, you could revoke my decision, but we *both* know what *that* would entail."

"Indeed," Supreme Brother said smoothly, elated that Superior Brother had made such a momentous mistake. "For usurping my authority in making this decision, our Patrons would demand your death. I am amazed that you — who show such excellent judgement otherwise — made such a serious error." Inwardly, Supreme Brother was relishing the fact that he now had a legitimate hold over Superior Brother's life, or death. They exchanged a glance that told each that the other was fully aware of the fact.

Suddenly, Supreme Brother chuckled: a dry coughing sound which betrayed that it was a very rare occurrence. Superior Brother frowned, unsure how to react to this development.

"Well, I have to admit that if you had submitted this to me my reaction would have been the same as yours. Let us assume that I authorized your decision — for the present."

Superior Brother realised that he was being offered a lifeline for reasons which he didn't fully comprehend, until he saw the glint in Supreme Brother's eye. Then he knew that the price of his life was total cooperation with Supreme Brother: more, that *that* cooperation had to be freely given. He marvelled at Supreme Brother's cunning, and then grinned as he realised that it would have been exactly his reaction were he in Supreme Brother's shoes. With new respect for each other, each smiled a genuine smile of warmth.

"And what was the second proviso?" Supreme Brother queried, curious despite himself.

"It was that the Initiation Ceremony be altered slightly."

"In what way?"

"Well, under normal circumstances a candidate must wear

the Brown Robe of an uninitiate before taking his vows before our Patrons, and then ceremonially casting the Robe aside, he dresses in normal clothes and takes his place among the assembly. Of course, in Britain that would mean joining the First Circle." He broke off as Supreme Brother nodded impatiently.

"I know the Ceremony of Initiation better than most," he observed. Superior Brother smiled. "Of course. Well, the second proviso was that a woman wishing to take vows may not be allowed any clothing until the meeting after her vows have been taken. Forgive me, I explained that pretty badly. A potential Sister must go through her first meeting, the one at which she will take her vows, naked. Once her vows are taken, and the meeting over, she may dress."

Supreme Brother frowned. "But that makes no sense. Our Patrons are *always* ready to take advantage of circumstance, but I don't see what they can possibly get out of this."

"I have not quite finished," Superior Brother admitted, gazing levelly at Supreme Brother, attempting to gauge just how his next piece of information would be taken. "After she has taken her vows, the Sister must prove her worth to our Patrons. She must give herself to each of them for thirty minutes."

Supreme Brother *stared* at him for a disconcertingly long time. "Are you *mad*?" he finally asked.

Superior Brother smiled confidently. "I might be, I never really considered the possibility. Frankly, I was shocked by what our Patrons demanded."

"Then why did you consent to it?" Supreme Brother demanded.

"Because it would take a very strong-willed woman to come through that ordeal — a woman who could consciously agree to do such a thing will think nothing of the more mundane tasks which she is given in the service of the Society. Such women make *very* dangerous opponents for our enemies. I allowed it because, it seemed to me, we can make good use of any who could go through such an ordeal. They would be unlikely to go to pieces at the idea of a mission which would normally be considered degrading or humiliating — not after the experience of our Patrons. I decided that it would benefit our Society, and based my decision upon that."

Supreme Brother digested this information silently. "What of those who don't come through it?" he asked.

"They don't leave the meeting alive."

Supreme Brother frowned. "I was wrong. I merely thought you devious. Now I understand you to be ruthless as well."

"It goes with being leader," he replied.

Supreme Brother nodded.

"I must confess to a certain amount of surprise," Supreme Brother murmured. "How many Sisters are there?"

"Seven in the equivalent of the Third Circle, and another sixteen at lesser ranks."

"And they went through that ordeal willingly?" Supreme Brother asked, incredulous.

"Yes. Of course most are frightened to the point of petrification, but for some reason that I don't understand, each woman who has come through the experience successfully seems to undergo some subtle alteration in their character. They become fearless, almost. It seems to give them an inner strength which they lacked, originally; a sense of purpose, of single-minded directness within the confines of our Society. Many of the best suggestions for further endeavours come from our Sisters, and they are always ready to undertake anything which they might suggest. They allow no outside influences to deflect them from our service. I have never been given cause to regret my decision."

Supreme Brother thought this over for several minutes. "What you say makes sense. I remember one Sister advising you to kill us quickly shortly after we interrupted your meeting. Even after she knew exactly who we were she seemed strangely unaffected by her actions. Most people would fear the consequences of such insubordination."

Superior Brother smiled. "You refer to Sister Margaret. She is, perhaps the best example of what I have been saying. She didn't fear for herself because she knew that her actions had been done with the safety of the Society in mind. It would be a very harsh leader who punished her for taking her responsibilities too seriously."

Supreme Brother nodded, deep in thought. "Her loyalty is

beyond question?" he mused, quietly.

"Absolutely," Superior Brother confirmed, intuitively knowing that something he had said had rooted in Supreme Brother's mind. He guessed that it had to do with Sisters generally, and one Sister in particular. It was obvious that the whole question of admitting Sisters into the Brotherhood was secondary now, that his reasoning had been listened to and accepted. He let out an inaudible sigh of relief, knowing that for the past few minutes he had been in a very awkward position which Supreme Brother could have exploited mercilessly, had he been so inclined.

"Like a new variable in the equation," Supreme Brother whispered.

"Pardon?"

Supreme Brother smiled, distantly. "I agree with your course of action," he confirmed. "And I endorse it, without reserve."

Superior Brother gazed into Supreme Brother's eyes, attempting to fathom what was happening in the shadowy depths which he focussed upon.

Ignoring the obvious question which Superior Brother wished to ask, Supreme Brother spoke. "Of course, you want to know just how long you are going to have to put up with me."

"But....."

"Dan," Supreme Brother said mildly, addressing Superior Brother by name. "Don't try to deceive me. Were our roles reversed, I would find you an irritant. As I am overall leader, you would prefer me at arm's length rather than breathing down your neck. There is some truth in the saying that absence makes the heart grow fonder. You feel that I inhibit you, that I stifle your almost absolute authority. I know this to be true, because I suffer from similar feelings, much as I like you, personally."

"O.K., Paul," Superior Brother said, copying the informal tone which Supreme Brother had allowed to enter the conversation. "Cards on the table. I am used, as you, to being a law unto myself. It annoys me that whilst you are here I must continually look over my shoulder to check that you approve

24

my actions. Under normal circumstances I wouldn't give a damn what you thought, unless it involved a major decision which could be made by nobody else. I look forward to the day when I will be rid of you, and to that end I will give all the aid that I am able. The way things are at the moment, no one knows exactly where they stand, and that unsettles our Brothers. The boundaries between each Society are clearly defined, yet your presence here shatters those boundaries and creates all kinds of dangerous precedents — dangerous for you as well as me — and the sooner you return to Britain so things may return to some kind of normalcy here, the better I'll be pleased."

Supreme Brother stared intently into Dan's eyes, before nodding almost imperceptibly. "Not only are you devious and ruthless, you are astute, too," he sighed. "I accept what you say; I am as eager to leave America as you are to get rid of me. The sooner I can take an active part in the rebuilding process the happier I will be, and that can only be accomplished in Britain.

"Provisionally, I suggest that we, that is Brothers Jerome, Richard and myself should return to Britain no later than the beginning of next month. But before we do leave, we will need to have a general discussion about what we intend to do, and what kinds of aid we may call upon you to provide. Just so we don't take you by surprise. The three of us should meet with you, and one other, someone whom you can trust. A *Brother* whom you can trust," Supreme Brother added, almost as an afterthought. "One with sufficient authority to authorise that aid if you, for some reason, are unavailable."

Superior Brother nodded, smiling faintly. "No problem," he said.

"Further," Supreme Brother murmured, "I may need to borrow some members of your Society. I trust that that will not create any problems?"

Superior Brother thought this over. "I don't foresee any problems, but I would prefer that no more than twenty be seconded to you at any one time — and no more than seven from the equivalent of your Third Circle. Would that be sufficient?"

Supreme Brother frowned slightly, assessing how many he

might need. "I think that that will more than suffice. I was thinking in the region of five to ten — after all, the last thing I need is to be surrounded by twenty American-accented Brothers."

Superior Brother laughed, a genuine deep laugh. "You know as well as I that their accents would be no problem. Have you any idea which Brothers you might need?"

"I have had one or two thoughts on the matter," Supreme Brother admitted, "but I would like to discuss this with Jerome and Richard first, before finalising any selection."

"Fine. So, when shall I set up this meeting that you want? I would like to get this matter cleared up with a minimum of delay, as I said earlier. Nothing personal."

"I understand. Let us meet this coming Saturday evening. That will still give us ten days more for any last minute details or ideas. It also means that you will be rid of us in just under two weeks."

Superior Brother nodded. "I assume that you will keep in close contact with me? I'd like to know just how quickly the rebuilding is being accomplished. It promises to be fascinating to watch our Society re-form and to fulfil its ultimate destiny."

Reminded of his defeat, Supreme Brother's eyes darkened and smouldered dangerously.

"Yes," he replied in his accustomed frigid tone. "It will be *fascinating*, but from the Baron point of view *it will be lethal*."

***

The Saturday evening following this frank discussion between Superior Brother and Supreme Brother saw five men sitting in casual chairs, sipping coffee.

Superior Brother had formally introduced Brother Gerald, who would, in his absence, authorise the aid which had been agreed upon between them. Brother Gerald's face held a serious expression throughout the meeting. He stood over six feet tall, and was slim to the point of thinness. His complexion was unnaturally pale, giving the impression that he might be a reanimate corpse. His thin, gaunt face radiated intelligence, however; none doubted that Superior Brother had chosen him wisely.

Throughout that meeting, Brother Gerald sat, contributing

nothing unless in response to a question, or to clarify a point on which he was unsure. His eyes flicked to each as they spoke, and each, in turn was certain that he missed *nothing*. Supreme Brother wondered whether Brother Gerald would be able to repeat the conversation verbatim weeks later. It would not have surprised him. He felt that Brother Gerald possessed some rare and valuable talent. His eyes more than made up for any signs of life that his complexion might lack. It seemed obvious that behind those eyes lay a considerable intellect.

"I have," Superior Brother was saying, "had the sum of ten million dollars transferred into those accounts controlled by what's left of the British Society, which should help meet any interim expenses until funds are again flowing through more normal channels."

"*Very* generous," Richard muttered.

Superior Brother turned his gaze upon Richard, unsure whether there had been a hint of sarcasm in his voice.

"We do not lack for funds," Richard explained. "Supreme Brother made very sound financial arrangements years ago."

"Then," Superior Brother smiled, "accept it as a gesture of goodwill."

Richard returned the smile. "No doubt the money will come in useful, but for the immediate future our need is for practical help in our rebuilding process. The donation of some of your Brothers means more to us than twenty times the amount of money you mentioned."

Superior Brother nodded, thoughtfully. "I agree. Have you decided exactly *who* you wish me to have seconded to you?"

Richard glanced at Supreme Brother before nodding and pulling a sheet of paper from his pocket. "Supreme Brother gave me an indication of the specific attributes which, he felt, might be needed. I have examined the data on each of your Brothers, and the results are listed here."

He passed the sheet of paper to Superior Brother, who glanced through it before passing it on to Brother Gerald. "There are one or two choices which I admit surprise me, but no matter. All *are* at your disposal. Decide who you wish to accompany you back to Britain, and the necessary arrangements will be made. You may summon any of the remainder when it is felt that they are needed. Inform either Gerald or me, and the required Brothers will be on the next available flight."

Supreme Brother allowed himself a frigid smile. "That is the most important thing. However, instinct tells me that in the future, before we are finished rebuilding, there may be some people who will have to be liquidated. It might not be feasible for our developing Society to take care of the matter. It will take time before our new Brothers will have the necessary experience for such matters. If, to destroy an unbeliever might bring unwelcome suspicion upon us, I would prefer the matter be handled by another — with *appropriate* circumspection."

Superior Brother frowned slightly. "I appreciate what you are saying, and what you are asking. More, I understand your motives." he thought for a second before adding: "If such an important circumstance comes to pass, let us have the details and the situation *will* be rectified to your satisfaction. I take it, however, that you are not including Anton Baron's descendants among those who might require liquidation?"

Supreme Brother considered before answering. "I cannot say that for certain. Obviously, if I require the murder of one of Baron's descendants, then you would have to bring about that death by occult means. Our Curse specifically prohibits us from taking more direct actions in *those* cases."

"Of course. In either eventuality you may count upon us."

Silence fell. The men sipped their now tepid coffee. Minutes passed in the same contemplative silence. At last, Jerome spoke.

"How much experience do those Brothers listed have in the recruitment side of your Society?" he asked, in his quiet, fanatical tone.

"That is something which need not worry you. All on your list — with perhaps three exceptions — understand exactly what recruitment entails. They know that they must be highly cautious; further, they understand how to sound people out. Many of them can detect a potential Brother after speaking with them for only a few minutes. They are as accomplished as you might desire or expect."

Jerome nodded impatiently. "And will their loyalty be to

Supreme Brother, or to you?"

Superior Brother smiled again, but this time his smile was a parody, demonstrating that he was unused to hearing such blatant insolence.

"Jerome," Supreme Brother warned, quietly.

But Jerome's eyes flared with the insane zeal which was so characteristic of the man. "Forgive me, Supreme Brother, but I must know where the loyalties of these Brothers will lie. If I am to work with them, I must trust them. I cannot trust them until I know the answer to my question." His voice was still quiet, but it could have been shouted through a megaphone, so forcefully did he make his point.

Silence stretched out again. The Brothers felt the undercurrent of tension which had suddenly invaded the meeting. Finally, Superior Brother nodded. "Under the peculiar circumstances, I suppose that you *have* made a valid point. For the period of their secondment, their loyalty will be to Supreme Brother alone. Once they return to America, their primary loyalty will revert to me. I will brief each of the candidates on this matter personally. I think, too, that it might be a good idea if, again for the period of their secondment, each Brother be subordinate to you, Jerome, and to Richard,"

He noticed the blaze which appeared in Jerome's eyes as he made this statement, and knew that he was on the right track. "After all, you two know much better than they just how things may be achieved in Britain. They will need help and guidance. Have no doubt that they will make suggestions, but you, guided by Supreme Brother, must make the final decisions. It seems to me that this is the only way your objectives will be achieved. I would be angry if I found that all our careful planning had been undone by one of my Brothers making a *stupid* mistake because he was unused to the way things are done, in Britain."

Jerome's eyes blazed out their approval of what he had heard. He even smiled. He turned his head to face Supreme Brother. "This is better than I had dared hope for," he said. "I am well satisfied with these arrangements, and I have no further questions to ask."

Supreme Brother smiled in return. A bleak, cold affair which told that he, too, was pleased with arrangements.

Richard nodded. "I will need information about Tony Baron's whereabouts, and any developments. I would like Brother George to accompany us to Britain, when we return."

Superior Brother's face displayed his concern. "You are not thinking of attempting to continue our Curse and rebuild your Society at the same time, surely?" he asked.

Richard grinned a genuine grin. "No," he replied. "But it would be useful to keep up to date about what is happening with Brandon, Hunter and Baron. When the day dawns for us to take up our Curse again, I don't want to have to begin searching for them. The more information which we have about them, the more predictable they may become. It was partially through lack of information that Baron managed to complete his journey to meet Hayter. I don't intend to let *anything* be left to chance next time."

Superior Brother glanced at Supreme Brother. "I'm impressed," he admitted. "I wish that more of my Brothers showed such single-minded purpose, such an insight into future probabilities."

"Richard is more valuable than you could ever imagine," Supreme Brother affirmed. "As is Jerome, in differing ways. They tend to complement each other. Each makes a formidable opponent. Together, they are a very powerful combination. I am happy, in *many* ways, that they are my *Brothers*, and not my opponents."

Richard frowned, uncomfortable under Supreme Brother's testimony. Jerome, however regarded his leader with his burning eyes, the praise tending to increase the intensity of his glare exponentially.

Silence returned. This time, it was relaxed and calm. Each sat, savouring the atmosphere.

"Is there anything else which needs to be discussed?" Superior Brother asked.

"One or two minor points. Nothing critical," Supreme Brother replied. "We leave shortly for Britain."

Richard smiled at Jerome. "At *last*," he said, "I've been eager to hear those words for six months," his eyes took on a hard glint. "And once we have rebuilt, then I look forward to renewing our acquaintance with Brandon, Hunter and Baron."

He glared into Supreme Brother's eyes. "At least *I* have the knowledge that I killed George Hayter," he spat. "I cannot wait to have similar opportunities for revenge upon them all."

"But you *will* wait, Richard," Supreme Brother returned, easily. "Let the knowledge that the day for vengeance will come sustain you. On that day, you may savour your opportunities. In the meantime, remember not only that it was *you* who destroyed George Hayter, but remember the manner of our Brothers' deaths. Let the knowledge fester secretly within you, so that when our day comes it will come with a savagery at least equal to the fury which you feel within you. Let your anger drive you. Do *not* let it possess you. Let your rage fuel your labours as we rebuild. Let it move you ever forward to that day when we will emerge victorious with our Curse fulfilled. I, too, am impatient for that day to dawn; but patience is one of the hallmarks of our Society. It is one of the many reasons why we will *never* be defeated.

"So, Richard, curb your impatience in the assurance of our final victory. We three, united, embark on something which has only been accomplished once before in the history of the Brotherhood. The *rebirth* of our evil; a *renaissance*, if you will. We have worked to complete our Curse for over five hundred years. What are a few years more on *that* time scale?

"But be assured, Richard, that both you and Jerome will be with me to witness the eradication of the Baron line. You will participate in that destruction. In fact, every day that you work on the rebuilding of our Brotherhood, you will be participating in the preparation for that annihilation.

"We have the aid which will make our task so much easier. Revel in the knowledge. *Glory* in it. For, one day, you will awake to the realisation that our rebirth is *complete*.

"And remember this, Richard. Not only are Baron and Hunter condemned by our Curse, but any *friend* of theirs, too. And, in the latter case, we are *not* constrained to bring about death by occult means. That simplifies things, somewhat.

"Time, Richard. Time dulls people's reactions. They become phlegmatic. They are less wary. They, Baron, Hunter and Brandon, must be *certain* that they succeeded in destroying us. They will believe that there is nothing more to fear. Time will work against them. But it will work for us.

31

They will not expect us to rebuild, and will not expect our strike when it comes. Time will mature our rage, like a fine wine, and turn it into the sweetest experience of our lives. The wait will be *more* than worthwhile.

"And so, curb your impatience. Mute your anger. Let it find release in your daily labours, until that day when it may be released in full fury, in vicious fulfilment of our Curse.

"But, until that day, Richard, *patience*."

Supreme Brother finally fell silent. He still held Richard's gaze, however, as though gauging what effect his words had had. He noticed, from the corner of his eye, Jerome, eyes blazing, nodding agreement with what he had said.

Still holding direct eye contact, which was never easy for anyone to do with the Supreme Brother, Richard replied. "I *will* be patient; I *will* attend to the rebirth of our Brotherhood. I *will* remember the way my Brothers died. I *will* savour the passage of time."

His voice dropped considerably in volume as he continued, in a savage tone: "And I will savour my rage and impatience. But most of all, I will savour the *consummation* of our Curse, and the *deaths* of Hunter, Baron, and Brandon."

Jerome smiled at him enthusiastically.

Supreme Brother nodded slowly, icy eyes locked upon Richard's face. "Good," he whispered.

Chapter Two: *Recollections*

Margaret Brandon stood alone in an area of the lawn enclosed by privets. Behind her, the small ornamental gate which gave access to this enclosure squealed on its hinges, as the wind swung it to and fro.

Margaret frowned at the distraction which the gate caused, glancing quickly at the rear of the mansion, which was about twenty metres away. Taking a deep breath, she refocused her attention upon the grave. She took in the colour of the single red rose which she had placed there, thinking, as she always did, just how inadequate a gesture it seemed to be.

She bit her lip, knowing it was the only gesture which she could make, to one dead. She knew that no matter how magnificent her offering to this grave, and to the person it contained, she would *still* feel that it was inadequate.

A sudden gust of wind buffeted her, blowing her long brown hair across her face. She shuddered with the sudden chill. How many times, she asked herself, had she stood here, in this exact spot, pondering the inadequacies of her token of remembrance? It was a question which she couldn't answer. She made the pilgrimage here frequently, never allowing more than a month to pass before standing here again, remembering a few days which had transformed her life. In many ways, it had been the occupant of the grave who had begun and encouraged that transformation.

Despite knowing him for only a few brief, oh so brief, days, he had affected her in such a profound manner, more than anything or anyone else ever would in her life that, even now, she found it hard, almost impossible, to accept the fact of his death.

Perhaps that was, in part, the reason she came here so often, to reaffirm that fact to herself. She locked her eyes upon the grave-marker.

***

GEORGE HAYTER

***

GREATLY MISSED AND

DEEPLY MOURNED

***

The words, though true, failed lamentably to express the depth of loss which she actually felt. It was an emotion so powerful and intimate that Margaret doubted that it could ever be satisfactorily translated into anything as mundane as language.

The sun came out from hiding behind patchy cloud, almost as if to reward her for finding time to spend with the dead, at a time when so many people were concerned with nothing but their lives. A time when it was fashionable to shed crocodile tears over the deceased, before carefully expunging memory of the dead person, lest the shadow of true grief overflow and impinge into life where, some believed, it had no place.

But Margaret had no fears about allowing her emotions to show. It had, after all, been Hayter who had taught her that she need not fear her emotions, that by recognising and understanding them, she might understand herself, and others, more easily. It had been a difficult lesson, but one made easier by Hayter's unorthodox and direct methods.

Despite the tears which rolled down her face as she remembered the old man, she smiled at the memories.

The smile died as she thought upon the price which Hayter had willingly paid for her life and freedom. A fragment of St. John's Gospel drifted into her mind. Hadn't he said something like: 'greater love has no man than this, that he lay down his life for his friends'?

She moved her gaze around the small enclosure; Hayter had, indeed, given his life freely, but not just to save her and Tony and John. He had somehow deduced that it was the only course of action open to him, one which would destroy the Brotherhood which had persecuted him for so many years. She found herself wondering whether Hayter would have made the same sacrifice if the annihilation of the Brotherhood had not entered into it. She knew, however, that Hayter would probably not have taken the same action in other circumstances. He had been too wise a man to make a heroic action which would, ultimately, have been futile. She supposed that she should be grateful that matters had coincided as they had. Yet, she still wished that the whole mess had been resolved in some different way.

Her abduction had provided Hayter with the key which he had been missing in his earlier deliberations. Shaking her head, Margaret knew that in some way which she couldn't begin to comprehend, the whole scenario had been mapped out years earlier. All that had been needed was for the three of them to come together within the mansion at the proper time. Fate, or Anton Baron, had taken care of the rest.

Margaret again felt the depression which musing upon Hayter and the Cult seemed to engender within her. Pondering upon these things, she was drawn inexorably to the conclusion that it hadn't mattered what actions she had or had not made, back then. Similar events would have come to pass whatever she had done. In some ways, the realisation made her feel inadequate. What was the point of having a free will when your every action had been planned out for you?

It seemed obvious to her that Hayter had had a free choice to make. He could have sacrificed himself, and saved the others or he could have refused that option; the consequences of the latter Margaret didn't want to think about. Anton Baron or not, she was certain that things would have worked out catastrophically, from her point of view.

She had not been very surprised when informed that she had been related to Hayter. They had been drawn to each other almost from the second they had met. She had felt so easy in his presence, had liked him instinctively. Taking into account all the unusual things which had occurred between them, Margaret would have been more surprised if she had been told that she *wasn't* related to Hayter.

The knowledge that she was of the Baron line, though, forced her to pose herself another question. Had Anton Baron's prophesy manipulated her into meeting Tony, in order that the last three descendants of Anton Baron could be physically united in one geographical location simultaneously? If that was not the case, she asked herself, what were the odds against the last of the American Barons joining the other two in order to complete a five-hundred-year old prophesy? Incalculable. The sheer scope of the scenario defied

35

comprehension. It was not, she thought, at all surprising that their enemies had failed to see through Anton's plan, until that plan had come to fruition, and destroyed them all.

Her memories of the time she had been held by the Cult were very vivid, perhaps more vivid than she would have liked. They only became vague from the point when Brother Paul had identified himself to her; whenever she tried to focus closely upon what had happened after that, her mind told her that she had been floating upon a sea which had no real existence. A calm place where nothing could harm her, nothing lay claim to her attention. Nothing, that is, until she heard Hayter playing the piano. It was indistinct, but had been enough to rally her determination not to stay where she was forever. The piano music had moved closer and closer until she could see a spectrum of colours. She had opened her eyes in surprise and fear, only to see Tony and John looking anxiously at her. Even though John's eyes had been bandaged, she had felt an absurd certainty that he was looking at her, that his bandages provided no handicap to his vision. The notion had disappeared almost as quickly as it had appeared.

The squealing of the ornamental gate interrupted her reverie, and she blinked, bringing herself back to the present. She cast another look at the grave-marker. "George, you've got a *lot* to answer for," she whispered, affectionately.

Another gust of wind cut through her clothing, making her shiver. She glanced quickly at her watch. Had she really been standing here for two hours? It always seemed that time fragmented when she stood at Hayter's grave, almost as though time itself ran differently, here. In some perverse way, Margaret thought that it would be correct for that to happen since Anton Baron had succeeded in mastering time. In actuality, she knew that it was simply a case of doing so much thinking on these visits, which made it impossible to keep track of the passage of time.

The sun disappeared behind a new patch of cloud. Margaret glanced at the sky, thinking that it would soon begin to rain. She glanced at the grave one last time, and smiled a sad, bitter-sweet smile, before leaving the enclosure, ensuring that the ornamental gate was secured.

It was an idiotic gesture, she knew, since ordinarily there was nobody to hear the squeaking noise which it made. It offended Margaret's sense of decorum, to leave the gate open and squeaking; implied that she did not care about the grave, when in fact it was very important to her. Margaret wanted to leave the grave serene, secluded and peaceful. The man lying beneath the grave-marker deserved peace and quiet; had more than earned it, she thought, as she moved away from it.

She made her way into the mansion, closing the door quietly behind her. She made herself coffee before moving to the room which had always seemed to welcome her, more than any other. It was the same room where she had first heard Hayter play. As soon as she entered it, she felt the aura of relaxation and calm which never seemed to diminish. She moved a dust cover from the huge leather sofa, before sitting and sipping her coffee.

She glanced at the piano, a slight smile crossing her features at the memories which drifted to her mind. Her gaze moved on around the room which she knew so well. It seemed almost too peaceful in the mansion; each time she entered it, she expected to encounter the emptiness of an uninhabited building. Whilst inside the mansion, Margaret never thought of herself as alone. She knew, irrational though it might seem, that Hayter was here. She could feel his presence in every object which he had touched; thought that she could, occasionally, sense his spirit in the air which surrounded her. Sometimes, she fancied that if she had entered a room a second earlier, or had turned a corner a *fraction* sooner, she would have caught sight of him. His aura seemed to be an integral part of the mansion, close and comforting, never threatening or oppressive.

It was partially this sense of Hayter's presence which attracted Margaret into such frequent visits to his grave, and afterwards, into his mansion. She always experienced a strange contentment within its confines, but never more so than when she sat quietly in this particular room, thinking about the man who had caused such dramatic changes in her life and in herself. She smiled, thinking of too few days spent with him. Although the mansion was now hers, she still thought of it as his, Hayter's.

Collecting an ash tray, she resumed her seat. Lighting a cigarette which she took from her shoulder bag, she thought of the look of disgust which crossed John's face whenever she smoked in front of him. She smiled. He had a way of making no comment which always made her feel guilty about what she was doing. The ensuing confusion upon her features usually made him laugh at her. She remembered Tony telling her that Hayter had called John's sense of humour infuriating. Margaret thought that she understood exactly what Hayter had meant.

She wondered what Hayter would have made of her relationship with John. At that time, she had been dating Tony, although she had found John disturbingly attractive. She sighed. No doubt Hayter would have been surprised by developments, but not so much so that he would have been unable to make some cynical comment about it.

She drew deeply on her cigarette, wondering just when things had begun to sour between Tony and herself.

After coming out of the coma, she realised that Tony had changed. They all had, and the changes which afflicted them were mostly subtle and difficult to define. But Tony had changed more obviously than any of them.

She remembered looking into his eyes, and seeing doubt, uncertainty and a haunted desperation there. It was almost as though he feared making eye contact with her. It took time for Margaret to realise that Tony blamed himself unmercifully for Hayter's death, no matter how often or forcefully it was pointed out to him that there had been no other option, and that Hayter had already made his decision. There had been nothing that Tony could have done to prevent the consequences.

But Tony's guilt went deeper than they could know or understand. He had convinced himself that, despite what they said, John and Margaret blamed him as intensely as he blamed himself. He had become prone to periods of negative introspection; he made no attempt to hide this from either of them, being unresponsive and lost within the darker aspects of his personality. Each time he returned to some semblance of normality after these detours into the depths of his psyche, it was with an unhealthy depression bordering on neurosis.

It seemed that proximity to either John or Margaret increased the frequency of these periods of soul searching. Tony's moodiness and irritability appeared to increase as the others made steady progress towards health. His visits to see them in the hospital had become slowly more sporadic; and when he did visit, it seemed obvious by his frequent glances at his watch, the long periods of silence which he not only did nothing to dispel, but seemed, rather, to be more comfortable with, that he was counting the seconds before he could decently make his escape.

More than once Margaret had caught the smell of alcohol upon his breath, and wondered whether he was attempting to drown his feelings and emotions by drinking heavily. In fact, Tony was suffering the pain of loss and the certainty that he had been responsible for most, if not all, of what had occurred. He had found that alcohol dulled his pain somewhat; yet it was only a temporary relief. As his system adjusted to the greater quantities of liquor which he consumed, he found himself drinking even greater quantities at more frequent intervals to achieve the same amount of relief from his own twisted sense of culpability.

Many of the times Tony failed to visit Margaret and John were actually a result of his being in a drunken stupor, unable to leave the mansion by virtue of his unconsciousness.

When questioned about his failure to visit, Tony lied about the reason, not wishing to admit to John and Margaret — and least of all himself — that he was becoming an alcoholic.

The lies came to him so easily, and he delivered them with such composure that neither of the other two realised that he was lying until much later.

Tony, himself, had noticed that his depression intensified during and after visiting the hospital, and he began to think of reasons for avoiding that particular scenario. Even so, he knew that if made too frequently John would demand to know the real reasons for his absences. It would be a demand which he knew he would be unable to answer to their satisfaction

It was at this point that Tony began to resent the depression which they caused within him. It was only a small step to begin resenting them for the pain which they, unknowingly, caused him.

John and Margaret, aware that something was wrong with Tony, but unsure what it was, or what they might do about it, had both attempted to broach the subject with him, yet their attempts met with a cynical and aggressive response which their patience and reason had been unable to pierce. On more than one occasion Tony had abruptly cut short his visit, escaping from their concern and solicitude, leaving them baffled and anxious for him.

His emotions towards Margaret became warped and perverted by his resentment of her; he still loved her, yet his love became a twisted and perverted thing which could only find expression in hurting and confusing her. His sudden friendship towards John had twisted much more quickly into a dislike bordering on animosity.

This relatively sudden reversal towards John, rather than towards herself, caused Margaret to begin rethinking her whole relationship with Tony. She hated what she was seeing; it was a side of Tony of which she had never really been aware. She tried to make allowances for him, understanding as far as she was able, the pressures and guilt which Tony seemed to have taken to himself.

Even so, as the weeks passed, Margaret felt a definite lessening in the strength of her emotions for Tony. As though every time he shrugged off her attempts to help him, some of the love which she had felt for him was lost. It was a peculiar sensation, but one which she seemed powerless to prevent.

Throughout this time, John was constantly there when she felt that she needed someone to talk to. He never attempted to take advantage of the unexpected circumstance to further his own claims on Margaret's affections, something for which she was profoundly grateful. At that time, she didn't feel she could cope with the break-up of one relationship at the same time as beginning another. Even so, as her feelings for Tony diminished, Margaret was aware that her friendship with John was deepening; becoming more intense, more intimate.

Tony was not slow to realise what was happening, which only fuelled his aversion to John. When Margaret attempted to discuss what was happening to their relationship, how Tony was irretrievably damaging it, Tony simply refused to listen, sneering at what he considered her simplistic grasp of events.

His visits became even less frequent. He made no attempt to hide his gnawing resentment of them both, making it seem that he was almost an enemy come to gloat over their misfortunes. John's patience had finally snapped, and he had told Tony that he didn't want any more visits from him. Tony had agreed with almost obscene eagerness. Margaret had not felt able to make a similar demand, which, it seemed, frustrated Tony.

More weeks had passed; Tony still visited Margaret sporadically, yet neither took any pleasure from these visits. Margaret began to dread them. Her recovery and period of observation were coming to completion. More and more, she was certain that her relationship with Tony was beyond salvage. They both knew it, yet neither had expressed these sentiments to the other, as though each were waiting for the other to take the responsibility for the failure of their liaison.

The final time that he had visited Margaret forced her to make the decision which she should have made long ago. When he appeared, Margaret and John were laughing and joking about the early days John had spent in the hospital, and the chaos which he had caused.

Their laughter and good humour died abruptly as Tony appeared in the doorway. John made a move to leave, but Margaret restrained him. Tony swayed on his feet, and both guessed at the same time that he was very drunk. The liquor had loosened his tongue, and the story of his guilt and resentment of them had poured out of him. He reviled them for their earlier laughter, when he was continually tortured by the past. His attitude had become more vitriolic, his anger more obvious as he told them exactly what he thought of them. Why, he had asked, should they have laughter and joy when all he had was darkness and depression?

John had stood, and groped his way blindly to Tony. He placed his hands on Tony's shoulders, and spoke. "We have laughter and joy, Tony," he had said, "because we accept the inevitability of what happened. We don't wallow in self-pity on things over which we had no control. We feel our loss just

41

as keenly as you - maybe more so, but we can't let our grief overcome us. If you thought about things carefully, Tony, you would realise that you don't need to find strength in a bottle. All the strength you need is inside you."

He took a firmer grip on Tony's shoulders. "Do you think you have a monopoly on guilt? I have more than my share to contend with; yet you don't see me shouting 'hey world, look at me. Isn't it tragic that I have to accept all this? Isn't it terrible that life will carry on whether or not I want it to?' If you want or expect pity Tony, you're in the wrong place. I'll tell you one thing, though," and John's voice took on a dangerous edge, "I never thought I'd hear myself say this, but I'm *glad* that George isn't here to see the way you turned out. He was counting on you to be strong but he miscalculated very badly. George wouldn't have been proud of this exhibition you've been putting up for the last few weeks, he would have *loathed* it, and he would have loathed *you* for being so spineless."

The mention of Hayter caused Tony's anger to erupt. John's voice forced him to look inside himself and see things from a perception other than his own, and he didn't like what he saw. When John forced him to see how his reactions had been a betrayal of Hayter, when forced to the understanding that Hayter would, indeed, have loathed the adjustment which Tony had made, he had reacted before thinking, which was very easy in his inebriated state.

He broke John's grip and landed a solid punch to John's jaw. It was so unexpected that John was forced over backwards. As he lost his balance he struck his head on the corner of Margaret's bedside table. He collapsed to the floor, unconscious.

The realisation had sobered Tony quickly, and he moved to John's side, checking respiration and pulse. "I think he's all right, Margaret..." he had begun to say. As he locked his eyes on hers he saw the fury within them, her disgust at his action, and knew that their relationship was finally, irrevocably, dead.

Ignoring him, she pressed the 'call' button, and then moved to examine John for herself. Tony backed away, knowing that he no longer had any place here, that his acceptance of his melancholy and depression had cost him dearly.

He left the room and the hospital quietly, deep in thought. That dark side of his personality had done an excellent job of destroying his relationships with those who once had been closest to him.

As he drove back to the mansion, that night, he made many connections and revelations about himself. For the first time, he knew how much he had hurt John and Margaret, and knew that there was nothing he could do to redress the balance. He convinced himself of the fact. There was, he decided, only one way to try and atone for his actions; never to intrude upon either of them again. George Hayter had been notoriously difficult to unearth. Tony felt that he would be able to emulate his Great-Uncle in this, if in nothing else.

**

Margaret drained the last of the coffee from the cup, wondering where Tony was these days. Since that night, over ten years ago, neither she nor John had heard from him. They had attempted tracing him, but as with George Hayter, so long ago, they had been unsuccessful.

She stood and wandered over to the piano. She removed the cover, and opened the lid, before sitting, looking at the keys which she had been unable to manipulate properly on her first visit to the mansion. Since then she had taken lessons, and although not up to Hayter's standard, she was a passable pianist.

But playing, here in this room, somehow became easier. She found that she didn't have to concentrate upon what she was doing, freeing her thoughts to dwell upon the past. She understood exactly what Hayter had meant when he had told her that playing helped him concentrate upon difficult matters.

Swallowing a lump which suddenly rose in her throat, she began to play Grieg's Piano Concerto.

As she lost herself in the music, she thought back to events of years previously.

**

Nurses had answered her summons, and hoisted John unceremoniously onto Margaret's bed. Some smelling salts had quickly brought him back to consciousness. Starting up, he had demanded to know where Tony was. It was only then that Margaret realised Tony was no longer there. John was furious, threatening what he would do to Tony when he managed to get his hands on him, when he suddenly broke off, confused.

Margaret had asked him if he was O.K., but he had ignored her question, tilting his head comically to one side, as though listening intently. His hands moved to rub his eyes through the bandages. He shook his head quickly, as though to clear it of the last traces of ammonia, but his look of incredulity remained.

"I think I can see," he whispered, as though to give the thought stronger utterance might negate what he was saying. He began fumbling with the bandages, until a nurse gently, but firmly, pulled his hands away. "Let me get these bloody bandages off," he had demanded, but the nurse was adamant. The bandages would be removed under the supervision of John's doctor.

But John was not content to wait. He insisted on his doctor being summoned there and then. He was so excited and insistent that the nurse finally agreed.

Some two hours later, John, his bandages removed, sat gazing at Margaret as though he had never seen her before, and was memorising every detail of her face for a future painting. She found this frank appraisal a little unsettling, but accepted it, caught up in John's almost childlike joy at the gift of sight.

From fury at Tony, John now wanted to thank him for the punch which, it seemed, had returned his sight. He admitted that he had goaded Tony simply because he was tired of his cynical attitude, but John was certain that Tony would like to hear the good news.

However, by that time, Tony was driving away from the mansion and out of their lives.

With him out of the picture, Margaret and John slowly came closer together, each supporting the other when a painful reminder of past events brought the shadow of depression, which had temporarily engulfed Tony, into their minds.

They were both released from hospital on the same day the following week. By unspoken agreement they returned to the mansion. There was no sign of Tony. They had made their way to John's wing of the mansion, where they sat, discussing events and deciding what to do.

Hayter had been *far* wealthier than anyone had suspected. He had divided his wealth between the three of them, with a few other bequests. The mansion he had left to Margaret, with a proviso that John be allowed to continue to occupy it for as long as he so wished.

The rights to his occult works had been left to Tony, along with the last of Hayter's unpublished works, to be published or not at his discretion.

John had been left a flat in London which he hadn't known that Hayter possessed.

As they talked over what they might do in the future, each felt a physical pain at being in Hayter's mansion. Hayter's death seemed, if anything, more profound. Neither of them could face the prospect of living there so soon after the old man's death.

They visited his grave, each standing silently, lost in their own memories of him.

They had travelled to London the next day, John to look over his flat, Margaret to renew her acquaintance with the flat which she rented. The fact of her wealth had not yet been absorbed. She spent the morning renewing various acquaintances by phone. She had resigned from her job whilst still in hospital, knowing, vaguely, that she would never again have to work at a job which she detested.

She had met John for lunch even though he was half an hour late. He was enthusing over his flat which, he assured her, was more luxurious than he could ever have imagined. It even had a room which he was certain would make an excellent studio. He had insisted on taking her to see it.

As weeks turned into months, they saw each other virtually every day. John planned to open an art gallery, and was never so much in his element as when he was working towards this end. Margaret helped as much as she could, helping him choose suitable premises and assisting in the choice of decor.

Eventually, eight months after they had been discharged from hospital, John's art gallery was ready for its grand opening. He had invited several critics and artists to a celebration of its opening, and it was there, as the celebrations drew on into the night, that he proposed nervously, holding a diamond and ruby engagement ring out to her, as though he was stunned at his own audacity. Margaret hadn't needed to think about his offer, simply accepted it.

Five weeks later, they were married quietly in a civil ceremony, witnessed by an associate of John's, and an ex-workmate of Margaret's. Both had hoped, secretly, that Tony might take advantage of the situation to attempt to heal the rift which lay between them, but he didn't appear, nor sent any indication that he might have known they were getting married.

***

Margaret realised that the Concerto had ended some minutes ago, and that she had been sitting there motionless, arms by her sides, thinking over the past. She left the room to make another coffee, then sat again before the piano.

Her fingers glided over the keys, Chopin this time, and again she thought back to the past.

After touring Europe on their honeymoon, they had returned to the hard work of running the gallery. It was not essential, from a financial point of view, that the gallery made a profit, but John relished the challenge of making certain that it did do so.

Many of John's own paintings were sold there, and Margaret was persuaded by John to contribute some of her own drawings and sketches. When they sold quickly, for what seemed to Margaret to be an astronomical price, she began sketching more regularly for the gallery. However, knowing they would be sold for the kind of prices which John placed on her work, Margaret often became guilty of trying *much* too hard, rather than sitting languidly, tranquilly, and allowing her natural gifts for sketching to take over and dictate what she drew.

Margaret demanded and forced her talent to come and aid her whilst she was sketching, but more often than not the pressures and demands which she placed upon herself resulted in the quality of her sketches suffering drastically.

Many of these Margaret shredded in disgust. It was a good

thing, she thought, that she wasn't under contract to John to produce sketches of a certain quality.

When she felt at peace, happy and tranquil deep inside, and she sketched with no conscious preconceptions of how much they might earn, Margaret created her best, her most beautiful work.

However, she found it hard to draw and sketch without thoughts of the amounts John would charge for her sketches to float into her mind and so ruin her efforts, to John's irritation and, paradoxically, Margaret's amusement.

But Margaret began to be bored by this existence. It satisfied her creative abilities, but she began to feel that there were other, more important things which she could do.

It was this restlessness which led her to the Orphanage.

She had walked into the gallery to overhear part of a conversation between John, and his Gallery Manager, Steve Preston.

"....of course, there isn't much chance for the poor thing. She's been left paralytic and incontinent. Very few people would be willing to undertake the kind of intense care that she would need. She'll spend the rest of her life in care," Steve had said.

"God. Poor kid," John replied, shaking his head. "That's no life. It's not even an *existence*."

"Agreed. But there is no one. All her family were killed in the accident. Most she can hope for is that she dies quickly."

"What?" John demanded, incredulously.

"Well, how would you feel, in bed twenty-four hours a day, with no way of amusing yourself, and nobody even to come and visit you?"

John had thought this over; Margaret could imagine the thoughts which were running through his mind: memories of his own enforced confinement.

Of course, he had had the use of his limbs, and people to visit him, but even so the enforced monotony had nearly driven him mad.

"Is there anything which could be done for her?" John had asked. Steve had laughed at that. "Oh, yes. If the Orphanage

47

had twenty thousand to splash out on this one of the sixty that they cater for, but funding isn't what it might be."

Margaret had broken in on their discussion. "What are you talking about?"

John smiled faintly. "Steve has just been telling me about a girl who's been admitted to the Orphanage where his wife works. She was with her family driving to Wales. Their car was involved in a horrific crash. Her parents and two brothers died. She survived, but is virtually paralysed from the neck down. She has no other relatives. I think that you heard the rest."

Margaret looked at them. For moments, speech eluded her. "It's barbaric," she finally said. At the blank looks which were flashed at her, she continued. "That anyone could be left to rot like that. Doesn't anyone care?" she demanded,

"Slow down, Margaret," John urged. "If nobody cared, she *wouldn't* be in the Orphanage."

"Of course people care, Margaret," Steve added. "But the money just isn't available."

"Then it should be made available," she snapped back at him.

Steve looked at her, refusing to be drawn into an argument. John placed his hand on her arm and led her into his office. They sat. "Margaret, I understand your feelings, but there's no need to bite Steve's head off about it. He was expressing the same feelings as you before you came in,"

Margaret rubbed at her forehead. "I'm sorry, John. You're right. I just get so annoyed when I hear things like that."

"I know the feeling," he replied. "It's a pity we can't do anything."

"Why can't we?" she demanded. "We wouldn't miss twenty thousand."

John frowned, "We soon would if we started donating that kind of money to every deserving charity we heard about."

Margaret sighed. "I suppose so," she admitted. John glanced at her, eyes narrowed. When Margaret agreed with him so quickly, it usually meant that she had thought of something, but not necessarily something of which John would approve.

"But this could be a one-off," she said, smiling at him. "What's the use of money if we just let it sit there — especially when it might improve the quality of that girl's life."

John sighed heavily, knowing that nothing he might say would dissuade her. He had learned many things from Hayter, one of which was the ability to concede defeat gracefully. "It's your money, Margaret. If this is what you want to do, I can't stop you — and I wouldn't try."

Margaret smiled at him. "That's one of the reasons I love you," she said.

"Why?" he asked. "Because I'm so reasonable?"

"No," she replied, grinning at him. "Because you let me get my own way."

He made a move towards her in mock anger, but she eluded him, fleeing from his office, laughing. John looked at her, through the open door, seeing her talking to Steve apologetically, yet making a note of the details. He scratched his head. He had an uneasy feeling about this.

***

Margaret stopped playing abruptly. She smiled. John had confessed to her how uneasy the whole idea made him. With hindsight, his fears had proved unjustified; as she became more involved with the Orphanage, John began to take a deeper interest in her activities.

It was this, more than anything else which provided the fulfilment which she needed so badly. She glanced at her watch. It was time to head back home. Almost regretfully, she replaced the dust covers as they had been and left the mansion, locking the door behind her. She looked at the mansion, and the land surrounding it, before getting into her car and beginning the return trip to London.

She lit another cigarette as she drove, remembering her first journey to the mansion; the inn, the fog. Her mind settled itself back into the train of thought she had been following inside the mansion.

***

She had made an appointment to see the Director of the

49

Orphanage the next day. She was, for some unfathomable reason, surprised that the Director was a woman.

Margaret was early for her appointment, but the Director saw her anyway, asking in what way she might be of help. They sat.

"I'm sorry, Mrs. Anderson," Margaret said, "I didn't explain why I wanted to see you. It's not what you can do for me that I want to talk to you about, it's what I *might* be able to do for you."

Mrs. Anderson frowned. She looked to be in her fifties; her face was pleasant, creased with laughter lines. Not attractive, Margaret thought, but more intriguing. Margaret intuited that, although this woman had a pleasant personality, she could be a formidable opponent. It was only after Margaret had got to know her better that she realised Mrs. Anderson was used to fighting bureaucracy in order to get higher funding and better equipment. She had the welfare of all her charges at heart, and anything that threatened that welfare caused her to react as an angry mother protecting its young.

This knowledge endeared Mrs. Anderson to Margaret. Equally, when Mrs. Anderson realised that Margaret, too, thought only of improving the lives of the children within the Orphanage, the two became firm friends.

An ally with so much money was a rarity, yet Mrs. Anderson didn't value Margaret just for that, but more so for the publicity which she and her husband could generate to highlight the plight of the Orphanage.

Although Margaret regularly made donations, Mrs. Anderson valued Margaret's friendship much more highly. She was someone to whom Mrs. Anderson could turn when she needed a sympathetic and understanding ear when problems with the Orphanage weighed heavily on her mind.

Margaret re-ran that first conversation through her mind.

"I'm afraid that I don't understand."

"A friend of my husband's was telling him about a girl who was involved in a road accident, and is paralysed. They were saying what an appalling tragedy it was."

Margaret fell silent. Mrs. Anderson nodded. "Yes, although

Mrs. Preston doesn't exactly work here. She is a volunteer who visits the orphans from time to time, sometimes takes some of them out for the day. She has special clearance from the Board, of course."

"Her husband and mine were saying that if the money was available, things could be done to make life....easier for her."

Mrs. Anderson laughed, drily. "Mrs. Brandon, that is a very big 'if'. We simply do not have the resources to buy the type of equipment which would be needed. We are talking specially adapted electric wheelchairs, a computer, a complex..."

"How much?" Margaret interrupted.

"Pardon?"

"How much do you think you would need?"

Mrs. Anderson looked at Margaret quizzically. "I don't have an accurate figure available. I believe, in the region of fifteen thousand or so."

Margaret locked eyes with the Director. "You have the money."

Mrs. Anderson's eyes became hard. "If this is some kind of sick joke, young woman...."

"It's no joke, Mrs. Anderson. I'm very, *very* serious."

The Director's eyes became less aggressive. Her expression became one of bafflement. "But *why* should you want to do this? I'm not saying I'm convinced you mean what you say."

"My husband was saying that it's a pity nothing can be done. Well, I am in a position to do something. I won't sit back and let this child suffer any more than she already has done."

"Bravo," Mrs. Anderson said, quietly. "It's a pity other people can't adopt the same attitude." She glanced down at her desk before continuing. "But, of course, you know that I couldn't possibly accept your offer — even if it *is* genuine."

Margaret's face fell. "Why ever not?" she demanded.

"Because there are rules, Mrs. Brandon. I cannot divert any donation to one of our children rather than another merely because the donor expresses a preference. You must understand what a dangerous precedent that could create."

"And if I donate the money to the Orphanage?"

Mrs. Anderson took a deep breath. "Then it would be used just like any other contribution. To buy equipment which is needed by the majority of the children in our care. I could not justify spending such a large amount of money on equipment which is needed by only one of the children in this institution. Not when there are so many other things which would benefit many, many more of these children."

Margaret took a cigarette from a pack in her handbag. "Do you mind?"

The Director smiled, "No. In fact, I'll join you."

"There must be a way around this," Margaret insisted.

Mrs. Anderson shrugged. "I wish I had a pound for every time I've said that myself."

"What if," Margaret began. "Yes, Mrs. Anderson, what if you gave me a list of what is needed. I buy the equipment and *then* donate it to the Orphanage."

Mrs. Anderson blew out a lungful of smoke. "It's highly irregular," she said, "but not without precedent."

"Then that's what I'll do," Margaret declared, "And," she added, becoming caught up in the expressions which were chasing each other across Mrs. Anderson's face, "I'll donate a further ten thousand to the Orphanage. That way, nobody can accuse me of any prejudice or bias."

Mrs. Anderson's mouth fell open. Margaret had to struggle not to laugh out loud at the reaction her offer had elicited.

"*Jesus*," Mrs. Anderson finally said. "You *are* serious, aren't you?"

"I said earlier, Mrs. Anderson, I'm very serious."

"I think you'd better call me Sue," she said.

"I'm Margaret," she replied, with a smile.

Sue frowned. "Forgive me if I ask an impertinent question, Margaret."

"Go ahead."

"Why? Most people go out of their way to avoid making donations. Many don't want to admit to the existence of children whose lives are empty of love, of care. *Why* do you want to help them?"

Margaret frowned, looked down at her knees for a moment, and then looked into Sue's face, before continuing: "I could say that it felt like a good idea at the time, but there is more to it than that. I was physically abused by my father, as a child. There was no one there to help or to protect me. I understand what it's like to be alone and afraid: I never knew my mother — she died when I was little more than a baby.

"I remember, for doing the least, most *trivial* thing wrong, my father would force me to strip naked, and then, using a particularly heavy leather belt, he would beat my buttocks and the backs of my legs until I collapsed. He would belt me so viciously with it — until my legs just couldn't support me anymore." Tears came into Margaret's eyes as she brought these particularly hideous memories to mind and shared them with Sue.

Sue seemed about to comment but Margaret forestalled her by continuing: "And *sometimes*, as I lay on the floor after collapsing, whilst I was still shrieking and screaming and sobbing in agony, and begging him to stop, he would carry on beating me *brutally* with that belt, not caring where it landed on my body. The pain went *beyond* excruciating; and sometimes he only stopped after I lost consciousness — presumably because it wasn't as enjoyable for him when I didn't scream and yelp and *beg* him to stop beating me." Margaret pulled a tissue from her handbag and dabbed the tears from her eyes before they could begin trickling down her face. She took a deep breath, and then continued: "I remember feeling so isolated and alone; and I *knew* that no one loved or cared about me."

The expression which appeared upon Sue's face told Margaret that what she had related had been understood. "And so, if I can do anything to help these children, I want to. I have been *very* lucky. I'm happily married, I have money. I have everything to live for. Most of these children will not be as fortunate as I have been."

Sue's eyes held Margaret's. "Thank you for confiding in me," she said. "If you hadn't, I would have been questioning your motives and drawing the worst conclusions. Would you like a coffee?"

"Please," Margaret replied, taking a deep breath and trying to shake off the emotions which thinking about her childhood invariably generated within her.

"It's the least I can do for someone who has just offered the Orphanage twenty-five thousand pounds," Sue said. "You know, Margaret, I'm suddenly very pleased that I decided to see you."

Margaret laughed. "When could you let me have the list of what equipment is needed?"

"Tomorrow," Sue replied. She left the room, excusing herself, and returned a few minutes later with two cups of coffee.

"Could I visit her?" Margaret asked.

"Georgina?" Sue groaned. "I know that this is going to seem very ungrateful, but our rules are very strict on that. No unauthorised visiting is permitted. I'm afraid that I would be in hot water if I made an exception."

"But I thought volunteers visited the children, took them out."

"Yes. But *cleared* by the board of Governors."

"How would I go about getting clearance?"

"By applying for it. It would need to be approved by a member of the Board before they would consider it, though. And once approved there would then be a mandatory background check."

Margaret sighed. "And I would have to manage to run one of them to earth and convince them that I am genuine before they would approve my application for consideration by the Board?"

Sue nodded, and then grinned. "But I happen to be a member of the Board, and, although it's unusual, I will endorse your application."

Margaret looked at her, gratitude written over her features.

"I'll get you the necessary forms before you leave. If you can get them back to me before Friday, I can present them to the Board on Friday evening. Honestly, Margaret, having just promised such a sizeable donation, I can't foresee any problems whatsoever. It will mean that the mandatory checks can begin that much more quickly, too."

***

Margaret pulled up at a red light. The rain which the sky had promised earlier had materialised, a fine drizzle. She yawned. The traffic lights changed, and she moved off, winding her window down slightly to let some fresh air into the car.

It had taken less than two weeks for the Board of Governors to approve Margaret's status as an authorised visitor. John had mentioned cynically that the clearance had come through the day after her cheque had cleared. Margaret preferred to think that that was just coincidence. She had mentioned to John that she was now, officially, a member of a very select band.

"Must be very bloody select if it takes twenty five thousand pounds just for membership," he had replied. She had glared at him and asked if he would like her to add a few finishing touches to his latest paintings.

Although she was only joking, the threat had the desired effect. He stood in front of her, as though to prevent her getting anywhere *near* his studio.

"All right, I take it back," he said.

"Are you sure?" she asked, innocently.

"Very sure. Sure enough that you don't even need to *think* about going near my studio."

She stepped away from him, swaying her hips provocatively. "That's what I like," she said.

"What's what you like?" he demanded, guessing what was going to happen.

"A man who knows when he's defeated," she said, grinning impudently.

"And you think that you've defeated me, do you?"

She nodded. "Unless you can think of some way of asserting yourself. After all, if you don't, I might begin to think that I can get away with anything."

"Is that so?" he said, quietly, advancing upon her. She began to move away from him. He darted towards her, and she tried to elude him. He was lucky, guessing which way she was

55

going to turn. He held her close to him, although she struggled to free herself,

"Well, I can't have you thinking you can get away with anything," he said to her. "Now, I wonder just what would be the best way to assert myself." He grinned and took a long, long look at her, from head to toe.

He transferred her wrists to his left hand, and, as she continued to struggle, he began slowly, leisurely almost, to undo the buttons of her blouse. She almost tore free, but he recaptured her, and bore her to the floor. He continued undressing her, her fake struggles becoming weaker as she surrendered to the feelings building up within her. Her mouth sought his, and they dissolved into each other.

Margaret smiled at the memory. Although there was no way of proving it, she was certain that she had conceived from that particular act of mutual seduction.

She had been stunned when her pregnancy was confirmed. It was the last thing which she had expected. Margaret wanted children, but, for some reason, she had never imagined that she would become pregnant. The news had elated her, as she had known it would John. Although she couldn't wait to tell him, her deeper instincts had instructed her to choose the right moment carefully.

She had wanted an intimate and relaxed atmosphere. She wanted, and needed, to see the look upon his face as she told him. It would, she knew, be something which she would remember for the rest of her life.

It was, but not for the reason she thought. She had prepared a romantic dinner for two: candles, soft music. She had known that John would be home by six thirty, and laid her plans accordingly.

At seven thirty he had not appeared. She had tried calling the gallery, but there was no response.

At eight thirty, the dinner was ruined, and so was Margaret's mood. At nine fifteen, the front door had opened, and John had called her. She had taken a deep breath, attempting to bite down her irritation. True, the evening meal was beyond salvage, yet she could, surely, recapture the romantic mood she had been in earlier.

She had entered the living room, a welcoming smile upon her face. It had disappeared abruptly as she caught sight of Steve Preston and a man who she didn't know.

"Oh, Margaret," John had said, "sorry I'm a bit late. This is Stuart Audley," he had indicated the unknown man, who had seated himself in the nearest chair. "We're discussing the possibility of displaying some of his work."

John noticed the look on Margaret's face. "Is everything ok?" he asked her.

She had forced a smile: "Fine."

John had held her gaze for a second, before turning back to Mr. Audley. She turned, heading towards the kitchen. She knew John would expect her to brew coffee and stay out of the discussion. Margaret's business sense left much to be desired, and John always handled anything connected with that side of running the gallery. Although he frequently sought her opinions in private, before making any decisions.

She had brewed coffee. She had taken it in on a tray, allowing them to pour their own. John was extolling the virtues of his gallery, when she caught his eye.

He broke off what he was saying with a slight frown at her.

"If you want anything else, could you get it yourself? I'm going to bed."

"Do you feel all right?" John asked her, a slightly worried frown on his face. It was the first time she had ever absented herself from any of these discussions, although she tended to take no active part in them.

"Fine," she replied. "I've just got a headache."

John nodded at her, obviously not convinced. "We won't be long," he assured her.

But Margaret knew better. John was a ruthless businessman, and as tenacious as a bulldog. He would spend hours in such discussions, getting the best possible deal for himself and the gallery.

In any other circumstance, John was as easy going as was possible to imagine. But, where business was concerned, his personality seemed to undergo a total reversal. He had an instinctive understanding of how far he could push potential clients, when he had obtained the best possible terms. He took an almost sadistic delight out of these proceedings, and Margaret understood that his business dealings provided a harmless outlet for any feelings of frustration which might have built up within him. He tended to accumulate his feelings of annoyance, when a painting wasn't going as well as it could have been, when the gallery had had a bad week, when he, himself, felt under the weather.

John never released these feelings upon Margaret; he tended, instead, to hide these emotions deep within himself, only allowing them release in a situation where they could be released relatively harmlessly.

So, John and Steve and Stuart Audley discussed business; John with his usual ruthlessness, Steve agreeing John's points, suggesting alternatives when it seemed that the other two had reached an impasse.

Eventually, the three of them had come to agreement. John had brewed more coffee, and they sat talking and laughing. Stuart Audley grinned at the sudden change in John Brandon's attitude now that their business had been concluded.

"Are you always so aggressive in your business dealings?" he had wanted to know.

"I suppose so," John laughed, as he caught Steve nodding his head vigorously. "It's a cut-throat market. You have to be quite aggressive to survive."

Stuart had nodded. "Well, Mr. Brandon, I look forward to a mutually profitable association. I'd better be going, it's late."

"I'll give you a lift," Steve said. He added, as an afterthought, "If Margaret's still awake, tell her I'm sorry about her headache." He hesitated. "John, it's not for me to comment, but Margaret seemed upset."

John nodded. "I thought so, too. Maybe it's a migraine."

The others made their exit, leaving John alone in the sitting room. He carried the tray back into the kitchen. Now that he no longer had a potential client to think about, he was more alert to unusual things in the kitchen than he had been.

He saw the candles. Frowning, he wondered what they were doing there. As comprehension dawned, he looked

58

tentatively into the oven. He saw the remains of dinner there. He took a deep breath. Margaret's sudden headache was explained, he thought. Yawning, he decided that he would make it up to her tomorrow.

Entering the bedroom quietly, he undressed and slipped into bed, being as careful as he could not to disturb Margaret, who, by this time, would be asleep.

He relaxed, feeling himself begin to drift along into sleep. However, something prevented him. He shifted position irritably. He felt the bed shake.

"What the...?" he said, rousing. It took him a second or two to realise that Margaret was the cause of the shaking. She was sobbing, quietly.

John sat up in bed, switched on the bedside lamp, and put a hand gently upon her shoulder. "Margaret?" he asked, "what's wrong?" He moved closer to her, managing to put his arms around her. She turned into his embrace.

"Margaret," John repeated, "what's wrong?"

"Nothing," she lied.

John grinned at her. "Come on, tell me. And I don't want to hear about your non-existent headache, either."

Her sobs had diminished to the point where she was able to answer. "Was it that obvious?"

"Probably not to Stuart, but Steve told me that he thought you were upset. I found the candles and some unidentifiable dinner in the oven. I can put two and two together. I'm sorry, I should have rung and let you know that I'd be late. I didn't know you wanted a quiet evening alone with me. If I had I'd have made other arrangements with Stuart."

Margaret sighed. "I had something that I wanted to tell you."

John pondered this. "Something you wanted to tell me, eh? And you wanted a romantic setting. Must have been important."

She sat up, looked into his eyes. "I thought so at the time."

He sat, regarding her. It was obviously more than important to her. She was not the kind of person to overdramatise things. Tired as he was, John decided that there was only one thing which he could do. Her tears still glistened on her lower eyelashes. He wiped them away, carefully. To his knowledge, Margaret had never cried as a result of one of his actions until now. It told him how desperate she had been to communicate her news to him. He got out of bed.

"Where are you going?"

"Out. I'll be back soon." He smiled at her. "Brew some coffee, and we'll have that romantic meal when I get back, just as you planned it. Well, nearly," he added, thinking of the ruined mass in the oven.

He dressed quickly and left the flat. Margaret blinked back her unshed tears. She, too, got out of bed and got dressed. She went into the kitchen, washed the cups which John had left there, and brewed the coffee.

She was just setting the tray down as John returned. "Chinese take-away. Best I could do at this time of the morning."

Five minutes later, they sat opposite each other, eating John's improvised meal. He had rescued the candles, and they cast a soft light upon the scene. He turned on the music centre, and quiet background music filtered through the room.

They locked eyes. Margaret flashed a dazzling smile at him. He grinned.

"You save that particular smile for when you're really happy," he observed, bringing a forkful of rice to his lips.

"I suppose I do" she replied. "And I'm *very* happy."

John glanced at her, curiously. "Is that what you wanted to tell me?" be asked, sounding slightly deflated.

She broke eye contact, and looked hard at the table. He placed one of his hands over hers. "Well, love, whenever you feel ready. Not before."

Her eyes met his again, shyly, tentatively. She felt absurdly self-conscious; something which she hadn't felt since the first few days spent in Hayter's mansion.

John continued eating. He smiled at her. "I love you," he said, so softly that she only just heard him.

"John, I'm..." she faltered.

"You're what?" he asked.

"Pregnant."

His eyes jerked to hers. She saw several expressions run across his features. Disbelief, incredulity, shock. They gave way to exhilaration, joy, love.

He opened his mouth to speak, but found that no words would come. He was unable, at that moment, to express his feelings. He was, too, unaware that his face was talking for him, and was showing Margaret all the things which she had hoped to see.

He stood, and walked around the table to her. She stood, and he wrapped his arms around her in a bear-like embrace. "When did you find out?" he wanted to know.

"A few days ago, but I wanted to tell you when we were alone. I wanted to remember this for the rest of my life."

He groaned. "And I ruined it," he said.

She smiled at him. "I thought so, earlier, but this is perfect."

John's face radiated his feelings as he picked her up and took her back into their bedroom, the remains of the take-away forgotten. They made love, they talked, and they made love again. Finally, as full dawn broke, they slept, their bodies nestled together as closely as possible.

***

Margaret parked the car outside the flat. She locked it, before moving to the main entrance. She made her way to the flat, softly humming one of Rachmaninov's preludes.

"John," she called out as she entered. There was no reply. She frowned. Linda would be in bed, but John would never have left her alone. "John," she called again.

He appeared from the door which led to his studio. "Hi," he said, wearily.

She took in his appearance, noting the many stains upon his overall. He stretched and rubbed the back of his neck.

"You look tired."

"I am," he agreed, absently.

"Is anything wrong?"

He frowned. "I suppose not. Would you like a drink? I'm parched."

"Please," she replied. She followed him into the kitchen. "So, what's annoyed you?"

He glanced at her. "Well... after you'd gone, this morning, Linda had one of her school friends over. They were messing around in her room. Anyway, I remembered that I meant to look over Audley's revised contract, and that I'd left it at the gallery. Came to me as I was finishing the farm landscape. I told Linda I'd only be thirty minutes, and I was.

When I got back, she was sitting in the living room. Her friend wasn't anywhere to be seen. I knew there was something wrong as soon as I saw her face."

"What was it?" Margaret demanded. She was strict with her daughter, but not unfairly so. Usually, she found that a stern telling off was all that Linda required. Her daughter, she found, tended to listen to reasoned argument, and it was seldom after a scolding, that she repeated an offence. Upon occasion, Margaret felt that stronger measures were called for. If anything, John, she felt, was too lenient with his daughter.

However, at the moment, John was looking a little abashed. They made their way into the sitting room. As they sat, John resumed.

"I asked her the same question. She looked really frightened. Even when she knows that I've caught her doing something wrong, she doesn't look that frightened. So I knew that it was something serious."

"Well, what had she done?" Margaret asked, a little irritably.

"After I'd gone, her friend was asking about my painting. Because I'm not in any of her school text books, she can't believe that I make a living at it."

Margaret locked eyes with him. "She didn't take her friend into your studio?"

John nodded grimly. "But not just that. They started larking about; my landscape ended up face down on the floor. Not only that, Linda tripped over it, somehow. The whole thing was smeared beyond salvage."

Margaret took in a deep breath. "Can I see it?"

John nodded. They went to his studio. He indicated a

canvas against one wall.

Margaret turned it to face her. He had not exaggerated; if anything it was worse than he had indicated.

"Couldn't you sell it as an abstract?" she asked, flippantly.

He glared at her. "If it's of any consequence, that one has been commissioned. I might add at fifteen thousand pounds."

Margaret held up her hands in mock surrender. "Sorry, John. I was just trying to get hold of my anger before I went to see her." They returned to the sitting room. "How many times have we *both* told her that she is *never* to go into your studio?" Margaret asked.

"That's one of the things I asked her," John said.

"What did you do?"

He took a deep breath. "I was angry, Margaret, fuming. Perhaps I should have sent her to bed until I'd calmed down." He paused, looking directly at her.

"But you didn't?"

"Send her to bed? Yes, but not before I'd given her a real hiding — I'll tell you this, Margaret. I'll bet, after the spanking I gave her, that she'll never even think of going in there again."

Margaret looked at him for a long time. "Good," she finally said.

"What? I thought you'd be annoyed at me."

"Why? Because you did exactly what I would have done under the same circumstances? I've told you before, John, that you're not strict enough with her. You punishing her like that has probably hurt her far more than I could ever have done, and I don't mean physically. She deserved it, and that's the end of it."

"Then why do I feel so guilty about it?" he demanded.

Margaret smiled at him. "Because you're not as used to it as I am. Just accept it, John. At least some good will come of it. You won't have to worry about her going into your studio again."

He nodded. "How was the visit?"

"Fine. I stopped by the library, first, and got some books that I want to read through."

His grin became a smirk. "Don't tell me, let me guess. They are all by George Hayter."

She nodded. "I forgot to bring them in with me — I'll get them later."

John drained the last of his coffee. "Well, back to work. I don't think I'll be coming to bed tonight."

She frowned at him. "The landscape?"

He nodded. "The bloody thing has to be finished by the twenty-third. That means I've got less than two weeks to re-create it. I'm sure I can get it done in a few days, but I'd rather get it finished as soon as I can, or I'll start worrying about whether or not I'm going to meet the deadline, and you know what I'm like when I get worried."

She nodded. "Like the proverbial bear with the sore head."

He managed a grin over his shoulder at her, as he returned to his studio.

Margaret followed him. "Do you think Linda's still awake?"

John nodded, "I'm sure of it." He glanced down at his hands, then back at her.

"I think that I'll go and ask her to explain herself," Margaret said.

John nodded. "Might be an idea," he agreed.

She headed towards Linda's bedroom. At the door, she hesitated. She normally knocked before entering. Perhaps, Margaret thought to herself, if she withdrew that privilege amongst others, Linda might begin to understand that if she wanted such adult privileges, then her behaviour must be of a particular standard.

So, Margaret entered without knocking. Her daughter lay in bed, the light on, fully illuminating the room. Linda's eyes jerked to her mother's as she entered.

Margaret noted the redness surrounding her daughter's eyes, and the look of dejection upon her face. Linda broke eye contact first, guiltily looking down at the bed covers. Margaret felt a surge of compassion build up within her; it wasn't difficult for her to imagine the feelings and emotions which must be passing through her daughter's mind.

Biting down the surge of empathy, Margaret approached the bed, noting as she did so that Linda's clothes lay strewn haphazardly upon the floor. It was almost, Margaret thought, as though Linda had undressed and thrown her clothes to the floor in anger at the double punishment of the spanking and being sent to bed. In fact, this was exactly what had happened.

Margaret sat at the foot of the bed, saying nothing until Linda finally looked up at her. "Has Daddy told you what happened?" she asked, in a tone that was more a whisper than speech.

Margaret nodded. "I can't believe that you were so disobedient. I can't remember how many times you've been told *never* to go into Daddy's studio. What made you do it?" Margaret demanded.

"Claire wouldn't believe that Daddy was a painter. I told her that he is better than Picasso, 'cos you can tell what Daddy paints, just by looking at the paintings."

Margaret struggled, only just successfully, to stop herself from grinning at the idea that John was a better painter than Picasso. "But, if Claire didn't believe you," Margaret continued, allowing none of the sudden amusement Linda's statement had made to enter her tone of voice, "that still didn't give you permission to go into Daddy's studio."

Linda looked down at the bed covers again, absently rubbing at the shoulder of her nightie.

"Did it?" Margaret demanded.

Linda swallowed, before shaking her head.

"Pardon?" Margaret snapped at Linda, refusing to allow her to answer by nodding or shaking her head.

"No," Linda said, in a voice so low it was almost a whisper.

"Well, we agree upon that. Now what about the painting?"

"I didn't..." Linda began, then lapsed into silence. She gulped a breath, and swallowed again.

Margaret began to feel irritated. "You didn't what?" she asked.

Linda kept her eyes glued to the bed covers, as though too ashamed to meet Margaret's eyes. She shrugged her shoulders.

65

The silence stretched out; Margaret's anger reasserted itself. Her daughter's refusal to answer fuelled it still further. "Well, Linda, you've got a choice. You can either answer my question, or you can have another spanking and then answer it. It's up to you."

The threat worked. Linda's head jerked up. She looked into Margaret's eyes, almost as though she was trying to assess whether or not this was an empty threat. What she saw convinced her, however. Even so, she hesitated.

"All right, Linda, get out of bed and come here," Margaret said in her sternest 'Mummy is not amused' voice.

Linda made no move towards Margaret. Tears came into her eyes. "I didn't mean to knock Daddy's painting down," she blurted. The tears began to roll down her face. "I tried to pick it up, but I tripped over my shoelaces, and I fell on top of it."

Margaret frowned. "And how did you manage to knock it down in the first place?" she wanted to know.

Linda looked down at the bed covers again. "I pushed Claire. She pushed me back. I overbalanced, and knocked the painting down."

"So it wasn't Claire's fault — it was you who started it?"

Linda nodded, then, remembering Mummy had become more angry when she hadn't spoken, and the threat of a further spanking, which, she hoped, Mummy had forgotten about, she added, "Yes."

"Daddy told me he gave you a spanking. He is *furious* at you. I just hope that he punished you as severely as he said he did."

The look which crossed Linda's features told Margaret that John hadn't exaggerated the severity of her punishment.

"I'm angry at you, too," Margaret continued. "And I'm ashamed of you. We try to treat you like an adult, and this is how you respond. Like a four year old. Did you tell Daddy that you were sorry?"

Linda looked at her for several seconds, before admitting, "No."

For a couple of seconds, Margaret was sure that she had misheard.

66

"Why not? *Aren't* you sorry?"

Fresh tears began trickling down Linda's face. "Yes," she cried. "But Daddy was so angry that I didn't get a chance to tell him. And then he sent me to bed. I don't want Daddy to be angry at me anymore."

Margaret relaxed, a little. "Do you want to tell him that you're sorry?" she asked.

Linda wiped the tears from her face. "Yes," she said.

Margaret left the bedroom, and went to John's studio. She knocked.

"Yes, come in," he shouted.

Margaret entered to see John busily painting. "John, Linda would like to apologise to you."

John glanced at her. "Tough," he said.

"John, she tried to earlier, but you didn't give her a chance. She knows what she did was wrong. She's upset that you're so angry with her."

"She should have thought of that before she came in here."

"John," Margaret insisted, "she feels frightened. She needs to tell you that it wasn't deliberate. She needs to know that, although you're angry at her, you still love her."

John stopped painting, and turned to face her. "That's very articulate for a nine-year-old," he observed.

"There's no need for sarcasm," she snapped. "I know how she feels."

John considered. "I suppose you do," he said, "O.K." He put his paintbrush and palette to one side, and followed Margaret to Linda's bedroom.

As soon as she caught sight of him, Linda sat up in bed. "Daddy, I'm sorry. I didn't mean to do it."

John took a few paces closer to her. "I know that you didn't mean to do it. I'm glad to hear that you're sorry, too." Linda smiled at him, as he continued. "I love you Linda, nothing will *ever* change that. Being sorry about it helps, but it doesn't undo what you did. Do you understand?"

Her smile faded.

Linda stared at her father, dismay written over her face.

Seeing that he was waiting for an answer, she said, "I...I think so."

John managed an irritated smile at her, before turning and leaving the bedroom.

"Daddy," Linda shouted after him. John returned, frowning. "Are you too angry at me to kiss me goodnight?" she asked, timidly. His frown erased itself. He took a deep breath. "I suppose not," he said, approaching her, and kissing her cheek.

"Goodnight, Linda," he said.

He stood, looking down at her until Margaret broke in. "If you don't mind, John, I still have some things to do here." She was surprised by the attitude he had adopted towards Linda, but wouldn't let that surprise show in front of her daughter.

John glanced at her. From Margaret's expression, he knew that there were other things concerning Linda on Margaret's mind. He nodded at her. "I'll be in my studio," he said as he left, closing the door behind him.

"Mummy," Linda said immediately John had left, "what can I do to make it up to Daddy?"

Margaret thought about how she should answer. "You're going to have to work that out for yourself. Daddy's trying to teach you that if you do something wrong, you have to take responsibility for what you have done — and being sorry doesn't take that responsibility away from you. Daddy has to have that painting ready in ten days or else he might not able to sell it. I shouldn't tell you this, but the painting you knocked down and ruined was to have been sold for fifteen *thousand* pounds. Now Daddy will have to stay up all night painting it again. That's why he won't let you off with being sorry."

Linda's mouth fell: "Fifteen thousand pounds," she whispered, awed. She frowned. No wonder Daddy had been so furious with her — or that he had treated her so uncharacteristically harshly.

Margaret looked directly at her. "I think you've got more immediate things to worry about," she said.

Linda looked at her, uncomprehending.

"Linda, when I've told you not to do something, and you

do it, what happens?"

Linda frowned in confusion. "Sometimes you tell me off."

"And if you do it again?" Margaret wanted to know.

"You smack me."

Margaret nodded. "And what happens if I tell you to do something, and you don't do it?"

Linda looked at Margaret warily. She wasn't sure where this was heading, but she didn't like it. "You smack me," she repeated slowly, reluctantly. Margaret nodded again. "Can you tell me how many times I've told you to fold your clothes before getting into bed? How many times I have told you off about it?"

Linda guessed what was about to happen. She returned her gaze to the bed covers, feeling queasy. Two spankings in one day was unprecedented. "Lots," she whispered.

"And about ten minutes ago, what did I tell you to do?"

Linda swallowed. "To get out of bed and come to you."

"And what did you do?"

She continued avoiding Margaret's gaze. "I didn't do as I was told," she confessed, an anguished tone in her voice.

"So what am I going to do?" Margaret asked.

"Smack me?" Linda said, half in question, half in statement.

"I don't want you to think you're being punished again for what happened earlier," Margaret said. "Daddy punished you for that. I'm punishing you for disobeying me. You understand me?"

Linda nodded, albeit reluctantly.

"Good," Margaret said. "Now, come here."

***

Margaret sat up in bed, George Hayter's treatise on Demonology propped up on her knees. In the time since she had first been introduced to his writings she had made a lot of progress. She could absorb Hayter's reasoning and conclusions without having to give his premises a second thought.

As she finished the chapter she was reading, Margaret took a deep breath. Her own occult abilities had deepened and matured remarkably quickly. She had found that she had an instinctive grasp of occultism. Where others might have to memorise difficult incantations, or meet specific requirements, Margaret had found that she could usually achieve the same ends by focussing her will upon what she wished to achieve. Her instincts then took over.

It had become obvious to her that she was a 'natural' occultist. In many ways, her occult abilities reminded her of Hayter. Had he passed some of his power on to her, she wondered, or was it something which had always been there, but of which she had been unaware? She felt a little smile upon her face. It wasn't really fair, she thought, that she should have this ability, whilst others must undergo years of gruelling study to achieve half of her abilities.

And those abilities had come in very useful on more than one occasion.

Margaret laid the book to one side upon the bed, and lay back against the headboard, thinking back.

***

Soon after her clearance had been approved, Margaret had taken advantage of it to visit Georgina, the girl whose plight had first interested her in the Orphanage.

There were four dormitories, each housing fifteen children. The dormitories were split into cubicles to present at least a modicum of privacy. Margaret had thought that the space in each cubicle was too small, but it was better than nothing. Each child knew that their cubicle was their own private territory, where they could retreat in free time, without much chance of intrusion.

However, due to her obvious medical problems, Georgina was housed in the hospital wing. Sue had taken Margaret there. She introduced Margaret and then left, discreetly. Now that she had achieved her desire to visit, Margaret found that she hadn't got a clue about what she should say.

Georgina lay flat on her back. She managed to turn her head slightly in Margaret's direction, a questioning frown on her face. "Are you the new nurse?" she asked. "I know Mrs. Anderson introduced you, but I don't know you, do I?"

Margaret shook her head: "No, Georgina, you don't know

me. I'm not the new nurse; I came here to visit you. Didn't Mrs. Anderson tell you that I wanted to visit you?"

Georgina managed a nod. "She said that someone wanted to, but I didn't believe her. Was she talking about you?"

Margaret nodded. "I think so. I'm......a friend."

Her eyes narrowed, became hostile. "Are you?" she sneered.

Margaret intuited that she would have to win her friendship. She was grieving, perhaps feeling guilty that she had survived when her family had not. This apart from the feelings of helplessness and depression which she must be prone to. Margaret knew she could not be less than honest.

"Yes, Georgina, you're right. I'm not your friend."

The girl's face betrayed the shock which Margaret's statement had generated.

Margaret smiled. "That didn't come out quite right. What I meant to say was that I'd like to become your friend, if you'd like that."

Georgina's face softened. "I don't have any friends," she said, softly.

"But you must have," Margaret said. "Surely you had some friends before the accident." As soon as the words were out of her mouth, Margaret could have kicked herself.

Georgina winced, but answered. "I thought I did. They were such good friends that not one of them has been to see me."

Margaret bit her lip. "Perhaps they couldn't get permission to visit you," she suggested.

Georgina looked at her, a calculating look on her face. "That's not true," she said. "I overheard Mrs. Anderson telling the doctor that she had been to see each one of my friends. She wanted them to visit me and cheer me up. They all refused. I said I don't have any friends, Mrs. Brandon, and I don't say things that I don't mean."

Margaret realised that this child, which was the wrong description of the teenager in the bed, was very astute and intelligent. She became aware of the silence and of Georgina studying her at the same time.

"Maybe you're right," Margaret said, hoping that her frankness wasn't going to be taken the wrong way. Her instincts told her that that was so, but she was still uncertain about trusting them. "Maybe you don't have any friends. But I'm asking to be allowed to be your friend, to come and see you. To be someone you can talk to, if you want to."

"And to tell everything I say to Mrs. Anderson, so they can assess whether or not I've got any psychological problems," Georgina deduced in a flat, uninterested tone.

Margaret moved a chair closer to the bed and sat. "No. Nothing like that. If you want — ever — to say something to me as friend to friend, then I promise it will stay between us,"

Georgina looked a little puzzled. She had been expecting some spark of anger. "Why?" she asked. "Why should you give a damn about me? I might as well be dead as lying here. I've got nothing to live for," she added, bitterly. "It's all right for you, you can walk out of here when you get bored, I can't. I can't do a thing. You just don't understand what it's like. Why don't you take your pity and give it to one of the other kids here? Why pick on *me*?"

Margaret thought about this. "How old are you?" she asked.

"Thirteen. Why?" she spat back.

Margaret held her gaze for many seconds. "You're intelligent, and I think you might be old enough to understand. Georgina, I think I have a very good idea how you feel."

"How could you?" But Margaret detected a curious tone to the question.

"Well, until recently I was in a coma in hospital. Once I regained consciousness, if I hadn't had friends to visit me, I think I would have gone mad. But, more than that, I understand what it's like to be *hurt* and *alone*, with no one to turn to."

Georgina looked at her, sullenly. "Do you?" she asked, but the curious tone was still there.

Margaret sighed. This was not going to be as easy as she had supposed. "Georgina, if I tell you something about myself, something so personal that I wouldn't normally talk about it,

72

can I trust you to keep it to yourself? You might understand then how I can say I know what it's like to be lonely and afraid."

Georgina's face remained neutral, but there was a flicker of interest in her eyes. "You can trust me," she said.

Margaret thought about how best to begin, and then spoke. "When I was a child......"

As she related the story of her childhood and the abuse she had suffered at her father's hands, Georgina's face slowly lost its neutrality. She became absorbed in what Margaret was telling her. As Margaret related stories about the things which her father had subjected her to, Georgina's mouth opened in surprise and shock. Her eyes locked on to Margaret's, interest and intrigue expressed upon them.

She didn't interrupt Margaret once, simply lay listening. Margaret, for her part, found the telling compulsive. She included details which she wouldn't have related to a thirteen year-old-girl, under normal circumstances. She finally reached the part of her story when she had left home. She paused, realising that she had been talking for over an hour. She felt parched.

She excused herself to get a cup of coffee from the staff room. When she returned, Georgina was ready for her.

"Did he find you?"

Margaret frowned. "My father? Well, yes, eventually."

Georgina became impatient. "What happened?" She wanted to know.

Margaret sipped her coffee. "I'm not sure that I *should* tell you any more — let's just say that it wasn't pleasant."

Georgina shook her head. "You've told me so much - you can't leave it there." Her eyes sparkled, "not if you're going to be my *friend*."

Margaret looked at her sharply. She had, she realised, been trapped absurdly easily by this youngster. If she didn't complete the story, the initial point of relating her childhood would be lost. She could sense it.

She put her coffee upon the bedside table, and took a deep breath. "O.K., but this is all strictly between us two."

Georgina managed a nod. "Promise," she said.

Margaret took another deep breath. She avoided mentioning Hayter or occultism, and told the version of the story which Tony had given to the police. She described her humiliations whilst held by the Cult, but was careful not to give any indication that anything other than natural (but perverted) forces had been at work.

It took a further hour for Margaret to finish the story. She felt queasy herself, reliving all the experiences of her childhood and those at the hands of the Cult. She noticed Georgina's eyes, wide open, a mixture of admiration for Margaret and disbelief of the story obvious in them.

"Could you pour me a drink of water, please?" Georgina asked. Margaret did so, and gently held the plastic beaker to Georgina's lips so that she could sip it. As Margaret replaced the beaker, Georgina asked, "but how did your husband find you?"

"I wasn't married to him then," she replied. "As far as I understand it, he, and Tony, managed to follow one of them to the crypt."

"Very convenient," Georgina commented.

Margaret glared at her, sharply. "You mean you think I'm lying?"

Georgina nodded. "It's a good story, though. Very well thought up."

Margaret's glare intensified. She stood. "OK, Georgina. You won't believe me. That's up to you. I'm leaving now, and I won't come and see you again. But *before* I go, there's something that I think you might like to see."

Margaret took off her jumper, and began unbuttoning her blouse. Georgina's face mirrored her surprise at this turn of events. As Margaret removed her blouse, and stood facing her, she saw Georgina's eyes widen as she took in the scars which her flogging at the Cult's hands had left. They stood out vividly white against her darker skin. She turned, exposing her back to the girl's view. She heard her sharp intake of breath.

Margaret replaced her blouse, buttoned it, and pulled her jumper on.

Confusion and shock were obvious on Georgina's face. "But," she stammered, "but that means..."

Margaret stood for a few seconds, gravely staring into her eyes: "Goodbye, Georgina," she said, as she turned and headed for the exit.

She had only taken a couple of paces towards the door, when Georgina called after her. "Mrs. Brandon! *Please, don't go.*"

Margaret detected the sob.

She turned back towards Georgina, without speaking. She retraced her steps to the chair and sat. She watched the expressions which crossed Georgina's face in silence.

Georgina locked eyes with her. "I'm sorry, Mrs. Brandon. I thought you were trying to trick me; I'm just so confused. How did you get through what happened to you without it affecting you?"

Margaret smiled wryly. "Oh, it affected me, certainly. If you're asking me how I can *live* with the knowledge of what happened, then that's a different thing. I simply accept the knowledge. I can't do anything to alter the past. So, I think of the future. I'm lucky, really. I have a husband who is very understanding."

Georgina pondered this. "I hate being so helpless," she said. "I can't even go to the bathroom. I have to wear nappies."

Margaret nodded.

"It's so embarrassing, too. I don't think that I'll ever get used to strangers changing me. They try to make it less humiliating for me, but it doesn't really work. I can't do anything about my periods, either; I think that *that* hurts me more than not being able to move. You know what I mean?" Georgina's face reddened at admitting this to a relative stranger.

Margaret shook her head. "I can only try to imagine it. I think it's something that you can only comprehend when you've been in a similar position. Georgina, have you ever thought that the people here might find it as embarrassing as you do?"

She frowned. "No," she admitted.

"Unfortunately, Georgina, it's something that has to be done. I don't think the staff are trying to make things more humiliating for you. Imagine how mortified you'd become if they didn't look after that side of things for you."

Georgina's face creased into a frown as she considered what Margaret said. It was obvious that she hadn't thought of it this way before.

"If you think of it that way, then perhaps in time, you won't feel it as keenly."

Georgina grimaced. "I don't know. Maybe. But it's not easy."

Margaret nodded. "I didn't say it would be easy."

They fell silent. Margaret shifted position in her chair.

"Why was he like that?"

"Who?" Margaret asked, caught out by the sudden change of subject.

"Your father. Why was he so *cruel* to you? What made him do all those things you told me about?"

Margaret sighed. "I don't know. I wish I did. I don't know why he hated me; and that is the right word. He *hated* me."

"You know, Mrs. Brandon, I find it hard to believe."

She locked eyes with Georgina, who hurriedly corrected herself. "No, I believe what you told me. I don't understand why he treated you like that. My parents never use physical punishment..." she broke off, aware that she had used the present tense. "No, that should be 'used', shouldn't it? They are *dead.*"

She drew a shuddering breath, and seconds later was crying freely. Margaret left her chair and sat next to Georgina on the bed, gently stroking her soft, dark brown hair.

"That's it," Margaret said. "Let it out, Georgina. It's better to let these feelings out. Keep them inside you, and they'll eat away at you." She reached for her handbag and took out a packet of paper handkerchiefs. She gently dabbed the tears away from Georgina's face, as the girl continued sobbing uncontrollably.

At that moment Sue Anderson entered. She glanced quickly at Margaret sitting next to Georgina, comforting her.

Margaret returned the glance and indicated the door with her eyes. Sue understood. She nodded almost imperceptibly and left as quietly as she had entered.

Gradually, Georgina's sobs decreased, and finally stopped. She lay breathing quickly, suddenly seeming very hurt and vulnerable. Margaret wiped away the last of her tears. She continued stroking the girl's hair.

As Margaret gave her a small smile, she noticed the look in her grey eyes. She saw appreciation and gratitude; but, more importantly, as far as Margaret was concerned, she saw acceptance of her friendship.

"Feel any better?" she asked, gently.

Georgina nodded, than blushed self-consciously. "I'm sorry I was awkward with you before. Mrs. Anderson told me someone kind would probably be coming to see me. I thought it was arranged just to cheer me up; that's why I didn't think you were genuine. It seemed like some weird trick."

Margaret grinned. "What changed your mind?" she asked.

"Well, the things you told me. If it was a trick, you had to be making them up. If what you told me was true, then you either don't mind telling anyone about what happened, or you are genuine. You didn't want to tell me about what happened when your father found you. The scars you showed me, and the way you were ready to leave made me realise that what you'd told me was true.

"But there was something else," she added, shyly.

"What was it?" Margaret wanted to know. "If you don't mind telling me, that is."

Georgina blushed again. "When I started crying, I saw the expression on your face. It wasn't pity, it was compassion. No, it was more than that. It was as though you were sharing my grief, drawing it out of me and into yourself. That's what it felt like, anyway. It was as though you were looking at one of your closest friends and *sharing* her pain. That's when I knew that you really meant what you said about wanting to be my friend."

Margaret felt stunned.

"And I know that Mrs. Anderson was right. You *are* kind."

Margaret broke eye contact. "If we are going to be friends, then you'd better get used to calling me Margaret."

Georgina frowned, uneasily. "Mrs. Brandon, that doesn't seem right. It makes it sound as though I'm being cheeky. My dad is — *was* — very strict about things like that."

Margaret nodded. "I understand that; but it's not as though you've not been *asked* to call me Margaret. Don't you think friends should be on first name terms? How would you like me to start calling you Miss Thompson?"

She frowned. "All right: Margaret. How long are you going to stay?"

"Sounds like you want to get rid of me," Margaret said, smiling.

"Oh, no. I *didn't* mean it to sound like that."

Margaret glanced at her watch. "Gods! Actually, I've got to get moving."

A frown of annoyance crossed Georgina's features. "I've been here four hours already — I've got to go."

"I understand," Georgina said, with evident reluctance. She hesitated: "You *will* come and see me again, won't you?" she asked, earnestly.

Margaret nodded, "You try stopping me." She stood, picked up her handbag, and headed towards the door. As she reached it, she turned back to the figure lying in the bed. "I'll come again soon," she promised.

"Margaret," Georgina said, in a soft, gentle voice, "*thank you.*"

Sue had been waiting for Margaret. "How is she?" she asked, quickly.

She fell into step beside Margaret. "Fine, really. All I did was get her to release some of the anger and grief she feels. I suppose that it's a start."

"You seem to have got more of a reaction in a few hours than anyone else here has managed in several weeks," Sue observed. "Would you like a coffee?"

"I'd love one, but I can't. I've got to meet John at the gallery."

Sue nodded. "I won't keep you, then. Next time you visit,

though, I'd appreciate a talk with you about Georgina."

Margaret stopped walking. "What about her?"

Sue's face became serious. "Well, if what I saw was anything to go by, she likes you: trusts you. We are not having an easy time getting through to her. What I'm asking is that you let me know how she is. You may well find out things which she might be unwilling to confide in us."

Margaret looked straight into Sue's eyes. "Let me get this straight. You want me to tell you everything she might confide in me? To *spy* on her for you."

Sue's expression hardened. "I wouldn't put it that way. I'm thinking more of her needs."

"She needs someone she can trust not to hurt her," Margaret said. "She knows about your attempts to get her so-called friends to visit her. Do you wonder she finds it hard to trust people? She needs someone who will talk to her and listen to her and be there because they want to be. The last thing she needs is to find out that I'm repeating her every word to you."

Margaret made to carry on walking, but Sue took hold of her arm, gently. "I don't think you understood what I was saying, Margaret," Sue insisted. "What I am getting at, is this. If, when you visit her, you think she is more depressed than usual, let me know. I don't want to intrude on your private conversations. God knows that she doesn't get much in the way of privacy. But if I know she's feeling more depressed than usual, then I can make time to spend with her. I can let the staff know and ask them to be *more* patient with her. If I don't know about things like this, then there isn't a lot I can do; my hands are tied. I'm only trying to think of Georgina, Margaret. Am I being so unreasonable in that?"

Margaret turned to face Sue. She examined what she had heard. "My mistake, Sue. Of course you are right. I just don't want Georgina to think that I'm less than sincere about why I'm visiting her."

"I agree. I think that it's essential that there is someone that she feels she can trust; someone outside the Orphanage. I'll be very discreet about what you tell me, though. I'll make sure that she doesn't guess that you're giving me hints, every so often."

"As long as you don't expect me to start telling you everything she says," Margaret insisted, "because I won't do it."

They continued walking. They exchanged pleasantries before taking leave each other, at the entrance.

***

Margaret focussed on her bedroom door, as it opened cautiously.

"I thought you might have gone to sleep," John explained, as he caught sight of her sitting up in bed. He noticed the book on one side of her.

"Finished it?"

Margaret shook her head. "Oh, I got through the chapter that I wanted to examine, but my concentration seemed to be slipping. I was thinking about the first time that I visited Georgina."

John nodded, absently.

"You haven't finished that painting already?"

"No. I'm just making some coffee. I thought I'd ask you whether you wanted one."

"Please, John."

As he disappeared, Margaret reached for her cigarettes. She cursed as she realised that she hadn't got any here. She got out of bed and retrieved a pack from the living room. She took an ash tray with her.

When John returned, carrying her cup of coffee, his eyebrows shot up at the sight of Margaret smoking in bed. He placed the coffee on the table beside her. Immediately after, he went to the window and opened it to its widest extent. A sharp, cold wind blew into the room.

Margaret shivered. She glared at John, and thought she could *just* see the briefest of smirks on his face. She knew that if she complained about the open window, he would close it, but would dispose of her cigarette first. He stretched, and Margaret heard the click of joints popping.

"Are you taking a proper break, or drinking your coffee as you paint?" she asked.

John rubbed his eyes. "No, I think I'll stop for half an hour or so. I'm starting to see double. If I don't take a break, I'm going to make a mess of it."

Margaret smiled at him. "What are you going to do for the rest of that half hour?" she asked, moving slightly to make the bedcovers slide down and expose her breasts through her thin nightie.

John's gaze slipped down from her face and he grinned appreciatively. "Well, there is something that I fancy doing," he said.

Margaret crushed her cigarette out in the ash tray. She looked down at the bed, waiting for him to approach her, anticipating the seduction to come.

John advanced on the bed, retrieved Hayter's treatise on Demonology, and, before Margaret had realised what he had done, was leaving the bedroom.

"John?" she called, feeling absurdly frustrated, "what are you doing?

He turned to face her. "It's years since I've read this," he said.

"But, I thought that you were going to spend your break with me."

He grinned at her, slyly. "Lord, no," he said. "You'll taste of tobacco; the room reeks with it. I can't think of a better turn off." He turned and left the bedroom, chuckling.

"You *swine*," Margaret called after him, as the door closed. She glared at the stub of the cigarette. She knew how much John hated the smell of tobacco, and normally, smoking in their bedroom was forbidden. She took a resigned breath. She could understand his actions. Almost involuntarily, she smiled. She got out of bed and closed the window. The room had cleared of smoke. She returned to bed.

She realised that she had nothing to read, now that John had made off with Hayter's treatise. She didn't feel tired. She got out of bed again. She went to the living-room and selected a CD. Returning to the bedroom, she placed the CD in the CD player, and, seconds later, she was listening to Chopin's etudes, as played by George Hayter. The quality wasn't quite as good as the original recordings. Margaret felt that the originals were too precious to risk in everyday use, and had duplicated them all.

As the music took a firmer hold on her perceptions, calming and relaxing her, as these CDs by Hayter always did, she lay back in bed, closed her eyes, and her thoughts returned to the past.

***

Georgina had made Margaret feel a little nervous. When the girl's grief had broken, and Margaret had sat next to her, comforting her, she had realised that this was a golden opportunity to utilise her abilities by helping to alleviate some of Georgina's pain.

The physical contact between them had made it a simple matter for Margaret to attune her own finer perceptions to Georgina's. From there, it was a simple matter of drawing what Margaret tended to think of as negative emotions from Georgina and into herself.

She knew that she had to be very gentle and delicate about how she did it. The last thing Margaret wanted was for Georgina to have some idea that things were more than normal; Margaret sensed that Georgina would be very unresponsive to the idea of occult powers being used upon her. She had been very gentle. It was a simple operation not really demanding much in the way of concentration. Margaret had felt Georgina's fear, anger, despair, depression and grief slowly leave her, to be absorbed by Margaret's own self. It added a tremendous burden to Margaret, but one with which she felt able to cope. She knew that she would be able to neutralize all these emotions without any difficulty. She was basically a well-balanced woman, and extreme emotions had very little part to play in her psyche. Margaret could have banished each emotion individually, but that would have taken time, quiet, and concentration. She knew of an easier way, however.

All she had to do was sit and listen to Hayter playing Grieg's piano concerto, Hayter's favourite piece, and the darkest emotion would immediately be banished from her. It was as though no amount of dark emotion could withstand

Hayter's joy and happiness generated by the music which he had loved. It seemed that he had transformed his intangible emotions into a powerful weapon via the medium of music. In times of deep thought, Margaret intuited that Hayter had left her this legacy, almost as though he had been saying, 'To you, Margaret, whom I love, who knows what suffering is like, no more depression. I am with you, if only through the music which I play.'

That same night, she had put on a pair of headphones, and listened to Hayter's playing, and felt all Georgina's emotions leaving her, unable to find any anchor point in her personality for their presence. Even if there had been such an anchor, they would have been unable to withstand Hayter's onslaught.

It had seemed, Margaret thought, that Newton's law held in other areas than physics. To every action there is an equal and opposite reaction. From the feelings of grief and despair which she had absorbed, the pendulum now, having listened to Hayter playing, seemed to have swung the other way. Margaret felt invigorated, joyful, happy to be alive. How much of that was the theory of the opposite reaction, and how much was sheer absorption from George Hayter, Margaret could never readily define. It did give her an insight into just how Hayter must have felt after he had performed similar operations. He had never had the time to explain to her how using occultism had affected him, but she understood that he had gained immeasurable pleasure from using his considerable abilities to aid other people, despite his mind being constantly occupied by the threat which the Brotherhood had represented.

Now that was over, the Brotherhood just a bad memory. Margaret was more and more aware of the power which she could wield. She knew that she was not in Hayter's league (she didn't have the faintest idea about how to relocate herself, and was certain that she wouldn't be able to do it if she tried), but she was determined to utilise and refine those abilities which she had discovered she possessed.

She devoured every occult opus Hayter had produced, and, surprising her, she found that they made sense. She progressed rapidly, much to John's surprise. He, himself, had some occult ability, but it was not instinctive. He would struggle to get through most of Hayter's works, although he had little difficulty grasping the theory behind them. But John was happy not to attempt developing his own limited skills. He remarked on his lack of interest by reminding Margaret of his brother. Occultism, he had said, made him think of how his brother had been murdered by the Cult, and it was a subject which he never liked to think too deeply upon.

Margaret accepted this, but was surprised that John took a keen interest in her own progress, encouraging her when she seemed to hit some problem or other. Margaret had asked why he took such an interest in her progress when, as he had pointed out, it was a painful reminder of his brother.

John had smiled at her. "George once said that when a Baron began studying occultism, no power on Earth could prevent them. George, as you know, wasn't prone to exaggeration. That apart, if I know what you're doing, I'll feel easier in my own mind. George was a great one for making dangerous experiments, despite my objections. I don't want you to copy that trait; so, if I think that what you want to attempt is too dangerous, at least I'll have the opportunity of talking to you about it. After all, I know a lot about occult theory. Remember, I used to proofread George's output. I remember how annoyed he used to get at himself — and at me — when I spotted a mistake in what he had written." John had laughed at the memory; Margaret had joined in, trying to imagine Hayter's expression when corrected by John on the field of his expertise.

Having played the CD, Margaret had taken off the headphones, and thought about her encounter with Georgina. Margaret still found that she was more than surprised by Georgina's reaction.

Margaret had been as gentle as she could when taking over Georgina's emotions, but the girl had perceived what Margaret had done with unerring accuracy. The thing that bothered Margaret was that it should not have been possible for Georgina to make that connection. Not unless...

She sat up in her chair as the thought hit her. Now that she thought about it, it became obvious to her that Georgina must have some latent occult ability. She smiled, slightly. She had perplexed Hayter in almost the same way.

She knew, however, that Georgina would react towards occultism in a similar way to Margaret, before she had met Hayter. Margaret found that she could understand that, but she knew that she would have to be even more cautious about using occultism where Georgina was concerned.

It was almost two weeks before Margaret got around to visiting the Orphanage again, partly because she was nervous about Georgina making further connections about what she had done, and partly because John was insistent about her providing the gallery with four more sets of six sketches.

Margaret's visit was prompted by the phone call she received ten days after she had visited Georgina. John had answered it, and called her over: "Sue Anderson wants to speak to you."

Margaret took the receiver. "Hello, Sue?"

"Hi, Margaret. How are you?"

"Not so bad. What can I do for you?"

"Well, I was wondering, when are you next planning on visiting Georgina? She keeps asking me, and I have to tell her to be patient. I know that you've lots of things to do, but every day that goes by without a visit from you makes her more irritable. She won't communicate with us. To be honest, I'm getting worried about her."

"I'm sorry, Sue. Honestly: I intended to visit last week, but John insisted that I provide some sketches for the gallery. I've only just finished the second set, and he wants four sets."

"I see," Sue said. Margaret could imagine the frown on Sue's face. "So you won't be visiting for another couple of weeks?"

Margaret shook her head. "Erm... wait a second, Sue." Margaret put the phone down and had a quick conversation with John.

"Hello, Sue?" she said, having returned to the phone, "I'll be down tomorrow."

"But I thought you had to finish your sketches."

"I do, but I've told John that I'm taking a break tomorrow. What's the use of being the gallery owner's wife if you can't use your influence to get some time off?" Margaret laughed.

Sue's voice became warmer. "Thank you, Margaret. I appreciate it. By the way, Georgina has a couple of surprises for you when you get here."

"Really? What kind of surprises?" Margaret asked.

Sue laughed. "I'm under orders not to tell you. Georgina says that you will be so intrigued that you won't rest until you come here to find out."

"That young woman is devious," Margaret replied.

"I'm glad that I'm not the only one who's noticed. Will you be here in the morning or afternoon?"

"Yes," Margaret replied.

"Pardon?"

Margaret laughed again. "Well, I've got the day free, so I'll spend the day there. Perhaps that'll make up a little for the wait Georgina's had to put up with."

"You know, when I tell her that, she won't rest until you get here. She'll be running around everywhere. By the way, the offer of that coffee is still there."

"Thanks, Sue. I'll drop by your office before I go on to see Georgina."

"I'll look forward to it," Sue said. "See you tomorrow, Margaret."

As she replaced the receiver, she became aware of John standing behind her. As she turned, he placed his hands upon her shoulders. "So, you *think* you can use your influence on the gallery owner to get time off, eh?"

She smiled at him. "Oh, I'm sure I can."

He kissed her. "Damn right you can," he muttered.

Next day, Margaret drove to the Orphanage. The sun was shining, there was not a cloud in the sky. Margaret parked, and then made her way to Sue's office.

"Morning, Margaret," Sue said. She looked tired and drawn.

"Sue, what *have* you been doing? You look half-dead," Margaret observed, suddenly concerned.

She smiled. "It goes with the job. I've been burning the

candle at both ends, recently."

Margaret shook her head. "You look *terrible*. Why not go home and get some *sleep*? You look as though you need it."

She shook her head. "No, I'm fine. I might finish early, this afternoon, though. I do feel a bit under the weather."

Sue stood and left to get coffee, waving aside Margaret's protest that she could get it just as easily. Sue brought two steaming cups to the desk, and sat down heavily. She rubbed her eyes.

"How are things?"

"Hectic. Our physiotherapist is off sick, and our resident doctor has had to leave at short notice. His mother's died, apparently. So, we've a queue of kids waiting for physiotherapy, and I've been ringing around to find a doctor who is free to cover."

"Any luck?" Margaret asked.

"Yes, surprisingly. Dr. Paul Rheece. He lectures in one of the hospitals in London. He was in private practice until recently. Anyway, he sold his practice, and now he lectures. He said he would welcome a return to more practical medicine, even if it was no more than treating sore throats. He's even offered to cover for our physio whilst she's off sick."

Margaret frowned. "That *was* a stroke of luck."

"Indeed. Mind you, we were due for some. They say bad things come in threes. Well, we've had two. I was expecting this to be the third; I suppose that shows just how cynical I'm becoming in my old age."

"When is he starting?" Margaret wanted to know.

"Today. I saw him yesterday; gave him a tour of the place. He seemed impressed. The thing that really affected me was the way he made time to talk and play with some of the children - especially the handicapped ones. I get the impression that he's the ideal man for the job."

Margaret nodded. "Sounds good. Mind you, many doctors, these days, seem able to look through physical disability and see the potential of the person behind it."

Sue nodded. "True," she said.

Margaret drained her cup of coffee. "How's Georgina?"

she asked.

Sue frowned. "The last two weeks she's been moody and irritable. She kept asking when you were coming to see her again. I told her that you have many things to keep you occupied. She insisted that you are her friend and would be back to see her soon.

"Then, I suppose when she'd had time to doubt her certainty, she wanted me to phone you so she could speak to you."

"Why didn't you?" Margaret asked.

"Margaret, you've made a very large donation to the Orphanage — we are very grateful. You've begun visiting Georgina; no doubt, in time you'll be visiting all the children here," Margaret nodded. "But that *doesn't* give the children the right to disturb you at home. And," Sue added, with a rueful grin, "I don't think that it says in my contract that I have to act as a secretary or a telephone exchange."

Margaret grinned back at her. "I understand what you're saying — or rather, what you're *not* saying," Margaret said. "You were afraid that once she was allowed to speak to me over the phone, she'd be doing it every day. And then, that led you to think that I might get tired of it and disappear into the bright blue yonder."

Sue frowned at Margaret quizzically. "Do you read minds as a side-line?" she asked.

Margaret realised that she was using her intuitive occult abilities without being aware of it. Keeping her composure, she managed a laugh at Sue's suggestion. "I'm afraid not," she said. "But it was obvious that was what you feared by the way you tiptoed around it."

Sue snorted. "I suppose it was."

"Sue," Margaret said, "if Georgina wants to call me anytime, let her. I won't mind. I'll give her my number when I see her."

"That won't be of much use to her," Sue observed.

"No, maybe not. But it *will* show her that I have asked you to let her phone me."

"Well, if you're *sure*, Margaret."

"Positive. Well, I'd better get moving. She won't thank me for keeping her waiting." Margaret stood and moved towards the door. "Oh, I've been thinking."

"Yes?"

"Well, you can always use extra funds, right?"

"Too true."

"Well, I *think* I could persuade John to donate a couple of his paintings, and he's on good terms with quite a few artists. I think he *might* be able to get them to donate some of their work, or loan them to the gallery at the very least. Then, we could have a sort of charity day at the gallery, with *all* the proceeds to come here. What do you think?"

Sue lowered her eyes. "Margaret, if I didn't know you better, I'd swear that you're after my job. Knowing you better than that, all I can say is that if your husband agrees we *won't* be able to thank him enough. Don't forget, I've never met him, only spoken to him on the phone. It's not as though he's shown any interest in what we do here. If you can persuade him, we'd all be so grateful."

"I don't think it will be very difficult. I'll speak to him and let you know what he says."

Sue nodded. "I think it's a good idea, then. But, in keeping with my cynical nature, I won't get any hopes up until we know what your husband thinks of the whole idea."

Margaret nodded. "I'll see you later," she said.

"Maybe," Sue muttered. "I might have gone home before you leave."

"Well, if you have, I'll be in touch."

Sue nodded. Margaret left the office, and made her way to the hospital wing. She knocked at the door to the room which Georgina had inhabited the last time Margaret had been there. When there was no reply, Margaret opened the door. The room was empty, the bed stripped. There was no sign that the room was in use.

As she closed the door, Margaret heard a low electric whine. She turned in time to see Georgina grinning at her wickedly, her electric wheelchair powering down the corridor at a good five miles per hour.

"Margaret," she shouted. "I didn't think they'd remember to tell you that they've moved me to a different room."

The wheelchair drew to a halt. Margaret noted that there was a metal band running around the back of Georgina's head and terminating at her temples.

"Neat, eh? I only need to move my head and I'm off."

Margaret smiled at her. "Why did they move you?" she asked.

Georgina grinned. "That room was too small. There's so much equipment that it wouldn't all fit in there. They had to find me a bigger one." She turned the wheelchair in a half circle. "Come on, I'll show you."

Margaret walked beside her, as she took her to a room further down the corridor. As she had said, it was much bigger than the other. Margaret looked around, amazed at all the gadgets which she could see.

"I know," Georgina said. "Difficult to take in, isn't it? I've got people coming to see me almost every day to explain what each one is for, and how it works. The computer's the only one I can use properly, and I still have lots to learn."

Margaret found a chair and sat. "Looks like you've been kept busy," she said.

Georgina pulled a face. "I was *hoping* that you'd come sooner. I *couldn't* wait to show you that I can get around again."

"I'm sorry I took so long. I've had a lot of work to do the last couple of weeks."

"What do you do?" Georgina asked, then added self-consciously: "I'm sorry, it's none of my business."

Margaret smiled. "I help my husband with his gallery. He's a painter. I do some sketching; anyway, I've got to produce some sketches for him."

"Could I see some of them?"

"I've not got any with me. If you really want to see some, I'll bring them next time I come."

She nodded. "I'd love to see some of them. Margaret, could we go for a walk?"

Margaret looked at her. "You aren't really dressed for it,

you know," she said. "It looks very nice out there, but there is a cold wind blowing."

Georgina pondered this. "What if you put a dressing-gown around me?" she enquired.

Margaret shook her head. "No. If you really want to go outside I'll get someone to help you dress."

Georgina frowned, impatiently. "That'd take ages." She thought for a moment. "Why don't you dress me?" she asked. "There are some clothes in that wardrobe." She saw Margaret's hesitation. "I don't think that I'd be as embarrassed with you," she said. "If you don't *mind* doing it," she added, doubtfully.

Margaret nodded. "O.K.," she said, "but you'll have to tell me the easiest way to do it."

Georgina smiled. "First you'll have to undo the harness that stops me falling out of the chair. Then, I think it's easiest if you lift me onto the bed. Take my nightie off, put my clothes on, then lift me back into the chair, fasten the harness, and that's it."

Margaret nodded. "I think I can handle that," she said.

Margaret found the operation surprisingly easy, although she did feel a little uncomfortable when she saw that Georgina wasn't wearing a bra. Immediately, she eased the blouse she had placed within reach onto the girl, buttoning it, covering her small breasts, before turning her attention to her skirt.

A few moments later, Georgina sat in her wheelchair, grinning as Margaret locked the harness in place. "I was right," she declared. "I didn't get embarrassed." She caught the look on Margaret's face. "Did you feel embarrassed dressing me?" she asked.

Margaret fell into step beside her, as she moved off in the wheelchair. She knew that Georgina was waiting for an answer, and that she would detect it if Margaret was less than honest with her.

"Yes, a little. I can't say that I'm at all used to exposing and dressing thirteen-year-old girls. If I was used to doing it, it probably wouldn't have bothered me."

Margaret held the door, as Georgina manipulated the

91

wheelchair out onto the lawn by the side of the building. She stopped by a bench, where Margaret sat.

"So, it did bother you?"

Margaret nodded. "A little. The important thing is that you felt comfortable about it."

"No, I didn't," Georgina admitted. As Margaret glanced questioningly at her, she continued with a grin. "I didn't feel anything at all."

Margaret grimaced. "I asked for that. You know what I mean."

Georgina nodded. "I didn't get embarrassed. I've been doing a lot of thinking about what you said to me last time you were here. I guess it made me understand that there are people out there far worse off than I am. It helps, knowing that, but I still feel sorry for myself. I lose my temper quickly. I get angry at myself and at everyone else. I'm trying not to lose my temper so much, though."

Margaret nodded slowly. "Would you like to be able to phone me when you feel like that?" Margaret asked.

Georgina looked at her, a frown of surprise on her face. "Yes, I'd love to — but Mrs. Anderson won't let me."

"She's changed her mind," Margaret said.

Georgina stared at her. "How did you manage that?" she asked.

Margaret frowned at her: "Sue Anderson isn't as bad as you're making out, Georgina. She wouldn't let you phone me because she wasn't sure whether or not I'd get annoyed at being disturbed at home. I just told her that I don't mind you phoning me — but *not* every five minutes," she added.

Georgina giggled at the thought.

"Margaret," she said, regaining her serious expression, "I would like to phone you, but I won't call every day. I promise."

Margaret smiled. "In that case, Georgina, I'll give you my number before I leave.'

Georgina spoke again. "Margaret.... If I ask you a question, will you give me an honest answer?"

Margaret felt that she knew what was coming. Matching

Georgina's seriousness, she said, "Of course I will — if I have an answer."

"Will I *ever* be able to use my arms and legs again?"

Margaret sighed and broke eye contact. After a few seconds, she began speaking. "From what I've heard, it's extremely unlikely. They don't say that it's *impossible*, but it *is* improbable."

Georgina digested this silently. A couple of minutes passed, before she spoke again.

"You know, Margaret," she said despondently, "I always took my arms and legs for granted until now. I never understood just how much I relied on them. I suppose it's the same with most things. You don't realise how lucky you are until you haven't got them anymore."

"Can you feel your limbs at all?"

Georgina nodded. "Sometimes, I think that I can. I have a sort of numb feeling around my shoulders, but I can't feel anything lower than that."

Margaret swallowed. "As long as you don't ever give up."

"How do you mean? I'm getting used to the idea of being like this for the rest of my life. Wouldn't it just be torturing myself for no good reason to begin thinking that I *might* walk again?"

She fixed her eyes upon Margaret, almost daring her to contradict what she had just said. Margaret nodded. "It probably seems that way, to you, and I'm not surprised. Even so, you must never, ever give up hope. Miracles do happen, you know."

"Not to me, they don't."

"Georgina, I do know that if you believe strongly enough then there is a chance you will recover. It might be a *remote* chance, but any chance is better than none at all."

She frowned at Margaret. "You aren't giving me false hope, are you? You aren't the sort of person to get somebody's hopes up for no reason. You're too honest to do that." Her look became appraising. "What do you know that you're not telling me?"

For a moment, just a moment, Margaret was tempted to tell

Georgina of her abilities, of her occult powers. However, her finer perceptions warned her against such an action. But Georgina had caught the look which had momentarily crossed her face.

"You *do* know something," she declared, with a certainty which Margaret found unsettling.

She knew that again Georgina had caught her out. Margaret was amazed at the girl's deductive abilities, until she realised that this was a part of her latent occult powers. She knew that she would have to say something, but thought carefully before she began.

"It's not something I know, as such. It's a *belief* which I have. Do you remember I told you of Tony's Great-Uncle Robert?"

Georgina nodded.

"He was a very clever man: very wise, very brave," she added in a whisper. "In the few days that I knew him, he taught me all kinds of things which I would have laughed at if they'd been said by anyone else. It wasn't until after he'd died that I realised just how *wise* a man he was. One of the things that he impressed on me is that there is never, ever, any excuse for giving up hope. He said that if you believe in something *strongly* enough, with all your *mind* and *heart*, if you want it badly enough, it will come to you. I believe that, too. I believe that if you want it desperately enough, if you believe deeply enough, then you will recover. It's as simple as that, although it won't sound nearly as simple to you."

"It sounds *weird* to me," Georgina commented. "There's *nothing* I want more — but look at me. I'm still a cripple."

Margaret gazed at her levelly. "That's because you doubt that you can overcome your disabilities. Become certain that you will walk again, and I think that you might surprise some people - yourself included."

She knit her brows. "You believe that?"

As Margaret nodded, she said, "I don't know. It sounds so complicated."

Margaret was about to answer when a shadow fell over her. She looked up to see a small man, about five foot four of him, standing in front of them. His hair was grey. He looked to be in his fifties. He smiled at them.

"Georgina Thompson?" he asked.

Georgina managed a nod. "I'm Dr. Rheece. It's time for your physiotherapy."

Georgina's face fell. "Can't we do it tomorrow?" she begged.

He shook his head. "No. You've already missed two sessions. We have to exercise your muscles. I'm sure you understand that."

Georgina nodded, reluctantly. "How long will it take?"

"About two hours; maybe a bit more."

She looked annoyed. Then moving her gaze back to Margaret she asked: "Margaret, how long are you staying?"

Margaret grinned at her slyly. "About another two hours, maybe just a bit more."

"*Hell*," Georgina spat venomously, her temper beginning to flare despite her resolve. "So you'll be leaving just as I finish this physio session?"

"I'm sorry," Margaret apologised, with a broad smile. "I was just teasing you. I'm here for the rest of the day."

Georgina's face brightened.

Dr. Rheece regarded Margaret, a friendly smile on his face. "If you'd like to, and if Georgina doesn't object, you can sit in on the session."

"Object?" she demanded, "Margaret, I insist."

Margaret had sat in on the physiotherapy session, asking questions of Dr. Rheece, encouraging Georgina to be patient. Whilst doing this, Margaret focussed her inner awareness upon Georgina. She felt certain that she could repair the damage that her spine had sustained. Not all at one go, she decided. A rapid recovery would probably be looked upon as one of those mysteries of nature. An immediate recovery would provoke intense interest. Margaret wanted to avoid that if she could.

The rest of the day passed pleasantly. The two of them discussed Margaret's beliefs further, and Georgina finally conceded that it did have a kind of warped sense about it. Margaret was reminded of how many times she'd thought, herself, of how warped Hayter's logic could seem to be.

Margaret had left promising to visit again the next time she had an opportunity, emphasising that it would probably not be for another two weeks, much to Georgina's irritation.

***

Margaret smiled absently as she loaded another CD. She had taken a couple of days to re-acquaint herself with what Hayter had written on the subject.

She had made innocent enquiries about Georgina's physiotherapy sessions, and made an unannounced visit to the Orphanage three days later. She had made her way casually to the room where Dr. Rheece was patiently manipulating Georgina's arms.

Margaret had moved away from the room, so she wouldn't easily be detected by anyone glancing through the glass windows in the upper half of the door. She had concentrated upon Georgina, drawing in her will, and releasing it quickly, knowing that the sudden resultant pain on Georgina's part would mask Margaret's actions.

She heard the ear-piercing scream an instant later. She saw Dr. Rheece jump as though he had been stung. It appeared that Georgina had fainted. He quickly began examining her.

Margaret turned and left the Orphanage quickly, a smile of satisfaction upon her face.

She returned to the flat, and went about her sketching with a lightness of spirit which she hadn't felt for a long time. Her sketches reflected her mood, and, by the time John returned from the gallery, she had completed four of them.

He had inspected them, over her shoulder.

"My *God*, Margaret," he exclaimed, picking up the finished sketches. "These are *superb*. You've *excelled* yourself."

She smiled. "I think so, too. But in more than just those sketches."

"Tell me about it," he said, sitting without removing his jacket.

Margaret grinned at him. "I went by the Orphanage today. I'm expecting a phone call any minute to tell me that Georgina has made unbelievable progress."

John absorbed this, silently. Suddenly, his eyes widened. "You didn't...?"

She nodded.

He glanced at her from the corner of his eye, thinking very carefully what to say to her. Margaret began to feel uneasy. "John?" she asked, "what is it?"

"Look, love, I don't want to start yelling at you. But please, in future, let me know before you pull any more stunts like this."

"Why?" she had demanded.

"It's dangerous," he replied, trying to keep his voice both gentle and calm, although truly, he felt neither.

Margaret laughed. "Oh, come on, John. You're being melodramatic. I've checked up on what George had to say, and I took *all* the necessary precautions."

John slipped his arm around her shoulders. "I remember telling George that he'd got it wrong about Anton's prophesy. The solution was so obvious that he didn't see it. This is a similar thing. The danger is just as obvious, to me, yet you missed it."

"What danger?"

John fixed her with his serious gaze. "You know that when you do something like this, there can be an opposite reaction within yourself?"

"Of course. But I can deal with those emotions."

John sighed. His fear forced him to snap angrily back at her, and he regretted his tone of voice the instant the words left his mouth: "Are you missing the point deliberately? You are *pregnant*, Margaret. What you did could have caused a miscarriage. If that had happened, I doubt that George himself would have been able to prevent it."

Margaret's hand flew to her mouth as comprehension dawned. "Jesus. You're right. I didn't even think of that."

John nodded. "Well, no more. Not until after our son's born."

Margaret nodded her agreement. "Georgina will continue to make rapid progress. I did the whole thing in one go. It will just seem like an unusually rapid recovery from what was considered a permanent disability."

He shook his head. "I hope you know what you've done."

She scratched her head. "I've given Georgina her freedom back. You can't understand how that feels - but I promise I won't do anything else that might harm our....." she stopped in mid-sentence. "What makes you think it'll be a boy? She demanded.

"What else could it be?" John retorted, her promise having destroyed his anger, and restored his usual good nature.

"A girl?" she suggested.

"No, it's got to be a boy. You're *not* to have a girl."

"It's not really something that I can control, you know," she pointed out to him.

"Surely George must have written something to make *certain* you'll have a boy," John mused. "Who would want a baby girl?"

Unfortunately, the twinkle in his eye gave away his teasing, and Margaret wrapped her arms tightly around him. "I promise I'll be more careful in future, John. I won't take any chances," she whispered to him. "I just didn't think it through. I love you so much, John."

He moved to kiss her as the phone rang.

"For *you*, I think," he said.

"And I'm sure it will be a girl," she grinned at him as she moved to the phone.

Margaret picked up the receiver. "Hello?"

"Margaret, it's Georgina. I can feel my hands. Really. I was in physiotherapy today, and I got such an incredible pain in my back. I must have passed out. When I came to it felt like my arms were on fire. You know, you were right? I'd just started to convince myself that I would walk again, and this happens. I think it's thanks to *you*. If you hadn't told me what Tony's Great Uncle had said, and convinced me that you believed it, this might not have happened."

"You're sure?" Margaret demanded, as though she couldn't believe what she had heard. "What does Dr. Rheece say?"

Georgina giggled. "I thought he was going to have kittens," she said. "He says that he has seen something similar before.

He's arranged for me to have lots of tests to see if they can find out why it's happened. I don't think that they'll find out though. I think it's just like you said. I wanted to recover badly enough, and I believed enough."

Margaret smiled. "This calls for some kind of celebration. I'll come and see you as soon as I can."

"You'd best check with Mrs. Anderson first. I'm going to be taken to see lots of specialists for those tests. I don't want to miss you."

Margaret blinked back tears.

***

She opened her eyes, surprised to feel tears trickling down her face. She wiped them away. As she had forecast, Georgina had made fast progress, which the specialists were at a loss to explain.

About five months later, Margaret saw Georgina take her first faltering steps since her accident, to many cheers and much applause.

Dr. Rheece had taken Margaret to his office. "You know, Mrs. Brandon, if I wasn't a man of science, I'd say that there was more to Georgina's recovery than meets the eye."

Margaret began to feel slightly nervous. "In what way?" she had asked. He fixed her with a piercing stare. "I've seen similar things before. I won't speak in riddles. There has been some other force at work here, and I think that you *know* what I mean."

Margaret's unease intensified. "I'm not sure that I do," she said.

"Georgina told me what you said to her about believing that she might walk again. I can put two and two together, Mrs. Brandon." He continued staring at her, a grim frown upon his face.

"I'm sorry?"

"It makes you feel a little insignificant when something like this happens. When all the laws of medicine say that it can't. It just goes to show that the power is within you."

Margaret swallowed, certain that he had deduced, somehow, exactly what she had done.

"And me," he finished.

"I'm not sure that I understand, doctor."

His gaze transfixed her again. "The power of *God*, Mrs. Brandon. What has happened to Georgina is a miracle."

Margaret suddenly understood that Dr. Rheece hadn't, after all, managed to put the pieces together; realised that his scientific training would make it difficult for him to do so. Margaret had to prevent herself from letting out a heavy sigh of relief. "Yes," she echoed quietly. "I suppose it *is* a miracle."

Dr. Rheece nodded, sagely.

Chapter Three: *Tragedies*

Sandra Logan clutched at her abdomen. She grimaced. Cold sweat ran down her face. Wiping it away, she became conscious again of just how hot her forehead and face were. She staggered and took a deep breath.

She walked unsteadily along the road which she inhabited each night; not that a heavily pregnant woman made much from prostitution: apart from the odd one who had never had sex with a woman in her condition. It was, she guessed, more the novelty value of having a pregnant whore.

Her vision fragmented, and she grasped a convenient lamppost to help herself stay upright. After a few moments, once her sight had settled again, she continued on her journey.

Circumstances had forced her into selling herself; it was the only way she could gain sufficient funds to feed her habit. Her introduction to hard drugs had come via a mutual acquaintance. At that time, it had just been harmless fun. Harmless, until she had felt the withdrawal symptoms.

From then, it had been a vicious circle. Amos, her supplier, had refused to give her more to counter the feelings which told her that her whole body was on fire, slowly being cremated.

He had demanded payment: a hundred pounds. It was a *generous* discount on his normal prices, but calculated to make her even more dependent upon him.

He was a massive Negro. Someone who you would not like to encounter on a dark night, unless with several armed friends. For him, drugs were side-line. His main income came from the girls he owned, body and soul, from their prostitution.

From her introduction into the marvels of hard drugs had come this life of utter misery. Less than two weeks after her first withdrawal symptoms had manifested themselves, she was walking the streets for Amos. By day she lived in a decrepit boarding-house which he rented as bedsits.

The whole place was filthy. He charged exorbitant rent, which he deducted from the whores' share of the money. To those women willing to cater for the more unusual male perversities, Amos gave a greater share of proceeds. They tended, most weeks, to be able to buy some small luxury for themselves.

However, Sandra was not one of these. When, some weeks, she made less than Amos thought she should have, he would withhold the drugs she craved. He used this situation to humiliate her into promises she would not otherwise have made. He made her beg him to take her, to do things to her which — afterwards, when the drugs had been supplied — made her feel physically *sick*.

When in a good mood, Amos would just manipulate her into begging him to beat her for not having made enough money.

She had contemplated suicide frequently, but the idea of terminating her own existence nauseated her almost as much as the things to which Amos subjected her.

In retrospect, the whole association with Amos had been a relatively brief one. As soon as he discovered that she was pregnant, he had *insisted* on aborting the unborn child.

A furious row erupted at her vehement refusal. He had promised that the operation could be done that very night. He had friends willing to perform such illegal abortions with no questions asked or expected.

He had lost his temper when she had turned down his offer. Having promised, rather kindly from his point of view, to keep her supplied with all the drugs she might crave whilst recovering, her refusal struck him as ingratitude in the extreme.

He threatened to drug her into unconsciousness and have the abortion performed anyway. He had not expected her reply.

"You can do it, Amos. I know I couldn't stop you. But I swear to God that I'll grass you up. I'm sure the pigs would like to know how you make such a good living. You'll have to kill *me* as well as my baby."

His rage had overcome him. He beat her viciously, before flinging her bodily into the street. He made threats against her, warning her not to come near him or his girls, ever again.

So, penniless and homeless, she had wandered London's

streets. Her only way of making enough money to survive was prostitution. Her early months had been difficult. She thought that it was the drastic changes in her body, coupled with the craving for the drugs which caused the rash that appeared spontaneously over her body.

But the rash had disappeared fairly quickly; the sores around her genitals — which had been an irritation — healed. Sandra believed that she had nothing to fear — or rather, she *made* herself believe that she had nothing to fear. But deep down, she knew that she was *very* ill.

She wanted to go to hospital for a checkup, but knew that a blood test would show up her addiction. She would have to give a false address. She feared that they would check up on her. Once they found out that she was homeless, and a prostitute to boot, the social services would become involved.

She shivered at the thought. She had heard some terror stories about the NHS and detoxification; although wildly exaggerated and inaccurate — of which fact she was unaware — her resolve not to put herself into such a situation was born.

She met other prostitutes. She was surprised that her story about Amos gained her such sympathy with her fellow night workers. Some had known him — others had heard that he was someone to be avoided.

She gained the friendship of several of these women; usually by referring a potential client to one of her friends who would consider catering to his specific depravities.

Often, she found a bed for the night from a grateful friend, if it was only the floor of the bedsit which the friend rented.

A tall, red-haired woman, whom she knew only as Mandy became Sandra's closest friend. Her pregnancy was becoming obvious, and Mandy wanted to know what Sandra would do when the time came.

Sandra always shrugged off the question, not having any idea of what she would do; or of how she might be able to provide for herself and the child. She still could not bring herself to cater for the more exotic sexual perversions, and refused to consider the suggestion.

She found a deserted row of terraced houses, one of which she broke into and used as a home. She didn't care about the other inhabitants; rats who scurried away at her approach, but became bolder when she slept. One, braver than the others, had decided to find out what this intruder's flesh might taste like, and had bitten deep into her leg to find out.

The sudden agony had roused Sandra. After that, she kept an old cricket bat which she had found, near her. The rats seem to learn quickly that too close an investigation of this intruder was not advisable. They soon learned to avoid her, and the bat which she wielded.

It was not long after the rat bite that she began to feel sick. The pains in her stomach sometimes doubled her over in their intensity.

Despite her feelings of nausea, she still went out at night, hoping to earn a few desperately-needed pounds. She remembered vividly the night she had thought she was going to *die*.

She had turned down a scruffy man for no better reason than she didn't like the look of him. He had returned hours later, with friends.

She hadn't guessed he was there until she was half in the car. He had pulled her from within. The other, who had suggested she get in his car, had shoved her forward. She was quickly gagged. The car moved off. She struggled, but the three men in the back of the car had been *more* than a match for her. Finally, in a secluded grassy area, they had stripped her naked; one had held a knife at her throat whilst the others took turns raping and sodomizing her. Her ordeal seemed to go on and on. Then they had beaten her unconscious and left her, laughing at this demonstration of their masculinity.

Another contraction hit her, as she continued down the road. Absurdly, she noticed that there was not a car to be seen. Normally the road was very busy.

Eventually, she noticed movement from her left. She glanced quickly in that direction, to see Ann moving towards her.

"Sandra?" and as comprehension dawned, "the baby?"

She managed a nod as she fell to her knees. "Where's Mandy?"

"I'll get her," Ann reassured her, and hurried away.

Sandra vomited weakly, distressed to see the thick threads of blood intermingling with her vomit.

Whether or not she passed out she didn't know. The next thing she was aware of was Mandy slapping her face gently. "Sandra, we've got to get you to a hospital."

The sudden onrushing fear gave her strength which she hadn't known she possessed. "No," she struggled to her feet. "Take me to my house, Mandy." She saw the doubt and uncertainty in her face. "Please, I *beg* you," she pleaded in an anguished voice.

Reluctantly, Mandy nodded. Supporting Sandra, they began the journey to the derelict row of houses.

Sandra made her way forward as best she could, her vision swimming disturbingly in and out of focus. She began to hallucinate. Then came a period of lucidity, when she was able to walk unaided, taking a gasping breath when another contraction hit.

Once they were inside the house, the lucidity vanished abruptly. Sandra was seized with wracking coughs which brought blood splashing onto her lips. She collapsed to the floor, gasping for breath, crying out with the intense pain which seemed to erupt from her stomach.

The hallucinations returned. At times, she thought she was being tortured mercilessly. Other times, she remembered *all* the man who had bought her. Their faces came into her mind faster and faster, until it was one vast whirling kaleidoscope of faces and leering grins.

One face stood out among the others. Amos stood in the room, grinning at her, savouring her suffering.

"Should ha' had that abortion," he said. "'Cause me, I think yo's dead."

She opened her mouth to scream at him as yet another contraction tore into her consciousness. When she looked again, the spectre had vanished.

"Sandra, I've *got* to call an ambulance," Mandy pleaded with her. Sandra shook her head.

Mandy stood, fully intending to do as she had said, when

Sandra vomited again. She knew that she *should* call an ambulance, but she couldn't leave Sandra alone here. She stayed.

The pain became a constant in Sandra's mind. She was vaguely aware of Mandy moving her legs apart, at the same time trying to assure them *both* that things would be alright.

The pain suddenly diminished, and Sandra became aware of a weak, thin crying. It sounded so weak, she decided, merely because her own breathing sounded so harsh and ragged.

Her stomach churned again. She fought against it weakly. Her breathing became shallow. "Let me hold my baby," she managed to whisper.

Mandy only just heard the plea. She carefully deposited the small, helpless bundle into Sandra's arms. Through fragmented vision, Sandra saw her baby. "She's beautiful," she whispered. "I'll call her Kim."

Mandy smiled at the sight of mother and daughter. The infant continued to wail.

Mandy frowned. At last Sandra's breathing had quieted. But it was *too* quiet. She moved forward. "Sandra?"

There was no reaction. Mandy put her fingers to Sandra's throat. She could feel no pulse.

"Jesus!" she whispered, backing away from Sandra's body. She fled into the night.

***

Twenty minutes later, PC Davies turned his police car into Uxor Street. He glanced at his companion wearily. "I'll bet you *anything* that it's a false alarm."

His companion, WPC Knight raised one eyebrow. "Don't tell me. It's your years of experience talking."

"Damn' right, Rachel. When you've been on the Force as long as I have, you develop a sixth sense that you come to rely on."

She regarded him sceptically. "You've only got two years on me, Stu. I think it's kosher."

"Take the bet?" he asked, grinning.

"Stakes?"

"Dinner at your place tomorrow. And a flash of your tits."

"Not a chance," she assured him.

"Dinner at your place, then."

"Agreed — and if I'm right you can take me out for dinner, all at your expense."

He nodded, grinning. "Just make sure you've not forgotten how to cook."

They left the car and approached one of houses. The door was locked. "Have to break in," he muttered.

"Try the back," she suggested.

He shook his head and charged at the door. He was solidly built, and felt a pleasurable sensation as the door flew open with a harsh squeal under his onslaught. Rachel passed him a torch and they entered, every movement they made echoing back to them.

"I'll take the upstairs," he said quietly.

Rachel nodded, clicking on her own torch. She examined the downstairs rooms, and found nothing but dust and a thick, cloying odour.

Stuart joined her as she moved into the kitchen.

"You see, nothing. A practical joke." He snorted a laugh.

Rachel nodded glumly, knowing that not only had she lost the bet, and would have to cook dinner, but also that she would not hear the end of the story. It would be all over the station before their shift ended.

"I should have insisted on higher stakes," Stuart was saying when they both heard a cry: a thin wail. They stopped as one, moving their attention to an alcove which they had not inspected at all thoroughly.

Rachel moved into it. "Stu, there's a door here. I think it must go into a cellar."

"Want me to take it?" he asked, knowing that cellars weren't her favourite places.

"No, I'm okay," she replied, opening the door and starting downstairs. He followed her, she blocking his view as they came to the foot of the stairs.

"Jesus! Stu, quick," Rachel yelled, running forward and

lashing out with her torch.

He moved forward quickly, although it took his eyes a few seconds to register what he was seeing. Rats, seemingly hundreds of them, although there were only nine or ten. They squealed and scurried away in fear at this unexpected attack.

It was then he properly took in the scene. The corpse of the woman, showing many signs of the meal which her body had been providing before the intrusion. Blood all over the floor.

His stomach tightened. He saw what looked like an afterbirth.

The wailing attracted his attention as he saw Rachel stoop and retrieve something from the floor.

"Rachel," he snapped. "You know better than to disturb things."

She turned on him angrily. "What d'you expect me to do? Leave the baby on the floor until those rats come back for her?"

His mouth fell open. "Christ," he yelled.

"When you've finished, do you think you could radio in and get an ambulance? And bring the blanket from the car. The poor thing's *freezing*."

Stung by the fact that she was now dictating his course of action when it was usually the other way around, he being the senior of the two, he nodded irritably.

Kim Logan had come into the world surrounded by pain and anguish and darkness and rats. About 30 minutes later, some five miles away, in a private maternity hospital, Linda Brandon came into the world surrounded by joy and love and light; and every medical aid to make the birth as easy and safe as possible.

***

They sat watching as the ambulance pulled away. Stuart let out a deep breath. Rachel shook her head.

"You all right?" he asked her, kindly.

She managed a nod. He pulled out into the road, following the ambulance. They drove in silence, each affected by the discovery of the baby and the corpse in differing ways.

"What a way to have a child," Rachel finally said.

Stuart nodded. "This is going to make the bloody report awkward. I hate paperwork. Give me patrol any time."

"So you can use your sixth sense that you've gained over so many years on the Force?" she asked, innocently.

He closed his eyes and gripped the steering-wheel more tightly. He ground his teeth. It wouldn't be long before this got out at the station. He would be a laughing-stock.

"How did you know it was genuine?" he demanded.

"I suppose you could call it female intuition," she answered lightly. "More to the point, when a friend takes me out, I *really* enjoy myself. Last time, I had a five-course meal, and I still could have eaten more."

He paled slightly, thinking of the charges made by the class of restaurant to which she would expect him to take her. "You *didn't*?" he pleaded.

She nodded. "And I just *love* vintage wine," she added.

He groaned out loud, much to her satisfaction. A moment later, his thoughts began running along other lines. "If your bloody intuition is so good, perhaps you can explain what we found in that cellar?"

She shook her head seriously, all trace of humour gone. "Stu, I can't imagine. I suppose the baby will go into care?"

He nodded. "After the hospital's checked it over and giving it a clean bill of health."

"Baby," she corrected.

"What?"

"A baby, not an 'it'," she said.

He muttered something unintelligible as they arrived at the hospital.

They sat in reception, waiting for both news of the baby, and for the arrival of a social worker. Stuart pulled a battered cigarette from his tunic. Rachel nudged him, indicating the no smoking signs.

"Sod," he said, standing. "I'll wait outside for a few minutes."

As soon as he disappeared through the exit, a white-coated doctor entered from a door leading off to examination cubicles. He walked across to Rachel.

"Are you the officer who found the baby?"

She nodded and shook hands. "WPC Knight. I believe the Social Services are sending someone over. How is the baby?"

He ignored the second question. "Yes, I believe so. They've been held up."

She smiled: "So what's new?"

He grinned at her, suddenly. "Well, if Social Services think that they're going to whisk that child away, they've got another think coming."

Rachel opened her mouth to comment and ask her question again, when she caught sight of Stuart re-entering the building. She paused to let him reach them before continuing. "That means the baby's ill?"

The doctor shrugged. "It's too early to start listing illnesses, but my preliminary examination was disturbing." He rubbed his hand absently across his forehead. "Blood pressure alarmingly low; the initial results of the blood test that I took indicate that we have an addicted baby to deal with.

"There seems to be little mobility in the legs; I think there has been some kind of muscular wastage during the mother's pregnancy. If, as seems likely, she was a junkie, then that would probably account for it."

The two officers absorbed this silently.

"Add to that respiration weak, pulse irregular, and we have a very poorly child to look after. There may be some infection from the rat bites — and I'll bet that there is some disease other than from that source."

"Will she survive?" Rachel wanted to know.

The doctor smiled a tired smile. "I'm a doctor, officer, not a miracle worker. All I can say is that we'll do everything we can, but if you want my honest opinion, I doubt it. That said, I *have* been known to be wrong in the past. If she survives the next week or so I'll be a lot more optimistic; all I can say at the moment is that it's *not* looking good."

"Kim," Stuart said.

Rachel and the doctor stared at him.

"The woman who rang the police wouldn't give us her name, but she said that the baby was called 'Kim'." He broke

110

off, absurdly embarrassed about what he had just said.

"Kim, eh?" the doctor said. "I don't see that there's any reason for you to wait around. You'll just get very bored."

"Will you let us know how she is?" Rachel asked. She noticed Stuart give her a puzzled look from the corner of her eye.

The doctor nodded impatiently, then sighed. "Look, officer, like most doctors in the Health Service, I'm overworked and underpaid. I might well forget to get in touch with you — non-medical matters tend to get crowded out of my mind. It might be better if you were to get in touch with me — if you *really* want to know how she is progressing — or otherwise."

Rachel nodded. "Thanks," she said.

Outside, they sat in the car quietly. Stuart noticed the frown creasing Rachel's features.

"Don't get yourself involved," he murmured. "You'll only get upset."

"What do we know about the mother?"

"Very little. Her name was Sandra Logan, and she was a prostitute. We won't know the cause of death before the post mortem."

Rachel smoothed out her skirt over her legs. "I want to know why she felt she had to do that."

Stuart's eyebrows raised themselves. "Do what? Become a prostitute or die?"

"Mostly why she had her baby there, rather than calling an ambulance."

Stuart shook his head. "I somehow doubt that you'll *ever* know the answers to those questions. I get a strange feeling about this one. Somehow, I simply *know* that we won't find out *anything* worth knowing. I guess the reason that she prostituted herself was the same as many others."

"But they don't have children in rat-infested cellars," Rachel snapped back at him, angrily.

"Don't they?" he queried gently. "You mean, as far as we know they don't. Most avoid pregnancy by one means or another, I grant you. Those that choose to have a child do seem

111

to take advantage of the NHS, though. I suppose that's the weird feeling that I get about this. I've only had *this* kind of intuition once before."

"When was that?" Rachel asked, intrigued.

He glanced at her sidelong. "I haven't told you this: if it gets out that I *have*, I might just find myself out of a job and inside prison."

She took in his expression. She knew that this went beyond the trust normally expected between colleagues. "You have my word," she said.

He held her gaze before nodding. "I'd been seconded to another Force: never mind why. It was about two years ago. We were suddenly ordered to search the grounds around an old ruined church. We found bodies; hundreds of them. As far as I could find out, there had been some kind of earth tremor. Those people happened to be in some caverns underneath the church at the time. Most of them were unrecognisable, but I got the *damnedest* feeling that we would find out next to nothing about the incident. There was some initial press coverage, of course; but barely two weeks later, we were told that the investigation was at an end, that all necessary information had been gathered.

"All our records and files were sent to the Home Office at their request. Weirdest of all, all officers who had been connected with the investigation were interviewed by top brass from Scotland Yard. We were told that what we had been investigating was covered by the Official Secrets Act. We were warned that if we spoke about any aspect of the case, we faced dismissal from the Force, and criminal action."

Rachel made a face. "That sounds unbelievable."

"Even *more* unbelievable is the way the press seemed to lose all interest in the case. I'm getting a similar feeling now."

Rachel shook her head. "Investigating the death of a prostitute sounds a bit mundane after that story. Are you saying that you feel this will be taken out of our hands?"

He shook his head. "No, I'm not saying that. What I think will happen is just that there will be no information for us to uncover. I think that we already know more or less all the facts available to us. Sounds idiotic, but that's what I think."

"Using your sixth sense?" she laughed at him.

"No, this is *totally* different."

"You wouldn't like to bet on it, I suppose — after you've taken me out?"

"Oh, I'll take you out all right. And yes, I will bet on it."

"Stakes?" she asked.

"Terms, first. The bet is that one week from now, we don't know significantly more about the woman who died, why we found her in that cellar — apart from cause of death, of course."

She shook her head. "What do you call 'significant'?" she wanted to know.

"Things about her private life — things other than date and place of birth, and name and age. Things about her recent past say, within the last six months."

Rachel thought about this. "Okay," she said. "You're on. Stakes?"

He grinned at her, wickedly. "Dinner at your place — and a flash of your tits."

She hesitated before replying, with an equally wicked smile: "All right, I agree — but if *I* win, you do a streak through the station in the middle of the day shift."

Stuart thought about this, his face whitening at the thought of what might happen should he lose and be caught streaking by the Inspector. He took it for granted that Rachel would ensure as many female officers as possible would be around at the time. Still, she had never agreed to his original stakes before, and he had thought that she never would. It was more a joke between them than something either of them took seriously.

And his instincts *screamed* at him that they would find nothing, no matter how hard or diligently they searched.

He nodded. "Agreed," he said. "I'm looking forward to dinner at your place next week."

"Not as much as I'm looking forward to seeing you streaking through the station," she replied as he turned the ignition, engaged gear, and moved off smoothly.

Chapter Four: *Revisions*

John added the last brush-stroke to the farm landscape. He blew out a long breath. Laying his palette and brush to one side, he stepped away from the painting, appraising it critically. His vision blurred. He rubbed his eyes irritably.

"It's *good*," he muttered to himself in some surprise.

He moved to either side of the painting, keeping his eyes glued to it. He nodded approval as it passed this inspection. His vision blurred again, causing him a moment of panic. He knew what meant to be blind, and was frightened of losing his sight again.

He stretched, hearing his spine click. His legs ached; his neck ached; his eyes ached. As though to round off all of his suffering, he suddenly realised that he had a headache as well. He chuckled aloud at this realisation.

In the six days since the original had been destroyed, John had worked day and night on re-creating the landscape, drinking coffee by the pint, eating only sporadically, despite Margaret's objections. In that time he had snatched only a few hours' sleep. He had passed the point of feeling unreal, and of feeling tired. His compulsion to complete the landscape had transcended all other considerations. He hadn't even left the flat to go to the gallery, trusting to Steve Preston's ability to run things smoothly. John knew that Steve would contact him if there were any problems.

Feeling pleasantly exhausted, he made his way to the kitchen and brewed yet more coffee. He returned to the living-room, where he sat heavily upon the sofa. He smiled. True, he felt totally shattered, but the satisfaction which he felt at the completion of the landscape more than compensated for the extreme exhaustion and various aches which he felt.

Sitting comfortably, he sipped his coffee, mentally comparing the two versions of the landscape. The second, he decided, was much superior to the first. Why that should be, he couldn't decide. If it hadn't been for Linda, he would never have made a second attempt, he realised, but would have been content with the first.

The comparison made him aware of the fact that the first

painting had been only mediocre, by his standards. The version which he had just completed possessed that subtly compelling trait which was a hallmark of his work. For some undefinable reason, observers felt a subtle urge to look at his paintings until they had absorbed every detail of which they were capable.

It was this trait which made John's work so popular: he hadn't realised that he infused his paintings with such a compulsion until he had shown some of his work to Margaret, long ago.

He felt a pang of regret at treating Linda so harshly after her disastrous visit to his studio; especially since it had resulted in an improvement in the painting. He yawned. Not only had her visit improved the landscape, it had resulted in a lot of intense effort and hard work on his part, placing him under a lot of stress and pressure which he could have done without.

He shook his head. The exhaustion which he was feeling made it impossible for him to decide whether he had been too severe with Linda. He resolved to consider the matter further after he had had some sleep. He would discuss it with Margaret, he decided. He was certain that she would be able to put his conflicting feelings regarding Linda into perspective.

He glanced at the clock: 2:14 AM. He yawned again, rubbing his forehead with the back of his hand. Perhaps it was simply the relief of knowing he had completed the painting before the deadline, or that his tiredness was simply getting the better of him; John's eyelids began to close.

He felt himself drifting towards sleep. He opened his eyes, suddenly feeling the strain and fatigue which demanded oblivion. He managed a faint smile, attempting to savour the feeling of floating between the two states of consciousness and unconsciousness.

He drank the last of his coffee. With a heavy, tired sigh, he returned the cup to the kitchen. From there, he went to Linda's bedroom. She lay upon her side, breathing evenly, her light brown hair fanned out around her head. He kissed her, gently. Stifling another yawn, he entered the second bedroom. He frowned at what he saw. Margaret lay sleeping as peacefully as Linda, diagonally across the bed. John knew he would be unable to get into bed without disturbing her, and that was something which he was loath to do.

He returned to the living-room and settled down upon the sofa. He glanced quickly at the clock: 2:22 AM.

John allowed his eyes to close. As before, he tried to savour the strange feeling of being on the border of two states of consciousness. He thought about the gallery, about the landscape, about Hayter.

Sleepily, he glanced again at the clock: 3:22 AM. His eyes registered the information and he had begun to drift into sleep before his mind latched onto the incongruity. Had he slept an hour without realising it?

If that were the case, had he actually finished the landscape, or merely dreamed that he had? John shook his head in confusion. Everything seemed unreal. He found himself unable to differentiate between events of the last few days which had actually occurred, and things which he only imagined had happened. What was real, and what was an illusion? Irritated suddenly, he heaved himself off the sofa, an action which seemed to require all the strength of which he was capable. He made his way, on legs suddenly unsteady, to his studio.

Turning on the lights, he felt suddenly blinded by the harsh illumination. Blinking to help his eyes adjust, he swayed before taking a drunken, listing step towards the landscape.

He lifted the landscape's cover. It was just as he remembered it; if anything, it was better. He replaced the cover, feeling eerie overtones to what he was doing. He knew that there was something wrong, but he couldn't readily define what it might be.

Exhausted as he was, John found it almost impossible to think coherent thoughts. On an impulse, he raised the cover of another of his paintings. It was just as he had left it. He moved to the next painting, forgetting to replace the cover on the last.

It was a personal painting, one which he had no intention of selling. A view of the mansion where he had lived for many years, set in the summer-time; the gardens in full bloom, the wood adding a mysterious dimension to the whole — implying shade and coolness, and yet a subtle danger. John smiled. He had a lot more work to do on it, but he knew that, when completed, it would be a stunning, exceptional painting.

His feelings of unease intensified slightly. He stepped back from the canvas, looking all around the studio in an attempt to ascertain exactly from where this feeling of unease emanated.

The feelings of impending doom had become noticeably stronger when he entered the studio. He felt certain that the source was in here.

His eyes fixed themselves upon a large painting which stood apart from the others. For moments, John stood staring at the shape of the canvas beneath the cover. Suddenly, he knew with an inner certainty which seemed to thrust itself ruthlessly into his consciousness, that *that* was where the strange and eerie sensations originated.

He hesitated a few seconds more before moving firmly forward and throwing the cover to the floor. Whatever John expected to see, he was disappointed. He looked over the painting, the most difficult he had ever attempted, and the one upon which he lavished most love and care. A portrait of George Hayter, gazing calmly out at the observer, a slight smile upon his features. John closed his eyes, attempting to calm his thudding heart.

He looked again at the painting, taking in all the details; the subtle mixing of colours in the background, the way Hayter fixed him with his piercing stare...

John's eyes had moved on before his brain made the connection. The expression in Hayter's eyes had changed: or was that yet another illusion?

John locked his eyes upon the portrait, onto the eyes that glared furiously back at him. The painting had changed — he was certain of it. He would never have painted Hayter in any other mood than calm and relaxed, mainly because that was how John liked to remember him; the way George had been during most of their association.

Absolutely baffled, John scratched his head. Someone must have tampered with this painting. His anger surged within him at the thought. As his fury mounted, he attempted to remember the last time he had looked at his portrait of Hayter. Not since the original landscape had been ruined, he decided. Since then, he had been working so exclusively upon re-creating it that all other endeavours had been put on hold.

But who?

Linda? No. He shook his head. That was absurd.

Margaret? He doubted she possessed the necessary skill to do such a good job — and anyway, why would she? The question had no answer. His head throbbed painfully as he attempted to find a rational explanation for what he was seeing. His fury resolved itself into confusion.

He attempted to rationalise it a second time.

It was at that instant that the portrait moved. The head turned slightly, bringing the eyes into more direct contact with John's. The gaze intensified into a look of outrage and abhorrence so stark and powerful that John took a couple of paces backwards. He could not believe what he was seeing.

The canvas seemed to shrink, unable to hold the bulk of the figure which it contained. The figure which the canvas had held seemed to solidify, to take on a three-dimensional appearance. The portrait of George Hayter stood a few paces from John, the slight smile gone from his features, and in its place was an expression of such horror and savagery which, along with the fury that the eyes conveyed, made John fear that his mind would be unable to withstand what it was perceiving.

He realised that he was gasping for breath, as though he had just been on a long sprint. His heart was beating so rapidly and powerfully that he was certain he was on the verge of heart failure. His terror was such that he could hear his own heart beating as though it were being amplified through a megaphone.

The spectre which bore Hayter's semblance made no move toward him, but simply stood its ground, still wearing that same expression which had, if anything, intensified.

Making a conscious effort to get hold of himself, John whispered, "George? Is it *really* you?"

The spectre opened its mouth, whether in an attempt to answer John's question or not, he could not be sure. In either event, no sound reached John's ears.

"George?" he asked again, his fear and shock now under

some semblance of control. "George, it's me, John."

The eyes continued to regard him, but John thought he saw a glimmer of recognition cross them. Then he was sure that they softened slightly. He knew, suddenly, that the rage which apparently surged through this spectre was not directed at him. If that was so, who should be the recipient of that insane anger? He had no time to ponder the question as the spectre, maybe aware that it couldn't communicate as well as it would have liked, frowned in evident annoyance.

Its arms reached behind itself and returned into view holding an old and battered-looking book. The spectre's eyes locked on John's in a gaze somehow both compelling and pleading.

John took a hesitant step forward. "George, what do you want? How can I help you?"

He saw no answer to his question reflected in the demeanour of his ghostly visitor. Frowning, his eyes were drawn back to the book which the image of George Hayter held before him. John didn't recognise it.

He took another pace forward. "George, what is the book? Will it tell me what you cannot?"

The spectre seemed to consider this question. Slowly, it raised its arms, holding them out to John, indicating that he should take the book.

Virtually mesmerised, John moved forward, closing the distance between them. He hesitated only slightly before raising his hands to take the book.

As his fingertips came into contact with it, everything seemed to fragment; a sudden flash of blinding white light — making the florescent lights seem dark by comparison — erupted, temporarily blinding him. He shook his head, rubbed his eyes.

As his vision returned, he looked around again to get his bearings.

He was standing in the studio, before the portrait of George Hayter, his fingers actually resting against the flat canvas. They felt sticky and wet.

Moving his hand away, he turned the palm to face him. It

was covered in paint. He frowned in total incomprehension.

He returned his searching gaze to the portrait. Suddenly, before his eyes, the paint appeared to blister; and then it seemed as though all the paint had become unfixed, or so diluted that it could no longer defy gravity.

Slowly, almost delicately, the paint began to slide, run and splatter down the canvas, and finally to drip to the floor.

John stared incredulously at the disintegrating painting of George Hayter. The way the paint trickled down the canvas made it seem that Hayter himself was decomposing, and weeping tears of every colour of the spectrum. The face was the last part of the portrait to break up, leaving behind it a totally blank canvas.

John glanced down at the floor, baffled when he saw no paint there. He looked again at the canvas: the *blank* canvas.

"NO!" he shouted, jerking up from the sofa.

Sweat ran down his face, his heart hammering within his chest. He ran his hands over his face, as though he could erase the memory of the nightmare as easily as he could erase the perspiration from his forehead and neck.

He glanced at the clock: 4:22 AM.

He sat down, shaking, attempting to take slow deep breaths to calm his agitated heart. It didn't seem to do any good. His nerves grated upon him.

He sat unmoving for over half an hour. He was about to make himself another coffee when the thought occurred to him that what he had experienced might have been more than just a nightmare. There was only one way to find out.

He went to his studio and opened the door. The room was in darkness. Feeling more nervous by the second, he switched on the lights. All the canvases were covered. Swallowing the lump which had risen to his throat, he made his way directly to the portrait of George Hayter. Removing the cover, he saw his painting, exactly as he remembered it. Hayter stood, gazing calmly out at the observer, a slight smile evident upon his features.

John felt an overpowering sense of déjà vu. It had been at this point that in his dream he had noticed a change in the portrait. But this time, it remained exactly the same. John let out the breath which he had unconsciously been holding.

It had only been a nightmare after all, he decided. The product of overwork and copious amounts of coffee. He replaced the cover with an amused chuckle. He had almost taken it seriously.

He left the studio. Having made a cup of tea — he resolved to cut down his coffee intake after the nightmare — he sat again in the living-room thinking of what he could remember of his experience.

His nerves continued to grate upon him. Noticing a pack of Margaret's cigarettes, he lit one, making himself cough in the process. Margaret claimed that smoking calmed her. John found that it seemed to make him feel worse. Nevertheless, he finished it, attempting to understand what, if anything, his dream might have meant.

On the face of it, it could so easily be explained by his overwork and lack of sleep, except that he didn't normally experience such dramatic dreams. As he thought closely upon it, John found that he could still experience that extreme sense of impotent fury and desperation which had pervaded the whole event.

If it was more than a bad dream, John wondered what it had meant. What could have occurred to make George Hayter forsake his rest to return to John in such a spectacular — and terrifying — a manner?

The Cult?

John dismissed the thought almost as soon as it formed within his mind. The Cult had been annihilated. Destroyed. Expunged. Anton Baron had made certain of that. Hell, John had been there; he could not claim to have witnessed the annihilation, being blind at the time, but he had heard what had happened. He had been assured that the Cult had, indeed, finally bitten off more than it could chew.

And, drawing on his own knowledge of the Cult, and how the Brotherhood functioned, he knew that once the Supreme Brother had been destroyed, the Cult could no longer exist.

Their Pact was definite on that point. A Supreme Brother could only be succeeded by a Brother whom he had nominated. Ordinary Brothers could not elect a successor.

John knew that the Supreme Brother could not, despite his formidable powers, have survived the earthquake. It followed that he was dead, and all of his unholy Society with him.

No, there would have to be some other reason for Hayter's return.

He frowned, attempting to make sense of it. He found that he couldn't; not unless it had something to do with Tony Baron. If he was in trouble of some kind, would that have been sufficient reason for Hayter to resurrect himself?

Irritably, John shook his head. Knowing Hayter as well as he had done, he knew that George would not have returned to intercede in some problem which affected Tony. Indeed, he would have been nauseated by the very idea of interfering in another person's problems — unless his better judgement had been swayed by his sense of compassion.

John bit his lip. No, he could not imagine Hayter going to such extremes merely because Tony had ended up in deep water. After all, what could John or Margaret do to help someone they no longer knew?

Neither he nor Margaret had any desperate problems.

There was simply no sense to his feelings that there was more to this than met the eye. Logic told him that what he had experienced was nothing more than a normal reaction to the pressures under which he had placed himself.

Annoyed now, John attempted to assess whether or not it was possible from an occult point of view, for what he had dreamed to be some attempt at communication from Hayter, from beyond the grave. He grunted.

Yet, to be certain, he knew that he would have to do some research on the subject, and he would have to do so without arousing Margaret's curiosity.

He knew that if he was secretive about it, and Margaret found out, she wouldn't rest until she had prised the reason for his secrecy from him. John felt that there was no purpose in telling her of his dream. It would, he guessed, only serve to worry her and probably for no good reason. After he had done the necessary research, and found that his dream could be nothing to do with occult phenomena, he could tell her of his nightmare, making light of it, laughing at his own fears.

But not until then. She had managed to put her experiences with the Cult into perspective, into the background. It never seemed to play on her mind (*'although,'* he supposed, *'there must be times when it does.'*); he could not, and would not, take the chance that premature allusion to what had happened, before he could refute absolutely all possibilities other than natural, might bring all those memories more actively to the surface of her mind.

If she jumped to the conclusion that the Cult had not, in fact, been destroyed, she would worry herself sick until she had irrefutable proof either way.

And that, he thought, would put immense pressure on their relationship. He had spent many years with Hayter, constantly looking over his shoulder, lest the Cult attack. They had both become paranoid about it. He sighed. He would not be drawn into becoming paranoid again for no reason — and refused to say anything to Margaret which might have a similar effect upon her.

And what effect might it have upon Linda? He shook his head again, a shattered, defeated gesture. No, he loved Margaret and Linda much too much to consider being the cause of such misery.

John lay upon the sofa, all these thoughts running amok within his mind. He turned onto his side, certain that with all of this to think about, he would never sleep. It was his last conscious thought, as he was asleep almost before completing it.

***

Over the next couple of weeks, he spent most of his time in his office within the gallery, carefully assimilating what Hayter had had to say about the possibilities of a disincarnate soul overcoming the barrier which death represented in order to pass on warnings of danger.

He was surprised that Hayter had had so much to say on the subject. He had cross-referenced his articles to parallels in his other works, and to those he had quoted from his source material.

123

There were many apparently authenticated cases of dead husbands, wives and lovers who had transcended death and communicated such admonitions. Hayter stated unequivocally that he believed the bond of love made such communication possible.

But of this type of communication between friends, no matter how close, John only found oblique references. He made notes of the more salient points which he felt were worthy of deeper consideration, but made only slow progress.

After these two weeks of research, he found that he had to conclude that visitations of the type he had in mind were not possible under normal circumstances.

If either he, or Margaret, was in desperate danger, it might have been possible for Hayter to have returned to deliver a warning, but as they weren't, John was forced to the conclusion that he had been the victim of nothing more unnatural than going too long without sleep.

He wondered whether he might be dismissing the idea of danger too lightly. Sitting there, he thought back to the old man he had grown to love, understanding that a part of him wanted his vision to be true; to feel that death hadn't separated him from Hayter as finally as it, in fact, had.

His thoughts moved on to Barry, his brother, whose murder had led John into the situation where he had met Hayter. He frowned. If only his brother had let him know what he had been researching, he might not have been killed. John closed his eyes as a wave of pain hit him. It had been the first — and last — time that they had had any secrets from each other.

He thought again of the vision of Hayter. Logic demanded that he dismiss it, but there were two things which he didn't understand. First, the extreme emotion evident in the spectre's demeanour. Something disastrous, of cataclysmic proportions, would have had to occur for Hayter to become so irate. The second thing which puzzled him was the book which he had reached out to take. He hadn't recognised it at the time, yet now he had a vague feeling that he had seen it somewhere before.

He hit his desk in frustration. The action seemed to bring another thought into his mind. He had been very close to

Hayter. He knew that if George had attempted to communicate with him, then he would be in no doubt about it. Yet, he was.

Keeping that thought in mind, he saw things from another perspective. "Yes," he muttered. He sighed heavily. It was the final nail in the coffin. He smiled at the unintentional pun. There was one more test to be tried. He thought of the envelope which Hayter had left him, with instructions that it was to be opened: 'When the time is right'.

If he held that envelope, he thought, and felt that it was, indeed, the time to open it, then it might provide some answers. If he got no such impression, then that would be the end of the matter.

He nodded to himself. He thought of all the time he had spent on trying to unravel his nightmare's secrets; now he was virtually certain that his dark dream had had no secrets to be unravelled.

He sighed again as Steve Preston knocked and entered the office.

"You aren't expecting to be interviewed, are you?" Steve asked.

"No," John replied, placing Hayter's book and his notes into a drawer. "Why?"

Steve frowned. "There's a Miss Emma Carter outside. She says she's a freelance writer, and wants to interview you."

John took the card which Steve offered to him. It contained no additional information, apart from an address.

"Do you want me to get rid of her, or shall I make an appointment for her to see you?"

John thought briefly. "Make her an appointment. The gallery's doing well enough. We don't really need the publicity."

Steve shook his head. "Sorry, John. She doesn't want to interview you about the gallery."

John's eyebrows raised themselves. "Then what the bloody hell *does* she want to interview me about?"

Steve hesitated. "It makes no sense to me, but she says she wants to talk to you about George Hayter." Steve's voice was full of curiosity.

John's face registered his shock. He recovered quickly. "Perhaps you'd better show her in," he said. With a surprised gesture, Steve nodded.

A moment later he returned and introduced Miss Carter. Steve excused himself as she offered to shake hands with John, apologising for not having made an appointment.

John appraised her, critically. She was about five feet eight, wore her red hair long and was, he thought, very attractive. As he motioned her to sit, he took in her dark green eyes. He found them fascinating.

He suddenly realised that she was waiting for him to ask in what way he could help her. He coughed to cover his appraisal of her.

"Miss Carter," he said. "I'm not sure that I can be of much help to you. Mr. Preston said that you didn't want to talk to me about my gallery."

She smiled at him. "That's right," she confirmed. "I want to ask you some questions about George Hayter; you knew him very well, I believe?"

He frowned. "Yes, I did," he admitted. "But that was a long time ago. I don't understand why you want me to discuss him with you."

"I'm doing a series of articles on famous occult authors. I plan to expand them into a reference work when they are completed. But when I came to George Hayter, I came to a full stop. There are no biographies of him that I could find; his publishers can't tell me anything, and they suggested that I contact you or Tony Baron. I've tried everything I can think of to trace him, but I've had no luck. You are the only other person his publishers could suggest contacting, and so here I am." She smiled at him: 'I hope you won't mind helping me by answering some questions?"

John considered this. Her eyes seemed to smile softly into his, and his first reluctance to discuss Hayter began to fade. The soft, green eyes seemed almost mesmeric, and John began to see Miss Carter as more than attractive. Her green eyes, and long, red hair complemented each other perfectly. John realised that she was stunningly lovely.

His eyes travelled down the front of her blouse, openly

appraising her breasts, what he could see of them through the thin fabric.

He didn't notice Miss Carter's smile broaden slightly as his gaze locked more firmly upon her breasts. She sat back in her chair, stretching the fabric more tightly across them.

John could imagine that soft skin under his hands. A moment later, he could just see the darker circles of her areolae and he realised that Miss Carter was wearing no bra: for the briefest of instants, he *thought* he could make out the slightest protrusion of her nipples against the thin, stretched fabric. John's breathing rate became slow and regular as, in his mind's eye, he undid the buttons of her blouse, freeing those breasts and fondling them, caressing them, kissing them, licking them, sucking them, the nipple becoming *very* dark as it hardened, *engorged* with blood.

And at that moment, John would have given *anything* to have Miss Emma Carter in his arms, to be undressing her, and fondling and kissing those soft, sweet breasts.

Without his being aware of it, John's eyes closed a fraction.

As these thoughts and fantasies took deeper root in his mind, John's eyes closed a little more....

Emma Carter smiled as John's eyes closed even further. She formulated in her mind the questions she wished answered, ready to ask them as soon as Brandon was *completely* hypnotised; thirty seconds or so, she estimated.

The door opened abruptly, breaking the spell which she had been weaving, and leaving Emma cursing inwardly as John Brandon's eyes snapped open, and gazed past her to his gallery manager. "Sorry to interrupt, John — I'm going to go early for lunch. Anything I can bring you?"

Emma began to prepare the spell again for the instant the door closed. However, she caught John Brandon looking suspiciously at her. "Yes, Steve," he replied slowly. "Wait there a moment, will you?"

And John returned his gaze to Emma Carter, but this time he avoided looking directly into her eyes. '*Is he* aware *of what I tried to do*?' she wondered.

"Supposing — just supposing that I agreed to talk about him, what kinds of things would you want to know?" John asked her, obviously in response to her initial question. "There are certain things about which I have no desire to talk. The circumstances surrounding his death, for one."

She shrugged, very aware of the fact that the gallery manager was still standing in the doorway behind her. She could not try to take on both of them, especially when one was out of her eye-line, she knew.

"Obviously that was one of the things I wanted to ask about; but mostly I want background about the man himself. How he went about his research, how he was capable of such an enormous output. And I don't understand why he was such a total recluse. If possible, I would like to look around the mansion where he lived, see where he wrote, the things with which he surrounded himself; if possible, I'd like to visit his grave. He's buried behind the mansion, I believe?"

John smiled grimly at her. "I'm afraid that is impossible. The mansion belongs to my wife. She would never agree to your request, and I would use all of my influence with her to reinforce that decision."

"But why?" she asked, a surprised expression in her tone. She understood that Brandon would not repeat his mistake of allowing himself to be left alone with her, so she had to play out the rest of the scenario by pretending to be what she had claimed to be.

John considered before he spoke: "The time which we spent with George in the mansion is a very personal and private thing. We share those experiences and memories with each other, and with no one else. For you to visit the mansion would be, to my mind, a violation of George's privacy. That may sound a little eccentric to you, but George shunned people in life; I see no reason why his wishes should *not* be respected in death."

There was a long silence. "But you don't object to answering my other questions?" she asked.

John nodded. For some reason which he didn't understand, he was taking more of a dislike to Miss Emma Carter by the minute, despite the fact that she was so intriguing and appealing. "In fact, I do. The only things I will discuss are general background. The methods George used whilst writing were his, not mine. If he had wanted them disclosing, he would have done so before he died."

Miss Carter frowned. "Are you saying that he had a premonition of his own death? That must be what you are saying, otherwise it would be possible that he merely thought he would divulge these things eventually but died before doing so. You're saying that, before his death, he made certain that he had done all that he wished to do; had set all his affairs in order?"

John became angry at the insight which he had unintentionally given her. However, he kept his face impassive as he replied: 'If you wish to draw that inference, you may. I cannot confirm or deny it. However you are being somewhat patronising when you say that he had done all that he wished to do. Does any man — or woman for that matter — get to do all that they wish to do in one lifetime? I doubt it."

She digested this silently. "You aren't going to tell me anything useful, are you?" she said in a tone which revealed to John that his reply had muddied the insight which she had thought he had given her.

He smiled at her. "I'm afraid not. You'll find that that goes for my wife, too. And, I wouldn't be at all surprised if Tony's feelings aren't somewhat similar."

Her eyes opened wide. "You know Tony Baron's whereabouts?" she demanded.

Although his anger was now somewhat muted, John couldn't resist needling her. "Oh, yes," he said.

Eagerly, she took a pad from her pocket. "Would you give me his address? I can at least write to him and ask if he's willing to help me."

Locking his eyes upon hers, he said: "Tony's address is somewhere on Earth. I've not heard from him in close on eleven years. Now, Miss Carter, if you'll excuse me, I have a lot to do."

She stood, disappointment written all over her features. They shook hands again. "Well, thank you for your time, Mr. Brandon. If you ever change your mind, you can get in touch with me care of the address on my card."

He shook his head slightly. "I don't think so. Goodbye, Miss Carter."

"Goodbye," she said as she left his office.

He sat pondering her visit. She would have no luck finding information about Hayter, he thought, simply because there was no information available. It might take her a couple of months to realise that, John thought, with a smile.

Then his smile faded. There was something about Miss Emma Carter that he didn't like, despite her attractiveness. He glanced at Steve, who was still waiting patiently by the door. "That woman is *never* to be allowed in here again. And ban her from the gallery, too," he instructed.

***

"Hello? I appear to have the wrong number. I am calling my sister, Margaret."

After a few seconds the connection was made.

"It's as we thought," she said, without preamble. "He doesn't have the information. Yes, I am certain. I will do so."

She left the phone box, moved to her car and set off, driving away from the gallery.

***

That evening, John retrieved the envelope from the wall safe. He gazed lovingly at the neat copperplate writing which adorned it. '*For John, when the time is right*', he read.

He needed to do no more to understand that the envelope was not to be opened. He replaced it within the safe, as Margaret entered.

"John? What are you doing?"

He smiled at her, guiding her to the sofa. They sat. She looked at him quizzically. "What's going on? For the last two weeks, you've been so *distant*."

He looked at the floor. "I've lied to you," he admitted. "I've had something on my mind that I didn't want to worry you with until I was certain about it."

He looked back at her, relieved to see that she seemed calm and relaxed. "Well?" she prompted.

130

"Well," he said, "I had the damnedest nightmare, just after I finished the farm landscape, about *George*...."

Thirty minutes later, his story told, John waited for her reaction. When it came, he stared at her in disbelief. She started laughing. She continued until her sides ached.

"You're not serious," she begged, as a fresh peal of laughter hit her.

He nodded. "I was, and it's not *that* funny."

"But it is," she gasped. "If only you'd asked me about it two weeks ago, I could have told you that it was just a nightmare."

He frowned: "How?" he demanded.

She managed to control her laughter. "Something on that scale would create tremendous occult vibrations. Even if it hadn't woken me at the time, I would have been aware of the residue for days. Don't forget, I'm in sympathy with George more so than with anyone else. It comes from what happened to me in the mansion."

John frowned. "I didn't think of that," he admitted. He grinned suddenly, "I'm an idiot."

She kissed his cheek. "Well, you're a lovable idiot."

"Thanks! Oh, funny thing happened today. I had a freelance writer come to see me at the gallery. Wanted to know everything about George, wanted to visit the mansion — and George's grave."

"What did you tell him?" she asked, a harder tone creeping into her voice as she stroked his hair.

"Her," he corrected with a grin. Seeing her expression, he added, "Red-haired, very attractive. I told her that I wasn't willing to discuss George, and that there was no chance of her being allowed to poke through the mansion, or to visit George's grave. I referred her to Tony."

Margaret stopped stroking his hair. "But you don't know where he is," she objected.

Smiling, he nodded. Margaret caught the joke and laughed.

Feeling suddenly aroused, he kissed her. As her mouth opened under his, he pulled her blouse from her jeans and undid it. He felt her breasts under his hands.

131

He kissed her throat and neck, moving hungrily down to her breasts, her nipples.

Under the sudden onslaught of their passion, as they completed undressing each other, neither of them caught the sigh of defeat which almost *rippled* through the flat.

And neither of them could have been aware that, beneath its cover, the portrait of George Hayter seemed to close its eyes in anguish. Seconds later, blood-red tears as substantial as their love-making appeared beneath the closed eyelids, and then trickled slowly down the portrait's face.

Chapter Five: *Initiations*

The Supreme Brother entered his private cavern, which he used for changing into ceremonial robes, to find Brothers Richard and Jerome waiting for him. Supreme Brother gestured to some chairs set about a crude wooden table. They sat.

For several minutes nothing was said. Jerome's eyes were somewhat muted, as though he had bad news to relate. Richard's face was unreadable. Dark rings stood out starkly around his eyes. It was obvious that he had *not* had enough sleep.

Supreme Brother let out a long slow sigh. He seemed completely relaxed, content that all was going as it should be. Despite his aura of calmness, his eyes betrayed his deeper feelings. This was a rare occurrence, and one which demonstrated his total confidence in these two Brothers.

Whilst renewing their Society, he had given orders strictly prohibiting any attempt at continuing the Curse upon the Barons, desiring to solve one massive logistical problem before embarking upon another.

In the nine or so years during which their rebuilding had been in progress, Richard had been in charge of gathering information about the Barons who still lived. However, he had managed to find no trace of Tony Baron. He had tried everything possible during those years to locate the man who had been with Hayter within the mansion and had participated in the near-annihilation of the Cult. His failure to find any lead, no matter how insignificant, annoyed him.

It was the first time he had *ever* been unable to fulfil a mission with which he had been entrusted, and he feared Supreme Brother would mistake his failure for incompetence.

Supreme Brother broke the silence, startling Richard back into the present.

"It's something of an occasion, Richard."

Richard glanced at him, confused for a second, until he realised that his superior was referring to the coming meeting. He nodded slightly, still preoccupied by his failure.

"Richard," Jerome broke in quietly, "you take too much guilt upon yourself."

Richard flashed an irritated look at Jerome. He rarely said anything which didn't have a direct bearing upon their Society. Richard managed a weak smile, but said nothing.

"No, Richard, that smile of yours doesn't fool me. I think back over the time since we returned from America: the time when our Brotherhood was in ruins. The time when, despite the aid from America, we had to work virtually twenty-four hours a day. You did as much in that rebuilding as I. And, when *I* was ill, who took over my duties and completed them as well as completing his own, without any word or gesture of complaint? And who was it undertook to trace the Barons — again despite the *other* duties which you had to perform? Who was it had to be *ordered* to rest by Supreme Brother, because he was almost dead on his feet, and had lost over two stones in weight?

"In these last years, Richard, you have performed the work of four Brothers superbly, to my mind, and yet you are annoyed that one piece of information eludes you? *Why*? Don't you think we have noticed your past labours? I know that if you cannot obtain this information, then nobody can. Even James or Gregory could not have done more than you. I know it, and *you* know it. So, tell me, Richard, *why* do you insist on feeling guilty about it? Is it merely the knowledge that you are not superhuman? Or could it be that this charade of guilt is nothing more than self-pity, no matter how misguided?" Jerome asked, softly.

Richard stared into Jerome's eyes. He felt a surge of anger, but quickly suppressed it. "You presume *too much*, Jerome," he hissed.

Jerome glanced mildly at him. "No, I don't think I do. I merely point out that no one has worked harder than you, and you deserve *all* credit for that. You should feel proud of your achievements. You have *my* admiration. I do not like to see you, Richard, blaming yourself for something which is *not* your fault. My words weren't meant insultingly."

Richard ran a hand through his black hair. "Jerome, you're right. I have worked hard towards this day. It's not self-pity which haunts me, but *anger*. I know, in the not-too-distant future, Supreme Brother *will* give the order for the continuation of our Curse, and then we *will* avenge so many of our Brothers. Yet our revenge cannot be completed until we have run Tony Baron to earth. But how do we do that? I can find no trace of him. It is *this* which haunts me — that our vengeance, so long delayed, must be delayed even further."

Jerome locked eyes with Richard. "No, *my Brother*," he said, using a particularly intimate form of address, "I realise now that I was wrong. I assumed your emotion to be guilt — I should have known that you would have had our vengeance at heart. I understand your feelings; but remember, no one can hide from us forever. Eventually, Tony Baron *will* make a mistake, and that will prove fatal for him. When it happens, Richard, you will make him pay for the annoyance he has caused *all* of us, for the deaths of so many of our Bothers — before he dies, very slowly."

Supreme Brother watched them impassively. He turned his gaze upon Richard. "I recall, years ago, in America, I gave you something of a lecture on the virtues of patience. Do you remember it?"

"Yes," Richard admitted.

"You do well to do so. As Jerome says, I know how hard you have both worked in the past. I know you have done all possible to find Tony Baron. For the moment, he is not important. He *will* surface eventually; when he does, we will be ready. It is upon the subject of our Curse that I wished to speak to you both.

"You know that today's meeting is *very* special; we renew and reaffirm our Pact with our Patrons. Our extensive recruitment campaign may now be relaxed. It would seem reasonable to expect our Society to move back into those endeavours which were curtailed by our defeat. Unless we actively promote our evil, we stagnate. I intend to begin measures which will force our Brothers into a more active participation in all our labours. They must take responsibilities at *least* equal to those undertaken by yourselves, in times past. Our Society must move once more into top gear. We have made sound preparations for this, and I want the transition to

135

be as smooth as possible."

"And our Curse?" Richard asked.

Supreme Brother smiled his icy smile. "I am unsure whether to authorise the continuation of our Curse at the present time. I don't think our newer Brothers are capable of the dexterity of thought and action which may be required. I would prefer them to have more experience of working with each other — of relying upon each other.

"And it must be recognised that things have become more complicated since our return from America. We must not, this time, allow anything to be left to chance."

Richard frowned. "Don't you think you're being a little over-cautious? I think our newest Brothers would benefit tremendously from being involved in the execution of our Curse. They would, I am sure, mature very quickly from exposure to our vengeance."

"I don't agree," Jerome cut in. "We cannot be too careful. It was, remember, our manipulation by Anton Baron which almost destroyed us. Had we been more circumspect, things might have ended very differently."

"I know you to be no coward," Supreme Brother observed, "but others might misunderstand what you are saying."

Jerome's eyes blazed. "Let them. There comes a time where wisdom advises caution: if any of our Brothers cannot see that then they should never have been initiated into our Society."

Supreme Brother allowed himself the smallest of smiles. "You are invaluable, Jerome. Your thinking echoes mine. None would, I am sure, think of calling me a coward."

Richard laughed. "Not if they value their lives. Have you come to any conclusion about when we should resume our Curse?"

Supreme Brother frowned. "Immediately!" he whispered. As both Brothers looked sharply at him, he continued: "But with caution."

Jerome nodded enthusiastically. "I understand: Brother Fidelis was right. You are devious." His voice carried an edge of admiration.

Richard looked puzzled.

Jerome grinned at him. "We are to resume our Curse by eliminating friends of the Barons," he said. "Supreme Brother is hoping that Tony Baron is watching over the Brandons. If he realises that their friends are being eliminated, murdered, he might come out of hiding. If that occurs, then we destroy the three of them, and then simply wait until the child is of an age where we may destroy her."

"And if this doesn't bring Tony Baron out of hiding?"

"Then," said Supreme Brother, "we destroy the child when she is of age. Tell me, wouldn't you go to comfort your friends if they had just suffered such a tragedy as losing their daughter? I think that I *know* Tony Baron. He is attempting to emulate George Hayter. And, like Hayter, he has a compassionate nature. He will not be able to prevent himself going to the Brandons' flat. Once in the open, he will be easy prey."

"Unless his abilities, too, are similar to Hayter's."

"But they are not. He is not a natural occultist. We have nothing to fear from him in that way."

"We *do* from Margaret Brandon, however," Jerome informed them quietly. "Since her possession, she has progressed remarkably. Perhaps her possession triggered something inside her mind, released some slumbering abilities, which were deeply hidden. Perhaps, if the possession had never happened, her abilities would have remained buried all her life. Remember though, she *is* a Baron — the potential for becoming a powerful occultist is always there — it simply requires the right stimulus to release it. Although she is not in Hayter's league, she is still extremely powerful and dangerous. Just think of the ease with which she cured Georgina Thompson's injuries. I know that there have been many others, too — not to the same degree, I grant you: but we would be stupid to overlook it, or to write it off as *luck*. In an occult context, such a thing does not exist. She will be aware of any form of occultism practised near her. We must avoid that at all costs. She must not suspect that we have re-formed, that not *all* of us were destroyed. She could be very dangerous to us if she understood our re-formation, and the threat which we now pose."

Supreme Brother inclined his head. "Very true, Jerome. We must keep that in mind at all times. When we eliminate these friends of hers — and of her husband's — we must ensure that there are no links to the occult, and hence, to us. Therefore the deaths must appear to have been caused by, say, burglaries gone wrong, for example. We could kidnap one or two, and allow our Brothers to enjoy themselves. It would seem to the authorities that a psychopath was loose in the community," he smiled at the thought.

"I have discovered that John Brandon does not know the whereabouts of Tony Baron," said Richard. "I used Sister Margaret. Her cover as a freelance writer is well established. I judged that Brandon could not make any connections to us, as in fact turned out to be the case."

"Do not worry, Richard. As I say, Tony Baron will come out of hiding sooner or later. Richard, after the meeting, I want you to go home and catch up on the sleep you have been missing."

As Richard nodded, Jerome spoke. "How many times has this ritual been performed?" he wanted to know.

"As I am about to perform it, *never*. The ritual itself has been performed once before, to my knowledge, but it has never been incorporated into initiations, and the sacrifice was performed separately. I am in effect merging three rituals into one. Of course, it means that the meeting will be a mammoth one."

Supreme Brother frowned as another entered the cavern. Sister Margaret inclined her head. "All Brothers and Sisters are assembled," she reported.

Richard and Jerome stood. They excused themselves, knowing that their leader preferred a few moments alone before performing any ritual.

Supreme Brother took a slow, deep breath. Sister Margaret approached him. He glanced at her with curiosity.

"Will you need me after the ritual?" she asked quietly.

He thought about it. No doubt after the ritual he *would* be feeling tired and strained. A little relaxation might be enjoyable. '*What was the point of being the Supreme Brother*,' he thought, '*if you didn't take advantage of the fact that there were Sisters within the Society now, sworn to do his bidding, to cater to his every whim?*' He smiled a cruel smile at her. "Yes, I think I might," he said. As she turned to leave, his smile faded. He detected a tell-tale grimace on her face as she turned from him, and he detected a slight favouring of her left leg.

"Margaret, remove your robe."

She turned back to face him but now he detected a trace of fear in her eyes. Undoing the six buttons, three just under each collar bone, the robe fell to the floor. Supreme Brother walked around her and wasn't at all surprised to see welts upon her back, buttocks and legs. "What did you do to earn these?" he asked.

She faced him again. "Brother Richard thought I needed to be reminded of his importance within the Society."

Supreme Brother said nothing, his eyes fixed upon her. Despite her usual poise with other members of the Cult, it was infinitely more difficult to stand before the Supreme Brother — naked or clothed — with those eyes boring into her. Without his needing to ask, she continued: "Apparently, he took offence when I failed to acknowledge him as I walked past."

Supreme Brother said nothing, nor did his expression change. Margaret could now feel waves of power pulsating from him and battering into her, making her will-power crumble to nothing. The pulsating waves became painful, pounding into her brain.

"Brother Richard isn't important within the Society," he said, to Margaret's confusion as she fought the nausea building up within her, her brain feeling as though it was being slowly twisted in upon itself.

"Brother Richard is essential to the Society, and you *will* treat him with the deference to which he is entitled. How many stokes did he order be inflicted upon you?"

"Twenty, Supreme Brother," she whispered apprehensively.

"Then he was being unduly lenient. You will treat all

Brothers with respect, deference and submission."

Margaret managed to nod her understanding and compliance. The waves of palpable anger subsided quickly, but Margaret still had a pounding headache as a memento of Supreme Brother's displeasure.

"You may cover yourself," he said, indicating the fallen robe.

As she was re-fastening the six buttons, Supreme Brother spoke again. "Brother Richard's punishment was absurdly lenient. You will seek out the Brother responsible for giving you those welts, and will explain that your punishment was not sufficiently severe. You will then tell him it is my command that you receive an *additional* forty strokes. Perhaps then you will remember to treat all Brothers here with suitable *respect*."

Margaret's gasp of surprise and shock echoed around the cavern, but she was wise enough not to argue or remonstrate with Supreme Brother about the severity of her punishment. Forty strokes more was severe; arguing the fact with him could easily cause forty strokes to become eighty or a hundred. She looked briefly into his eyes, which seemed to bore into her. She dropped her gaze swiftly as he continued: "You are dismissed, Margaret."

Thanking him, she left the cavern, trembling. However before she found herself within the area where the ceremony and ritual would be performed, she had mastered her fears and nothing about her gave any indication that she was anything but her usual self.

Alone, Supreme Brother thought of his sexual dalliance with Margaret. Jerome and Richard had been startled by it, but were reassured when they realised that their leader kept Margaret very much in her place, according her no preferential treatment.

Supreme Brother had allowed both Jerome and Richard similar privileges, to emphasise their standing within the Society. Jerome, however, seemed not inclined to exercise his new prerogative.

Pulling on his ceremonial mask, and adjusting the dagger at his side, he left the cavern, emerging a moment later in the vast chamber where all were assembled.

140

He made his way to the elevated dais; all murmurs died away as he sat, sweeping his eyes over the two hundred and eight members of the Brotherhood. There had been over a hundred more members of the original Brotherhood before its destruction. However, he felt that there were enough now to make the organisation once more a force to be reckoned with.

Gracefully, Supreme Brother stood. "Brothers," he said, "and Sisters, you *all* know the significance of this meeting: or you think that you do. I am convinced that our rebuilding process is now virtually complete, and other matters now supersede it in importance. Matters such as undertaking the duties and responsibilities which your various ranks demand.

"You were allocated your present positions by Brothers Richard and Jerome. Now, you must earn them. Those of the First and Second Circle who believe that they could undertake the tasks and responsibilities which promotion to the next Circle demands may, after this meeting is concluded, inform these two Brothers. They will assess your abilities, perhaps ask you to prove yourselves by performing some labour on our behalf. The results will be submitted to me, and those I feel worthy of promotion will receive it. Those of the Second and Third Circles who cannot fulfil their current duties satisfactorily will be demoted to the relevant Circle. Again, this decision will be mine. This will be the only occasion when Brothers will be invited to apply for promotion. Does anyone have a comment to make? Any question to ask?

There was a muted mutter which quickly died away. Supreme Brother frowned as a Brother from the First Circle stood.

"Brother Thomas?" he asked, drawing on his encyclopaedic knowledge of the Brothers he had initiated.

"I would like to ask a question, *if* I may?"

Supreme Brother inclined his head.

"You said nothing about direct promotion from the First to the Third Circle, bypassing the Second."

There was some muted laughter. Supreme Brother looked at Brother Thomas. "What you suggest is *very* rare. Do you believe you could achieve such a transition?"

A flicker of doubt crossed Thomas's face, but it was gone

141

in an instant. "I do."

Supreme Brother caught sight of Richard struggling to suppress a grin. He, too, felt a *trace* of humour at what was being suggested. "See me after the meeting is concluded. *I, myself*, will set you a task to perform, to assess whether you are one of those rare Brothers capable of making such a massive leap."

Brother Thomas sat, seemingly undaunted at the prospect of a task being set for him by Supreme Brother himself.

When no one else rose, Supreme Brother continued: "We are here to renew and reaffirm our Pact, and to initiate five new brethren. Further, we are to resume our Curse upon the descendants of Anton Baron, as modified by myself.

"We will begin by attacking friends of Baron's descendants, but we will act with all caution. Most of you know of our near destruction. You know of the aid given to us by our American Brothers. You know of the marriage of John Brandon and Margaret Hunter. They have complicated our revenge by producing a child; Tony Baron cannot, at this time, be located. So, as always, we must bide our time. Brothers — and Sisters — will be selected to take part in our vengeance."

He fell silent, appraising the assembled throng once more, relishing the feeling that he *was* once more, the Supreme Brother.

"And so, Brothers, to our Pact, and our re-dedication," he whispered.

Raising his arms, Supreme Brother began the ritual, calling first upon their Patron Demons to attend, and then restating the terms of their Pact.

That ritual culminated in the sacrifice of a six-month-old baby. Supreme Brother performed the sacrifice with relish, feeling years of inactivity drop away from him. As the sacrifice was completed, he felt waves of strength pouring into him. He smiled grimly. This was the reciprocal part of the sacrifice, where the Patron Demons shared some of their power with him.

He cleansed the chamber of the blood, and relocated the corpse away for later disposal. Almost immediately, he called for the prospective Brothers and Sisters to be admitted.

They were ushered in, the prospective Brothers wearing the brown robes which signified that they were not, as yet, initiates. The prospective Sister was naked. All were blindfolded.

Supreme Brother allowed the tension to build before motioning for them to be brought forward. As they reached the dais, he asked: "Who wishes to be first?"

The woman took a pace forward. "Me, Supreme Brother," she said, loudly and firmly.

He locked his hard, frigid gaze upon her. Despite the fact of her blindfold, she felt his gaze and shivered. "Well said," he murmured, "but *not* possible."

The woman took a deep breath. One of the men stepped forward. "Me," he said.

"Remove your blindfold," Supreme Brother ordered. The man obeyed and blinked several times. Supreme Brother's eyes bored into him.

"You are here of your own free will?"

"Yes."

"You renounce all authorities other than mine?"

"Yes."

"You place yourself totally, body and soul, in my charge?"

"Yes."

"You understand that you may not renounce these, your vows?"

"Yes."

"You accept these, our Patron Demons as your total Lords and Masters?"

"Yes."

"Tell me why we should accept and admit you into our Brotherhood?"

"Because I belong here."

"You have already demonstrated that; had you not, you would now be dead."

The man glanced into Supreme Brother's eyes, his expression unreadable.

Taking a chalice from the dais, Supreme Brother offered it

143

to the man. "Drink it all," he commanded.

The man did so, gasping as he forced the foul concoction down his throat. He turned white.

"Now recite, of your own free will, your ritual dedication of yourself in the knowledge that, once uttered, you are irrevocably bound to us, and to our Society."

The man did so. The Demons signalled their acceptance with an ear-piercing shriek and a swirl of chaotic colours which seemed to engulf him. He cried out once in fear, surprise and pain, then gained control of himself, and refused to let any other sound pass his lips.

Eventually, the Demons moved back to their position behind the dais. Supreme Brother drew his ceremonial dagger. He held it to the man's throat, pressing slightly so that he drew blood. The man stood his ground.

"You acknowledge my right to slit your throat? To mutilate you should it please me?"

Taking a deep breath, the man nodded, "I do, Supreme Brother."

Supreme Brother sheathed his dagger. He looked a moment longer at the man before him, saying: "I, Supreme Brother, name you Brother Gregory. The last Brother to have that name excelled all here. I do not expect you to do likewise, but be worthy of the name."

Taking a second chalice, Supreme Brother offered it to Brother Gregory.

The Brother took it, saying, "I, Brother Gregory swear loyalty to you, Supreme Brother, and to all assembled here." He drained the chalice.

Supreme Brother embraced him cursorily. "Brother Gregory, take your place." As the Brother stripped off his brown robe, he added to the assembly: "We have a new Brother."

There were several cheers and enthusiastic applause. Jerome stood. "Welcome to our society, Brother," he said, smiling, eyes blazing. Brother Gregory, now donning the robe of a fully-fledged Brother, smiled back.

"Brother Gregory," Supreme Brother said, completing the

formalities, "take your place, and welcome."

As soon as the new initiate had taken his place in the First Circle, Supreme Brother spoke. "Who will be next?" he asked.

Each initiation took around three-quarters of an hour. At length, only the woman was left. Supreme Brother dabbed at his forehead with a cloth, then turned his attention to her. "Remove your blindfold," he ordered her.

She did so; he noticed that she, too, was sweating. Whether through the heat within the chamber, or through fear of the coming ordeal, he couldn't decide. Being a Sister in the male-oriented Society wasn't easy, demanding a very strong personality. Supreme Brother used the initiation ceremony to test a potential Sister's determination and strength of character.

As she looked timidly at him, Supreme Brother wondered if she could possibly be as innocent as she appeared.

She was of medium height, and was slim. Her short, curly auburn hair seemed to emphasise her face which was thin and yet elegant. Her light brown eyes seemed timid and shy, yet he knew that this was an illusion.

He considered her, thoughtfully. His eyes travelled over her body, lingering on her firm breasts, her legs, the triangle of dark brown hair. He found her extremely attractive.

His eyes retraced their route to her face. She blushed. Still he stood, surveying her, refusing to begin the ceremony until his thoughts had run to their conclusion.

Then he began the initiation, closely watching her, listening carefully to her answers. He could not fault her. The initiation differed in that the Demons did not signify their acceptance with the harsh ululation which had been heard when the men were approved.

In the case of a woman, this was the point at which the initiation diverged.

"Are you willing to give yourself to our Patrons?" he asked her.

She hesitated barely perceptibly before answering, "Yes."

"And you do so of your own free will?"

"Yes."

He motioned her to the dais. "Lie there: open your legs,

145

and yourself, to our Patrons."

She made her way slowly to the platform, her breathing rapidly increasing. Her fear and terror were total; only sheer willpower *forced* her to obey his command.

Supreme Brother sat, watching her. The Demons swirled above her, colours changing madly as they worked themselves up. One darted towards her. Her legs were forced further and further apart until it seemed that they must dislocate.

She screamed horribly as the Demon took her. Her hips were raised to an impossible angle as the Demon disappeared inside her. She screamed again. Supreme Brother casually noticed her fists clenched so tightly that there seemed to be no blood inside them. They were incredibly white.

Abruptly, she was on her back again, the Demon on top of her, *probing, nipping, possessing.*

Supreme Brother watched as she was manipulated like a marionette, her body placed in various positions; every millimetre of her body examined minutely; *every* orifice explored and exploited.

The whole situation was made even more eerie by the fact that it was conducted in dead silence, except for the screams and gasps which escaped the object of the Demon's lust. All the assembly watched in total silence, in morbid fascination at the test which was being enacted.

Finally, as exactly thirty minutes elapsed, the first Demon left her reluctantly, making way for the other.

However, the other made no move towards the woman. Instead it communicated with Supreme Brother.

"I waive my right - *for the present*," it said.

Alarm bells began to go off in the Supreme Brother's mind. "You may *not* do so," he returned firmly. He felt a palpable wave of anger, but brushed it aside. "The terms of our Pact are clear. You may have her now, or waive that right *forever*. The choice is yours."

The demon chuckled. "Very well, Supreme Brother. I *will* exercise my right — but do *not* be surprised if she doesn't survive the experience," it hissed.

Supreme Brother felt his anger building. "*So be it!*" he

snapped back, in his mind. "But it will be the last chance you ever have, so savour it. Should you harm her beyond what is customary, I will allow no more women to be initiated into either society. I doubt that your companion would thank you for that."

In he felt an unadulterated wave of fury, quickly mastered. The Demon considered.

"Very clever, Supreme Brother," it praised him grudgingly. "I *will* adhere to the terms of our Pact — not because of your threat, but because I acknowledge that you have *never* attempted to cheat us; that you honour our Pact.

"It has been *long* since you sacrificed to us," it added, with a trace of regret.

"I understand," Supreme Brother returned, "but for *that* you may thank Anton Baron and his accursed offspring."

The Demon gave the equivalent of a nod before approaching the woman, who lay gasping for breath.

The swirling colours changed into vaguely human form as the Demon grabbed hold of her, its phallus swiftly attaining enormous proportions. It rammed itself into her so powerfully that her whole body was moved over a foot along the stone dais. Minute fragments of the rough-hewn stone split and splintered into the skin of her back and legs causing a multitude of fine lacerations which immediately began to bleed. However, it is doubtful the woman was more than vaguely aware of these; the demonic member was of a length and girth which stretched and dilated her vaginal passage far beyond its normal limits. She screeched in pain and shock; the phallus was deathly cold, making her feel as though she was being raped by a gigantic jagged icicle. Simultaneously, she was certain that whatever was penetrating so deeply into her was wrapped in barbed wire. The thrust felt as if it was scratching and lacerating and tearing the delicate vaginal wall. She cried out in anguish as another set of barbs seemed to cut across the lesions already created. She wondered, in a panicking desperation, whether the Demon would harm her sexually beyond her abilities to heal.

She had known all along that she would have to come through this somewhat extreme ordeal, to prove herself worthy

147

of a place within the Society. She had thought long and hard about it, and had concluded that she would be able to withstand the experience. Other women had come through it, so why not she? And after all: how bad could the ordeal possibly be?

Her screams of agony redoubled and echoed around the cavern. She realised that she was being provided with a very painful and humiliating answer to her rhetorical question.

Taloned hands grabbed her breasts in a grip of steel; the grip was so tight and the pain so intense that she was certain the talons were penetrating and cutting deeply into her breasts. Another shriek of pain forced itself from her vocal chords as the swirling, colourful talons changed position, and gripped her breasts from a different angle, cutting deeply into flesh which had not, as yet, been shredded or lacerated. Rivulets of warm blood trickled down both breasts and onto her sides.

Before she could rationalise this the Demon moved and was forcing itself into her anal passage, stretching the delicate tissue wider and wider until she could feel it ripping and tearing, and could feel more blood oozing down her anal passage as the barbed phallus continued its freezing shredding of any tissue with which it came into contact.

The taloned hands scraped their way down her legs, leaving bloody lacerations in their wake, a testament to its examination of every inch of her body. She found herself jerked and pulled in different directions by invisible tethers, being placed in impossible positions at impossible angles. At times the Demon seeming to be mostly outside her body, only that numbingly cold phallus tearing and shredding whatever flesh it came to touch; at other times it seemed that a reversal had taken place and the Demon seemed to be almost entirely inside her. She could feel the insubstantial being inside her, seeming to be amusing itself by examining the internal nature of her body. She found the notion utterly revolting and struggled to prevent herself from throwing up. She struggled to breathe when it turned its attention to her lungs; she coughed up blood and tried not to panic. '*After all*', she thought to herself, '*if the Demons were not satisfied with her, her life would be at an end anyway*'. She wondered, momentarily, how

Supreme Brother would organise that.

Abruptly, as the thirtieth minute dawned, the Demon left her. The Demon chose to leave her body via her mouth; she felt both sides of her mouth rip and tear, as it gave her a contemptuous fellatiol thrust by way of farewell, leaving a cold, foul, bitter secretion behind in her mouth. She fought *not* to wonder what it might be.

Even Supreme Brother was shocked by what was done to her. He saw blood trickle from her mouth; had watched as her breasts were gripped in taloned hands so fiercely that blood was drawn immediately; as she was raped in every conceivable way (and in a few which were quite *inconceivable*) he wondered how she could possibly accept what was being done to her, and yet retain her sanity. It was impossible, Supreme Brother thought, that any human being could take such torment, such unadulterated suffering.

Blood flowed from her; from her breasts, her anus, her legs, her neck, the corners of her mouth.

Her shrieks continued, intensified, became a constant within the cavern.

Both the Demons then approached Supreme Brother. "The initiate is satisfactory," they reported before moving back to their position behind the dais.

The silence was complete except for the gasping, sobbing, wailing cries which still came from the woman. Supreme Brother hesitated visibly before calling firmly to her: "Come here."

She made no move to obey him, was lost in a world of humiliation, expecting yet another assault to begin.

He frowned, and yet could understand such a lack of response after what she had endured. He took a pace towards the dais. The woman turned her head a little and locked her eyes upon him. She gulped, trying to gain some control over her sobs.

"Stand, and come here," Supreme Brother repeated more softly.

Slowly, she stood, blood still running down her skin, her face and body swollen, demonstrating the abuse which she had suffered — and survived.

Limping heavily, grimacing at every step, she managed to make her way to the Supreme Brother. She swayed upon her feet, but retained her balance. No one moved to help her, knowing that such help was forbidden until she was formally accepted and named.

Her eyes sought his, attempting to bring him into focus. "Am I acceptable?" she asked.

Supreme Brother's eyes actually softened slightly. "Our Patrons have found you so, as do I," he said. "Is it still your wish to be admitted into our Society?"

She licked her dry and cracked lips, smearing the blood in the process. "*Yes*," she whispered.

"Then recite, of your own free will, your ritual dedication of yourself, in the knowledge that once uttered, you are irrevocably bound to us, and to our Society."

She nodded, slowly speaking the required words.

Supreme Brother held his dagger to her neck. "Do you acknowledge my right to slit your throat, to mutilate you, should it please me?" he asked, for the first time ever feeling that this part of the ritual was more than a little redundant after what she had allowed to be done to her.

"Yes," she whispered, staggering on her feet.

He understood that she was close to collapse. Despite his normal ambivalence towards women, Supreme Brother found himself admiring her. She was *determined*, *courageous*, even *fearless*. He caught himself wondering where she got those qualities, and smiled inwardly at the answer.

"I name you Sister...." he paused for a second. "Angela," he finished, liking the irony.

He took the *second* chalice from the dais and offered it to her. She took it and drained it.

The Supreme Brother embraced her, not caring about the blood which transferred itself from her to his ceremonial costume. "There has never *before* been a Sister Angela," he said. "And I wish you well."

He released her, and she swayed again. Supreme Brother turned his now once again icy eyes upon the assembly. "We have a new Sister," he said.

As one, the throng stood, cheering, applauding Sister Angela for the ordeal which she had endured.

She opened her mouth to complete her part of the initiation, but found that the cheers and applause drowned her voice. Supreme Brother held up a hand, and there was immediate silence.

"I, Sister Angela, swear loyalty to the Supreme Brother and to all assembled here," she said.

"Sister Angela," Supreme Brother said to her, "take your place, and welcome."

As she moved slowly towards the First Circle, the cheers and applause broke out again. A Brother appeared at her side and supported her the rest of the way.

Supreme Brother's eyes sought Richard's. Richard nodded and moved towards his new Sister. He needed to be sure that her injuries were, if serious, attended to immediately. It was not unusual for him to provide any care newly initiated Sisters might need; however, it *was* unusual for Supreme Brother to require him to check a new Sister before the assembly had been formally dismissed.

Their Patrons had treated her with unusual brutality; Richard wondered why that was. No doubt Supreme Brother would know the reason, and would share it with him should he need to know it.

Supreme Brother resumed his place upon the dais, patiently waiting for the noise to die down. It had been a very long and exhausting meeting: almost nine hours. He rubbed his eyes, feeling the strain catching up with him now that there was little more to do.

As the silence returned, Supreme Brother dismissed the Patron Demons and then returned his attention to the assembly. "Our rededication is complete. We have four new Brothers and a new Sister. There are many matters needing discussion but they must wait until our next meeting. I wish to see Brother Thomas and Sister Angela immediately this meeting is dissolved.

"Does any here wish to say anything which cannot wait

until our next meeting?"

When nobody spoke, Supreme Brother nodded. "Then I adjourn this assembly. *Be evil*, my Brothers — and Sisters."

Supreme Brother left the dais and returned to his private cavern. He sat and blew out a long breath. He rubbed his eyes again. His fatigue fell away from him as Brother Thomas entered quietly.

Without preamble, Supreme Brother spoke. "You believe that you should be promoted from the First to the Third Circle: why?"

Thomas considered. "Because I am able to perform to your satisfaction any task which you set me."

"You are confident at least," Supreme Brother replied, locking his eyes upon Thomas's. "I *will* consider promoting you, but you must earn it."

"How, Supreme Brother?"

"You know of our Curse. This is your task: kill Steven Preston, John Brandon's gallery manager. But do so in such a way that no suspicion may point even remotely in our direction. Should you fail to do this to my satisfaction...." he left the sentence hanging. "But succeed, and you will have your promotion. You may decline if you don't feel capable of attempting this mission," Supreme Brother added softly.

Thomas thought carefully. "How much time do I have to accomplish this task?"

Supreme Brother smiled his frigid smile. "*Very* astute. How much time do you think you would need?"

"No more than three weeks," he said, *oozing* confidence.

Supreme Brother nodded. "Three weeks it is. But remember, *no* links to our society. Inform Richard privately of your mission; he will be able to give you useful information. You may go."

Brother Thomas inclined his head and left the cavern. Supreme Brother grinned mirthlessly. He had a feeling that Thomas would, indeed, manage to complete his mission within the guidelines which he had stipulated.

He changed back into more normal clothing. Soon after, Richard entered. "Sister Angela is outside, as is Sister

152

Margaret."

"Tell Sister Margaret that I will be with her presently. How is Sister Angela?"

Richard frowned. "Cuts, abrasions, shock she seems *very* resilient. I don't understand why our Patrons treated her so harshly. They were much more vicious than they have ever been before," Richard's tone implied *more* than a purely medical interest in Angela. When Supreme Brother volunteered nothing by way of explanation for the way Sister Angela had been treated by their Patrons, Richard added: "She should be kept under medical observation for twenty-four hours or so. If you've no objection, I'll undertake the task myself."

"But Angela has suffered no permanent harm?"

Richard glanced at him shrewdly. "Physically, no. She'll be in a great deal of pain for a few weeks, I should think. I can prescribe analgesics to help with that."

Supreme Brother, now in normal clothing nodded thoughtfully. "Send her in," he said.

Richard left the cavern. A few moments later Sister Angela entered, wearing a skirt and blouse. She inclined her head to him. "You wanted to see me, Supreme Brother," she said.

He looked at her, noting that she was still in considerable discomfort. "Sit," he said, indicating the chair opposite himself. She sat, refusing to make eye contact.

"It has been a *long* time," he said

"Yes, Supreme Brother, it has," she agreed formally. He frowned in annoyance.

"The meeting is over, we are alone. We cannot be overheard. Forget, for the time being, that I am the Supreme Brother."

She looked at him then, locking her eyes on his, her lips opening slightly. "Did it surprise you, to see me waiting for initiation, father?" she asked with open curiosity.

He smiled a more natural and warm smile than the frigid affairs which his face normally wore. "*No*, Rachel. Even *before* you were approached as a possible candidate for initiation, I knew of it, and gave my approval."

She absently massaged one of her legs. "Rachel. It sounds strange hearing you use my Christian name. I don't suppose I'll ever hear you use it during meetings.

"Being the Supreme Brother doesn't really sound like you. You were never that methodical and orderly at home. Most of the time you seemed.... distant, preoccupied."

His smile faded. "Marriage is a totally different life. And it was a long time ago."

"Why didn't Mother ever take you to court?"

The smile reappeared. "I persuaded her not to," he replied quietly.

"Is that why she divorced you?"

"Yes: although she didn't cite the real grounds for wanting the divorce."

"I never understood how she found out — we were so *very* careful. "

He shrugged. "She always *was* a suspicious woman. I believe she saw us together in bed. It must have been a shock for her."

Angela blushed. The conversation was becoming *much* more frank than she had expected it to be. She noticed him smiling, savouring her discomfort.

"Or *had* you forgotten?"

She shook her head, "How could I?"

"Do you resent me, or hate me for seducing you?"

She felt the blood drain from her face. "No," she whispered, "I love you for it."

"Why didn't you get in touch with me after your mother died?"

She bit her lip. "Because I was certain that you'd murdered her, or had her murdered."

He straightened. "*Not true,*" he retorted angrily.

"Father," she pleaded, "that was what I believed at the time. I know *now* that I was wrong."

She stretched her body carefully, grimacing.

"Yes, our Patrons wanted to be certain you would be an asset to our Society. Equally, it isn't *every* day that they get to

154

defile the Supreme Brother's daughter. Are you okay?"

"I'll live. It was *much* worse than I'd expected, that's all."

"It might be an idea for you to talk with some of our Sisters. They will be able to help you put it into perspective; *especially* Sister Margaret."

Angela nodded. "I will," she affirmed.

"You understand that this will be the only time that I will talk to you as father to daughter? After this, you will simply be another Sister, and may expect no special treatment from me."

She stared at him. "I didn't expect any. I don't need *you* to help me."

He slowly inclined his head. "You have grown into a very attractive young woman."

"Thank you, father," she said, self-consciously.

"And you *don't* have any boyfriends?"

"No."

"I'm sure there will be plenty of applicants among our Brothers."

She frowned. "They'll be disappointed."

"Why?"

"I find that I prefer father-figures," she murmured pointedly.

"You wouldn't be trying to seduce *me*, would you?"

"Of course not; no. I just thought the knowledge might...*interest* you."

He drummed his fingers upon the table.

"I always wondered why you and mother married in the first place."

He thought for a few seconds. "I was a lot younger then," he mused. "I had not, at *that* time, achieved my current position within our Society. I believed, wrongly as it turned out, that I loved her. But she loved me: too much, if that is possible. Our marriage was doomed from the start, partially from my dedication to the Brotherhood. And of course, then *you* were conceived. In many ways, you were all that kept us together, until our incest was discovered. By then, all pretence had gone. The rest, I think you *know*."

"But there are *so* many things you've missed out," she protested.

He looked at her starkly. "Because they are none of your business, do you think?"

She accepted the rebuke silently.

"You *may* find that Brother Richard has developed an interest in you," he observed.

"That's his problem."

His tone becoming sharp, he added, "Not so. It's more your problem. One of the rewards which he enjoys for his past labours is the right to sleep with *any* of our Sisters — you included."

She frowned at him. "And you will allow him to....to force me?"

He sat back, smiling his accustomed frozen smile. "Yes; a few minutes ago you said that you didn't want any help from me. Even if you did, I would not provide it. You swore loyalty to our Brothers and to me. Let this be the first of many tests of your ability to overcome adversity."

Angela took a deep breath.

"I'm afraid that your thoughts give you away."

"What?" she asked, suddenly apprehensive.

"You concluded that Richard could sleep with you, but could not force you to enjoy the experience. Be careful that your thoughts don't lead you to active disobedience. The punishments for such are severe."

"But he can't force me to enjoy it," she said emphatically.

"I'm afraid that you underestimate Brother Richard's abilities. No doubt you *will* learn that for yourself. Richard is a surgeon, and has told me that you need to be kept under observation for twenty-four hours. Richard has volunteered to undertake this duty himself. Report to him when you leave me."

Angela opened her mouth to protest, but then thought better of it.

Supreme Brother glanced at his watch. "Time for me to resume more important duties," he observed, acidly. "Sister Angela, as you leave tell Sister Margaret that she may enter."

156

Angela stood, knowing that the interview was at an end. "Yes, Supreme Brother," she said, as she stood and turned to leave.

"Oh, and one more thing, Sister Angela," he called after her.

"Yes, Supreme Brother?" she turned back to face him.

"I expressly forbid you to reveal, or to imply, that you are related to me, to any of our assembly." His eyes bored starkly into hers.

"I understand, Supreme Brother," she whispered as she left the cavern.

Chapter Six: *Introductions*

Kim Logan made her way along the corridor to the games room humming to herself as she went. Her crutches, which she manipulated with the ease of extreme familiarity, formed a beat to her melody.

She entered the room and looked around. It was deserted, which was unusual for a Saturday. Frowning, she remembered the football match which would soon be starting outside. Most of the other children would have gone to watch it, she supposed. Absently, she placed the book, which she had been carrying, down upon a table.

Football *bored* her. Other children could talk of nothing else, yet she could see no *point* to the game. Kicking a ball around a pitch for ninety minutes held no interest for her whatsoever.

She retrieved a chess set from a cupboard and set the pieces in position.

Taking a deep breath, she gazed at the board. She opened the book at her marker and studied the problem which confronted her. She frowned.

The authors *assured* the reader that there was a checkmate solution in five moves, but she couldn't see it. It puzzled her, since she has been able to solve *all* the other problems within sixty seconds of seeing them — no matter how devious the solution. She had not even needed to set the positions up and play the solutions through — but this particular problem defied her.

She placed the pieces in their indicated positions, removing those which were not essential to the problem. She gazed hard at the board, concentrating deeply.

A moment later, she laughed delightedly. Once seen, it was painfully obvious, involving a pawn promotion, but taking a knight rather than the more usual queen. She wondered *why* she had not spotted the solution earlier. She smiled, pleased with herself.

She looked up as Billy Simms entered the room.

"Hi, Kim," he said. "No one here?"

"No," she replied, wanting to point out to him that his question was not necessary, but knowing, deep within herself, that he would never understand what she meant. "Do you want a game?" she asked, indicating the board and pieces.

"Only if you let me win," he replied cautiously.

She shook her head.

"I'm going to watch the football; coming?" he wanted to know.

She shook her head again as he disappeared out of the doorway. She continued staring after him long after he had gone; he was a couple of years younger than she, but he would never reach his teens.

She thought, intuited, of the way Billy would never again as happy as he was at the present time. She knew that he would be dead within three years; that he would be beaten to death by his foster parents, although she couldn't have explained to anyone, least of all herself, how she knew.

Nor, she knew, could she share her strange insights into other people's probable futures with anybody.

With a sad sigh, she returned her attention to the chess board, and the defeated black king. Why was it, she wondered, that the black king got beaten far more than the white, in these problems? She found that she could easily win whether she played black or white.

Frowning again, she turned to the next problem. The solution was obvious. She moved on to the next and looked up in surprise. The authors claimed a four move checkmate solution, but she was *certain* that she could do it in less. She set up the position.

Confidently manipulating the black pieces, she placed the white king in checkmate in three moves. She glanced at the book again; it was the first mistake that she had found.

She wondered whether she should write to the authors and tell them of her solution. A moment later, she dismissed the notion. She thought that they might become angry at her for pointing out their mistake: after all, she didn't like it when she made a mistake in her school work and was told about it.

'No,' she decided, *'I don't want to upset them — not after*

all the time they must have spent writing *the book in the first place.*' It never even *crossed* Kim's mind that the authors might be grateful to her — as well as *very* surprised: that future editions of the book would be corrected and that she would be credited with discovering the faster solution.

She continued to wade through the problems, rarely taking more than a couple of minutes to solve any of them. She became so engrossed in what she was doing that time seemed to pass quickly, without her being aware of it.

She had just put the white king in checkmate, and was regarding the board critically, wondering how *anyone* could leave their king so open to attack, when she became aware of another presence in the room.

She looked up quickly and saw a woman watching her, a smile upon her face. Kim *had* seen the woman about the Orphanage occasionally, but had never spoken to her. She smiled tentatively in return.

"Hello," the woman said, approaching Kim. "There must be a match on outside. Normally, this place is *crowded.*"

Kim nodded. "There is," she replied.

"It's Kim, isn't it?" And as Kim nodded, she continued, "I'm Mrs. Brandon. Why aren't you outside watching the match? Don't you like football?"

"No, it's *boring.*"

Mrs. Brandon laughed; a good-natured, almost musical sound. Kim suddenly realized that she liked this woman.

"I'm glad you said that, Kim. I can't *stand* the game myself, but everyone else here seems to love it. What are you doing?"

Kim glanced down at the board self-consciously. "Solving chess problems," she replied shyly. Kim often felt *awkward* and *shy* with adults, especially with adults she didn't know.

Mrs. Brandon sat opposite her, glancing at the book, and then at the board. "You know, I never *could* solve things like this," she said conversationally, "you must be very good."

Kim shrugged: "Not really. I don't get much of a chance to practice."

Mrs. Brandon looked at her for a second and then surprised

160

her by asking: "Would you *like* a game?"

Kim's eyes opened wide and she smiled. "Yes, please," she replied, "if you have time. *Sometimes*, chess games can last *ages*. I don't want to make you *late* for anything," she added awkwardly.

Mrs. Brandon smiled at her again. "Let *me* worry about that. I have the *rest* of the morning free - and after all, this *is* why I'm here."

Kim looked at her, obviously puzzled.

Mrs. Brandon laughed at Kim's confusion. "No, I didn't mean that I came here specifically to play chess with you. I'm one of the Board of Governors of the Orphanage, and I try to spend as much time with the children as I can. Sometimes we play games, sometimes we just talk; sometimes they need a *friend* that they can *talk* to."

Kim considered what Mrs. Brandon had said. She understood, somehow, on a *very* deep level, that an offer was being made, but in such a way as not to make her feel uncomfortable. She appreciated the fact. She locked eyes with Mrs. Brandon and suddenly felt a burst of such intense calmness and tranquillity that she gasped out loud. She saw a look of surprise on Mrs. Brandon's face, *swiftly* mastered.

The feeling of euphoria faded. Each regarded the other with curiosity. Time seemed to stretch out. Mrs. Brandon broke the spell by asking, "What about that game?"

Kim nodded and began to set up the pieces. Mrs. Brandon excused herself and returned a few minutes later with a drink.

Five minutes later the game began. Kim quickly guessed that Mrs. Brandon was holding back, not wanting to upset her with an *easy* victory. She smothered a smile. It was obvious to her that whilst Mrs. Brandon understood how to play and to develop an attack, she lacked the understanding of how the pieces *complemented* each other; of how a strong defence could absorb an attack, giving an extra move to the defender, which could *easily* turn the game.

As Mrs. Brandon sacrificed a knight, Kim couldn't resist saying: "I think *that* was a mistake - it's checkmate in four moves."

Mrs. Brandon glanced at her. "I think you're trying to bluff me, young lady," she smiled back.

Four moves later, Mrs. Brandon surveyed the remnants of her defence, and her king, which was defeated. She looked at Kim in time to see her attempt to hide the grin which had lit up her face.

"Was that *luck*, or was it planned?" Mrs. Brandon asked her.

"It was *planned*," Kim protested, a little upset that *anyone* would think she won chess games by sheer *luck*.

Mrs. Brandon began setting up the pieces again. "We'll see, shall we?"

This time, Kim realized that Mrs. Brandon was playing *much* more ruthlessly. That suited her. She noticed that Mrs. Brandon tended to think less about her defence when she played this way, leaving her vulnerable to a sudden attack. Kim realised that Mrs. Brandon's pieces were already in a dangerously weak position.

Less than five minutes later, Kim announced, "Checkmate."

Mrs. Brandon glanced at the board, then at Kim. She stood and left the room, saying nothing. Kim stared after her, wondering if she was angry at being beaten so easily.

A moment later, she reappeared with another drink. As she sat, she looked at Kim, "You know, you *must* play my husband sometime — he's a superb player."

Kim glanced at the board.

"Why haven't you set up the pieces again?" Mrs. Brandon asked her.

"I thought you might.... *might* have had enough," Kim lied, feeling guilty about the untruth.

Mrs. Brandon smiled at her. "No, I want to try and level the score."

Kim again felt a surge of happiness and tranquillity. She glanced at Mrs. Brandon as she set up the pieces and noticed that this time there was no look of surprise on Mrs. Brandon's face. She had never experienced similar feelings with anyone else, and suddenly understood that this was one person whom she could *trust* — she felt so strangely relaxed with her.

These thoughts continued to run through her mind whilst playing the next five games. Kim once thought of allowing Mrs. Brandon to win, but feared that she might guess what Kim had done. She didn't want to do anything to upset someone who was trying to be so nice to her.

They talked and joked as they played, as though they had known each other much longer than they in fact had. Although neither of them was aware of it at the time, they had become friends.

"Checkmate, Mrs. Brandon. I've won seven, and you've won..." she broke off slyly, "... a few less than seven."

She began to set the pieces up again as Mrs. Brandon glanced at her watch. "Good Lord! I didn't realise that we'd been playing so long. I'm afraid that I've *got* to go."

Kim smiled broadly, "I thought you might have had enough of being beaten," she said.

Mrs. Brandon regarded her, solemnly. "Next time I'm here, we'll continue this battle," she said, "and I think that I might even the score."

Kim grinned at her, shaking her head. She thought for a second and then added, cheekily: "Mrs. Brandon, I think that the only way you could beat me would be by putting me over your knee."

Mrs. Brandon stared at her for a *long* moment. For a second Kim thought that she might have gone too far; that her cheekiness was going to be taken the wrong way. Then Mrs. Brandon began to laugh. "You know, Kim, you might just be right."

Mrs. Brandon glanced at her watch again: "I really *do* have to go," she said. "It's my daughter's birthday, and she's having some friends over."

Kim's face became serious. "Really? What's your daughter's name?" she asked.

"Linda."

"Mrs. Brandon?"

"Yes?"

"Would you do me a favour?"

"If I can."

"Would you wish her 'Happy Birthday' for me?"

Mrs. Brandon smiled. "That's a kind thought. Of course I will."

As Mrs. Brandon turned to go, Mrs. Anderson entered. She seemed pleased to find Mrs. Brandon. She asked if she could speak with her in her office. As they made their way out, Mrs. Brandon turned to Kim. "Goodbye Kim. I *really* enjoyed playing you."

"Goodbye, Mrs. Brandon."

Alone, Kim finished setting up the pieces. She glanced at the book of chess problems. They seemed boring after so much time playing another person.

She sighed heavily, sadly, despondently.

She thought about Mrs. Brandon. There was something strange about her. Not frightening strange, but unusual: and nice. She found that she couldn't put it in words; she had felt safe and secure whilst Mrs. Brandon was there. Kim felt somehow attracted to her.

She *envied* Linda for having such a mother. It seemed, however, that parents of *any* kind were in short supply. She tried to imagine what it would be like to have some friends over to spend a birthday with her.

It was an empty feeling, knowing that nobody cared about you, that no one loved you, especially when you had no friends either.

Mrs. Brandon's innocent remark about her daughter's birthday had emphasised that so starkly. Kim knew that she was alone — utterly alone in the world, and there was absolutely no one who wanted her, or cared about her. It made her feel *so* isolated, and emphasised her loneliness so starkly.

Mrs. Brandon hadn't known that it was Kim's birthday, too. How could she have? *Why* would she have checked up on it? Even if she *had* known, what could she have said or done without it seeming obvious and false?

Plagued by these thoughts, Kim buried her head in her arms, sobbing quietly; the chessmen fell to the floor under this unprovoked attack, unnoticed by Kim, who was, for a few moments, overwhelmed in a world of despair, sadness, emptiness and unhappiness.

She sat up, rubbing her tears away upon her sleeve. Slowly, she retrieved the chessmen from where they had fallen. She set them in position finding herself envying them for having a place where they were *needed* and *appreciated* for being no more than what they were.

She took a deep breath, calming herself. It didn't seem *fair* that she should be so alone — although the knowledge didn't usually affect her to such a degree. It was one of those things to which there never seemed to be an answer.

She began to feel angry at herself for giving in to her feelings; was annoyed that she had acted childishly by crying over them.

At times though, she found it hard to behave in any other way. After all, she *was* only ten. She wondered if it got harder to act like a grown-up the older you got. And if that *were* the case, by the time you reached old age — around 30 — it must be almost impossible to act like a grown-up.

She bit her lip, vaguely wishing that things were different. For an instant she *knew* that things were going to change for her, but in the brief flicker of time that her impression lasted, she gained *no* insight into whether this change would be for the better or for the worse.

She frowned; it was strange that she gained such clear insights into other people's lives, yet *any* concerning herself seemed to be vague and to tell her next to nothing.

Why this might be, she didn't understand. She set up the next unsolved problem, and sat, staring listlessly at the board. Finding the solution seemed to be more trouble than it was worth. She wondered if she was catching a cold or something. It was so *rare* for her to find anything to do with chess less than exciting.

But she knew that she wasn't becoming ill; it was a feeling of helplessness and sadness. She couldn't understand why these feelings should *persist* within her, today.

Making a determined effort, she glared at the problem which she had set up with a new intensity, allowing none of her feelings to intrude upon her concentration. The solution came easily. She played it through angrily.

As she stared at the board, and at the defeated King, she became aware of the fact that her angry solution seemed to have released her from her unhappiness. Almost as though she had transferred her feelings into the beaten king.

She knew that that was impossible, but that was how it felt to her. Curious, she touched the piece, and pulled her hand away sharply as she received a tingling shock. What was it called? *Static electricity*? She reached out again to take it, but this time felt no unusual sensation.

She smiled at the defeated king; it was all alone, and she had a sudden feeling of *kinship* with it.

She replaced it on the board, still smiling, her earlier feelings of calm restored.

Automatically setting up the next problem, Kim wondered about Mrs. Brandon. She was sure that there was more to her than was obvious. And what was the strange thing that had happened between them?

She thought that Mrs. Brandon understood it, and could, perhaps, explain it to her. She decided that she would ask Mrs. Brandon — but not until she knew her a little better. Adults, she found, tended to be unpredictable, until you got used to them. And even *then* they could be erratic.

She had begun playing through the next problem when she heard someone enter the room. She glanced up, her eyes widening in surprise as she saw Mrs. Brandon standing there, looking down at her.

"I thought you'd gone!"

Mrs. Brandon sat down opposite her. "Kim, why didn't you tell me?" she asked *so* gently that Kim struggled to prevent tears filling her eyes.

"Tell you *what*?" she asked innocently, her heart thudding as though she had committed some crime.

"You *know* what I'm talking about, Kim."

Kim fixed her attention upon the board.

"Kim?"

"What good would it have done?"

"Well, it *is* a special day for you, too, Kim."

166

Kim fixed her eyes upon Mrs. Brandon. "*Is it?*" she asked, very softly. "It never has been before. It's *just* the same for me. If I'd told you, what could you have done — apart from saying 'Happy Birthday'? My birthday isn't *any* happier for me than any other day. There's nothing special about it." Kim asserted, seriously.

Mrs. Brandon took both Kim's hands into her own. The action was *strangely* comforting. "Kim," she said, "whether you feel it or not, it's a *very* special day."

Mrs. Brandon stood. "I haven't got time to argue with you to try to convince you. It's time for us to go."

Kim smiled at her. "Don't forget to wish Linda 'Happy Birthday' for me."

Mrs. Brandon returned her smile, but said: "I'm not going to do that."

Kim frowned, surprised and a little shocked. "Why not?" she asked her.

"Because," Mrs. Brandon said, packing the chessmen away, "you can tell her for yourself. Do you want to get changed before we go?"

Kim's mouth fell open. She wanted more than *anything* to go with her, but felt that she might have somehow forced Mrs. Brandon into making the offer. And how would *Linda* feel about a stranger intruding on *her* birthday?

"Thank you, Mrs. Brandon," she said, "but I can't go. Linda doesn't even know me; she might not want me there," she finished awkwardly, uncertainly, shyly.

"Kim, I can't force you to come if you really don't want to. As for Linda, I phoned her a few minutes ago, and she truly wants to meet you. She can't get over the fact that I know someone else who not only has the same birthday, but was born on the very same day as she was. If you don't come home with me, then Linda will be *so* disappointed."

The last sentence gave Kim the excuse which she felt she needed. "I don't want to do that. You're sure she wants me to go?"

"Positive."

"Then I'd better get changed. Will you wait for me?"

"Yes," Mrs. Brandon replied, adding, "need any help?"

Kim looked at her in surprise. "No, thanks," she said, hurrying out of the room remarkably quickly.

Kim could hardly contain her excitement as Mrs. Brandon drove away from the Orphanage. "How far is it?" she asked.

"Twenty minutes or so. I like your dress," Mrs. Brandon said.

"I've *never* worn it before. I chose it because it hides my legs," she admitted, confidentially.

"Do they embarrass you so much?"

"No, but they make other people feel uneasy; when they see how thin they are, the scars," she said, a tremor in her voice.

"You sound *nervous*," Mrs. Brandon observed.

"I am. It's the first time I've been taken *anywhere* on my birthday."

"There's nothing to be nervous about," Mrs. Brandon assured her. "Linda can't wait to meet you." Mrs. Brandon parked the car as she gave Kim this assurance.

A few moments later, she closed the door of the flat behind them.

"John," she called, taking off her coat. She took Kim's and hung them upon the wall, as a door opened and Linda rushed out into the hallway. Sounds of girlish laughter followed her.

"Mummy, Daddy's gone to his studio and says not to disturb him," Linda said.

"I think he meant that *you* weren't to disturb him," Mrs. Brandon corrected her.

"Maybe," she conceded. Her gaze travelled on to Kim, who managed a small smile, feeling horribly out of place.

Linda grinned back. "You're Kim, aren't you?" And before Kim could admit to her identity, Linda continued: "And you're ten today as well. That's neat."

The ice broken, Kim's smile grew in confidence.

"Linda," Mrs. Brandon cut in, "will you look after Kim? I want to have a word with Daddy."

Linda nodded. Mrs. Brandon headed towards another door,

knocking before entering.

Kim returned her gaze to Linda who was eyeing her crutches with open curiosity. "Did you have an accident?" she asked.

Kim shook her head. "No, I was born with weak legs. I don't really need them, but if I have to walk a long way, my legs get tired easily."

Oh," Linda said, unconcerned about such minor considerations. "Come and meet the others. Don't be nervous, they're okay; but they *can* be idiots sometimes."

As they approached the open door, Linda suddenly slowed and added, conspiratorially to Kim: "A few weeks ago, *one* of them got me in *real* trouble with Daddy. Claire, it was."

Kim was surprised by the sudden confidence and unsure *what* to say in response.

They entered the room; the talking and giggling stopped abruptly. Six pairs of eyes stared at Kim. As they took in her crutches, the eyes turned hostile. The atmosphere in the room became somehow charged. Linda seemed oblivious to the change. "This is Kim," she said. And indicating each in turn, she added, "This is Jane, Claire, Ann, Karen, Debbie, and Lisa."

"Hi," Kim said nervously. There was only a muttered response as she made her way to a chair and sat. Clare stared at her. "Linda, where d'you meet the cripple?"

The other girls giggled.

"That's *not* nice, Claire," Linda shot back, glancing at Kim in apology.

"So, why's she here? Where d'you meet her?"

"I haven't met her before — she's from the Orphanage where Mummy..."

"An orphan? And a cripple? And *we've* got to put up with her?"

"I invited her," Linda said. She glanced at the other girls, realising that they were following Claire's lead in being spiteful. "I want her here. It's her birthday, too."

Claire stood. She glared at Linda. "Then I hope you'll be happy with her because we're going."

The others followed Claire to the door. Glaring daggers at Linda, Claire said, "*Enjoy* yourself, Linda, with your *spastic* friend." She marched out, followed by the others. A few seconds later the front door slammed. Linda and Km looked each other, each, for the moment, not sure what to say.

"I'm... I'm sorry, Linda. I didn't mean to spoil things for you," Kim muttered unhappily into the silence.

"I meant what I said," Linda insisted, trying to reassure her. "It's *just* like Claire to do something like this She thinks it makes her look big. And the others are just as bad for letting her."

"Then why did you invite them?"

"Because *most* of the time they're okay. Then they do something stupid, like this!" Linda answered her.

"What do we do now?" Kim asked.

"Well, if you come over to the table we can play some games."

Minutes later they were laughing and joking together over the game. It continued until Mrs. Brandon came in. She frowned. "Where is everyone?"

"The others erm... had to go," Linda answered *lamely*, hoping that she wouldn't be asked to go into *any* detail.

Mrs. Brandon glanced at Kim who nodded agreement. Linda flashed a look of gratitude at her, relieved that her moral support made it unlikely Mummy would ask for a fuller explanation. Mrs. Brandon's gaze moved onto the game they were playing. "Can I join in?" she asked.

They played, laughed, joked; the afternoon passed quickly. Later, Mrs. Brandon remarked, "Kim likes playing chess."

Moments later, Linda was setting up the board, and telling Kim *just* how good a player she was. Kim glanced at Margaret, who smiled slyly in response.

"You can have white," Linda offered, generously.

"No, I prefer black."

Fifteen minutes later, Kim announced: "Checkmate," for the *fourth* time.

"Why didn't you tell me you were so good?" Linda asked.

"I don't think that I am," she replied simply.

"Mummy, *you* play her."

Mrs. Brandon sighed. "No, I've already lost to her seven times today."

Linda looked at Kim with a new interest. "How do you do it? Win like that?" she wanted to know.

Kim was about to reply when the front door slammed. A second later Mr. Brandon entered. He smiled at Mrs. Brandon and nodded to her. She smiled her understanding back at him.

"It seems, John, that it's up to you to rescue the family honour."

"This must be Kim. Hi," he said, sitting down. "The family honour?" he echoed, faintly.

"Hello, Mr. Brandon," Kim replied.

He winced. "Kim, *please* call me: 'John'," he said.

"Yes," Mrs. Brandon continued. "Chess! So far, Kim has beaten me seven times, Linda four. We need someone to balance things up."

"But why pick on *me?*" *he* protested.

"Mrs. Brandon did say I'd have to play you sometime, erm... John," Kim added softly.

He took a deep breath, looked from Mrs. Brandon to Linda and then to Kim. As she smiled timidly at him, he smiled back at her and nodded his agreement.

The game only took twenty minutes. As Kim slid her rook to the end of the board, she whispered, "Checkmate."

John grinned at her. "Well, you won. You don't seem very happy about it, though. Don't you like winning?"

As she locked eyes with him, John felt a disturbing sensation that her eyes seemed older and wiser than her years could possibly account for. The next second, the feeling had gone.

"Yes, I love winning; so long as I don't have any help."

John suddenly looked embarrassed.

"You castled too soon to give me time to attack, and then you deliberately sacrificed your knight when it should have been protected."

He glanced at Mrs. Brandon, guiltily. "She caught me

letting her win," he said.

"I don't think she needs any help." Mrs. Brandon observed.

"Okay Kim, let's play again — but this time, I play to win."

Kim's eyes sparkled. "Good. I like the way you play; you think about what you're doing."

"Thank you, Kim. You won't cry when I beat you, will you?" he teased her.

She stared at him. "No: will you?"

"Margaret, would you mind making me a drink?" he asked, keeping his eyes on Kim. As Mrs. Brandon left the room, he asked her, softly, "Where did *you* learn to be so cheeky?"

Immediately, Kim's face became serious. "I didn't mean to be, John... — Mr. Brandon," she stammered, confused.

He laughed. "It's John. Kim, I was only teasing you, you know."

Kim looked at him, unsure whether he was being honest with her. He winked at her, and she suddenly realised that John was trying to put her at her ease. Kim's face regained its smile. They finished resetting the board, and the game began, each of them taking care before making moves. Two hours later, it was still in progress.

Linda and Mrs. Brandon played cards, occasionally glancing over to the game of chess, trying to see who would gain an advantage.

After careful consideration, John made his move.

Kim smiled, "That's your first mistake, John, but it'll cost you the game."

He looked at her, then at the board. After a couple of moments' study, he nodded agreement. "You're a fine player," he complimented her. "For your age, your incredible."

She blushed under the words, not sure how to react to such praise, or what she should say in response. She was certain they could all see her face blazing crimson at the unfamiliar sensation of being praised, and the belief only made her embarrassment even worse.

John saw her plight and rescued her. "I was going to say that I must get back to my painting, but now I think I'd prefer a

172

chance to get my revenge."

Kim grinned her relief as her embarrassment subsided. As she reset the board, a thought occurred to her. "John, could I see some of your paintings, please?" she asked.

Linda giggled. They all looked at her. "Apart from Mummy, *nobody* sees Daddy's paintings before they are finished. No one is *ever* allowed in Daddy's studio," she told Kim.

"I know a young lady who had to learn *that* lesson the hard way," John observed pointedly, looking directly at Linda.

Linda blushed at the memory, hoping with all her heart that John wasn't going to tell Kim the whole story of her disobedience; or if he *did* tell her of it, that he wouldn't embarrass her *completely* before her new friend by relating how severely she had been punished.

John understood Linda's fears instinctively, and would never humiliate her by giving all those details to a friend — or potential new friend — of hers. His observation was merely to remind Linda that it would be unwise of her to forget that lesson.

"However," John continued, moving his gaze from Linda — who was relieved at that — and on to Kim, "as you are a very special guest, Kim, and as it's your birthday, too, I think I can bend the rules and let you visit my studio and see what I'm working on at the moment.... But I want that revenge game first."

John left the room for a moment, and taking advantage of his absence, Linda confided quietly in Kim: "You're the *first* person I've *ever* known Daddy agree to let into his studio. *Sometimes*, he won't even allow *Mummy* in there."

"*Really?*" Kim whispered back to Linda in amazement, suddenly realising just how special and rare a gift John was giving her. She was about to ask Linda more, when John returned and retook his seat in front of the board.

"John, thank you for saying you'll let me see your paintings: I really do appreciate it," Kim assured him, awkwardly. Kim was so unused to anything special occurring on her birthday that she felt overwhelmed by all of the attention. She began to have a faint understanding of what

173

Mrs. Brandon had meant when she had said that it was a special day.

John smiled at her: "You're welcome, Kim. We'll go and look at them as soon as we finish this game. That ok?"

Kim smiled and nodded eagerly. She moved her pawn to queen four, and the game began.

They were in the middle of it when the phone rang. Mrs. Brandon answered it.

"John, it's Sue Anderson. I've not been watching the time. Kim should have been back half an hour ago."

He looked up from the board, frowning. "So?"

"I'll have to take Kim back to the Orphanage; can you make a note of the positions?"

His frown deepened. He was enjoying the game and didn't want the continuity broken by saving the positions and then beginning the game again from this point at some time in the future. "Why can't Kim spend the night *here*? You can take her back tomorrow morning."

Although she was concentrating on her next move, Kim heard what John had said and looked up at him, her mouth open in surprise, her eyes shining in delight at the prospect that her first proper visit outside the Orphanage might be extended overnight. Her heart began beating faster in excitement and hope. She looked from John to Mrs. Brandon, desperate for permission to be granted.

Mrs. Brandon looked questioningly at John.

"You're a member of the Board, for God's sake: does Sue think we're going to kidnap Kim and emigrate with her?"

Kim stared at him, her heart thudding, hoping that he wouldn't change his mind about her staying the night.

Then John looked thoughtfully in Kim's direction. "But I'm assuming that Kim *wants* to stay the night with us: she might not want to."

"Oh, but *I do,* I do want to!" she assured him.

John grinned at her: "Margaret?" he asked.

"I'm sure there'll be no problem," she said, and returned to her conversation with Sue, explaining that John and Kim were deep in a game of chess, and that they would take care of Kim overnight and return her to the Orphanage early the following morning. Sue approved the plan, and Margaret's smile told Kim that her wish had come true.

The excitement of staying overnight interfered with Kim's concentration, and nearly two hours later she was painfully reminded of her mistakes as she took in John's superior position.

She analysed it, knowing that she could not win; suddenly, she smiled.

A little later, to John's consternation, she announced, "A stalemate by threefold repetition."

John sat back in his chair and fixed her with an unwavering stare. He knew the laws of chess, but it hadn't occurred to him that Kim might take advantage of any of the more obscure laws to force a draw the way she had.

Kim became uneasy, and glanced at Linda and Mrs. Brandon. Her gaze returned to John as he looked back at the board. "And I had you," he said, more to himself than to anyone else, "I had you beaten."

Kim nodded. "Umm, you did. That's why I played for a draw."

"That's....superb," he muttered, grinning at Kim, who smiled back at him, happily. She felt a warm glow deep inside herself which she had never experienced before. She could never recall feeling as happy as she did at that moment.

"John, it's getting late," Mrs. Brandon informed him, glancing at her watch. "Kim, you'll have to borrow one of Linda's nighties."

Kim nodded and moved over to the sofa. Mrs. Brandon left the room and returned a few minutes later with the nightwear. Linda immediately began to undress.

Kim glanced at Linda, then questioningly at Mrs. Brandon, and finally at John. She swallowed, unsure whether to follow Linda's example, and yet embarrassed at the notion by John's presence.

Mrs. Brandon hid her grin. "Time for you to leave, Mr. Brandon," she said.

John, his attention still upon the chess board, and the

stalemate which Kim had engineered, glanced up at her: "Pardon?"

Mrs. Brandon smiled at him. "One young lady here doesn't think it would be right for her to undress in front of you, and I agree with her."

His gaze met Kim's. She looked away from him, and then shyly down at her feet.

"Right," John said with a brief smile. "I've got something to attend to, anyway."

He returned some ten minutes later. Kim and Linda sat next to each other upon the sofa, chatting and giggling. Kim looked strange in Linda's nightie; vulnerable somehow.

"John, can I see your paintings now?" Kim asked, "Please?"

"Okay, but remember not to touch anything,"

The three of them made their way to the studio. As they entered, John flicked on the lights, then looked at Linda. "I don't remember you asking if you could come into my studio. I don't remember telling you that you *could* come in here, either." The twinkle in his eye told Linda that he was merely teasing her.

"Aw, Daddy! It's *my* birthday, too. I hardly *ever* get a chance to come into your studio with you."

John nodded at her. "Just this once, then."

Kim enthused over each of his paintings, seeming surprised that John had the ability to paint such masterpieces.

As John turned to the door, having displayed all the works he was currently engaged upon, Kim asked, "John, may I see that one?" and pointed to the portrait of Hayter which stood away from the others, a large cloth covering it.

John hesitated perceptibly before nodding and removing the cover.

"Ohhh," Kim breathed, moving closer to the painting. She tilted her head to one side. "He loved you very much, didn't he? He didn't like saying so, but he knew that you understood that. He was very sad at times, but you and Margaret... erm Mrs. Brandon, I mean.... and someone else.... made him happy."

Kim turned to John, who was stunned by what she had said. "I wish I could have met him; he was one of those people you only ever hear about, and never get to meet."

John re-covered the painting and led their way out of the room in silence.

"Kim," Linda asked as they reached the living-room, "how did you know all that about the man in the painting?"

John echoed the question. "Yes, Kim. How did you know?"

She frowned. If she tried to tell him about the insights which she gained, he would never believe her. He would think she was telling lies. She liked John immensely, and didn't want to say or do anything which might make him think she was lying to him. After all, if he thought she was a liar, he would think less of her. Wishing she could tell him the whole truth, Kim decided to try a middle course and tell him some of the truth.

"Sometimes, when I look at a picture, or hold something, I get an *idea* of what the owner's like. Other times, I get ideas about the person in the picture. Most times, I get nothing."

John digestive this silently. "How long have you been able to do it?" he asked.

"As long as I can remember," she admitted reluctantly, uneasy lest her admission lead to more difficult questions.

"It must be scary at times," John said, guessing that there was more which Kim was uneasy about sharing with anyone at present.

"It is," she assured him.

"You might want to tell Margaret about it," he said. "She knows more about things like this that she admits to."

"I don't know," Kim said, doubtfully.

"Well, think about it. You are quite right, by the way, about the man in the painting."

"He was a kind man, too," Kim said, softly.

John nodded as Mrs. Brandon entered. "I think it's well past time these two were in bed, John," she said, glancing disapprovingly at her watch.

He nodded. "You're right. But it *is* their birthday, after all;

and Kim *still* hasn't opened her present."

Kim stared at him, not comprehending.

He indicated the table. A card and parcel sat there.

"For *me*?" she asked, in complete disbelief.

Mrs. Brandon nodded, passing them to her. Sitting and opening the card, Kim read: "'To Kim, with every good wish for a happy birthday. All our love, John, Margaret, and Linda.'"

Kim sat looking at the card for so long that Linda prompted, "What about the present?"

Kim opened it, intrigued. As the wrapping-paper fell away, she took hold of what it had contained. She stared at the dedicated chess computer.

"I believe it has ninety-nine playing levels, and can store ten games in its memory," John said. "And I hope it beats you every time," and he grinned broadly at her.

Kim looked at them. "Thank you," she whispered, awkwardly: "*all* of you. I'll *never* forget today." She kissed Linda and then Mrs. Brandon, self-consciously. She made her way to John. Shyly, she kissed his cheek.

"And now it *is* bedtime," Margaret insisted. She led the girls out of the room.

John stared after Kim, a slight frown upon his face.

"John?" Margaret called softly to him.

He followed them into the bedroom. He kissed Linda. "Good night, Linda, sweet dreams," he said.

He noticed Kim watching him from the corner of his eye. Without hesitating, he kissed Kim's cheek softly. "Good night, Kim, sweet dreams. I've *enjoyed* your staying here — perhaps we could do it again, some time?"

"Could we, John; *please*?" she asked eagerly, breathlessly, her voice full of hope and excitement at the prospect.

He winked at her conspiratorially: "I don't see why not — but if I keep you talking, I'm going to be in serious trouble."

She smiled at him, "I wouldn't want to get *you* in trouble, John. Good night," she said softly, shyly.

***

She's a strange kid, isn't she?" John said, turning in bed to face Margaret.

"In what way?"

"Well, the way she plays chess. She's unbelievable; the type of person who turns into a grandmaster."

"That's strange?"

"Not on its own — but her reaction to my painting of George was eerie. She told me how much George loved me, that he never spoke of it, that he was often sad, but we — and Tony — made him happy. All from seeing that painting."

Margaret was silent for several seconds. John sat up.

"When I played her this morning, I had a strange experience." She told him about it

"So, what does it mean?" he asked her.

"Latent occult abilities becoming less latent. Either that or a sense of precognition. If it develops as she gets older what will she be like in ten years' time? It wouldn't surprise me if she was being less than honest with you about all that she can do. She's probably confused about it. After all, who wouldn't be, at that age? Maybe she needs someone to talk it through with her." Margaret frowned, thoughtfully.

"It would explain how she knew so much about George, and what happened when I was with her this morning," Margaret mused. "You know, John," she confided softly, "she intrigues me, too."

Chapter Seven: *Retributions*

"Come."

Andrew Thompson entered the Controller's office, wondering what he could have done to warrant the summons. Normally, praise or censure regarding his work was passed to him by his Project Leader.

The Controller, Mr. Fenly, didn't look up as Andrew entered, but seemed absorbed in a massive computer printout, the beginning of which lay untidily upon the floor in front of his desk.

Andrew sat, knowing better than to interrupt when somebody — especially the *Controller* — was following the complexities of a computer program. He sat, brushing a stray lock of black hair from his eyes.

Taking in the Controller's immaculate appearance, Andrew suddenly realised that he should have put on his jacket, fastened the top button of his shirt and adjusted his tie; not to mention rolling down his shirt sleeves.

He took the opportunity to ponder possible reasons for his presence in the Controller's office, as the Controller continued moving down the printout, adding sheet after sheet of continuous-feed paper to the pile at Andrew's feet.

Normally, Andrew went almost unnoticed by his colleagues. His slight frame and quiet manner tended to make him fade into the background; only his bright green eyes attracted attention. Sometimes, when the light caught them in a certain way, it seemed that they might have been painted on with luminous paint.

He often made a joke of it, pointing out that if there was ever a sudden black-out, he would *still* be visible in the dark.

Often, when his colleagues had problems which they couldn't find a way around, or couldn't trace, he came to their aid, finding the problem / solution almost instinctively.

He was highly valued by his colleagues for his abilities, but more so because he was *easy* to get along with; seldom irritable when things went wrong, always ready to pitch in and help with a ready smile and a joke — even when under the extremes of pressure and tight deadlines.

In all the time he had been working for the Ministry of Defence, he had glimpsed the Controller only twice, and had never spoken to him, or been spoken to by him.

Andrew moved slightly, again regretting his state of dress. The remainder of the printout fell to the floor. He realised that the Controller was looking at him.

There was a weird intensity about the Controller's eyes which made Andrew uncomfortable. He assumed that the Controller had not slept much lately.

However, when he spoke, the Controller's voice was remarkably quiet, and yet it possessed a strange quality which made Andrew certain that it would be heard in the midst of a cacophony.

"Ah, Mr. Thompson: Andrew. Thank you for stepping in. Very kind of you." The Controller's voice was warm, and as Andrew looked into his face the Controller smiled thinly at him: "No doubt you are wondering *why* I asked you here?"

"I suppose it has something to do with my work," he replied, "but I can't think what."

The Controller nodded: "I've just been familiarising myself with your part of project Arcturus." He indicated the fallen printout casually, as though it had not been designated 'Top Secret', but could have been a mere games program. "It really is first rate," the Controller added, still making no move to retrieve the printout.

"Thank you sir," Andrew replied, certain that the Controller had not yet come to the point. Under the praise his unease at being summoned to the Controller's presence drained away. He began to relax — as far as was possible when sitting opposite the head of the entire section. It seemed that his work had not only been noticed, but had come to the personal attention of the Controller.

"I've noticed that you spent a *lot* of time working on it," the Controller continued softly. "In fact, I understand that in the middle of the project, when there were several complex difficulties to overcome, you actually worked on eradicating those bugs not only very late into the evenings, but consecutive weekends, too."

"That's true," he replied, remembering the frantic and frenetic pace which had been forced on everyone when bugs and backup failures had caused the project to fall well behind schedule, and it had begun to look like it could not be finished within the allotted time frame, unless certain people were willing to work unpaid overtime. "I knew we couldn't hit the deadline otherwise. Everyone in my department worked overtime."

The Controller sat back in his chair, the glare in his eyes seeming to intensify slightly. "Oh, no, no, no, Andrew," he said. "I've looked into this issue carefully. The others only did what they were contractually obliged to do: but you gave up almost all of your free time."

"Sir, it was still very much a team effort," Andrew reminded him.

The Controller nodded. "Quite," he said. After a momentary silence he continued, "But, your wife?"

"What about my wife?" Andrew asked, puzzled. It was strictly forbidden for him to divulge anything about his work or the nature of the projects he worked upon. Andrew had no difficulties in keeping that rule, and his wife, Georgina, understood and respected it. His work sometimes kept them separated for weeks at a time, but rather than being a bone of contention and resentment, they both made the best of the time they had together. Their marriage had, if anything, become stronger as they made up for these periods of separation when back together.

"Didn't she resent the fact that she saw so little of you; that she was, in fact, taking second place to a computer?"

"Maybe," Andrew returned, smiling. "But she understands, as far as she can, that my work is extremely important, and may keep us apart for months. Of course, she knows nothing about the nature of my work, or anything about the projects which I may be assigned to."

The Controller accepted this silently. He appeared to consider for a moment or two, and then nodded to himself: "I don't think we need go any further with this. Tell me, Andrew, have you heard of project Erebus?"

Andrew had heard many rumours about project Erebus. It

182

had been awarded a massive budget, but the project had appeared doomed from the beginning. The original project leader had died suddenly; his replacement had only been in charge for two months — barely long enough to settle in and get things progressing the way he wanted them — before a routine medical examination had shown up a blood abnormality. Further tests had diagnosed an aggressive form of leukaemia, which had forced an early retirement. However, exactly what project Erebus was trying to achieve, what its remit was, was a closely-guarded secret. Andrew would have been horrified to have heard the merest whisper concerning the project itself: "Only vaguely."

The Controller glanced briefly at the discarded printout. "I've arranged for you to be fully briefed on your way to Belgium."

"Belgium?" Andrew repeated incredulously.

"You've impressed me, Andrew — and I'm not impressed easily. I think you are ready for promotion. Project Erebus has run into difficulties; I think we need someone over there who can devote all his time to solving those problems. You are the new Project Leader. Obviously, you'll be working closely with the Belgians, and from what I hear they don't know a ROM from a RAM unless it has fleece. Whatever possessed Government to develop this project jointly with them is beyond me. Anyway, you leave tonight."

"Tonight? But...."

"*Tonight*," the Controller insisted firmly. "Could your wife pack you some things and bring them here? If not, I can arrange for someone to collect anything you might need."

Andrew thought quickly. Another huge promotion opportunity such as this might take years to come along — if ever. "May I use your phone?"

The Controller nodded and began retrieving the printout.

Andrew dialled, and was somehow relieved when the phone was answered. "Hello, Georgina? Listen, I've just been offered the most unbelievable promotion. Yes. But it means I've got to fly abroad. No, I don't know for how long. I'm not sure." Covering the mouthpiece, he asked the Controller, "Can I say where I'm going?"

"Belgium will suffice."

"Somewhere in Belgium, that's all I can say. Can you pack me a suitcase and my passport and drop them off here? I know it's short notice, but I only just found out myself." He nodded, "Right, I'll see you this afternoon."

As he replaced the receiver, the Controller spoke. "Well, Andrew, all that remains is for me to wish you luck. I'm sure you'll soon be on top of the situation in Belgium. Hopefully, you'll manage to bring Erebus to completion within a reasonable time-frame and prevent the costs spiralling hopelessly out of control."

They shook hands. Andrew thanked the Controller again and left the office.

The Controller smiled, stood, and made his way out of the building. He walked briskly to the nearest call-box. He inserted his money, dialled, and after a few moments said, "Hello? I think I have the wrong number. I am calling my brother, Jerome.'

As the connection was made, the Controller's eyes burned with an insane zeal. "All is as discussed. He *will* be leaving the country tonight. His wife is driving to London. Yes. Yes, it is more than likely that she will. I will leave those arrangements to you. It is unlikely they will arouse any suspicion."

He made his way back to the building where he worked, barely aware of the curious glances he attracted, or of the way some people moved to avoid passing too closely to him. It was only when, having identified himself at the first of numerous security checks, where a guard asked him if he was feeling quite well, that he realised he must bite down on the exhilaration which he felt. He reassured the security guard and moved on, his exhilaration controlled, yet still savouring events to come.

***

Margaret answered the phone; a moment later a broad smile lit up her face as she recognised Georgina's voice. Georgina explained that her husband had just called and told her that he had been promoted to Project Leader by the Controller himself. In itself, that was almost unheard of. Andrew had been elated, Georgina told her. The only downside to this news was the fact that it meant a separation almost immediately, and who knew for how long? He had to travel abroad immediately, and had asked her to pack some things for him. As that meant having to come to London, she had decided that she would spend a few days in the capital. As it had been a while since they had been able to meet up and socialise, and Margaret was her oldest and dearest friend, was there any way they could meet up and spend some time together?

Margaret immediately reached for her diary and scrutinised it. Meetings filled the next two days. There was no way she was going to allow Georgina to spend a few days in the capital without their meeting up and spending some time with each other.

She checked the page for Saturday and found it empty apart from an unimportant appointment, easily rearranged. Her voice warm with anticipation, Margaret arranged to meet Georgina on Saturday.

Both young women were looking forward to seeing each other again, to catch up on events since their last meeting.

Georgina held a very special place in Margaret's heart; losing her family so suddenly, and then having such a bleak prognosis, Margaret's heart had gone out to her, and she had resolved to do all she could to help her. The result was, ultimately, Georgina's regaining the use of her limbs; the two women had shared a special bond ever since.

Margaret replaced the receiver, still smiling, feeling thrilled that she would soon, once again, meet Georgina. They would spend many, many happy hours updating each other on the latest developments in their respective lives.

But Margaret had no way of knowing that those few words were the last that she would ever utter to Georgina; that those same few words of explanation were the last she would ever hear her speak. For Margaret would never see the woman who had become her dearest friend, ever again.

***

Brother Thomas watched Steve Preston approach his house. It was secluded, set back from the other houses in the cul-de-sac. Preston walked quickly through the garden, stopping once to glance around.

Brother Thomas stepped back, out of view, as Preston disappeared.

The light was already failing. Brother Thomas returned slowly to his car, his thoughts revolving around what he would shortly do. He drove around aimlessly, in an attempt to quell the nervousness which he felt. It was a good sign, he told himself, in that it demonstrated the fact that his adrenalin was being released in anticipation. When the time came, he *knew* that he would act decisively.

The light faded completely. Brother Thomas pulled over, and poured himself some coffee from a flask. He unpacked some sandwiches and ate them mechanically. He glanced at his watch: almost time.

He drove carefully back towards Preston's house, parking some distance away. Locking his car and pulling on a pair of leather gloves, he completed the journey on foot.

As Preston's house came into view, Brother Thomas smiled to himself. He clutched his briefcase, approaching the house openly, however, the street lights illuminated him only vaguely. He didn't hesitate but rang the bell immediately.

After a few moments, the door was opened a few inches, held by a security chain. "Yes?"

"Mr. Preston? I'm Stefan Jarenski. We spoke yesterday, if you remember?"

"Of course, come in," Preston replied, disengaging the chain.

Brother Thomas followed Preston into the lounge. They sat.

"Forgive me for coming directly to the point," Preston began, "but I'm expecting my sister shortly. We're going out in an hour or so. I'd like to get this meeting finished quickly — or as quickly as possible."

Brother Thomas frowned; that cut his safety margin dramatically. He cursed inwardly. Having come this far, he had to go through with Preston's murder; but what if his sister arrived within the next few minutes, or even worse *during* Preston's murder?

186

Mistaking the frown which crossed Brother Thomas's face as an implied question, Preston continued: "My sister's got engaged and we're going out to celebrate," he explained.

The available time during which he had to do so many tasks had been reduced to an uncomfortably slim window of opportunity. Brother Thomas acknowledged Preston's remark, anxious now not to allow any time to slip away from him. "Would you prefer me to rearrange our meeting?" he asked, hoping that Preston would give away some indication of how much time he had available.

Preston glanced at his watch. "She said she'd arrive in around forty-five minutes, so as long as you don't need to talk with me for more than thirty minutes, we should be okay."

Brother Thomas smiled: "In that case I'll be as quick as I can," Brother Thomas promised: '*for reasons which you could never appreciate,*' he added silently, mentally, with a degree of gallows humour to himself. "I'm interested in commissioning a painting and a series of sketches," he offered.

"That's what I just don't understand. It really would be better if you negotiated directly with John Brandon. Certainly he could give you a better idea of timescale and price."

"Perhaps this will explain," Brother Thomas said, withdrawing a sheaf of papers from his briefcase, along with a twelve-inch knife, hidden from Preston's view by the papers.

Preston stood and moved closer to take them. Brother Thomas launched himself forward, taking Preston by surprise and knocking him to the floor.

Before he could bring the knife into a threatening position, Preston responded by throwing an instinctive punch which caught Thomas on the eyebrow. His eyes screwed up. Preston dislodged his assailant, knocking a coffee table over in the process.

Preston was first to his feet, landing a couple of kicks to Thomas's ribs before the knife flashed, and Preston felt warm, wet blood trickling down his leg.

He resisted the urge to look down and see the extent of the damage, keeping his eyes glued to Thomas.

Brother Thomas got to his feet, gritting his teeth against the pain in his ribs.

"Whatever you came here for, you won't get it," Preston bellowed at him.

Thomas charged at him. Preston attempted a sidestep, but his leg betrayed him, giving way as he attempted the manoeuvre. They fell to the floor, Thomas on top. This time, he had the knife at the ready. He held it to Preston's throat, making sure that the tip pierced the skin. He felt Preston's body tense, and then relax as he realised that any further attempt at attacking might easily cost him his life.

"I've no money here," he said.

Carefully, keeping the pressure on the knife, Thomas shifted position. "I want the keys to the gallery," he snarled.

Preston shook his head and then gasped as the knife was drawn slightly down, cutting effortlessly through his flesh.

Thomas glanced briefly at Preston's leg. "Of course, I'm not a doctor, but you *do* seem to be losing a lot of blood. All I want are the keys."

Preston withdrew a small bunch of keys from his pocket. Brother Thomas took them. He smiled, moving the blade from Preston's throat. "Nice doing business with you, Mr. Preston. But before I go, I do have a debt to repay."

Preston frowned, confused: "What?" he began to ask.

Brother Thomas plunged the knife deep into Preston's ribcage, twisting it as he did so. He withdrew the knife and repeated the action.

Preston's eyes bulged. Blood soaked quickly through his clothing. He coughed blood, fought to breathe air into his lungs, failed.

Brother Thomas moved away, staring at Preston's body, watching blood bubble from his mouth, fascinated by Preston's battle for life. He glanced at his watch. It had taken less than ten minutes. As Preston's eyes glazed over, Brother Thomas approached him again, and meticulously slit his throat.

Brother Thomas moved away from Preston's body, carefully appraising it and the room. He returned the knife to his briefcase. Glancing around again, he retrieved his sheaf of papers from the floor, consigning them to the briefcase, too.

He moved towards the lounge door. From there, he surveyed the room once more, slowly. He stood there for several seconds before nodding to himself, satisfied that he had left no obvious traces of his presence, but knowing that there would be thousands of minute particles within the lounge to keep the police forensic scientists busy.

He laughed softly at the image of those scientists labouring so intently in order to find a clue which might lead them to him — how could they know that they would be wasting their time?

He glanced one last time at Preston's body before leaving the room and the house.

He emerged into the insipid glare of the street lights, and moved away casually, glancing at his watch, instinctively keeping to the deeper shadows which the street lights did little to dispel.

He had almost reached the junction which gave access to the cul-de-sac when he was startled by the sudden roar of a car engine, and was, for the briefest instant, picked out starkly in the glare of the headlights as the car turned into the dead end.

He paused on the corner of the junction, looking back, curious as to where the car would pull up.

His lips curled in anger as the car stopped outside Preston's house. Two people got out and approached the house. One of them reached out and he could just hear the ringing of the doorbell.

"He must be in," Brother Thomas caught the words, a woman's voice which carried easily in the stillness of the night. A moment later the voice added: "I called him not half an hour ago."

Brother Thomas didn't wait to hear more. Obviously, Preston's sister had arrived early to pick him up, or surprise him, or something. Angrily, he began walking back to where he had parked his car. '*Women!*' he thought. Had she arrived just five minutes earlier she would have walked into him as he left Preston's house. He paled at the notion. Supreme Brother would have been *furious* had that happened.

As he walked, his mind worked overtime: could he complete the second half of his plan before the theft of the gallery's keys was discovered? He gnawed his lip; unless he completed his plan, as originally envisaged, Preston's death would be open to interpretation. Supreme Brother had decreed that no loose end should point in the Cult's direction. And if he abandoned his plan now, no loose end would do.

But he would not have completed his plan as originally conceived and outlined to Supreme Brother. He would receive lots of commendation for doing this much, he knew; but Supreme Brother might decide that he hadn't done quite enough to justify a promotion from the First to the Third Circle.

Such a promotion was almost unheard of, and those few who had succeeded in achieving it were viewed with awe and reverence and appointed to positions of tremendous importance, responsibility, and prestige.

And Brother Thomas wanted such a promotion very badly.

He reached his car. He cursed, fumbling for his keys, removing his gloves to obtain a better hold on them.

He accelerated away quickly, unsure now whether time was on his side or against him. Believing that fortune favoured the brave, he decided to continue with his original scheme, and to pray to all he held evil that his luck would hold.

Twenty minutes later, he parked near the gallery's rear entrance. The nearest street lamp did nothing to illuminate the car. All was quiet. Thomas smiled, pleased by the fact.

He made his way around to the gallery's main entrance, making no effort to conceal his movements.

Once inside, he made certain that he had disabled the various alarm systems, both key and coded.

He knew exactly which three paintings he wanted. Working rapidly, conscious that precious seconds were ticking away, he removed them from the walls, and then from their frames.

He clutched the three canvases, surprised by their weight. He made his way awkwardly to the rear of the gallery. He opened the rear door a few inches; felt elated that all was quiet and deserted. Barring some extreme calamity, his plan had been successfully executed.

He deposited the canvases in the boot of his car, and a

minute later was accelerating *away* from the gallery, a wide grin on his face at the completion of his mission. His promotion to the Third Circle was assured.

His grin spread even wider as he saw a police car, siren screeching, lights flashing, career past him at high speed in the opposite direction — towards the gallery.

***

"John, you look *awful*; why not go back to bed?"

He shook his head irritably. "The police want to see me again."

"But why? You must have told them everything you know a hundred times, by now."

John turned tired eyes to her. "I have," he admitted resignedly. "I think that they keep putting two and two together and making five."

Margaret stared at him, her curiosity obvious.

"I'm so tired I can hardly think straight," he continued, "but I keep getting the damnedest feeling that they don't entirely believe me when I say I have no idea who robbed the gallery — or murdered Steve."

"They have to believe you. The idea that you might have killed one of your closest friends and then robbed your own gallery is absurd."

"Tell that to D. I. Davies; sceptical doesn't even begin to describe him. I don't think he'd believe I went for a crap unless he had the used toilet-roll and three independent videos of the incident to substantiate it."

Margaret gently massaged his neck. He rubbed his eyes absently. "Christ, what a mess," he said.

"How's Steve's sister?"

"Devastated: under sedation, I believe. When he didn't answer the door she used her spare key to get in. She'd only spoken to him thirty minutes earlier, so was worried when he didn't answer the door. She walked into the lounge — and found him. He couldn't have been dead for more than a few minutes. If she'd arrived a few minutes earlier, the murderer might have been disturbed and Steve still alive. Or whoever was responsible might have attacked her, too."

He jerked angrily to his feet. "I just don't understand it," he burst out. "Who could have wanted those paintings so badly that they were prepared to murder Steve?"

"Do the police have any leads?"

He shrugged his shoulders. "I doubt they'd tell me if they did. The only thing they keep asking me is if I've ever heard of Stefan Jarenski. I haven't."

The phone rang. John answered it. "Hello? Yes, speaking. Yes, I know. But I've *already* told you everything I know about...." his eyes glanced at Margaret, and she could see the anger behind them. "I'm not trying to impede *or* obstruct your investigation. I've made myself available to you ever since...." he took a deep breath and listened to what was being said, and then shrugged his shoulders. "Okay — I'll be there in about twenty minutes."

He hung up. "The police want to see me yet again. What do I have to do to convince them that I've told them everything I know?"

Margaret sighed, shaking her head sympathetically.

"I don't know what time I'll be back."

"That's okay — I'm picking up Georgina shortly. Superb timing, isn't it?"

John smiled grimly. "At least you'll have plenty to talk about," he muttered as he left.

Shortly afterwards, Margaret got into her car and drove towards the hotel where Georgina had informed her she was staying.

She was less than ten minutes into her journey when the engine coughed, and the car shuddered in response. The engine died abruptly, leaving the car coasting under its own momentum. Margaret guided it to the side of the road, wondering what had happened, where was the nearest phone, and hoping that Georgina wouldn't assume that she had forgotten about their meeting.

***

"Excuse me, are you Miss Georgina Thompson?"

Georgina looked at the young woman who had spoken to her, failing to recognise her. "Yes," she admitted, wondering what this stranger might want and how she knew her name.

"Oh, good. I thought so. Margaret Brandon asked me if I would collect you. It seems that her car's broken down. My name's Emma: Emma Carter."

Georgina shook the proffered hand. "Oh, thank you. I hope you haven't had to go out of your way?"

"Not at all. However, I do have an appointment that I must keep before I drop you off; if that's okay."

Georgina noticed a second person — another young woman — waiting in the car. She got into the back.

"This is Angela, a friend of mine."

They exchanged greetings. As the car moved off, Georgina asked, "Do you know Margaret well?"

"Well enough. She's done lots of kindnesses for us in the past that we can never forget; so it's good to be able to repay her, if only a little," Emma said, smiling a little ironically. Angela nodded agreement and smiled, too.

"I read about the gallery being burgled, and about the manager being murdered. I just *can't* believe it. I met Steve Preston once; he seemed very nice, to me. He didn't strike me as the kind of man who would harm anyone. I can't believe he's been murdered. How's Margaret taking it? I tried phoning her, but I didn't get any answer."

Miss Carter nodded. "Yes: I believe that the press were ringing and asking for comments every two seconds. Margaret's terribly upset about all that's happened, and no wonder."

"I picked a lousy time to visit."

"I don't think Margaret'll see it that way. It's just a coincidence which nobody could foresee. You might be able to take her mind off it all."

They drove on in silence. As they left the capital, and the traffic thinned, Georgina began to feel a little nervous.

"Where are we going?"

Angela twisted in her seat to answer her. "To see my brother, Richard. He's a very eminent surgeon, not often in Britain. I never get to see as much of him as I'd like. I'm, sorry about dragging you along. It's not far now, honestly. As soon as Emma's dropped me off, she'll run you back to Margaret's."

As she gazed into Angela's timid brown eyes, Georgina felt a peculiar sensation of attraction. She wrenched her gaze away to cover her sudden confusion.

Angela smiled, but said nothing.

"You say your brother's not often in Britain; does he work abroad?" Georgina asked, recovering her composure.

"He lectures. As I say, he's a very eminent man, in many senses."

"How long is he staying for?"

Angela shrugged, "I dunno."

Moments later, Miss Carter pulled up outside a picturesque cottage. Even before the car was stationary, a door had opened and a slim man with black hair was hurrying through the garden towards them.

"*Richard*," Angela shouted, scrambling out of the car and literally *throwing* herself into his arms. The kiss which she gave Richard surprised Georgina more than a little. It seemed much more affectionate than the kind of kisses which she expected a sister to give to a brother. '*Perhaps she hasn't seen him for a very long time,*' Georgina thought to herself, a little uneasily.

Grinning, Richard disengaged himself from Angela's embrace, and approached the car. "Hello, Emma," he greeted her, with the enthusiasm of an old friend.

"I can't stop, Richard," Emma explained. "I have another passenger to drop off."

"I've just this minute brewed a pot of tea. Have a drink before you go — a quick one; your passenger, too," he smiled warmly at Georgina.

"I will, Richard — if Georgina doesn't mind?"

"No, I don't mind," Georgina admitted, unwilling to upset Emma by insisting that they start back for Margaret's immediately.

As she left the car and made her way through the garden, Georgina found herself thinking of her paralysis; of how she appreciated such simple things as being able to stretch her legs, to walk and to move her arms freely; to feel the breeze caressing her. She took in the pretty garden as she followed the others inside, noticing that Angela was holding Richard's hand affectionately.

Briefly, Georgina wondered if *she* would have had such a close relationship with her two brothers, had they not been killed in the accident. She sat, and glanced at Richard and Angela a little enviously as her tea was placed before her.

Georgina drank her tea quickly, grateful for the refreshment, but anxious to finish the pleasantries and continue the journey back to London to meet Margaret as quickly as possible. The others talked and laughed.

"How long are you staying, Richard?" asked Angela.

"Not long. You know me, I bring my work home!"

The other two laughed, as at some private joke.

"How do you...?" Georgina began, as the room began to tilt. "How do you manage...?" she looked from one to another, her vision blurring. Then she collapsed to the floor, unconscious.

The other three regarded her prone body for a moment, and then erupted into laughter.

***

Georgina blinked. Her vision blurred. She rubbed her eyelids. As her vision settled, she took in her surroundings. They didn't make sense.

Richard sat opposite her, regarding her with obvious amusement. In place of the picturesque cottage were the nondescript grey walls of a cave. Georgina looked all around herself, attempting to make some sense of what she was seeing. Her gaze returned to Richard. She frowned a question at him.

He smiled at her. "You passed out," he explained.

"Richard, where am I? Where are Emma and Angela?"

His smile slowly faded. "They aren't far away," he replied, which told her nothing.

Georgina stood, managing to ignore the queasy spasms which ran through her stomach. "Richard, where am I?" she demanded, managing to keep her voice steady.

"You've been kidnapped, Georgina." Richard replied

simply. "And I don't see that telling you where you are would serve any useful purpose."

"Kidnapped?" she echoed in disbelief. "Why? I'm not rich — and neither is my husband. You've made a mistake."

Richard's smile reappeared. He chuckled. "We very rarely do that. We don't want money. We wanted you, so we got you."

"You mean Margaret didn't have car trouble?"

"Oh, yes she did — we made certain of that. We knew that she was going to meet you, so Emma and Angela were instructed to meet you instead."

"Who're 'we'?" Georgina demanded.

Richard ignored the question. His smile broadened.

"You drugged me," Georgina accused him bitterly, realising suddenly that her tea had contained some tasteless sedative.

Georgina found Richard's smile infuriating. She looked beyond him to a rough wooden door. She sprang towards it, only to stop short as she realised that it opened inwards, and there was no door handle or anything else upon which to gain purchase. She turned back to Richard. He looked condescendingly at her.

"Georgina, there is no escape. Please, sit down."

"What d'you want?" she asked, moving towards the indicated chair but refusing to sit on it.

"A phone call," Richard answered simply.

"What?" she demanded in disbelief. This situation was getting more peculiar by the second.

"We want you to make a phone call, and to say what we tell you to."

"And you went to all this trouble just because you..." she trailed off. "Are you demented?" she asked.

"That's all we want of you. No more, no less."

"And if I make this phone call for you, you'll let me go?"

Richard shook his head slowly. "I'll be completely honest with you, Georgina. It's not a question of letting you go. You must realise that after making the call, we'll have to kill you."

Georgina stared at him for a long moment. Her heart started racing. "And if I refuse to make the call?" she queried, simply unable to comprehend what the alternative could be.

Richard shrugged and his smile reappeared. "We'll kill you," he told her.

"I don't seem to have any incentive to do what you want, do I?" Georgina pointed out, her fear now giving way to anger.

Richard nodded, "Oh yes you do. There are *many* ways to die, Georgina. There is the gentle drift into sleep, unconsciousness and death, totally painless and quite pleasant." His voice becoming cold and harsher in tone, he added: "But there are many other, more painful and excruciating ways to die."

"You know, you must be demented." Georgina replied, unable to believe that Richard truly meant what he had just said to her. "You can't just kill people and get away with it."

"Can't we?" Richard asked, slowly; his wry smile told of many crimes committed with impunity, with total contempt for both the police and the law. And Georgina suddenly knew, with an absolute certainty, that Richard had killed many other people, and that he did, truly, mean every word which he had said.

"Who do you want me to phone?" she asked.

"Margaret Brandon. All you have to do is to tell her to meet you at an address which we'll give to you."

"So you can murder her, too?" Georgina exclaimed angrily. This was surely some surreal, ghastly nightmare. Unfortunately, it felt more real, and more dreadful, than any nightmare which she had experienced, ever had.

Richard's forehead creased in a frown. "Let's just say that we have some unfinished business with Margaret Brandon," he said in a chilling tone.

Suddenly, Georgina made the connection. "YOU! You were one of those bastards who tortured Margaret years ago. I thought that she and the others made certain you all died."

Richard stiffened. Reference to the many Brothers — many of them intimate colleagues, friends, mentors — lost thanks to Margaret Brandon and those others added salt to a raw wound which had never healed. His voice sank very low, anger infusing it, as he answered her: "Oh no. However, it was a close thing. Many did die. They cry out for vengeance. Our Brotherhood has re-formed. Our occult powers flourish."

Georgina laughed. "Occult powers? You're deluded and demented. If you have any such powers, which I don't believe, why are you asking me to set Margaret up for you?"

Richard answered slowly. "Because she, herself, has some formidable occult abilities. She would detect any use of occultism near her."

"What? Margaret's a witch?" Georgina laughed aloud again, in a mocking tone, and was gratified to see a glint of anger in Richard's eyes.

"You should know," he snapped back at her. "Or did you believe that your 'miracle cure' was nothing more than that?"

Georgina opened her mouth and then closed it again as what Richard said hit home. His words had a horrid ring of truth about them.

She understood the truth almost instantly; Margaret did possess such powers. She had come into Georgina's life determined to make a difference — but her kind, warm heart had swayed her into giving Georgina back the gift of her life, and the true friendship which she had needed and continued to need.

As she assimilated all of this, a surge of love for Margaret flooded Georgina's being.

As Richard saw her stunned reaction to what he had just revealed to her, he misconstrued its meaning, and continued in his softer tone, "Ah, I see that you *didn't* realise. I apologise if I've shattered *your* delusions."

Georgina launched herself at him. His chair tipped over backwards. She had the satisfaction of clawing her fingernails deep into Richard's face and ripping them down it.

Richard threw her off him, regained his feet and bore down upon her, avoiding the kick which she aimed at him. He punched her viciously to the face, making her lose her balance and fall to the floor, blood suddenly streaming from her broken nose.

Georgina scrambled to her feet, but found herself unable to move towards him. She smiled as she saw the blood running down Richard's face, too, one of his hands clamped over an eye.

"You think that we tortured Margaret Brandon?" he roared at her. "Before you die, I promise that you will know the meaning of the word 'torture'. You will beg me for death many, many times before I will grant you the mercy of *that* release."

Abruptly, Georgina was alone in the cave. She tried to make sense of this situation, but couldn't. Her mind refused to accept the possibility that she had condemned herself to a slow, lingering, agonising death.

Chapter Eight: *Punishments*

Detective Inspector Davies frowned at the documents in front of him; he grunted irritably. Three unconnected incidents, yet he *knew* that they were connected in some obscure way.

He was sitting in what he fondly called his study, a box-bedroom which didn't contain enough space to swing a cat in comfort. He had further reduced his available space by insisting on having a small table and two chairs by way of furniture. He argued that it was essential to be able to sit and have some desk-space — or at least table-space — in which to work.

When presented with a problem, or deep in thought, he would often take to pacing the room, an action which both soothed and irritated him. Due to the severe lack of space, his second pace brought him to the bedroom door, forcing him to retrace his pacing in the opposite direction, and frequently making him lose his train of thought.

Although the room was cramped, and his area for pacing severely limited, he regarded it as a sanctuary. It was his domain: the only room in the house where he could secrete himself for hours at a time and remain undisturbed.

Lighting a cigarette, he returned his attention to the files upon the table.

The first was a report on the investigation into Steve Preston's murder. The file was not very impressive. Apart from the obvious link to the theft from Brandon's gallery, there seemed no real motive for the murder.

Surely the assailant/murderer could have used some less extreme method of keeping Preston silent for a couple of hours? Why resort to murder? The theft from the gallery had been immaculately timed, executed — he winced at the unintentional pun — with unnerving coolness.

If the attack on Preston had been solely to make the theft from the gallery possible, why compound the fact with murder?

If the *theft* had been the motive.

If the theft had *been* the motive.

If.

If.

If.

And there were no leads to follow. The paintings had not been fenced through any of the usual channels. The forensic search of Preston's house had yielded no useful clue. The investigation seemed stymied.

'*Jesus, Stu,*' he thought, '*six months since the poor bastard was knifed and we* still *don't know more than we did after two days.*'

Brandon claimed that he didn't know the Stefan Jarenski who was the last entry in Preston's appointment-book. He claimed that the gallery was very profitable, and that he and Preston were firm friends; that he could think of no one who might want to murder him.

D. I. Davies had wondered about the possibility of Brandon robbing his own gallery, but that line of reasoning created more problems than it solved. Brandon's gallery was doing very good business. Brandon himself was very comfortably off. What good would robbing his own gallery have done him? None at all.

Everything Brandon told him rang true. His gut instincts told him that Brandon had had nothing to do with the affair.

However, he also got the feeling that there was more to this than he could comprehend: that this crime was just the tip of the iceberg; and that feeling frightened him.

He replaced the first file and picked up the second.

Here was a mystery even deeper than that of the motive for Preston's murder. Georgina Thompson's body had been found on a building-site by a labourer who had decided to nip behind some bushes rather than walk to the other side of the site where the portable toilets were located. He tripped over the corpse: when he realised just what it was that he had kicked, his bowels emptied, he vomited and then fainted onto the body — what there was left of it.

D. I. Davies wasn't surprised. He visualised it, remembering that it was scarcely recognisable as human. Georgina's body was naked.

And parts of it were missing.

Swallowing back the bile which had risen to his throat, D. I. Davies picked up the copy of the post mortem and scanned through it. It made sickening reading. She had been subjected to prolonged and excruciating tortures, over how long a period it was impossible for the pathologist to say.

Her breasts had been cut off; an eye burned out, probably with a soldering iron; both eardrums perforated; acid had been sprinkled over her legs — one leg had been amputated below the knee, and had not been recovered; her anus and vagina had been seared by some extremely hot objects being forced into them; her genitals....

He dropped the report back onto the table. It ran on for page after page detailing torture upon torture, mutilation upon mutilation. What intrigued D. I. Davies was the fact that the tortures had not killed her. Whoever had murdered her had first taken a savage, sadistic delight in making her suffer extreme, excruciating pain, and had then finally garrotted her.

It had been established that she had not been killed where she was found. An exhaustive search had revealed no clue as to how she had been taken to the building-site.

Identification had only been possible by dental x-ray.

Two other points nagged at his mind. The pathologist had isolated traces of an unusual drug in her system: phyrosthene III. It was an experimental drug which, due to extreme side-effects, was no longer available in Britain.

Whoever had amputated her leg had been medically trained: the stump had been expertly cauterized.

D. I. Davies shook his head, wondering if they should be looking for a psychotic doctor who had a ready access to phyrosthene III. No hospitals in London had admitted to keeping a stock of the drug, and that interesting lead had taken them nowhere.

They were making no progress in solving this murder either. All clues proved ultimately to be dead-ends.

Two murders, both equally insoluble: and yet John Brandon knew both victims.

D. I. Davies thought back to his days on the beat; to his

secondment to another Force. He thought about searching the area around a ruined church, and the hundreds of bodies which had been found, crushed to death in a system of subterranean passages.

Those same perverts had kidnapped Margaret Brandon, although she had been Margaret Hunter at the time, and tortured her. She was rescued by Tony Baron and, surprise, surprise, John Brandon. He recalled the general dissatisfaction with which his superiors had greeted the story that Baron and Brandon had told them. Before any real clarification of details could be obtained, the Home Office had intervened, and issued orders that the case was to be closed.

Officially, it was not even to be discussed between officers, but P. C. Davies, as he had then been, had overheard enough to know that there were too many loose ends; that the given story did not tally with certain facts.

So, on the face of it, there were three unconnected incidents, yet John Brandon linked them all.

It was interesting that both Margaret and Georgina had been tortured, he thought. He wondered whether the doctors who had treated Margaret had found any phyrosthene III in *her* system. That would be an unbelievable coincidence. Weighing ideas in his mind, D. I. Davies became certain that Brandon knew much more about these matters than he had admitted.

All D. I. Davies' instincts screamed at him that these three incidents were linked by factors other than Brandon's involvement in them. Indeed, there was no evidence that Brandon was in any way connected with Georgina's murder.

However, no matter how he analysed what he knew, and suspected, he could not gain any insight into what those 'other factors' might be.

Another odd thing had come to his attention, too. The Brandons were fostering an orphan with a view to adopting her. Having made discreet enquiries, he had discovered that the child they were fostering was none other than Kim Logan, the baby he and Rachel had found in a rat-infested cellar, years before.

His gut feeling told him that this was a part of the pattern. That it was linked in some indefinable way to the other three events which he had been considering. How it linked in, and what the connection might be, evaded his comprehension. If anything, Kim Logan's appearance seemed to distort the tenuous threads which he held; made the whole thing distort and appear even more impenetrable than ever.

D. I. Davies stood and began pacing, two paces to the door, two paces back again. Try as he might, he could not force his mind to elicit any more clues from the information which he had available. Perhaps, if he questioned Brandon again but this time about all three incidents, he might let some information slip which would help in making sense out of the senseless; in making the connecting factors more attainable.

He could justify this questioning merely by pointing out Brandon's association with each incident. However, if Brandon went to his solicitor screaming about harassment, then D. I. Davies knew he might find himself prevented from further interrogation of Brandon without firm proof linking him to one of the two murders. He knew that no such proof would be forthcoming, since he was convinced of Brandon's innocence.

On an impulse he left his study and made his way to the living-room. His wife, former W. P. C. Knight, looked up from the book which she was reading.

"Come here and tell me about it," she said, patting the sofa next to her.

"About what?"

"Anything, as long as you sit close to me."

He sat and kissed her. "Sorry, Rachel. I didn't mean to ignore you. I got carried away up there."

"Well, you can always make it up to me now: and I *won't* complain if you get carried away with me, too."

He hesitated: "I need to talk to you."

"I'm listening," she replied quietly.

He told her about the murders, about his inner certainty that John Brandon held some of the answers. He told her of Brandon's involvement in the cases which had resulted in so many corpses being discovered.

Rachel listened patiently, pulling a face as he described the mutilations Georgina's body had been subjected to. Only after he'd finished did she speak.

"Well, Stu, if you're going to question Brandon again, it'd be an idea to do it gently. When you interview people you sometimes make them think you're just a hard-nosed pig who doesn't give a toss about other people's feelings. If you're aggressive when you talk to him, he's more likely to complain about you. You admitted that you haven't any real reason for questioning him again. I don't understand what makes you so certain that these three cases are all part of a bigger jigsaw."

"Me neither. There's another interesting point that I didn't mention. You remember the baby we found with that dead prostitute?"

"I don't think I'll *ever* forget it."

"I had a gut feeling at the time that we'd find no information about the mother, and that's how it turned out."

"I remember that, too," Rachel informed him ruefully.

Stuart dropped his gaze to her breasts. He smiled at the memory. "So do I — vividly."

Rachel felt her cheeks burning as she blushed.

His gaze flicked back to her face. "Do you know I *can't* remember what you cooked me that night. Must have had my mind on something else."

"Not just your *mind*, as I recall."

Caught out, he grinned and resumed, "the Brandons are fostering Kim Logan, the baby we found. Just like I knew we'd find out nothing about Kim's mother, I know that somehow she fits into everything. Whatever that might mean."

"You've lost me."

"*I've* lost me. Thanks for listening, Rachel. Just telling you about it has helped me to get it straight in my own mind, even though I don't understand what it is I've got straight."

He stood and lifted her into his arms.

"*Stuart!*" she protested.

"You said you wouldn't mind if I got carried away with you, so I am. I'm carrying you away to our bedroom."

Rachel giggled and kissed him.

***

John threw the paintbrush down. In the months since the murders, he had suffered extreme difficulty in capturing his inspirations and converting them onto canvas. He remembered a time — not so long ago — when he could paint solidly for hours, until exhaustion overcame him. Now it seemed that he could only paint in fits and starts, and instead of losing himself in his act of creation, his mind frequently wandered, his creative flow disrupted. It was so frustrating. Once away from his studio his inspiration would return in full force, only to disappear a few minutes after returning there.

He sat, looking around at his uncompleted paintings without really seeing them.

The deaths of Steve and Georgina had hit him harder than he cared to admit: Margaret no less so. The police seemed to be making no progress with either investigation. John smiled grimly: although he disliked D. I. Davies intensely, scepticism and arrogance personified, he had to admit, albeit grudgingly, that he was probably the best type of person to be in charge of these investigations.

The murders had been — were — so pointless. Steve had been a quiet, unassuming man who loved a good laugh and his work; the two had often gone hand-in-hand. He had been good at his job, relieving John of most of the problems and difficulties inherent in running the gallery.

He had been a dear friend.

John sighed bitterly. Georgina's death, the terrifying savagery of it, the waste of her young life, made him feel sick — and very angry.

To a point, he could rationalise Steve's murder, accept it more easily than Georgina's. The brutality with which she had been treated affected him very deeply; more than he could understand, at that time.

It reminded him, at a remote and subconscious level, of Margaret's torture, of the death that had been planned for her. With this unconscious recollection came an echo of the culpability and impotence under which he had laboured. It was almost reminiscent of the Cult, but that link, tenuous though it was, was also unconscious. For reasons which John never

206

understood, the connection never did manage to transcend his unconscious to his conscious mind until the evidence became overwhelming.

This resulted in his feelings of nausea and anger being amplified to the point where they interfered with his ability to concentrate; made relaxation virtually impossible, hence his difficulty in painting, which normally soothed and relaxed him. Such were the intensity of his emotions; they interfered with his *work*, his solace, and ultimately, with his perceptions.

In turn, this added to his confusion and anxiety. He could not comprehend why his emotions concerning Georgina's death seemed to be so out-of-control.

John's thoughts turned abruptly to Kim; his anger and distress fading.

For weeks after the discovery of Georgina's body, Margaret had consoled herself with the thought that she had at least been instrumental in helping Georgina to lead a normal life, and experience some happiness which would otherwise have been denied to her.

John thought it was this perception of Georgina's life, and death, which had nudged them towards adopting Kim. They had both felt that Kim would be able to adapt to, and become a member of, their family. The Orphanage itself presented no opposition to their application, other than to suggest that a period of fostering would lend weight to it, especially if it could be demonstrated that Kim felt settled and happy with them.

They had travelled to the Orphanage, Margaret feeling decidedly uneasy even though she was entering familiar territory. Kim joined them in a private office, her curiosity regarding their unexpected, unplanned and unannounced visit evident in her expression. She seemed to understand that there was more to this visit than the obvious.

She sat opposite them, looking from John to Margaret, unsure what she should ask.

"Kim," Margaret began nervously, "we want to talk to you, but I'm afraid that I don't know exactly what I should say."

Kim looked at John, and then at Margaret again, warily. "Am I... Am I in trouble?" she asked, quietly, doubtfully, unable to comprehend what she could *possibly* have done which was so bad that it had brought both John *and* Margaret to the Orphanage to see her.

'*Were they going to confront her with whatever it was she had done wrong?*' she wondered. But Kim couldn't think of anything she *had* done wrong. She noticed the serious expression upon Margaret's face, which was so unlike Margaret. She began to feel upset and afraid. She liked Margaret very much; Linda no less so. But Kim felt so at ease with John and wanted so much for him to like her and to have a good opinion of her, that the thought of having done something to make him upset with her made her feel sad and unhappy.

"Good Lord no; no! Nothing like that," John reassured her, breaking into a warm smile.

As soon as she heard John's gently reassuring voice and saw the smile, Kim broke into a dazzling smile in return. If she wasn't in trouble, then why had John and Margaret gone to all the trouble and effort to come to the Orphanage? And why were they seeing her in a private room? Nothing she could think of explained *any* of it.

"We have something that we want to ask you," he continued. "We want you to think about it very carefully before you decide — take as much time as you need. If you need to take days, or even weeks to decide, that's fine with us. Do you understand, Kim?" John asked her gently.

Kim nodded — now even more curious and intrigued at what this all might portend.

He glanced at Margaret and then continued: "Kim, how would you like to come and stay with us?"

"For the weekend?" Kim asked eagerly, her whole face lighting up as she broke into a big smile at the prospect.

"No, Kim. I'm sorry — I made a mess of that question," he explained gently. "I should have said: 'How would you like to come and *live* with us?'"

"How long for?" Kim asked, a trace of shocked disbelief in her voice.

"For ever."

She regarded them gravely for several minutes. She looked from John to Margaret and then back again. Her face slowly paled, and then became white as she comprehended what they meant, what they were offering her: the family life which she had *never* known, the feeling of belonging, of being loved, the security of she being their daughter, they her parents.

Margaret smiled slightly. "You don't have to say 'yes' now, Kim. Take as much time as you need to think it over. We *know* it's a lot to take in, and a *very* big decision for you to make. We want you to be a part of our family — and Linda does, too."

Swallowing hard, Kim stood and walked over to them. When she looked up at them, they saw her eyes had filled with tears, which then began trickling down her face.

"I don't need any time," Kim said. "I *want* to come and live with you.

"Can I?

"Please?"

She hugged them both and they her. They formed a perfect circle.

***

John grinned at the memory.

Kim seemed to settle in to the family life which she had never before known very quickly. He was particularly pleased that Linda didn't seem to resent Kim's presence at all. They seemed to have taken to each other.

At times, though, Kim puzzled him deeply. She sometimes made him think that she knew and understood far more than any ten-year-old should. However, for the most part she was a typical child, normally cheerful, seldom deliberately mischievous.

Although there was one important occasion which stood out distinctly in John's mind. It was an unsettling event. Looking back upon it, John found himself struggling to understand not only Kim's actions and disturbing insights, but his own as well.

He had been sleeping fitfully, nightmares about the murders permeating his unconscious mind. He woke up with the absurd feeling that someone had been watching him, as he slept.

Ten minutes later, he sat in the living-room, feeling tired, and listlessly attempting to summon enough concentration to read the morning paper.

Suddenly he frowned. Had the kids gone out? A quick check of their room and the rest of the flat provided the answer. They could have woken him to tell him where they were going, or at least have left him a note, he thought, irrationally irritated.

However, he grinned. Linda would never even think of doing that: she seemed to assume that he could exercise some form of telepathy to deduce where she and Kim might be found, since they spent so much time together. The whole concept of living within a family where parents might worry if they didn't know where you were was so new to Kim that he wasn't surprised that she hadn't thought of it either.

Humming unconsciously, he wandered towards his studio, hoping vaguely that he might somehow cast off his depression and put in several hours' work. Recently he hadn't been able to settle whilst painting and was, as a result, well behind schedule.

As he reached the studio door his humming died abruptly. He saw the reflected glow of the studio's lights from beneath the studio's door; he noticed, too, that the studio's door was slightly ajar. He listened and caught the sound of movement.

When he had earlier checked the flat he had not looked in the studio, for the simple reason that both girls knew that they were *not* allowed inside.

John's apathy was quickly replaced with annoyance. He remembered — vividly — Linda's disastrous visit which had culminated in the ruining of a commissioned landscape.

He opened the door. Linda came into view. She whirled around to face him and yelped in fear, eyes wide.

"Linda, you know you're *never* allowed in here. I'd have thought the hiding I gave you the last time was more than enough to make certain you wouldn't do it again. Obviously I was wrong, and you need *another* lesson to teach you *again* what happens when you go in here. You're going to be very sorry for yourself by the time I've finished with you," he assured her, angrily.

He grabbed Linda's arm and pulled her after him out of the studio. She began sobbing, terrified of what John would do to her after finding her disobeying him and breaking his strictest rule, *again*.

"John?"

Kim stood inside the studio's door, staring after them. John released Linda, shocked to see Kim standing inside the studio, and walked slowly back towards her.

"Please don't punish Linda," she begged him, in a very quiet voice. "She only came into the studio to try to make me come out."

"Kim, what were you doing in there? Why did you go in?"

Kim evaded his eyes. "I don't know," she whispered unhappily, dropping her eyes to the floor.

"I've told you, you are *never*, *ever*, to go in there," he scolded her, angrily. It was the first time he had *ever* raised his voice to Kim in anger, and he found himself hating the experience. Kim remained where she was, her eyes fixed firmly upon the floor.

"Kim, look at me," he demanded. She looked up, but John was certain that she was *not* looking *at* him, but a fraction to the side. With the light from the studio behind her, it was difficult to be certain. "Go and get undressed, put your nightie back on, and get back into bed. Stay there for the rest of the day."

As Kim, tears in her eyes, made her way back to the bedroom which she shared with Linda, John escorted Linda to the living-room.

"Was Kim telling me the truth?" he asked her.

Linda nodded.

"Tell me what happened."

Relieved that she wasn't going to receive the threatened punishment immediately, Linda said: "We were playing cards. All of a sudden, Kim walked off. I thought she'd gone to the bathroom. When she didn't come back I went to find her. She wasn't in the bathroom. The door to the studio was open. I looked in, and she was in there."

"What was she doing?"

"Nothing."

"She can't have been doing nothing," John protested in confusion. "When you looked in, what exactly did you see?"

"Nothing. Kim was just standing in front of that painting, looking at it."

"Which painting?"

"The big one of George Hayter."

"What did *you* do?"

"I told her she'd better come out, and that you'd be furious, but she wouldn't listen to me. I told her that if you found her in there she'd get a spanking, but she just ignored me. It was as if she didn't hear me. So I went into the studio and said it again. She just looked at me — then you opened the door."

John went back to the studio to check that no damage had been done. None had. He returned to the living-room, angry and confused. Linda looked timidly at him, unsure if she was still in trouble with him herself, or not. Afraid that if she reminded him of the fact that she, too, had been inside the forbidden room, he would *also* be reminded of the punishment which he had promised her, Linda suddenly found herself unable to stand the suspense any longer.

"Daddy," she asked hesitantly, "are you still going to punish me for going into your studio?"

John looked at her for a moment, realising suddenly just how scared Linda was of being punished for doing no more than trying to ensure that Kim obeyed his rule to stay out of his studio. Slowly, John went over to Linda and hugged her tightly.

"No, Linda," he replied. "Not this time."

"But before you knew Kim was in there, you were going to," she complained hesitantly, fearing it would sound like she *wanted* to be punished, which was, of course, the very last impression which Linda wished to convey.

John pulled her close and hugged her again. "Yes, Linda, I was." He sat her down on the sofa next to him and said: "But that was before I knew why you had gone in there. You did the right thing trying to get Kim to come out." He stroked her cheek gently with the side of his thumb.

"But you only sent Kim to bed instead of spanking *her*. It's *not* fair," Linda protested, sulkily.

John thought for a second before answering her. "Linda, Kim's not used to living with a family. It's very difficult for her. It's hard for her to realise that she is a part of our family now, and that we aren't going to disappear some time, and leave her behind and all alone. We have to give her more of a chance to get used to what she can and can't do. She's *still* being punished."

"I don't think it's fair," Linda insisted, her sulky tone now sounding more like anger.

"Perhaps it isn't fair, Linda," John agreed, casually. "You stay here. I want to talk to Kim."

He made his way to the children's bedroom, partly to make sure Kim had done as she had been told and had got back into bed, and partly because he wanted to know why she had gone into the forbidden room.

Kim was sitting on her bed, wearing a nightie. She looked up as John came in, not seeming at all surprised to see him. John got the distinct feeling that Kim had been *waiting* for his arrival.

"I thought I told you to get into bed," he said sternly, wondering why she had disobeyed him again. He sat beside her, waiting for her to answer his question.

"I *knew* you'd come to talk to me," she said softly, in a voice almost approaching a whisper.

"How?" he asked.

"I just knew, John," she said. John thought he detected a tremor in her voice, betraying Kim's own fears. Hesitantly, she added, again almost in a whisper, but one which still carried a sense of *terror* within it: "Sometimes, I know *lots* of things."

"What do you mean?" John asked, softening his own tone of voice and struggling to understand what Kim was trying to tell him.

Kim thought about it for a *long* moment. Finally, she

turned troubled eyes to him as she answered. "Sometimes I know .... *things....* *before* they happen."

As she spoke, Kim's eyes seemed to darken; seemed to be much, much older than her ten years.

"Like *now*," she continued, timidly.

"Kim, what is it that you know?" he asked her as gently as he could. He put his arm around her shoulders and drew her closer to him, to comfort her.

Her gaze somehow became abstracted as she tried to answer him: "It's like seeing lots of pictures lined up in two rows, one behind the other, some on the right side, some on the left side. If the first picture on one side comes true, then so do all the other pictures behind it on that same side. If the first picture on one side doesn't come true, then the first picture on the *other* side comes true, and *all* the pictures behind *that one* come true, too.

"So whenever I see the pictures, I know that everything on one side or the other *will* come true. If I can make the first picture on one side come true, then I know that all the pictures behind it will come true, too. Sometimes the pictures on one side have horrible things in them, so I *try* to make the first picture on the other side come true."

John held her close to him, stroking her hair softly as he spoke to her. "Have the pictures *ever* been wrong?" he asked her, softly.

Kim shook her head, slowly, sadly, seriously. "*Never*, John," she answered him in a voice little more than a whisper.

"Do they frighten you?" he asked, although he already knew the answer. He could *feel* Kim trembling and knew that she trembled with terror, pure and simple.

She nodded, adding: "It's like when I play chess and I can see check-mate in four moves. I don't know how I do it, but I'm never wrong."

John would dearly have loved Margaret to be in the flat, to reassure Kim, but she wasn't.

"What is it that you see in the pictures now?" John asked her, racking his brain for information on precognition.

"*Us.* Linda, you, Margaret and me. On *one* side, we're all

214

so very happy together. We're a *family*. We love each other. We care about each other.

"But on the *other* side...." she trailed off, an anguished expression filling her face. She looked up into John's face and he could see that tears had filled her eyes once more.

"Tell me about the other pictures," John urged her softly, gently. He took hold of her hands with both of his.

"They're *horrid*. It starts off with Linda *not* liking me. Then she starts to *hate* me. Then you and Margaret start to *argue*. Then you're *always* arguing," her words began to tumble out of her mouth in a breathless rush, and John could hear the fear and the terror which she felt. "And then.... *and then*.... something happens. Margaret and Linda *die*, and I have to go back to the Orphanage.... and then something else happens and *you're* killed; and then I'm all alone *again*."

"*Margaret and Linda die*?" John echoed, a sudden dread clutching at his heart. "How? What *happens*?"

John didn't seem to register the fact that Kim had just prophesied not just that he would die, but that he would be *killed*.

"Kim?" John questioned her into the silence, as all kinds of emotions chased themselves across her face.

Kim spoke softly, sadly, her voice trembling: "The pictures don't give me all of the details — they just tell me what *will* happen, and they are *never* wrong."

John took a deep breath, trying to make some sense of what she had said. It did not occur to him to doubt her. The expression upon her face more than convinced him that she believed every word of what she had said. After all the discussions he and Margaret had had about Kim's occult potential, John knew that he had to take what she had told him with deadly seriousness.

"John, you *won't* let Linda and Margaret *die*, and me go back to the Orphanage, *will you*?" Kim begged him, unshed tears in her eyes found release in her voice, which pleaded with John to ensure that the happiness which Kim felt to be just within her reach should not be snatched away from her: just as the emptiness of her life promised to be filled with the warmth and affection which Kim had always dreamed of —

215

that of a loving family.

"Of *course* not," he replied, with a certainty he by no means felt. "We'll just have to make sure that the other set of pictures come true. You said that if the first picture on one side comes true, then so do all the others on that side?"

Kim nodded glumly, apprehensively, dejectedly; she gazed unhappily down at her hands. It was obvious to John that Kim was afraid of something else.

"So," John continued, gently, "what's that first picture of?"

Kim was silent for a long, long moment. She bit her lip again hard, so hard it was almost sufficient to draw blood. John was just about to ask the question again, when she said, "It's of you. You're thrashing me for going into your studio."

John stared at her, unable to believe what she had said. "How could that possibly prevent all of those other things that you saw?" he asked her, incredulously.

Kim took a deep breath and then fixed her eyes upon John. Her tears, long unshed, began to stream down her face. John felt his heart go out to her, empathetically feeling her distress, fears, hopes and dreams, and above all, her confusion. As he tried to understand what was happening, Kim began to speak.

"John, it's like a row of standing dominoes. Once the *first* one has fallen, all of the others fall, one after the other.

"That's how Linda starts not liking me. She thinks it's *wrong* that she gets worse punishments than me. Then she starts to think that, whenever she's in trouble, or when she's late getting home, or when she's disobedient, that if I had done the same thing, I'd get away with it, or get a lenient punishment, yet she gets punished for it much more harshly than I do...

"That's when she starts to hate me. And then you and Margaret keep arguing about it. You can't agree, and *then* you're always yelling at each other...

"And *then*....." she turned and looked at John in anxiety, and a sob escaped her: "And then... and then *everything* else I told you about happens.

"I don't want to go back to the Orphanage, John. I want to stay with *you* and *Margaret* and *Linda*. I want us all to love

216

and care about each other. I *don't* want Linda and Margaret and *you* to die, John. — I *love* you and Linda and Margaret," she admitted to him for the first time ever, blushing through her tears. "I don't want to lose *my new family*."

"So you *want* me to spank you?" John said to her, understanding her logic, and feeling the desperation coursing through her, and underneath it all, the terror which she felt at the prospect of what would happen if John didn't inflict this upon her. John had never punished Kim physically, and felt hideously anguished at the prospect.

"No, I *don't* want you to," Kim told him desperately. "I *hate* the thought. But if you *don't*, then the *other* pictures will come true, so you've *got* to, John. John, you've *got to*."

John's mind whirled. It seemed that he had little option. He believed in Kim's ability to see aspects of the future. He felt as though he had been somehow manipulated into this insidious position. He caught Kim looking anxiously at him, obviously afraid of what he *might* or might *not* do.

Surrendering himself to whatever forces manifested themselves within Kim, and biting down the anguish churning within him, John nodded unhappily. He pulled Kim over his knees and spanked her every bit as severely as he had Linda the last time *she* had gone into his studio, loathing himself for it.

Kim's yelps of pain, her sobs and cries filled the room. Finally, John stood, squeezing Kim's shoulders softly, not knowing if she could even feel, or much less understand, his gratitude that she had insisted on experiencing this *excruciating* punishment to ensure the safety of her — and his — family.

Turning abruptly to leave the bedroom, John caught a glimpse of Linda desperately ducking back out of sight. How long she had been spying on Kim and himself through the partially-open door he had no idea. He did, however, remember telling her to wait in the living-room. He left the bedroom and quickly caught up with her.

On another occasion, Linda could well have found herself in serious trouble for being disobedient and spying on him, but at that particular moment John felt so completely nauseated, and his stomach was in full revolt.

"Linda!" he snapped angrily at her. "Since you insist on being disobedient, you can go to bed for the rest of the day, too. And whilst you're there, think how *you* would feel if I allowed someone to come and watch *you* being spanked."

A look of dismay crossed Linda's face at the idea. She hadn't thought of it that way. She opened her mouth to protest to John, but having witnessed what had just happened to Kim, and seeing the look of nausea upon his face — which to Linda looked like fury — she wisely thought better of it.

Linda moved to the bedroom from which Kim's sobs still echoed. John watched her go and, as reaction set in, moved quickly to the bathroom. He vomited copiously, and afterwards continued heaving for what seemed like *hours*.

***

Self-consciously, Linda closed the bedroom door behind her. She glanced guiltily at Kim's bed. Kim lay in bed, sobbing, her back to Linda. Linda swallowed hard, and made her way slowly to her bed, her eyes never leaving Kim.

She had stayed in the living-room for what had seemed like a long time, until her curiosity had overwhelmed her, and she had made her way to their bedroom. She heard Kim's terrified comment, but her voice was too low to carry to Linda. Yet, it sounded as though Kim was scared to death of something. Hesitating for a moment, she'd stepped closer in order to see into the room, and was just in time to witness Kim's punishment.

Linda's mouth dropped open as she witnessed the spanking; a deep pang of guilt stabbed into Linda's stomach. It was, surely, her fault that this was happening, wasn't it?

Being ignorant of what had gone before, she had been forced to the conclusion that John had acted on her complaint that Kim's punishment was not fair, not *severe* enough. After all, he had agreed with her before he left the room to talk with Kim.

Linda was, therefore, convinced that it was *her* fault that Kim had been spanked - and she *hadn't* been slapped lightly, but every bit as severely and harshly as Linda herself had been not that long ago. Linda now felt hideously guilty and sorry about it all.

Kim still cried and sobbed. Kim's body shook as she continued crying and sobbing, as though her heart would break.

Hesitantly, Linda approached Kim's bed.

"Kim?" she said softly, after a minute or two, tentatively touching Kim's shoulder.

For a moment, Linda didn't think Kim was going to acknowledge her presence, the same way that she hadn't in the studio. However, Kim rolled onto her back, almost in slow motion, and regarded Linda through tear-filled eyes, still crying, her eyes red and puffy.

"Kim, I'm *sorry*."

Kim frowned at her, not understanding. '*What did* Linda *have to be sorry for?*' she wondered. Or was Linda simply being sympathetic because Kim had been punished? However, Linda mistook the frown for a question.

"It's all my fault," she burst out, upset now because of what she had caused to happen to Kim. "I told Daddy I didn't think it was fair that he sent you to bed instead of spanking you. That time that *I* went in the studio before you came to live with us, he gave me a *really* bad spanking, *and* sent me to bed afterwards as well.

"But I didn't want him to come and smack you," Linda lied, confused about how her own feelings had swung so violently first one way, and then the other.

Kim rubbed her eyes. "*Didn't you?*" she asked bitterly, her voice heavy with accusation.

Linda opened her mouth to deny the accusation, but her words died as she took in Kim's expression.

"*Yes; yes, I did,*" she whispered the admission softly, guiltily, and quickly added: "but I didn't think Daddy would do it, and I'm sorry that he did."

Kim managed a small smile. "It wasn't your fault; I hadn't got into bed when John came in. That's why he smacked me," she said, feeling uneasy about lying, but knowing that Linda would insist on taking the blame otherwise.

Relief flooded through Linda. She had feared that Kim

would be angry at her; that they might not be friends anymore. Linda knew how John hated disobedience of *any* kind, and she could imagine John becoming more angry at Kim for this additional act of disobedience. Linda could envisage this being the catalyst for Kim's being punished so severely, rather than her simply being sent to bed.

Linda, despite her protestations to John about Kim's mild punishment, (as she had believed it to be), wanted Kim's friendship badly. She had always *longed* to have a sister with whom she could confide her secrets and desires and wishes, but that had never happened. Alternately, Linda wanted to have a close best friend with whom she could share *all* of her deepest secrets: and Kim might *be* that perfect friend, Linda thought.

Now that Kim had explained why what had happened was *not* Linda's fault, Linda began to feel her guilt and fears and worries draining away.

She sat on the edge of Kim's bed. Kim grimaced in pain as she sat up. "Does John know you're here?" she asked.

Linda nodded, "Yes, he sent me to bed, *too*," she admitted. She found herself dreading the questions which that statement was bound to generate. Sure enough, Kim spoke.

"Why? For going into the studio?" she asked, in a shocked tone of voice.

"No," Linda answered, suddenly feeling *very* embarrassed. She cringed inside as Kim tried to understand why Linda had been sent to bed. Unless she lied about it, something which she was very loath to do, Linda would have to own up to her actions.

"Why then?" Kim asked, puzzled.

Linda thought quickly. Realising that even if she *did* lie about it, there was always a possibility that John would tell Kim what she had done, anyway. She took a deep, *deep* breath, and then admitted: "'Cos I watched him spank you."

She blushed crimson, feeling thoroughly ashamed and embarrassed to have to admit to it.

Kim's face grew grave. "Did you hear what we said?" she asked immediately.

220

"No. *Why*? What *did* you say?" Linda asked, curiosity *burning* within her, as she remembered the sheer terror and anguish which Kim's tone had conveyed.

"That I was scared of being sent back to the Orphanage," Kim answered, truthfully enough.

"What was it like, living there?" Linda asked, taking the *first* opportunity which presented itself to change the subject from watching someone else being punished, which now acutely embarrassed her.

Kim shrugged her shoulders. "Not very nice. The grown-ups there hardly ever had time to spend with you. I was alone most of my free time. Until ... Margaret ... erm... *Mummy* came and played chess with me, hardly anyone else *ever* took time to spend with me." Kim explained, feeling very odd using the term '*Mummy*'; but now their relationship had *changed*, and unlike John, Margaret hadn't invited Kim to use her Christian name, so calling Margaret by name *now* seemed somehow disrespectful.

"What were the other children like?" Linda genuinely wanted to know.

"Okay, I suppose. They never really played with me, so I didn't make any friends. I spent most of my free time on my own. Until my — *our* — birthday," Kim smiled, "all I used to *dream* about was living with people who'd *love* me and *care* for me and *look after* me."

Linda detected the wistful, yearning tone in Kim's voice as she thought back, and suddenly realised how sad and alone and lonely Kim must have felt when living at the Orphanage.

"You're part of *our* family now," Linda insisted, after a moment's silence, attempting to reassure Kim in the light of what Daddy had said about it being difficult for Kim to adjust to being part of a family. "So doesn't that make us *sisters?*"

Kim thought about it. "I suppose it *does*," she said with a giggle. "But it means that we're *twins*."

Both girls started laughing and giggling. The noise of their laughter increased sharply.

"Shh," Linda hissed. "Daddy'll *hear* us."

They both looked furtively at the bedroom door, neither of

them wanting it to open.

"I bet Mummy'll be surprised to find out that she had *twins*," Linda observed, causing them both to erupt into more laughter, more giggles.

As the giggles stopped, Kim turned to Linda and asked: "Linda, *why* were you watching John punish me?"

Linda blushed again and took a deep breath. "I just wanted to know what Daddy was doing. I didn't *mean* to watch you...."

"It doesn't matter," Kim told her, *much* to Linda's surprise.

Linda looked at Kim. "Kim, will you ever forgive me?" she asked, doubtfully.

Kim looked at her for a *long* moment and then smiled. "You just told me that I'm your *sister*," Kim reminded her. "That's the *best*, the *nicest*, the *loveliest* thing anyone's *ever* said to me, Linda. If *I'm* your *sister* then of *course* I forgive you."

For a brief instant, Linda didn't believe it; then, impulsively, she *threw* her arms around Kim and hugged her, tightly. She *knew*, suddenly, that Kim *was* that friend with whom she could share *all* her most *precious* secrets.

"If John came in now *you'd* be in trouble for not changing into your nightie, *and* for not getting into bed," Kim reminded her.

Linda's eyes widened as she realised that she was as *guilty* of disobeying John's angrily-spoken orders as she had felt *Kim* had been. Her wide-open eyes reflected her sudden apprehension.

She didn't know *exactly* what John would do to her if he caught her out of bed, but *did* know — and only minutes ago had been reminded — that one of John's pet *hates* was disobedience; were he to come into the bedroom now, it was virtually *certain* he would view both her being fully clothed and out of bed as a *double* act of deliberate defiance — another thing which John didn't appreciate.

Linda wasn't at all interested in finding out what John's reaction to this perceived defiance would be. She would almost certainly find herself across John's lap — and Linda suddenly realised with a blush of shame, that John would punish her *in front* of Kim, so she might understand the embarrassment and humiliation which Kim must have felt when punished with a third person watching. John would view it as both ironic, and poetic justice. Linda *didn't* understand the exact meaning of either phrase, but knew it would be a lesson which John would be *eager* for her to learn, given *this* opportunity.

Quickly, she undressed and put on her nightie again, desperately hoping that Daddy *wouldn't* check on her before she had done so, and at the same time *dreading* that he would appear before she had managed to get into bed.

"You can get in with *me*," Kim offered, generously.

"But Daddy said I had to go to *bed*," Linda reminded her.

"You'll *be* in bed," Kim pointed out.

Linda giggled and nodded. Kim moved over to make room, wincing sharply as she did so.

"Does it *still* hurt?" Linda asked, curious, as she got in bed with Kim.

Kim nodded, "Yes — it's burning and throbbing horribly." She kept to herself the knowledge that this was the very *first* spanking to which she had ever been subjected. The intensity of the pain had come as a tremendous shock to Kim; one which she had decided she never ever wanted to experience again.

Linda looked sympathetically at her, knowing exactly what she meant, remembering from recent personal experience *exactly* how much pain and discomfort Kim was experiencing. "*Next* time, make sure it's Mummy who smacks you," Linda advised her, confidentially. "She doesn't make it hurt anywhere near as much."

The look which crossed Kim's face told Linda that she would remember *that* piece of information and advice.

They talked, giggled and laughed together in Kim's bed, sharing thoughts and dreams and wishes and *secrets*; one sister to another.

***

John smiled. Apart from that *one* incident a few months ago, Kim had behaved impeccably.

Margaret had been fascinated when he told her about

Kim's revelation. However, she understood very little of it, and was unable to give John any sound information upon precognition. They both worried about the effect this ability — assuming that it was genuine — might have upon Kim.

It emphasised to Margaret that Kim's gifts were already significantly stronger than she had supposed from the brief insight which she had gained when playing Kim at chess.

She began studying Hayter's exploration of the subject. Although she gained a *general* understanding of how certain people could attune themselves to the potential of future events, Hayter insisted that precognition was very vague and inexact, since he did not believe in the preordination of the future. One random factor could force subsequent events onto a tangential course, he argued, and he had never found *any* information to lead him to believe that future events could be consistently and accurately foreseen.

Of abilities such as Kim's, Hayter made no mention, which implied to Margaret that it might be unique. It did nothing to help her understanding of Kim's capabilities.

She attempted to analyse what she already knew, but it made little sense. To be able to predict one of two possible futures from one initial event was plainly ludicrous. It implied an ability to suspend the normal laws of temporal science, calculate all possible effects of random factors, compensate for them, and arrive at one of two possible outcomes.

Plainly impossible. Even for a George Hayter, it would *still* be impossible.

She discussed her lack of progress with John. He had no suggestions to offer; apart from making it plain to Kim that her strange gift, whether it caused her pleasure or fear, could be discussed with them.

However, Kim showed no such inclinations, much to Margaret's distress.

"It's as though she doesn't feel I'm trustworthy enough to share her confidence and talk with her about what she can do and how it affects her," Margaret complained to John one night.

"Don't push it," he advised her. "She's not used to confiding in anyone. It must be tough for her."

"I know, I know. I wish I could do more to help her understand it."

"How do you know she doesn't understand it already, in her own way?" John asked, rhetorically.

"I feel as though I'm letting her down." Margaret's hurt was obvious to John.

"Margaret, you're here. She knows she can talk to either of us if she feels she needs to. It might take some time for her to understand that and to feel comfortable with it. Until she does, I think we'll just have to be patient."

Margaret sighed but nodded agreement.

Kim never did take advantage of the offer to talk about her talents with them. She knew neither John nor Margaret would be able to understand them. You had to be someone *REALLY* special to do that.....

***

John retrieved his paintbrush with a sigh. He glanced at the canvases, noting that he hadn't made any progress whatsoever. None of the paintings before him stirred his imagination. It was almost, he thought, as though his creativity had been destroyed, stifled, *murdered.*

Wearily, he began cleaning the paintbrushes, wondering vaguely whether he needed a break from the gallery, from painting, from *everything.*

He glanced around as Margaret entered.

"Rough day?" she asked, taking into account the stiffness in his bearing. "Me, too. Did you manage to do anything?"

"Yes, I managed to stare at them. I just can't get into the mood. I stand here, but the inspiration just won't come. Perhaps we need a holiday."

"Not a bad idea," she approved as they embraced.

She led him to the living-room; they sat. "Kids in bed?" she asked

"Uh huh."

They sat in silence, Margaret feeling uneasy as she took in John's distant expression. "Do you feel as tense as you look?" she mused aloud.

He turned lethargically to face her. "Yes, probably. It's

been getting worse over the past few months. I feel on edge *all* the time I'm awake; I used to be able to lose myself in my painting, but I've not been able to do that recently."

"Steve and Georgina?" Margaret queried softly.

"I s'pose so. They aren't constantly on my mind, as far as I know; and yet, I keep asking myself the question, '*Why them*?', and I can't provide an answer that makes any sense. For some reason I don't understand, it makes me angry that I don't have the answer, and then I feel inadequate, on edge, depressed, because I know that I should have the answer. Not *an* answer. *THE* answer. Do you understand?" he demanded, grabbing her shoulders in powerful fingers, his eyes boring into hers.

Margaret gently removed his hands from her shoulders. "No, John, I don't."

The sudden animation faded from his eyes. "Neither do I," he admitted heavily.

She drew him into her arms, caressing him lightly. "Will you let me help?" she murmured.

John considered, negligently undoing the buttons of her blouse. "No," he said finally, "I doubt you'd be able to. I need to understand and comprehend what's happening to me. I think that the only way I can do that is to work the answers out for myself." He gazed briefly at Margaret's breasts, smiling, but making no move to free them from her bra. A faint, wry smile tinged his face as he slowly re-buttoned her blouse.

Pondering his reply, and his *lack* of interest in undressing her, she again wrapped her arms around him, hoping that such a simple action might reassure him. She longed to help him overcome this depression, but could only do so with his permission.

They stayed there, virtually motionless apart from Margaret stroking John's head and back.

Eventually, Margaret felt the tension drain from John's body; assumed that he was sleeping, his head upon her chest. She began to feel drowsy, too.

A sudden *explosion* of energy jerked her fully awake. Completely disorientated, she glanced worriedly at John, and then around the living-room.

John roused himself, somehow sensing that something damned peculiar had happened.

A second explosion generated a shocked yell from Margaret. She jumped to her feet, knocking John to the floor. He stood quickly, his face ashen.

Margaret's brain began functioning again. There had been no noise: not as such. The eruption of energy, which she had sensed without initial comprehension, was the result, she knew, of some *powerful* form of occultism. And it was very near. Someone had expended a vast amount of power to create such an *enormous* effect.

"John?" she whispered.

"I know. I felt it, too."

She glanced at him, surprised, "You *did*?"

He nodded and then abruptly stared at the living-room door.

Margaret's gaze followed his. The door handle turned very slowly.

Attempting to impose some calm upon her thudding heart, which was a major distraction, she began focussing her will, ready to unleash an assault upon whatever might enter. She was surprised when she realised that she was doing all this automatically, without thinking about it.

She noticed John, standing almost arrogantly, a strange half-smile upon his face; then it was gone, and she was certain that she had imagined it.

The door opened to reveal a man dressed in a suit, tie and overcoat. He looked directly at them as he entered. His fair hair was thinning. He wore a moustache and a long, untidy-looking beard. He took a step into the room.

Feeling behind himself for the door-handle, the man closed the door. He stood regarding them, saying nothing by way of introduction, nor making any threatening gesture.

As she stared at him, Margaret felt a trace of recognition; she struggled to recapture it, and then *realisation* dawned.

"Jesus Christ! I don't believe it. John, it's *Tony. Tony Baron.*"

As though he had been waiting to be named, the man

moved closer to them.

"You bleedin' *IDIOTS*," he snarled.

Chapter Nine: *Rebuttals*

Brother Richard made his way to the cavern where Supreme Brother waited. He was in a good humour. The society was rebuilt, and was functioning as a coherent whole. The promotions/demotions had been, almost without exception, finalised. The Third Circle were once again engaged in their nefarious activities.

Himself and Jerome excepted, of course. By virtue of the fact that they were the only survivors of the original Third Circle, it been decided that they should oversee the activities of the rest of the hierarchy.

It was only just, he reflected, that his and Jerome's *vast* experience should be recognised in this way. And, of course, when Supreme Brother decided that he had to look around to ensure he left a successor, where else would he look other than at the two Brothers who had shared the work of making the Phoenix rise from the ashes of destruction, and who were in titular command of the Brotherhood?

Jerome? Richard shook his head. He doubted that Supreme Brother would choose him. Whilst respecting Jerome very highly, Richard considered Jerome to be just a little too unstable for the job. '*Which leaves me*,' he thought.

His smile faded as he thought upon the enormity of the task. Of course, there were many benefits in being the Supreme Brother: the unnatural augmentation of one's occult powers by the Patron Demons one of the more desirable. Even so, the practical difficulties and ultimate power of life and death over so many Brothers staggered Richard's imagination.

Not that he didn't think he could cope in that position....

And things were going so well. The Curse on the Barons — and their friends — was nearing completion. The fulfilment was in sight. He laughed cynically. The last time they had thought that, Margaret Hunter had appeared, and turned out to be the last survivor of the American Barons.

Richard remembered, in his mind's eye, many of his Brothers and friends who had died. Gregory, Andrew, Paul, James: one by one he supplied names to faces. Sadness emerged briefly within him, only to be supplanted by fury.

They, the Brandons and Baron, were beginning to pay for what they had done.

Richard touched his cheek where Georgina had scratched him. The ridges were no longer there, but Richard could still feel them. She had dug her nails into his eye. He had managed to speed the healing process somewhat, but it had still caused him great discomfort for several days. Jerome had teased him about it, managing to make him see — or half see — the amusing side of events.

However, Richard had ensured that Georgina had nothing to laugh or gloat about. Taking immense pleasure in her screams and in the many agonies which he inflicted upon her, he had turned his mind to the problem of causing her the maximum suffering with the minimum of effort, whilst at the same time ensuring that her life wasn't in any way threatened. He had tried his utmost to create a living hell for her, ensuring that every conscious minute was a minute filled with excruciating agony, total humiliation, and absolute despair.

Richard had shown just how deeply his sadistic streak ran. He had induced such unbearable, indescribable agony within Georgina that he was elated when she begged him to kill her. Richard had then indulged in a cruel game with her, promising that if she begged him to do all kinds of things to her — no matter how degrading — he would inject her with an analgesic/sedative to give a brief respite from her pain. On a few occasions, Richard had even kept his word, thereby keeping Georgina mentally off-balance, and never sure if he would fulfil his promise to give her a period of freedom from the agonies she would otherwise be forced to endure.

Richard had refused to allow her to die until he had tired of his sport — and that had taken a long, long time. By then, even Margaret Brandon would have been unable to recognise Georgina.

It was good, the knowledge that he had struck a blow — although the word *lamentably* failed to sum up his actions — towards the culmination of their Curse, the immediate cause of his good humour.

He entered Supreme Brother's cavern. Glancing at his superior, who was immersed in reading many closely-typed pages from a folder before him, he sat and waited patiently.

Soon after, Jerome entered. He nodded at Richard.

Supreme Brother regarded them for a long, long moment before he spoke. "You have caused me a great deal of inconvenience: *both* of you. It is possible that you have even undermined the security of our Society," he rasped at them, his eyes hard and cold enough to freeze the air. Pure, naked anger radiated from him.

Amazed at the charge, Richard began to insist that neither of them could have done such a thing when he was shouted down.

"RICHARD!" Supreme Brother snapped, his voice echoing around the cavern. He struggled to control his anger. "I did not say it was done *deliberately,* but all the same, it was *done*."

Unable to understand what Jerome and he were supposed to have done, Richard racked his brain in a futile attempt to gain an insight into how he could have exposed the Society to danger. The answer, when it came, made no sense to him.

"Georgina Thompson's *murder*," Supreme Brother informed them.

Confused now, and a little irritated, Richard pointed out that the event had occurred over six months ago. If an indiscretion had been committed, he demanded to know why such a long time had been permitted to elapse before being confronted with it. He wondered whether the Supreme Brother might be playing some devious game of his own. Such an eventuality was *not* without precedent! However, his leader's tone banished the notion.

"Because I was presented with a *fait accompli*. At the time I reserved judgement to give events the opportunity to demonstrate my reservations more clearly; and they have done."

The cryptic nature of this response began to annoy Richard. Whilst attempting, unsuccessfully, to control his irritation, he heard Jerome ask, in his quiet tone, how their actions could have threatened the Brotherhood.

For a moment, Supreme Brother fell silent. He regarded them with an incredulous glare before he spoke: 'You mean to tell me that, even now, you have no idea? Have you two *no* deductive reasoning?"

Angrily Richard retorted that they had acted correctly in Georgina Thompson's case, ignored the warning hand which Jerome placed upon his arm, and reminded the Supreme Brother that they did not need his permission for what they had done.

"It is *only* because we three have endured so much together that I allow your *insolence* to go unpunished," Supreme Brother remarked slowly, emphasising each word. "I will not tolerate it again."

Richard took a deep breath, let it out slowly, and nodded understanding. His anger faded as Supreme Brother began to speak, to be replaced by curiosity, amazement, and finally, *anxiety*.

"What you said *is* true," Supreme Brother continued. "You did not need my permission. However, you would have been wise to ask for my guidance. There are several points which may seem insignificant alone. Together, they compound the error *immensely*."

He paused as though to order his thoughts. Abruptly, his voice gradually rising in volume, he continued: "First, you tortured Georgina Thompson so severely that even *I* shudder to think of it. In itself, that was innocuous; she was a victim of our Curse and paid the price. But in acting as you did, you left a parallel. You must always remember that if our Curse applies to them, they are either Barons or *friends* of the Barons. You may remember that once, we tortured Margaret Brandon — we must be the only organisation of which she is aware, who would be capable of such savagery." Unwillingly, a trace of pride — swiftly suppressed — entered Supreme Brother's voice.

"The only reason I can suppose for her failure to connect Thompson's murder with us is the fact that she believes us destroyed. However, I fear John Brandon may make the deduction. We cannot prevent it: not *this* time, which brings me to the second blunder. Why on earth did you relocate the corpse to a place where it was bound to be discovered? That was the work of rank amateurs. Oh, no doubt you *wanted* the find to hurt the Brandons. And so it did. But at what cost?"

He took a deep breath, and when he resumed, his voice took on that rasping tone which was so familiar. "You

232

presented the Brandons with the key to unlock the mystery of Steve Preston's death. Indeed, the extreme mutilations apart, you ensured that the police became fascinated by Miss Thompson's corpse, *and* the area where it was found. There were absolutely *no* indications of how she was taken there. It is sufficiently rare to find *no* clues at the scene of such a discovery to intrigue the most mentally inept detective, and unfortunately, the detective concerned is far from that. I will come to *him* presently.

"You, Richard, bear the brunt of responsibility. Normally, I would applaud your misuse of Georgina Thompson, and shout '*Bravo! Encore!*' *if* your actions had been motivated purely in response to our Curse. But that was *not* the case. You acted as you did because you wanted to revenge yourself upon her for all the pain and embarrassment which she had caused you. I remember once telling you to let your anger drive you, but not to let it *possess* you. Is that advice so *difficult* to act upon?"

Richard remained silent, inwardly cringing as the catalogue of faults continued.

"That, then, was the third blunder. Next, allied to the second, was in allowing the body to be found so soon after Preston's death. It must seem very coincidental to the police *and* the Brandons.

"I mentioned, earlier, the detective in charge of these investigations. How many connections he has made, I cannot tell. You both may remember that I protected our Society after our defeat by having all police files of any relevance forwarded to the Home Office, and held securely under the Official Secrets Act. It should disturb you to know that this detective, Davies, has formally applied for permission to view those files. For obvious reasons, I could *not* allow that; I was forced, at considerable inconvenience, to have those files 'accidentally' destroyed. My actions will provide yet another coincidence, but I would rather risk *that* than allow this detective to view them.

"You, Richard, used your *wonder* drug on Miss Thompson.

233

Why? She would have felt what *you* did to her just as keenly without it, I should think."

Feeling that he could defend himself upon this charge, at least, Richard interrupted carefully, and explained that he had not used it for that reason, but merely as a rapid means of forcing Georgina back to consciousness, when the extreme agony which he was inflicting upon her caused her to pass out. He was about to add more when Supreme Brother cut in accusingly: "And you left *enough* of it in her system for it to be analysed and identified. And that same inspector, Davies, has been attempting to find a source for this *rare* drug." He was gratified to see a flicker of alarm enter Richard's eyes. "Oh, yes, Richard," he continued smoothly, "the police have been in touch with many hospitals, wanting to know whether or not they have a stock of the drug. It's phyrosthene III, I believe?"

Richard nodded, wary now of attempting further justification until he had heard *everything* which Supreme Brother had to say.

"Then you might be interested to know that this same detective, Davies, has also applied to the hospital which treated Margaret Brandon after our encounter. He wants access to her medical records, no doubt to discover whether any phyrosthene III was used upon her. We *could* have those records destroyed, too, but that would make the good detective even *more* suspicious, after he finds that the Home Office cannot help him. And he will, of course, find that the drug *was* used. All in all, this must be recorded as one of the most idiotic shambles in the history of the Brotherhood. And it is *all*," he added venomously, "because the two of you didn't stop to think of all possible consequences before you acted. I expect much better of you," he said, shaking his head.

"Is there nothing we can do to salvage the situation? No act we may perform in reparation?" Jerome queried, his usually blazing eyes muted to the point where they looked almost normal.

Supreme Brother shook his head. "I don't think so. The damage has been done. If we eliminate D. I. Davies, another will take over and carry on where he left off. All we can do is hope, and frankly, I'm not very optimistic. We must now proceed as though our existence is known by our enemies, acknowledging that we have lost the element of surprise."

Richard frowned deeply. "If that is the case," he said slowly, "we may be able to gain an advantage, after all."

Supreme Brother and Jerome stared at him.

"We know about the Brandons' fostering of Kim Logan. Why not use her to force Tony Baron out of hiding?"

"Richard, you intrigue me; continue," Supreme Brother invited, quietly.

"Our Curse forbids us from harming Anton Baron's descendants until they reach twenty years. For that reason, we may not harm Linda Brandon. You have said, Supreme Brother, that our Curse ties our hands; but it is *not* so in the case of Kim Logan."

"Are you suggesting that we murder her?"

Richard shook his head, beginning to regain his confidence. "There is no need for that. We merely hold her for ransom. Once Tony Baron is lured from his hiding-place, the girl may be released. Killing her would *not* further our cause."

"It would have to be planned carefully. I agree that capturing Tony Baron is very tempting, and probably worth the risk, but we have no assurance that he would appear. Why would the kidnapping of a girl he doesn't know lure him into the open?"

"He would have to," Jerome put in, eyes suddenly blazing. "Consider the time he spent with Hayter. He cannot allow the Brandons to be destroyed by us. He would be alone against our might, in that case. He cannot be such a fool as to believe that he can evade us forever."

"He has done a *damned* good job so far," Supreme Brother snapped.

235

"Admitted: but we have had other things occupying us. My point is that Hayter was a moralist. So is Tony Baron. He will surface to come to the Brandons' aid. I would not be surprised to learn that he already knows of our existence."

"Hayter," Supreme Brother muttered casually, "he was a worthy opponent. He had the courage to stay within his mansion and scream silent defiance at us." Focussing upon Jerome again, he asked, "what makes you think that Baron knows of us?"

"The simple fact that he has disappeared so completely. *Why?* — It is *not* something easily explained unless you allow fear of us to enter your thoughts."

Supreme Brother nodded, thoughtfully. "Richard, if I authorise this abduction, what do you have planned for her whilst she is our guest?"

"I will accept your guidance upon the subject," Richard replied, pointedly.

"Jerome," Supreme Brother smiled — a truly evil smile: "you *like* little girls;" he murmured. "*Really* like them, I mean, don't you?"

A slow, cruel smile lit Jerome's face. Richard wondered suddenly if he had ever seen Jerome smile before.

"As Richard says, there is *no* point in killing her; not until Tony Baron appears, and even then, not without my express permission. Nor do anything which might endanger her life. With *that* understood, you may use her in any way you wish.

"However, I want no *more* blunders. Be meticulous in your planning."

For several moments they sat in silence. Supreme Brother frowned, and then suddenly asked, "Do you ever get the feeling that we aren't in control?"

Richard and Jerome exchanged glances, each puzzled by the question.

"Sometimes," Supreme Brother continued quietly, "I get the feeling that our actions are not our own; almost as though another intelligent force is somehow managing to manipulate events, and us, but in such an incredibly subtle manner that we simply aren't aware of being manipulated. Do either of you *ever* get that feeling?"

"No," they denied in unison.

Supreme Brother sighed heavily. For the briefest instant, Richard caught a look of hesitation upon his leader's face, and then it was gone.

"How does Brother Thomas?"

Richard grinned. "As you would expect. Elated at the success of his mission, *and* by the fact that he received his promotion to the Third Circle. He managed to make it seem a very easy thing to do."

"He handled his assignment with a competence which belies his experience," Supreme Brother agreed.

They all glanced at the cavern's entrance as Sister Angela, accompanied by Sister Margaret, appeared.

Supreme Brother motioned them closer, demanding to know their reason for interrupting his meeting in this manner. Richard and Jerome smiled privately at the fact that Sister Margaret tended to be treated more *harshly* by Supreme Brother, due no doubt to his sexual relationship with her; almost as though he was demonstrating to the entire Brotherhood that she did not influence him in any way.

Slowly, her face almost as severe as that of the Supreme Brother, whom she faced, Sister Margaret reported that Tony Baron had emerged from hiding and was, even now, with the Brandons. Richard and Jerome looked at her with new interest, but remained silent.

"Are you *certain* that it is Tony Baron?" Supreme Brother demanded.

Sister Margaret smiled, "Positive," she said, with a calm certainty in her voice. Supreme Brother frowned: "Do you have any more information?"

Sister Margaret shook her head and then asked if she was

237

required to continue watching the Brandons.

"No," Supreme Brother replied slowly. "I doubt that there is anything more to be gained; unless Richard or Jerome feel that there is particular information which they require," he said, indicating them.

Jerome stood quickly, glowering at the two Sisters. He was one of the *few* Brothers who resented the fact that women had been admitted into the Society. The various Sisters were under no illusions regarding his feelings. Sister Angela retreated a nervous half-pace. Margaret, however, stood her ground and stared back at him.

"I need no help from these *bitches*," he murmured.

Margaret's eyes flashed in anger, "I noticed you were happy enough to hear our information about Tony Baron, *Brother*," she said, coldly. "You note I address you by your title, as a common courtesy. Is such simple *courtesy* beyond you, *Brother*?"

Enraged, Jerome moved towards Sister Margaret, but Supreme Brother intervened.

"Enough, Margaret," he snapped. "Remember that these two Brothers are your superiors; and remember that your position in our Society is tenuous at *best*. Suitable punishments for lack of discipline are easily arranged — by any of us three."

Visibly biting back her anger, she apologised to Jerome, with considerable reluctance; and he accepted the apology with an ill-grace which informed all that he would watch Sister Margaret assiduously for her next breach of decorum.

Having dismissed the two Sisters, Supreme Brother gazed at Richard and Jerome questioningly. "Do either of you have a feeling of déjà vu?"

Jerome inclined his head slowly. Richard's brow creased thoughtfully.

"So, we can safely assume that the Brandons will know how to contact Baron *after* this visit. Doesn't the timing alarm

238

you at all? I have never believed in coincidence, and yet....." he broke off and then continued in a whisper, "....and yet, here we are *again*. It is *this* type of thing to which I alluded earlier. Are we being manipulated in a particular direction? Into taking a specific course of action?"

After a moment's thought, Richard spoke. "I don't believe in coincidence either. But I cannot accept that events are being manipulated. We had already decided to kidnap Kim Logan to aid in the capture of Tony Baron. The fact that he has reappeared does not manipulate us in any other direction than that which we had already decided upon."

"Whenever I mention this possibility, we seem to come to that same conclusion. Don't you find *that* surprising?"

Quietly, a trace of humour in his voice, Jerome informed his superior that reaching the same conclusion was inevitable when there was no other conclusion to reach.

"Are you saying that I'm becoming paranoid?" Supreme Brother asked, evenly.

"Yes," Richard laughed. "A certain degree of paranoia is essential for *any* Supreme Brother worth his salt."

Supreme Brother's eyes narrowed briefly, and then he laughed; a dry, coughing, rasping sound which echoed around the cavern. As the echoes died away, he asked, "Is the kidnapping then agreed between us?"

The other two nodded, although Jerome frowned. Supreme Brother glanced at him inquisitively, inviting him to say whatever was on his mind. Jerome acknowledged the gesture appreciatively.

Turning to Richard, and virtually ignoring the Supreme Brother whilst they spoke, Jerome asked him, "Richard, I wonder if you might do me a favour?"

Supreme Brother sat back in his chair, wondering what might be on Jerome's mind.

"If I possibly can, of course I will," Richard replied, slightly puzzled.

239

"In that case, Richard," Jerome continued slowly, "I would ask that you execute this abduction with extreme delicacy and care towards Kim Logan, treating her almost as though she might be made of *glass*. I do not want her to suffer, or to be *hurt*."

Richard stared at Jerome incredulously for several seconds. Concern for potential victims was hardly a common trait within their Society. With a sudden grin, Richard asked, "Does this mean you no longer have the *stomach* for our activities, Jerome?"

The expression which crossed Jerome's face made Richard laugh out loud. Without *any* display of unease or embarrassment, Jerome explained, "No, Richard, not that. I prefer to inflict the harm myself. You could never comprehend the amount of sexual gratification it invariably occasions before introducing the child — of either sex — into those other, more intimate forms of *pleasure* and *pain*."

Richard nodded: however, he found it impossible to understand Jerome's sexual preferences. They were Jerome's, of course, and not his. "I promise you, my Brother," he affirmed, using the more intimate form of address, "that if it is *at all* possible, Kim Logan will be delivered to you as you have asked — unharmed."

Jerome, eyes blazing, smiled at the reassurance.

Chapter Ten: *Abductions*

Tony Baron continued to glare at them. Margaret and John exchanged puzzled glances, neither responding to his initial statement. Letting out a breath explosively, Tony took *another* pace towards them. "Well?" he demanded angrily.

Without reacting to Tony's vehemence, John suddenly sat, indicating that Tony should do likewise. Tony hesitated slightly before sitting in the indicated chair.

"I think we need to talk," John said softly.

Tony nodded, but made no effort, then, to begin discussion. He looked around the living-room with evident curiosity. His gaze hardened as it took in Margaret, then flicked contemptuously away from her. He regarded John with deep intensity for long minutes.

"Yes, it's difficult to know where to begin, isn't it? Why not tell us what's been happening to you all these years before moving on to the important things?" John suggested.

Tony's eyes sharpened perceptibly, and then became wary. His old smile appeared fleetingly. He nodded slowly. As he spoke, Margaret noticed a creaky timbre to his voice, almost as though he wasn't used to speaking, and such communication was an effort for him.

"There isn't a great deal to tell," Tony said. "Perhaps I should say that there isn't a great deal that I *want* to tell you. Of course, I kept myself appraised of what was happening with you two. I suppose I should congratulate you on your marriage, but it's been a long time since I've congratulated anyone on anything.

"I would have come to your wedding, had it been possible, but it wasn't. In those days, I was really screwed up. After... what... happened, I didn't want to face life — couldn't, in fact. I loathed myself for what I hadn't done; for... *his*... death. I loathed both of you: *hated* you.

"But I detested myself more. In the end, I lost the will to

live. I tried suicide, and very nearly managed it. I was too drunk at the time to make a proper job of it. You see, I'm an alcoholic. I couldn't attend your wedding because I was recovering from my attempt to kill myself.

"I staggered around from one week to the next until something happened that shocked me so deeply that I couldn't even begin to tell you about it, even if I wanted to, which I don't. It affected me so profoundly that I've not been able to face alcohol since that night....

"I made myself impossible to find. Several people tried, you included. Oh, yes, I was very aware of those who were trying to locate me. I had to be. I thought... I thought that my disappearance might give us an edge.

"I kept tabs on you. I watched virtually everything you did. I waited so long for some sign that you had put the pieces together. But that didn't happen. When Emma Carter tried getting information out of you, I was certain. I knew that that would be the turning-point. I couldn't believe it when you didn't make the connection.

"And then the murders started. I understood immediately the motive behind them. The nature of the ploy. At first, I thought it was insulting, because a child could have seen through it. But then I realised that you couldn't see it. Then I had to re-evaluate things. The plot was more subtle than I had understood. I miscalculated. I expected you to be able to see what was right in front of you.

"The murders weren't just an attack on you, but were an incentive to draw me out of hiding, out of my cocoon, back into the real world. Oh, God, how I laughed at the idea. I could afford to, because I knew that you *must* see through events.

"*But... you... didn't.*

"You wasted so much time. Exposed us all needlessly. I sense that the danger is getting stronger with every second that passes. They can't wait much longer. They can't! Don't you see that? Are you both blind?

"And now, I don't know where this leads us. And do you

242

know what you've accomplished?

"You've forced me out of hiding, and they know it. Why did you do it? My plans depended on me staying out of the equation, an unknown factor. Now everything's warped: perverted.

"In fact, we're probably wasting our time, even now. Things have gone too far for us to make any real difference. I don't even know why I bothered coming here. The simple fact is that we've lost."

He fell silent, staring broodily at them. Margaret wanted to know what he was talking about. Tony glanced at her, very briefly, but made no effort to answer her. It was John who spoke.

"Our old friends are back. We didn't destroy them after all," he groaned. "Somehow, they've managed to rebuild themselves. We are back where we started, except that we don't have a George Hayter to help us out."

Margaret looked wildly from one to the other, old fears and terrors suddenly returning. "But you *did* destroy them. You *did*."

John looked her straight in the eye. "Apparently not. I was on the edge of deducing this for myself: Emma Carter, the *portrait*, the *murders*. Jesus, I've been so dense."

"Then the Cult killed Steve and Georgina?" Margaret asked.

"The trouble with women," Tony interrupted scathingly, "is that they never listen to something the first time it is said. Nor can they make deductions from what they have managed to hear. You'll probably have to spend the next hour explaining everything to her."

"You're in our flat, Tony, and a bit of respect...." Margaret began.

"Bit of *what*?" Tony demanded furiously, leaping to his feet. "Respect? *Me* respect *you*? I don't respect anyone. Maybe I did once, but not now. I despise you."

243

Margaret moved quickly in his direction, her hand raised to slap him. Tony's hand caught her wrist, moving so quickly that neither she nor John saw the action. He bent her arm back slowly, making her wince. His glare became dangerous. He moved his body forward, until his face was inches from hers.

"Don't ever even think of touching me," he spat at her, making no effort to conceal the venom in his voice.

"Tony, enough!" John cut in. "We can't fight amongst ourselves, not now."

Tony let go of Margaret's wrist, and ignored her seething anger as he turned his attention back to John. Slowly, surprise appeared in his eyes. "I think you're labouring under a misapprehension, John," he told him.

John frowned, "I am?" he echoed, plainly not understanding what he was being told.

"Yes!" Tony informed him, with evident amusement. "You imply that we're all in this together. We aren't."

John's frown deepened.

"Oh yes, the Curse is still in place, and it still applies to me. But I've been hiding somewhere they can *never* find me. Just so we understand each other, you two are on your own. I fought the Cult once and lived to tell the tale. I've no desire for a re-match."

"Tony," John's voice was shocked, "you can't just leave us."

"You want to bet on that?" Tony enquired slyly. "I've no feelings of loyalty to either of you. No feelings of love or any other such crap. The only person I care about is me."

Tony!" Margaret demanded, her anger now subordinate to the remnants of other, deeper emotions, which she had thought dead.

Tony shook his head, a cynical smile upon his face. "You betrayed me first, remember?" as he continued, a trace of the bitterness which he felt entered his voice. "All the time I was working my *nuts* off in the mansion, the two of you were together. I remember the time you went swimming. You took the first opportunity that presented itself to strip off for him. I can imagine what else you got up to. Don't deny it. It doesn't hurt me anymore. It actually helped me to learn not to trust anyone except myself. That's why I'm not interested in whether you see my lack of concern as a betrayal or not. In essence, it's a reaction which I learned from you."

Margaret opened her mouth to protest, but John caught her eye, and she hesitated.

"Tony, you've told us where we stand, and I thank you for that. But I just don't understand why you've gone to such trouble to warn us about all this."

Tony hesitated, frowning, almost as though he had not considered the question before. "I'm not sure," he confessed. "Maybe I just didn't like the idea of the Cult getting to you without you knowing who they are. If I know you, you'll give them a run for their money."

"But you won't help us?"

"No."

"When did you learn to relocate?" John asked, changing the subject abruptly.

Tony laughed at that. "Soon after... George's... death. I learned a lot of things. Perhaps I inherited some of... *his*... abilities."

"But if that's so," John insisted suddenly, "you could make all the difference."

"I've already said no. I mean no. I've done what I came to do, so perhaps this is the time to say goodbye," he said, glancing at them both.

"No, Tony," John urged. "Will you help by telling us what you know about them? I'm rusty on the subject."

Tony thought for a few seconds. "I suppose so," he said finally. "I think I can do that without..." he shrugged. "What do you want to know?"

"When did the Cult start recruiting women?"

245

"Ages ago."

John threw question after question at Tony, who replied with succinct answers which demonstrated his intimate knowledge of the Society. When John related to him the story about the portrait of Hayter, Tony's fascination became obvious and he asked to examine it.

Despite his reticence about allowing anyone into his studio, John escorted Tony there. He seemed enthralled by the portrait, and somehow disappointed that it didn't come to life and talk to him.

Margaret said very little as the time passed, wondering how the Tony Baron she had known and loved had changed into the cynical, embittered man who stood before her.

Returning to the living-room, John asked Tony about the book which Hayter had tried to give to him in his vision. Tony sat heavily, for the first time thinking carefully before he answered.

"It's a grimoire penned by Anton Baron himself. I was only ever permitted to see it once, and then only two selected pages."

"Didn't you ask about it?" John demanded.

"Yes, I did. But you know what George was like. All he would say was: '*The time is not right.*'"

"Do you know where George kept it? He had hundreds of hiding-places."

"Sorry, I don't. Looks like you're going to have to poke around the mansion."

"Think, Tony. Where did George go to get it?"

"I've told you all I can," Tony replied bitterly.

John shrugged. "We appreciate it."

"Don't. I helped you because my mood incline me to do it; for no other reason. Another day, I wouldn't have done. It's time for me to go, and I don't expect to see either of you ever again. I prefer my solitude to the warped existence that you lead."

He stood, breathing slowly, preparing to relocate as the door opened and Kim entered. Tony glanced at her, a questioning look upon his face. Concerned, Margaret moved towards Kim, asking her why she was out of bed. Kim didn't seem to be aware of Margaret's presence. Her eyes were locked upon Tony.

Slowly, Kim approached him, her expression unreadable. All the while, Tony watched her intently, his frown slowly replaced by look of incomprehension.

Kim stood directly in front of him, saying nothing, not having to. Hesitantly, he moved his hands out to her, palms upward. Kim looked from Tony's face to each of his palms, them back to his face again.

Smiling slightly, Kim moved her hands until her palms rested a few inches above Tony's. She tilted her head slightly, almost as though she was asking a question. Tony murmured a few words which were inaudible to all but Kim. Her smile grew in confidence as she lowered her hands onto Tony's.

John and Margaret glanced at each other, then at Kim. That some form of communication between Kim and Tony was occurring neither had any doubt, but what it might have been they could never have guessed. John opened his mouth to ask Margaret a question, but she gently placed her fingers on his lips, shaking her head. She regarded Tony; his eyes were closed, yet his forehead continually twitched, as though receiving a massive amount of information from Kim. From her position, Margaret was unable to see Kim's face, and was loath to move in case she somehow affected what was happening.

Minutes later, Tony's eyes blinked open. He stared at the little girl before him in apparent amazement. Kim gazed gravely back at him. Then, evidently satisfied, she moved her hands back to her sides. She glanced once again at Tony's palms, then back to his face. She smiled again as she turned and left the room.

Absolutely baffled and concerned, Margaret followed her.

"Tony, what was all that about?" John demanded. He didn't reply; seemed lost in some world of his own. John repeated the question, and Tony glanced abruptly at him. Then he engaged in a careful scrutiny of his feet, but said nothing.

Margaret returned, informing them that Kim had gone straight back to bed, showing no signs of being aware of what she had done, and now appeared to be sleeping deeply.

Margaret asked Tony for an explanation, but he refused even to demonstrate that he had heard her. She looked at John. "If he's too proud to speak to me, perhaps he'll tell you."

Tony looked up at John suddenly. "She's the girl you intend to adopt?"

John nodded, wondering how Tony had known that; he said nothing, hoping that Tony's curiosity might encourage him to talk.

"Has she done anything like this before?"

Margaret cut in, "Like what? What did she do? Tell us. We have a right to know."

Tony glared at her. "You've no rights as far as I'm concerned," he snapped back. "Will you ever learn to stay out of what you don't understand?" To John he added, "If you want my help, answer my questions — and I'd appreciate it if you got that wife of yours to keep her mouth shut. Otherwise, I'm out of here, and you're on your own: understood?"

Margaret stormed angrily out of the room.

Swallowing his own irritation with difficulty, John said, "Ask your questions, Tony. But your help had damned well better be worth it."

Ignoring the implied threat, Tony asked about Kim, wanting to know everything about her, but especially anything remotely connected with the occult. He was very patient with John's answers, asking for further clarification when he was unsure what John was telling him. Even so, it seemed to John that Tony was struggling to understand what he was being told.

"Margaret could properly explain it better than I," John

couldn't resist saying.

Tony stood began pacing the room. "I doubt it. At the moment, the very last thing I want is to have your wife prattling on about something she can only half-grasp and colouring it with what she thinks it might mean."

"How did you become so bitter, Tony?"

"You think I'm bitter *now*? You should see me on a bad day."

He sat again, suddenly deep in thought. He ignored everything else John said to him, until his thoughts had run their course.

"This is what I want you to do. No, don't interrupt," Tony cautioned, coldly. "I've no idea how much time the Cult will give us. Not much, I'm certain. I need you to look through the mansion for that grimoire which... *he*... seemed to want to give you. It must be hidden in the mansion. You know that place better than anyone else so I want you to find it. As soon as possible. It has to have some of the answers we need.

"I think that that's the place to start. Let me know when you've located it." He stood, obviously believing that the conversation was at an end.

John stood, too. "You've not convinced me that your help is worth all the trouble that you're going to cause."

"Perhaps it isn't. The choice is yours." He placed a card upon the sofa. "If you find that grimoire, and decide you do want my help, you can contact me on this number — but only for the next two days. If I don't hear from you, well, to be frank, I won't lose any sleep over it."

"Tony, you bastard, I want some answers..." John began, as Tony relocated himself, leaving John alone. Shortly afterwards, Margaret returned to the living-room, not at all surprised at Tony's absence.

"What did he say?" she asked.

"Sod all, apart from wanting me to find that grimoire."

"Are you going to?"

He sighed heavily. "What other option do I have? Neither of us has any idea what we might be up against. He does."

"Did he tell you anything else? About Kim?"

John shook his head and reiterated their conversation.

"He's an embittered swine," Margaret observed, finally venting her anger.

"Perhaps he has reason to be. I wonder what it was that gave him such a shock that he stopped drinking. I meant to ask him."

"John, do you really think that we need his help?"

He shrugged. "Maybe, maybe not. He might just be able to prevent the Cult from killing us — or worse. You know what I mean."

Margaret shuddered as she recalled the various humiliations which she had suffered at the Cult's hands. "You're right," she muttered. "Even if he is a cold-hearted, calculating... What are you going to do?"

"I'm going to the mansion. Christ alone knows where George might have hidden that bloody book. The sooner I start, the sooner I'll get it found."

"I wish I could help."

He shook his head. "I'll be happier knowing that you're here. Protect yourself every way you can think of. The kids, too. Don't go out unless you have to."

They kissed. "Good luck, John," Margaret whispered.

***

As he drove to the mansion, John's mind was constantly distracted by attempts to understand exactly how the Cult had managed to escape from the snare set by Anton Baron and primed by Hayter. It didn't make sense, John thought, that Hayter would have sacrificed himself the way he had, if there had been the remotest chance that the Cult would not have been destroyed.

With these thoughts still clamouring for understanding, John pulled up outside the mansion. Rather than entering immediately, he made his way to the lawn at the mansion's rear.

He entered the small enclosure and made his way to the grave. The early morning light cast a soft illumination over it. John stood silently, staring at the marker, remembering Hayter as he had been before Tony and Margaret had arrived, and the chaos which had ensued.

The fact that time was against him made him leave the grave sooner than he would otherwise have done. As he entered the mansion, his mind suddenly seemed to focus upon the reason for his visit: the location of the grimoire. John began listing, mentally, Hayter's hiding-places, in order of difficulty of access.

He closed his eyes as he brought to mind the sheer number of places which Hayter had utilised.

As he had expected, the safe in what had been Hayter's study was empty. Hayter would have considered it a much too obvious hiding-place. John swore as he began searching through the entire mansion, knowing that unless he was very lucky, or had a sudden inspiration, it could take weeks.

He made slow progress, since every room, each passage and hiding-place conjured up memories of Hayter. It was impossible, he found, to see and handle objects without them releasing some emotion generated by a half-remembered incident.

John continued his search, attempting not to lose time over anything which could have no bearing on the location of the grimoire. Even so, it was well into the afternoon before he realised it. A sudden growl from his stomach informed him that he was hungry.

He paused his search, ate a hurried meal and then returned to his seemingly impossible task.

He worked methodically, checking the more likely hiding-places on each floor of one wing before moving to the next. However, he found nothing which gave any indication that he was on the right track.

251

Later, lying on his bed in the wing of the mansion which he had once occupied, gave him a strange feeling. It made him focus upon the years he had lived with Hayter. Now, as then, the threat which the Cult represented was a constant problem. With these thoughts still whirling through his mind, John slept.

He dreamed of the painting of Hayter coming to life, unable to speak, yet still offering the grimoire to him, before the paint became unfixed and he was left staring at a blank canvas.

John woke early in the morning, and immediately returned to the job of locating the grimoire. Although he wracked his brain in an attempt to understand where Hayter might have hidden it, he had no more success than he had had the previous day.

Early in the afternoon, John sat in the lounge feeling absolutely depressed by his failure. He moved to the piano, struck a few notes randomly. '*George, where would you have hidden that grimoire*?' he mused to himself. Immediately, his mind replied: '*Where it would be obvious, yet not easily seen.*' The thought galvanised John. He ran towards the library.

He made his way to the centre of the room, gazing slowly at the shelves, and the books which they contained. He turned, certain now that he was at least looking in the right place. He compared what he saw with his memories of the library as it used to be, when he had catalogued the contents, and selected material which Hayter had requested, or which John had thought Hayter might find pertinent to the subject which he was researching.

Initially, John saw nothing which caught his attention. He scanned the shelves again, trying to open his mind to any peculiarity. He was halfway through his second circuit when he stopped dead. He turned to look again at the stack devoted to the works of George Hayter. Apart from five or six gaps where the books he and Margaret had taken normally resided, the entire stack was full.

But it shouldn't *have been.*

The bottom shelf had never been used, partly because Hayter had not quite written enough books to justify it, partly because Hayter himself disliked those shelves as being too awkward to reach easily.

Examining the bottom shelf, John found that the books there had been selected randomly from the rest of the library. He began opening each one in turn, and laughed out loud as he opened the fifth book. Hundreds of pages had been cut out, leaving space for Anton Baron's grimoire to be secreted. John recognised it instantly.

He lifted the grimoire carefully and opened it. As he focussed on the parchment, it seemed to John that the faded characters began moving on the pages, preventing him from reading. He stared more intently at the grimoire, but the words seem to disjoint into individual archaic letters which now swirled as though affected by a maelstrom. John felt a sudden surge of nausea. He tore his gaze away from the grimoire, astonished to find himself struggling to catch his breath and feeling totally disorientated. He managed to close the grimoire and replace it within the larger book. He sat, breathing slowly until his discomfort eased.

"George always *was* a cautious bugger," he murmured, suddenly aware that the grimoire would only allow its secrets to be unlocked by certain people. He managed a twisted smile. No doubt Tony had known that; which meant that the grimoire would behave the same way to anyone not of the Baron line. John grinned. Had Tony forgotten, he wondered, in his twisted bitterness, that Margaret was as much a descendant of Anton Baron as Tony himself was?

Tony had seemed to set great importance on reading through this book, and probably wished to keep most of the information to himself. If that was his plan, John knew that Margaret would be able to thwart it.

John hurried out of the mansion, his spirits suddenly rising.

***

"But *why* can't we go out, Mummy?" Linda asked.

Margaret wondered whether John had reached the mansion yet, or was he already scouring through it to find Anton Baron's grimoire? She glanced at Linda, pondering for the hundredth time how she could explain the Cult, and the danger which it represented, without frightening either child. She felt that she couldn't do it. Not only because she knew that her own fear would be obvious to them, but knowing that to explain the Cult's capabilities with any realism, she would have to tell them about her experiences whilst in their hands. It was simply something which she didn't think she could do.

Margaret bit her lip, recalling the time when she had done just that for Georgina. She had only been able to relate such personal information because it was essential to gain Georgina's trust.

The idea of reliving her experiences whilst relating them to her daughters — Margaret suddenly realised that she found it quite natural to think of Kim as her daughter — made her feel nervous and apprehensive. The children were too young, she thought, to be exposed to such barbarity, no matter who told them of it. And yet, to understand why they had to be careful from now on, they would have to be told *something*.

She sighed; perhaps, if she was careful, she would not have to tell them too much about what the Cultists could do. Maybe John could explain how they had hurt her without disclosing too many details.

It suddenly occurred to her that although Linda had seen her many times in various states of undress, she had never asked Margaret about the scars upon her body, a legacy from them, her torturers.

Both children, she felt, should be told about the Cult, but not until they were older, when they could cope with such horrors more adequately than they could at present.

Her instincts demanded that she do all that she could to protect the children, but she still felt other, conflicting urges; both to explain everything to them, yet to keep her first-hand experiences from them.

254

Margaret felt confused and frightened.

"We always go out on Saturdays," Linda insisted.

"I know you do," Margaret replied as the phone rang, interrupting her.

She hurried to the living-room, certain that it must be John calling. It wasn't. Sue Anderson sounded annoyed. Margaret asked what the problem was, vaguely afraid that the Cult might have struck at the Orphanage. When Sue explained, Margaret couldn't help laughing her relief. It seemed that Sue had visited a sick nephew in hospital, and he had given her measles.

Unable to see any humour in this situation, Sue snapped angrily at Margaret, who managed to control her laughter and commiserate with her.

Somewhat mollified, Sue went on to ask Margaret whether she would mind sitting in for her at the Orphanage until she was no longer infectious.

Margaret became suddenly suspicious about the cause of Sue's illness. Had their enemies been at work to bring this request about? Quickly, Margaret explained that she couldn't help out right now; that she had certain problems of her own.

Sue sounded surprised at that, but didn't press the issue, nor ask Margaret for clarification. They talked for a few more minutes.

As Margaret hung up, she remembered John once saying that becoming paranoid was a side-effect of working for Hayter. She knew now that that had been an untruth. When faced with the Cult, paranoid was the only safe way to be.

She realised that she was trembling. She had believed that Hayter, John and Tony had eradicated the Cult: cocooned herself within that belief, knowing that whatever disasters occurred in their future, they would pale into insignificance when compared to the Cult's depravities.

Now, she knew that she had been a naive fool. They generated such terror within her that, had she not got a family she loved dearly, she would seriously have considered copying Tony in hiding herself where she could never be found.

Only, they would find her. And the next time, Margaret knew that they wouldn't make the same mistake. She remembered what had been done to Georgina; why, she asked herself, hadn't she realised that the tortures she had been subjected to bore all the hallmarks of the Cult? Margaret couldn't believe how blind she had been.

Shaking her head, Margaret again pondered the best way to explain to the children why they couldn't go out. She made her way back to their bedroom only to feel a deep pang of dread stab into her. The room was empty.

Panicking, Margaret checked the flat, calling for them. Her cries went unanswered.

As she bolted out of the flat, Margaret remembered what she had said as Sue's phone call interrupted her. She gritted her teeth. No doubt, Linda had taken Margaret's incomplete sentence as implied consent, something which she was *very* adept at doing.

On occasion, when she wanted to do something and was told she couldn't, Linda would devote all her ingenuity into misinterpreting what Margaret or John had said. Obviously, having been told once that she couldn't go to the park, she had taken advantage of Margaret's distraction.

She had probably taken Kim with her, since Kim had not been there when Margaret had forbidden the excursion.

As she pounded along the road towards the park, Margaret could imagine Linda telling Kim that Mummy had said that she *knew* they always went out on Saturdays. Linda would think that Kim's presence would make it less likely that she would be punished.

Linda, Margaret suddenly realised as a stitch began to form in her side, could be very devious. As Kim hadn't known that she couldn't go out, she would only be scolded. Linda was hoping that the scolding would apply to both of them, and that no further punishment would be inflicted upon her. She was

256

using Kim to shield herself.

Margaret passed through the gates into the park at a sprint, fear and anger consuming her. She slowed to a fast walk, looking this way and that, her breath coming in gasps. The park appeared deserted.

Fifteen minutes later, Margaret spotted Linda standing against a tree, her back to her.

Relief flooded through Margaret, but sheer *fury* at her daughter's act cut through it instantly. Margaret opened her mouth to call Linda, but her shout died unvoiced and a sudden, *grim* smile appeared on Margaret's face.

Silently, she crept up behind Linda, taking into account that Linda's short skirt was ideal for her purpose. She heard Linda counting under her breath.

Taking careful aim, putting all her weight and strength into the swing, Margaret struck the back of Linda's leg with her hand as *viciously* as she could, which considering Margaret's emotional state, was considerable.

In one rapid action, Linda screamed, burst into tears, whirled around, stared at Margaret in disbelief, tears streaming down her face; her hand moved to rub her burning, stinging leg, but Margaret took hold of her wrist before she could do anything to reduce the white-hot pain which Margaret had inflicted on her.

Margaret found that she, too, had to stifle a yelp of pain. The slap which she had just landed upon Linda's leg made her own hand feel as though it had been scalded. She grabbed Linda by the shoulders. "I told you that you couldn't go out. Where's Kim?"

Linda was sobbing too hard to be able to answer.

"Answer me! Where's Kim?"

Linda still couldn't answer. Margaret's eyes glinted dangerously. She moved her hand, threatening another slap.

"She's... she's hiding," Linda managed to stammer between sobs, moving her hands quickly to protect the threatened leg.

"Hiding where?" Margaret demanded.

"I don't know."

Muttering darkly, grabbing Linda's hand, Margaret began to search for Kim.

***

Richard was absolutely amazed to see the two children appear unaccompanied. Surely this made his task easier? Supreme Brother had constrained him to be cautious, to take no risks. He had envisaged a period of reconnaissance before being presented with an opportunity to complete his task. But here, it seemed, was a heaven-sent opportunity. He grinned at the absurdity of that idea. Casually, he overtook the two girls and entered an empty call-box.

As the connection was made, he murmured, "Be ready," and hung up. Linda and Kim were ahead of him again. He made another call, to the speaking clock, muttering platitudes whilst surreptitiously keeping the girls in view.

He saw them enter the park. Absolutely unable to believe his luck, Richard slowly began to walk in that direction. He couldn't have wished them to go to a better place. They seemed to be doing everything to play into his hands: literally.

He entered the park at a slow walk, checking in his pocket for the wad which had been soaked in anaesthetic.

The girls were about twenty yards ahead of him, just off the footpath. They suddenly stopped walking, apparently to discuss something. Richard didn't even glance in their direction as he walked past them, although he did hear a snatch of conversation which gave him an inward surge of satisfaction.

"Let's play hide and seek. There's lots of trees and bushes over there," Linda said, neither child paying any attention to Richard as he ambled away.

"No, I can't run as fast as you."

"I'll let you hide first, then.

"Okay," Kim conceded.

Richard had increased his pace, and was soon well-hidden behind some bushes. He had checked carefully; there was no one else around. His heart-rate increased with excitement. This was becoming too easy.

He watched as Linda and Kim approached the wooded area and selected a convenient tree. As Linda turned her back, Kim moved towards a clump of bushes away to Richard's left.

It was too much to hope for, he thought, that she would have come directly to where he was waiting. Frowning slightly, he began quietly and cautiously to make his way towards her. He moved in such a way, taking advantage of every piece of cover, that neither Kim nor Linda, should she suddenly look, could get a glimpse of him.

Seconds later, Richard could see Kim hiding behind a bush. He moved closer and closer to her in absolute silence, expertly stalking her. Almost five yards from her, he froze behind a tree, his attention darting to the woman who had appeared.

It took him several seconds to recognise Margaret, even though he had been one of her principal torturers. Angry at this turn of events, he glanced quickly at Kim, who couldn't see Margaret from where she was hiding.

His mind performed rapid calculations. Richard gauged his distance from Kim, assessing whether he could complete his mission safely, or whether to abort it and wait for another opportunity.

Supreme Brother had left him in absolutely no doubt that he wouldn't tolerate any loose ends: that Richard was to take no risks, justified or otherwise. Although sorely tempted, he knew better than to risk Supreme Brother's wrath by disobeying him. Reluctantly, he decided the risk of something going wrong was just too great: Margaret Brandon might see him — and she possessed some formidable occult abilities. Equally, she only had to call the children, and Kim would probably bolt from her hiding-place: *damn it.*

As Richard began to edge away from Kim, he glanced at Margaret once again. He noticed the way she was approaching Linda: as cautiously and as quietly as he had been Kim. The expression upon her face left him in no doubt about what she intended to do. This distraction, he quickly realised, he could turn to his advantage.

He wondered, briefly, about the difficulty of relocating two people. It took an enormous amount of energy when there was only one person involved. Supreme Brother had warned him that it would take all his concentration and will-power to accomplish this task, but that physical contact between him and Kim would make the operation that much easier. Everything else seemed to be in his favour; Richard's confidence in himself increased dramatically.

Kim stood almost motionless, completely unaware of his presence. He retrieved the wad from his pocket, before stealing to within three feet of her, the bush shielding him from her view, should she turn her head in his direction.

Richard glanced again at Margaret; he saw her arm begin its swing, and moved behind Kim. The sharp *crack* of the slap landing, and Linda's scream shattered the silence. Kim jumped, turning towards Linda, but *away* from Richard.

He stepped forward quickly, clamping the wad over Kim's nose and mouth to stifle any sounds which she might make. She struggled, but Richard held her in a firm, tight grip: he felt Kim, in her panic, inhale deeply through her mouth, no doubt to try to scream; almost immediately, her struggles lost much of their strength. After just ten seconds, Kim's body slumped into his arms. After twenty seconds, she was deeply unconscious.

Richard held her close to him, exhaling in deep satisfaction. He was even able to take time to look at Margaret, and saw her holding Linda by the shoulders. He heard her furious voice: "Answer me, where's Kim?"

Richard grinned savagely. Their turn *would* come.

He tightened his hold upon Kim, praying that what he was

260

about to do would not prove too much for him. He concentrated deeply, visualising where he wished to appear in minute detail. With a gentle surge of power which would have astonished Margaret, had other emotions not stifled her perceptions, Richard relocated himself and Kim.

Richard's last thought, as they disappeared, was that Margaret had moved her hand to slap Linda's leg again.

***

John had just started away from the mansion when a police-car, lights flashing, appeared. It braked to a halt in front of him. John felt his heart suddenly begin to hammer. Only Margaret — and possibly Tony — knew that he was here.

The police constable got out and strode up to John's car. "Mr. John Brandon?"

John nodded.

"You are needed at home urgently. I'll give you an escort."

"What's happened?" John demanded.

"I can't say, Mr. Brandon. I've simply been told to get you home as *quickly* as possible."

As John hesitated, he added, "We're wasting time, sir."

John mastered his anxiety. The constable took his silence for assent.

At times exceeding the speed limit at a rate which made John feel uncomfortable, he followed the police-car; in an amazingly short time, considering the distance involved, he pulled up outside his flat.

The constable accompanied him to the door, ensuring he went inside, although he didn't follow.

As he entered the living-room, Margaret almost jumped into his arms, sobbing hysterically. "They've got Kim. She disappeared in the park. I looked everywhere for her. I had to call the police, John. I *had* to."

"Mrs. Brandon," another voice cut in, and John turned to face the tall, dark-haired man he had not had a chance to notice. "I'm Detective Sergeant Bradley," he introduced

261

himself, to John. "Mrs. Brandon, you said, *'They* have Kim'*,* do you have any idea who might be behind this?"

"What's going on?" John demanded, struggling to comprehend what was happening.

D. S. Bradley, and Margaret, between sobs, told him of Kim's abduction.

"Do you have any idea who might be responsible?" the detective pressed.

Margaret glanced at John. "No," she lied.

"Do you think you might leave us alone for a while?" John asked.

The detective nodded. "I'll find out whether the search has turned up anything."

They listened for the door slamming before talking.

"What do we *do*, John?" Margaret asked, *begging* him to have an answer.

John turned troubled eyes to her. "We can't tell them. It'd cause more problems than it would solve."

"But Kim might be murdered," and as the thought amplified itself, "Jesus, they might be doing... *anything*... to her."

John held her close, forcing himself to think rationally, not to give in to his emotions which threatened to tear him apart.

"Our only hope is the grimoire. I found it. Do you want to look at it, or should I call Tony?"

"John, how can you?" Margaret snapped at him. "You don't seem bothered that Kim's been kidnapped."

"Of course I am!" he snapped back. "But our *only* chance is to fight them on their own ground. The police cannot help us."

Margaret bit her lip. Slowly, she nodded agreement. "Get the grimoire," she said.

John retrieved it from his car. Margaret took it from him, a spark of curiosity in her eyes, despite her terror for Kim. She opened it, and read: '*Because toward essential and lasting*

262

demand almost oblique chance gathering none entreat....' she trailed off, reading to herself.

Her face falling, she said, "The damned thing's protected — I can't make *any* sense of it," her voice trembled.

John nodded grimly. "It was too much to hope for," he spat, turning to the phone. Glancing at the card Tony had left, John dialled the number.

"Tony says he'll be here soon," John announced, slamming the phone down.

Chapter Eleven: *Insights*

Tony Baron grinned mirthlessly. John's phone call hadn't surprised him in the slightest. So what if he had exaggerated about the contents of the grimoire being essential to solving the riddle of how to fight the Cult? He owed *them* — The Brandons — no loyalty. However, the grimoire was more than precious; it was *priceless*. Tony knew more about what it contained then he had admitted.

It had been penned by Anton Baron himself, and detailed ceremonies and rituals which made no sense. Not even *George* had fully understood them. When he had attempted to describe those obscure rites to Tony, pondering upon their meaning, they had seemed completely unfathomable. It wasn't until well after his death, and Tony's recovery from his alcohol addiction and suicidal tendencies, that Tony had realised exactly what those archaic and meaningless ceremonies represented. Nothing less than the understanding of *how* Anton Baron had managed to transcend death and the laws of temporal and spatial physics.

And who knew what else?

Once Tony had grasped the potential significance of the grimoire, he had coveted it with an unholy intensity. However, caution had demanded patience. He discovered, by chance, that the Cult were again active, and knew that John and Margaret — *bitch* that she was — would need him again. He could have attempted to steal the grimoire; after all, locks and bolts meant little to him — except for the fact that Anton Baron had gone to considerable lengths to protect the grimoire — and surely he would have protected it against theft, in some oblique way?

Therefore, Tony knew that he had to induce John or Margaret into giving the grimoire to him freely. After all, neither of them would be able to decipher its contents. He laughed at that thought.

He thought again about understanding Anton Baron's

temporal relocation. The grimoire might be the only document in existence to hint at how to relocate through time.

Not that Tony was so deranged that he envisioned himself jumping forwards and backwards in time; he merely felt that he didn't belong in this century. The frantic, frenetic pace of life, the petty considerations each day demanded irritated him. Everything he had ever had, almost everyone he had ever loved, had been warped or perverted. Now he loved and was loved by nobody. He trusted only in *himself.*

He would take the grimoire from them, fools that they were, and make some excuse to leave with it in his possession. Of course, it would take some time to unlock all the grimoire's secrets, but he had plenty of that: and quiet: and solitude. His hiding-place had *all* of those attributes. '*Not like this place,*' he thought, looking around the unfurnished bedsitter which he had rented. He had no use for furniture. He slept upon the floor. He sat, when he wished to, against a wall, never feeling uncomfortable. It did mean, however, being surrounded by people. Tony loathed people passionately. It was another thing that bitch had forced him into; another reason not to help her.

But, with luck, this would be his last day in this miserable place. They would give him the grimoire, of that he was in no doubt. Then he would betray their trust. It was poetic justice, really. As he had said to Margaret, she had betrayed him first.

And the beauty of it. The simplicity. The Cult wouldn't be able to find him — they had tried for years with little success; and John and his bitch wouldn't be around to make the attempt, either.

Tony supposed that he should feel sad about that, but he didn't. He couldn't afford to, since to be sad about them — or about anything — he had to care in the first place.

Whistling cheerfully, Tony stood, his plans made, and prepared to go to John's flat. He could afford to walk. After all, it wasn't as though there was any urgency about these matters. Relocation drained him, and he didn't want to advertise his location to the Cult now that he was no longer in hiding.

***

Brother Richard glanced around the cavern. He deposited Kim carefully upon a chair before collapsing next to her. His vision swam in and out of focus; his breathing sounded ragged and harsh. For a moment he thought he was going to throw up. He felt physically weak, mentally drained. Concentrating on anything — even thought — took the equivalent of a gigantic effort.

Relocating two people, he decided, was something only to be attempted in an emergency, or as a last resort.

Richard and Jerome had discussed various methods of abducting Kim, from the subtle to the ridiculous. Jerome had even suggested relocating into the Brandons' flat, grabbing Kim and then relocating out again. Jerome had smiled as Richard had asked what Margaret Brandon would be doing whilst all this occult activity was going on. And, he had asked, how was he to manage to perform two relocations in rapid succession, when the second would be three or four times more difficult than the first?

Jerome's smile had widened as he pointed out that that was not his problem....

The best plan, they had decided, was a mixture of caution and audacity. Wait for an opportunity for the kidnapping to be effected, and then take advantage of events. Success demanded the abduction be performed in relative seclusion; the only safe way of incapacitating Kim, Richard had stressed, was by anaesthesia. In certain circumstances, Margaret Brandon might be close by. Attempting use of anything other than natural means to render Kim unconscious might, it was agreed, be unwise.

Adopting these tactics demanded that Richard be prepared to relocate Kim away. He envisioned a multitude of problems connected with carrying an unconscious Kim to his car, or any other form of transport. He couldn't think of a better way to make himself conspicuous.

He had discussed the difficulties with Supreme Brother, who had emphasised the need for close physical contact with Kim. He warned Richard that afterwards he would feel completely exhausted, mentally, physically, and emotionally.

Richard opened his eyes wearily. Supreme Brother hadn't exaggerated, he realised. He glanced at Kim.

Struggling against his fatigue, Richard checked Kim's eyes and pulse. He sighed. She would be unconscious for a while yet.

He longed to be relieved of Kim so he could snatch some sleep. He still had the second half of his mission to complete, but at least that wouldn't take place until tomorrow. Once Kim was in their hands, Supreme Brother had, in theory, agreed that more direct approaches to the Brandons were in order, to disorientate and unnerve them. Richard looked forward to that task. To face Margaret again after all this time; to remind her of their last meeting....

But what he would savour most would be...

Richard's thoughts scattered as he realised that Jerome was standing in front of him. He started, knowing that he had begun to drift towards sleep. He smiled at Jerome. "Completely unharmed," he said, waving a hand lazily in Kim's direction. "Just as requested."

Jerome's eyes blazed as they devoured Kim. He appraised her from head to toe, and back again.

"Superb, Richard," he approved, still allowing his gaze to wander all over Kim's body. "Absolutely superb. My Brother, if ever you should require a favour of me, which is within my power to grant, *it is yours*," Jerome vowed, which showed exactly how *thrilled* he was at Kim's arrival.

"Right now, all I want is sleep," Richard said, yawning.

"Then I will look after our guest. I will remain with her until matters are — resolved."

"Take care that you don't go *too* far, Jerome."

"I will. How long will she sleep?"

"Difficult to say. Between six and twelve hours. Let the anaesthetic wear off; don't try waking her."

Jerome grunted acknowledgement.

"I'll be back for her clothes tomorrow."

"They will be ready for you. Supreme Brother wishes to speak with you before you leave."

Carefully, Jerome lifted Kim into his arms.

Richard made his way to Supreme Brother's chamber. His leader motioned him to sit.

"I see you found it difficult."

Richard agreed, and yawned.

"I don't want to keep you, Richard. I take it there were no problems. Do you still feel that a visit to the Brandons' flat tomorrow is the best way to proceed?"

Tiredly, Richard assured the Supreme Brother that his views hadn't changed, that he thought a personal visit to present their terms for Kim's return would be the best way to demoralise their enemies.

Supreme Brother nodded agreement, a faint smile crossing his features. "Yes, *I* see it that way, too. To be presented with one of us, yet unable to do anything to harm him: shrewd and cunning thinking, Richard. Let it be so."

Standing, Richard excused himself.

"You have done an excellent job, Richard. I will remember it. Go now, get some sleep. You deserve it."

***

Jerome carried Kim to one of the punishment chambers which had been prepared. That meant the cave boasted a rudimentary bed of wooden planks.

Gently, Jerome laid Kim upon the bed before closing the door. He moved the only chair next to Kim's bed. With deft fingers, he moved her hair, untangling it, smoothing it away from her face. No less gently, he fastened a button on her blouse which had come undone. He lifted her into a semi-sitting position, allowing her upper body to rest against him as he gently removed her coat.

His fingers slid slowly, lightly down her body, tucking her blouse into her skirt. He completed this operation with great care, his breathing becoming more rapid. Smiling, he carefully returned her to her former recumbent position.

Jerome took a long, long look at Kim before straightening her skirt, then moving his fingers down her legs to her socks, he pulled them up. Nodding approval to himself, he covered her body with her coat to keep her warm.

Satisfied, he sat in his chair, softly stroking Kim's hair, murmuring comforting phrases to her.

If anyone could have seen Jerome, at that moment, and assumed Kim to be his daughter, he would have thought that Jerome presented a perfect picture of paternal devotion.

***

Margaret sat upon the sofa, tension radiating from her. John sat next to her, drawing her into his arms.

"What are they doing to her, John?" Margaret asked softly.

John held her more tightly, wanting to reassure her, yet knowing that she would see through any words of comfort which he might utter. His tone matched hers as he replied, "I don't know, Margaret. My mind won't stop tormenting me. Those bastards will be sorry if they hurt her. I swear to you."

"She might be dead already, John."

He didn't answer her for a moment. She looked at him and saw the tears in his eyes as he whispered, "I know."

"I've never been so angry at Linda in my life," Margaret said, knowing that if John broke down, she would, too. "I've told her that she has to stay in bed, but I've not finished with her. I'm too frightened for Kim to worry about what Linda did."

"You aren't blaming her for what happened to Kim, are you? You know how the Cult operates."

"No, I'm not. I'm blaming her for disobeying me and trying to use Kim to... to..." despair flooded through her

269

again, cutting through the barrier which she had attempted to erect.

"What are we going to do, John?" she asked.

"We're doing it. Waiting: waiting for Tony."

Immediately he had spoken there was a knock at the door. John jumped to answer it. Moments later, he returned to the living-room, frowning.

D. I. Davies followed him.

"May I sit?" he asked, sitting down before permission could be granted or withheld. John resumed his seat next to Margaret.

D. I. Davies moved uncomfortably, as though ill at ease. John and Margaret regarded him, unconsciously making his visit more difficult for him. Abruptly, the detective glanced at his watch.

"I don't have a great deal of time," he explained cautiously. "D. S. Bradley spoke to me earlier. He suspects that you may know more about this abduction than you admit."

"Really?" John broke in sarcastically. "D. I. Davies, admitted at the moment we're only fostering Kim, but we fully intend to adopt her. I'm more worried about her than I've ever been about anything in my life. We both are. Tell me why either of us would keep anything from the police?"

D. I. Davies sat back, crossing his legs. "Mr. Brandon, I *know* that you don't like me. I'm just an old-fashioned copper who has to get to the bottom of the cases he's presented with. Being hard-nosed gets to be a habit. I knew, within a day or two of the investigation starting, that you had nothing to do with Steve Preston's murder. But I had to cover every angle, no matter how unlikely. If you resent me for the way I interrogated you to establish your innocence, then I'm sorry.

"I'm not here in my official capacity; not exactly. I want to talk to you *off* the record. A moment ago, you asked me why you would keep information from the police. I think I might be able to answer your question. For the same reason that you lied

270

about the circumstances surrounding, *and* the death, of George Hayter."

The detective watched them closely, noting their reactions. He detected a stiffening in John's posture. Margaret's eyes widened. He smiled inwardly. So, they *had* lied about it.

"Did I give false information?" John asked innocently, recovering his composure almost instantly.

"I might not be able to prove it, but yes I believe so. I remember those events, since I was one of the PCs who had to recover those bodies from the ruined church. Those which could be recovered."

John and Margaret said nothing.

D. I. Davies sat forward in his chair, and as he spoke he gestured for emphasis. "Look, all that happened a long time ago. As I said, I'm not here in an official capacity. When you've been a police officer for as long as I have, you come to trust your feelings. And I feel that you're both in very deep trouble. Believe me, I want to help you."

John hesitated, touched by the sincerity which the detective's words conveyed. "I don't know how you came to that conclusion," John answered him slowly, "but we can't help you. And you can't help us."

"Wait, Mr. Brandon," the Detective appealed, "let me tell you what I've pieced together so far. Somehow you, your wife, George Hayter, or whomever have got on the wrong side of a powerful syndicate. One powerful enough to infiltrate the Home Office at the highest level.

"You have something which they want. I don't know what. Information; an object maybe; and they want it badly. They've tortured your wife, murdered your friends, and now they've kidnapped the little girl you intend to adopt. And those are just the things which *I* know of.

"Am I right?"

John glanced at Margaret, and then at D. I. Davies.

"Am I right?" he repeated softly.

John hesitated before shaking his head. "Not really," he said.

D. I. Davies frowned. "Then explain it to me. I can't help you if I don't understand what's happening."

With heavy emphasis, John replied, "D. I. Davies, you don't *want* to know. You could never accept or believe it."

"I'm listening."

"You have your career. Maybe a wife and children. If you did help us, which you can't, you would be risking their safety, and your career," John explained patiently.

"I'm *still* listening."

Annoyed now, John stood and began pacing. "All right, but you asked for this, remember that.

"Let me tell you a story. Five hundred years ago...."

As John related the history of the Baron family, D. I. Davies sat back in the chair, no emotion crossing his face. John told the story as quickly as he could, finishing with the account of Hayter's death which he had originally suppressed with Tony's help.

He said nothing about recent events, partly because John didn't know all the facts himself, and didn't want his factual account coloured with his own speculations; and partly because John knew that what he had said sounded absurd enough without attempting to explain to the Detective such things as how Tony could suddenly relocate himself, or how Margaret could cure Georgina Thompson.

John finally fell silent, and locked eyes with D. I. Davies.

The detective returned the stare. Standing, he said, "You're right. I can't accept it. I can't believe it. Mr. Brandon, I'm a police officer. I need *facts*, not fairy stories and demons and bloody *wizards*. It's bull! *I* know it, and you know it. I've tried to give you an opportunity to level with me. If you want to persist in playing your trivial games, fine. I can't help you if you won't trust me."

He moved towards the door, then turned and added, "If you

change your mind, you know how to get in touch with me."

"D. I. Davies," Margaret said, suddenly.

He looked questioningly at her.

"Will you do something for me?" she asked him.

"If I can," he replied cautiously as John moved to answer another knock at the door.

"Then think about what John has told you. Really think about it. Ask yourself if some of the unexplainable things that have happened — especially recently — becoming more explainable when you consider them in terms of what you've just been told."

Tony entered the room, asking John over his shoulder, "Have you *really* got it?"

"This is Detective Inspector Davies," John introduced them, hurrying back into the room. And, to the detective, he said, "This is Tony Baron."

D. I. Davies eyed Tony suspiciously. "Nice to meet you," he said with a trace of sarcasm. Then: "I've got to be going."

"Think about what I said," Margaret pressed him.

D. I. Davies glanced at the three of them. "I can find my own way out," he said.

As he made his way to the street, the Detective found himself wondering what it was that Tony had wanted. He had asked John Brandon: 'have you *really* got it?' eagerly enough.

Could he have been referring to the syndicate which was pursuing the Brandons? Was he referring to whatever it was this syndicate wanted from them?

His forehead creased in concentration, the Detective wondered whether Tony Baron could be a part of the syndicate. He dismissed the notion. It was more obvious than ever, he thought, that John and Margaret knew more than they would tell.

And John Brandon's story? Occult battles, things that go bump in the night? Crap!

However, he wondered what Rachel would make of it. It

might be an idea to get her perspective on it. It couldn't do any harm, except to waste time.

Perhaps a discreet tap of the Brandons' phone might be useful, he mused, as he got into his car.

As the door closed behind D. I. Davies, Tony glared at John. "What was he doing here?" he demanded.

"He wanted to know about the Cult, so I told him."

"You did what?"

"He didn't believe me, Tony. Don't get so worked up."

Tony sat in the chair which D. I. Davies had vacated. "You found the grimoire, you said?"

John nodded.

"And you tried to read it, didn't you? And so did she," he laughed. "And neither of you got anywhere. It made you feel sick to look at it, and she couldn't make any sense of it.

"You," he said, pointing a finger at John, "thought she would be able to read it, 'cos she's a Baron?"

"That's right," John admitted. "*Why* couldn't Margaret make any sense of it?"

Tony looked directly at Margaret for the first time. "You were right. It can only be read by Anton's descendants. But at the time Anton was writing and protecting the grimoire, you have to remember that women were considered vastly inferior to men; were thought of as having no real value. Come to think of it, they weren't *so* wrong in those days."

Tony hesitated, puzzled that his jibe had elicited no reaction from Margaret. He continued, "So, it was natural for Anton to limit access to his grimoire to males of the Baron line. You could say, I suppose, that she," and he grinned sneeringly at Margaret, "couldn't read it, 'cos she just hasn't got the *balls*."

Tony couldn't understand why Margaret was refusing to respond to his baiting. He lost his train of thought as John handed him the ancient grimoire. Tony looked at it for a long time before opening it. He read for several minutes.

"Don't tell me, you're not going to read it to *us*, Tony?" John asked cynically.

"Not a chance," Tony replied. "This information is only for males of the Baron line, and I'm the *last*."

John nodded shrewdly, suddenly understanding what had made him feel vaguely uneasy. Placing a hand upon the book, John said, "You may not borrow it, *nor* take it away from this place."

Tony started angrily. John had trapped him, he realised. If he left with the grimoire now, he would never be able to unlock the protection against theft, would never have access to Anton's secrets. However he decided that a bluff might work.

He handed the grimoire back to John. "Fine: solve this whole mess by yourself. I'll say goodbye now, 'cos I don't think we'll ever meet again."

"John," Margaret interrupted, worried, "we *need* his help."

John flashed a warning glance at her. She recognised the determined expression John wore when conducting business meetings.

Tony stood to leave. John said, "Then this is goodbye, Tony. There's just one thing I want you to see *before* you leave."

A grim smile upon his face, John picked up a table-lighter, and held it beneath the grimoire. Tony stood dead still. John flicked the lighter.

"NO!" Tony yelled, leaping across the space between them and dashing the grimoire from John's hand. As Tony regained his balance, John swore. "I wondered just how much the grimoire means to you. You were too eager for me to find it. I'll bet it doesn't even have any information which will help us?"

Tony glared at John but said nothing.

"The grimoire was all you wanted, wasn't it? You unscrupulous bastard. I've a good mind to destroy the damned thing."

"No," Tony snapped.

"What does it contain?" John demanded, retrieving it.

"Information about Anton's temporal relocation," Tony admitted reluctantly.

And nothing which might help us?"

"Maybe; I don't know."

"And this is the *only* copy?"

"Yes," Tony muttered unhappily, scared that if he lied now and John found out, he might carry out his threat to destroy the grimoire, after all.

John smiled. "I think we can do a deal. You help us and the grimoire is yours."

"And if I refuse?"

John picked up the lighter again. "As you so rightly said, I can't read it, Margaret can't read it, and if you refuse, I'll destroy it so you can't read it, either."

Tony sat heavily. "Then I've no choice. I'll help with information, but I won't battle the Cult again. What use would the grimoire be to me if they killed me? As soon as you decide to attack the Cult, I'll consider myself free to take the grimoire and disappear. If that's not good enough for you, then destroy it now." John knew that this was the best deal he would get from Tony, no matter how hard he pressed. He moved closer to Tony, offering him the grimoire. John held one end, Tony the other.

"Ownership of this grimoire passes to you once we decide to attack the Cult, providing you have given us reasonable help: agreed?"

"Agreed, although if you are killed before making that decision, the grimoire still becomes mine?"

"Agreed — so long as you aren't behind our deaths." He lowered the grimoire to Tony's knee.

"You know, John, you're an absolute *git*," Tony observed, with a certain grudging admiration.

"Start reading, Tony. I want to know anything which might

276

help us."

"Tony," Margaret interrupted hesitantly, unsure how he would react to her after being trapped so perfectly by John. "Have you any idea why the Cult would kidnap Kim?"

Long seconds passed. Margaret wondered whether Tony was so immersed in the grimoire that he hadn't heard her, or was merely ignoring her. However, Tony slowly raised his head. For the first time since he had reappeared, Margaret felt that Tony was taking her seriously.

"When was she kidnapped? Why didn't you tell me earlier?" he demanded.

"What good would it have done?"

"It would…" he began, and stopped abruptly. "So that's why the detective was here?"

"Partly," John admitted cautiously. "Tony, we were hoping that you might know of a way to get Kim back."

Tony looked at them, suddenly understanding why Margaret hadn't reacted to his jibes; comprehended their terror and anxiety for what Kim might be subjected to. He found it impossible to empathise, but did remember, vaguely, his own feelings after Margaret's capture.

"You know, *he* would have told us not to react the way the Cult wants. They're attacking you where you're most vulnerable. I don't know of any way to get Kim back, but there must be one. I doubt that the grimoire can help, but I won't know until I finish reading it through."

He returned to the grimoire with a new intensity.

John and Margaret could do nothing to help him. They sat next to each other, sharing their ghastly fears and heartache in silence, paradoxically comforting each other at the same time.

Neither could have said how much time passed as they sat in almost total silence, the only noise the creaking of the pages as Tony progressed through the grimoire. John remembered a similar feeling of impotence when he had been blinded, and could not help Hayter in his desperate search for the knowledge which he had needed.

It had taken hours, he remembered. Now it seemed to John that they were fighting a losing battle, time being their enemy as much as the Cult. He wondered if Kim was still alive. He was under no illusion as to what they were capable of doing. '*If she is still alive,*' John thought, '*what torments and degradations must those depraved perverts be subjecting her to?*' he prevented his mind suggesting answers to his question by a profound effort of will. John found himself wishing that Kim had been granted a swift death, rather than the prolonged torture at which the Cultists were so expert.

John felt Kim's abduction keenly: it was as though he was responsible for it. He had brought her into his family, made her a part of it, and then failed to protect her. Ultimately, he felt, he was responsible for every hurt and terror inflicted upon Kim. His misplaced feeling of guilt tended to exacerbate the other emotions which he felt, leaving him feeling utterly desperate and virtually inconsolable.

Margaret's emotions were more straightforward. Her fears for Kim had the very real foundation of her own experiences. She knew what the Cult could do, and the lengths to which they would go. They would baulk at nothing.

She didn't believe that Kim was dead: refused to believe it. The Cult might have killed Steve Preston quickly, but not Georgina. The male-oriented Society, she knew, rejoiced in torturing women — and little girls, she realised bitterly. Her mind, perversely pointed out each of Georgina's mutilations, and asked the fruitless question, '*Has that been done to Kim? Has she been* tortured*, her body* mutilated*? Has she been hurt in... in...* other *ways? Has she been beaten senseless, only to be revived and beaten again? Has she been degraded,* raped*, sodomised, brutalised?*'

Margaret rubbed tears from her face; could not stop them flowing. She drew in a gulping breath as she lost control of her emotions. She barely registered the fact that John held her in his arms, rocking her as he might do a young child. As he

278

might do *Kim*, she thought, her soundless weeping increasing in intensity.

Tony looked up from the grimoire, his face unreadable. He didn't react, merely returned his gaze to the book.

Eventually, by degrees, Margaret managed to gain some control over her anguish. She glanced at Tony, then at John, who shrugged.

"*That's* interesting," Tony said suddenly. "I don't know that it helps you directly, but you never know."

"What, Tony?"

"Here, Anton says... No, let me read you the passage. It says:

"'*Understand that our eternal enemies are Brothers, with one of their number ruling supreme. The position of the Supreme Brother is without doubt a curious one. He may elect a successor from within the ranks of the hierarchy, but Supreme Brothers appear reluctant to exercise this right — with good reason. Successors apparent tend to become ambitious, and more than one has attained the rank of Supreme Brother by assassination of his predecessor.*

"'*Yet it remains the duty of a Supreme Brother to nominate a successor before the whole assembly of Brothers, giving any dissenting Brothers the opportunity to voice their dissent before having them put to swift death.*

"'*The Brothers' occult powers are augmented by their Patron Demons through their leader. His powers receive the greatest augmentation; ordinary Brothers vastly less. There is no direct augmentation from Patron Demons to Brothers. All is accomplished through the Supreme Brother.*

"'*Hence, if a Supreme Brother were to die without a nominated successor, chaos would ensue. A Supreme Brother may not be elected. And, with no Supreme Brother to act as a channel to the ordinary Brothers, the unnatural augmentation of their occult powers would cease. Further, a Supreme Brother who dies without a nominated successor would have broken the Pact with their Patron Demons, who would have to withdraw their support from our enemies. The Pact could not, once broken, ever be renewed.*

" 'Yet be assured that a Supreme Brother is phenomenally powerful, reflecting, as he must, the might of the Patron Demons. Allied to this, he is deeply cunning, highly intelligent, very devious and absolutely ruthless. The concept of mercy, for example, is alien to him as we understand it.'" Tony stopped reading and looked at them.

"Interesting *yes*," John agreed. "But it doesn't help much with regard to Kim."

Tony raised his eyebrows, a resigned gesture.

"How is it, it reads in modern English?" Margaret asked.

"I'm not sure how he did it, but it translates itself as you read it. Your eyes see archaic characters, but your mind understands it as though it was written yesterday."

"Anything else in there?" John asked, hopefully.

"Not yet," Tony replied, his eyes dropping back to the book.

Silence returned to the room, Tony reading, John and Margaret doing their utmost to contain their emotions which tore at their consciousness in furious demand for acknowledgement.

Soon afterwards, Tony looked up sharply. He frowned. Margaret glanced at him.

"You've got a *visitor*, John," Tony said. "One of the Cultists, if I'm not mistaken. He hasn't come here to harm either of you."

"What do I do?" John asked Margaret. "Let him in?"

"*NO!*" Margaret snapped, jumping to her feet.

"Yes," Tony contradicted her. "They're either getting too bloody sure of themselves, or they want to talk. The Cult are rarely stupid enough to take any risks."

"How many of them?"

"Just one."

"Right," John said grimly. "I'll listen to him before beating him to death."

Tony caught John's arm. "Do anything to him, and what do you think his friends'll do to Kim?"

The question made John snarl in anger, but he accepted the logic of what Tony said. He made his way to the door, opened it, and motioned the Cultist to enter.

Brother Richard walked into the living-room. He carried a plastic bag. He waited until John had moved to stand next to Tony and Margaret.

"May I at least sit down?" Richard queried.

"No," Margaret spat back. "I might have to listen to you, but I don't have to make you feel welcome, you bastard." Margaret's eyes seemed almost black, radiating her utter fury. John hoped she wouldn't act precipitously, for Kim's sake. The atmosphere became so heavily charged John marvelled that the Cultist could stand there, apparently unperturbed.

"Get down to business," John advised. "What do you want?"

Richard smiled. "In good time. My name is Richard."

Margaret's eyes fixed themselves on him even more intently. She clenched her fists, knowing that she had to restrain herself, despite her hatred of this man who had been instrumental in the tortures to which she had been subjected when *she* had been captured by the Cult. In fact, this was one of the two men who had seriously injured John, rendering him unconscious, before chasing Margaret, capturing her, and using a wad of anaesthetic to render her unconscious.

When she had regained consciousness, her tortures had begun, culminating in a terror so great that even now, Margaret detested bringing it into focus.

"*I remember you,*" she said, in a low voice filled with loathing and hatred. Her gaze never left Richard's face, her glare leaving no doubt about what she would like to do to him, given an opportunity.

281

However, Brother Richard just smiled at her: "I expect you do," he replied mildly, seeming unconscious of her glare, or of the utter hatred which it conveyed.

"Is this an occasion?" he continued. "Margaret and John Brandon and Tony Baron all together in one room. I should congratulate you, Mr. Baron. You did a first-rate job of hiding yourself!"

Tony frowned. "Enough of this; say what you've come to say."

"You know," Richard continued, ignoring Tony's demand, "there's only Linda I haven't met."

"*Try it!*" Margaret snarled, venom filling her voice.

Richard didn't seem in the least intimidated. He knew that as long as they had Kim, they held all the aces. "We have Kim," he said, looking at each of them in turn. "We all know it." He placed the plastic bag upon the sofa. "I brought these in case you wanted proof that we do have her."

John reached into the bag and pulled out Kim's clothes. Silently, he passed them to Margaret. She looked at each item. "That was what she was wearing," she whispered.

As one, the three of them turned hostile eyes upon Richard.

"The Supreme Brother is willing to release Kim to you."

"Her body, you mean," Tony interjected.

"I assure you..."

"Your assurance is less than worthless," Tony interrupted him.

"I give you *Supreme Brother's* word: Kim is alive."

Tony nodded to John almost imperceptibly. Margaret noticed the action.

"And just why would your leader be willing to release her?" John asked.

"Perhaps because you are willing to meet the ransom for her."

"Which is?" Margaret cut in.

Richard spread his hands, half-shrugging. "The Supreme

282

Brother proposes a straight swap. Kim Logan for Tony Baron."

John and Margaret looked at each other in consternation, then at Tony, who showed no reaction.

"And if I agree?" Tony asked quietly of Richard, "what then?"

"Then we will make the swap, and Kim will return home to John and Margaret, and that will be the end of the matter."

"Tony, you can't," Margaret almost shouted. "You can't trust him."

"He wouldn't give Supreme Brother's word if he was lying."

"Wait," John insisted. To Richard he added, "You can't expect us to make an instant decision."

Richard agreed. "I understand," he said. He took a map from his pocket and dropped it onto the sofa. "The place is indicated on the map. If you decide to agree to the swap, be there in six hours' time. The exchange will then be made. *Supreme Brother* grants you safe passage there and back and promises no tricks."

Richard looked at each of them again, then turned to leave.

"Tell me what you've done to Kim!" Margaret hissed.

Richard turned back to face her. "*Nothing* at all. I saw her only a few hours ago and she was fine. Although..." he lapsed into silence.

"Although what?" Margaret demanded, her voice low.

Richard sighed. "Although I can't guarantee that she *won't* be harmed during the next few hours. You see," he explained lightly, "Brother Jerome is looking after her. He *likes* children.

"*Especially* little girls — *if* you follow me...."

Margaret started towards Richard, but John restrained her. She bit her lip as Richard smiled broadly at her, turned, and left the flat. Margaret felt blood trickle into her mouth.

Tony sat and took the grimoire from his pocket, where he had hidden it. Margaret couldn't believe he was as unaffected

283

as he appeared to be.

"Tony, what are you doing?" she asked him.

He glared at her. "The offer is genuine," he said. "He came here to throw us as far off balance as possible: into confusion: except *I* am in full control of my emotions. I have six hours to find something useful in here, otherwise I'm dead."

Margaret and John started at him. "You *can't* be serious, Tony!" John exclaimed.

Tony closed his eyes for a second. "I am. Not that I want to do anything for you — or *her*; I don't," he glanced at Margaret. "I wasn't kidding when I said that I loathe and despise you both. But I have *nothing* against Kim. *She's* got the rest of her life to live. Life is nothing to me. Neither is death."

"I can't let you do it, Tony," Margaret insisted.

Tony actually smiled at her. "You can't do anything to stop me."

Margaret folded Kim's clothes. "They didn't even let her keep her underwear," she whispered, caught between fear and hope, and guilt at the hope which Tony's statement had generated.

"Do you know what you're letting yourself in for?" John demanded. "Torture is the least of it."

"Would you check that map, John, and tell me how long it will take to get to the rendezvous? And by the way, I probably understand what they will do to me far better than you."

"I don't understand you, Tony. You're offering to sacrifice yourself for a girl you've only ever seen once."

Tony looked at him then. "What's that got to do with it? I've made a decision; I find it amusing that you'll both think of me as performing some great sacrifice when I'm not. I'm not doing it for you. It's for *Kim*."

John studied the map. "It should take about forty minutes."

"Then I've got at least four hours to study the grimoire — barring *further* interruptions."

284

His rebuke stung them both. They sat in agitated silence as Tony studied. Although they tried not to, they couldn't stop themselves watching the clock, counting down the time before John and Tony would leave to hand Tony over to the mercy of the Cult. Margaret thought of what Anton Baron had said about mercy being an alien concept to the Supreme Brother.

The hands of the clock moved, it seemed to Margaret, almost as though they were in a race. Only three hours left.

Two hours.

One hour.

"Tony," John said softly, "if you haven't changed your mind, we'd better get moving."

Tony stood, handing the grimoire to John. "No, I haven't," he said. Indicating the grimoire, he added, "I didn't find anything else, but I didn't manage to get *all* the way through it.

"For *Christ's* sake, cheer up. Kim will be safe soon."

John passed the book back to Tony. "It's yours," he said.

Tony laughed with genuine humour. "I doubt it will do me much good now. I'll leave it here. It's not the sort of thing one presents to our Cultist friends."

Tony flashed a quick glance at Margaret. "Let's go," he said to John.

Margaret moved up to Tony. She hugged him tightly. "*Thank you*, Tony," she whispered to him.

Tony broke her embrace. He stared at her for an instant, then turned to leave the flat, and to give himself up to torture and death at the Cult's hands.

Chapter Twelve: *Perversions*

Brother Jerome continued stroking Kim's hair, although he had stopped talking to her over an hour earlier. He stifled a yawn. Kim showed no signs of waking up, but Jerome placed much too much trust in Richard's competence to do anything which might speed her return to wakefulness. And, after all, Jerome had plenty of time ahead of him, alone with Kim.

He turned his head casually as the door to the cave opened and Supreme Brother entered. Normally Jerome would have stood, but Supreme Brother gestured him to relax. Silently, he crossed the room to stand next to Jerome. He looked down at Kim.

"She'll be very pretty when she gets older," he observed, conversationally.

Jerome stared at his leader in some surprise. It was hardly the type of statement which one associated with the Supreme Brother.

"Don't you agree, Jerome?"

Jerome shook his head. "As she gets older, she will lose her innocence. It is that which appeals to me; not physical features."

Supreme Brother smiled: "There is that, of course."

"When you say, 'When she gets older,' does that mean you intend to release her whether our terms are accepted or not?" Jerome enquired informally of his leader.

"No:" Supreme Brother replied slowly, "they will meet our terms. They have little choice. She will not be our guest for long: strange, really. Margaret Brandon apart, she will be our only guest *ever* to leave us with her life."

"With her life, yes," Jerome said slyly.

Supreme Brother frowned at him. "Richard will give the Brandons my word that Kim will be released to them alive."

Jerome understood. When Supreme Brother's word was given — with his permission, for who would dare that without consent? — it could, under no circumstances, be broken. "Richard has already cautioned me not to go too far with her. I will be careful."

"If I did not trust you so implicitly, Jerome, I would forbid you to touch her: as it is, I leave her to your discretion."

Jerome's eyes blazed at this demonstration of Supreme Brother's confidence in him.

Supreme Brother lifted Kim's coat off her. He glanced at her cursorily before lowering her coat, once again, although it didn't cover her body as well as it had formerly. "Richard has told you he wants to take her clothes with him tomorrow?"

Jerome nodded: "They will be ready for him."

"Good. Do you intend to spend all your time here? If so, I will arrange for a Brother to bring you food and drink."

"No need, Supreme Brother; I prefer to attend to that myself."

"As you will, Jerome," Supreme Brother said, leaving the cave.

With extreme gentleness, Jerome smoothed Kim's coat over her, ensuring, as far as possible, that no heat could escape.

He resumed his seat, and continued stroking Kim's hair. He jumped as she moaned suddenly, unexpectedly, and turned onto her side. He readjusted her coat, which no longer covered her back, smiling now. It was the first indication that the anaesthetic was wearing off.

Over the next few hours, Kim appeared more and more restless. Jerome glanced at his watch. It was nine hours since Richard had given his estimate of how long she would be unconscious.

Jerome sighed. Perhaps he was merely becoming tired himself, but time seemed to be dragging. He sat back in his chair, his eyes fixed to a point upon the wall above what served as Kim's bed. It was basically several planks of wood interlocked together and covered with a sheet. It was far from

287

comfortable, and Jerome hoped that this discomfort would help speed her return to wakefulness.

His thoughts drifted over events past and present, to Brothers alive and dead. He smiled as he thought of the original Brother Gregory, and of his meteoric rise from Second to Third Circle, and then to the rank of Brother Fidelis, the Supreme Brother's successor. He hadn't enjoyed his new rank for long, however, and his death had been a particularly horrific one.

Kim dreamed that she must have fallen out of bed and be sleeping upon the floor. It was strange because she couldn't feel the carpet under her hands or face. Her nightie felt strange, too. Unsure now whether she was awake or asleep, she wondered how she had got into bed in the first place. She had been outside playing with Linda.

Kim opened her eyes and abruptly screwed them tightly shut again. What her eyes saw looked like a view from an out-of-control carousel. It made her feel queasy. Slowly, she opened her eyes again. The view tilted alarmingly. She blinked rapidly; her vision slowly settled into focus.

Without moving, attempting to understand what she was seeing, Kim's gaze moved over what she could observe whilst keeping her head still.

The ceiling looked rocky: grey. To one side, she saw a rock wall. Straight ahead was another. No, she suddenly realised, that wasn't right: the wall and ceiling didn't join. It looked like a cave. But that just couldn't be true! How could she have got into a *cave*?

As she wondered about that, she noticed that there was another person here, sitting in a chair next to what she was lying upon. It wasn't a bed. Beds were soft, and warm, and comforting, and cosy. This wasn't. She looked at the chair — a wooden one — and then at the person who occupied it. The man sat motionless, his eyes — Kim couldn't tell what colour they were — seemed to be staring at something above and behind her. She didn't know the man, had never seen him before in her life.

Alarmed, and totally confused, Kim attempted to make sense of the situation in which she found herself. She couldn't. She became aware of her terrible thirst. She looked at the man again, and was even more alarmed to see that he was no longer gazing into the distance. His eyes were locked upon her; watching her.

"Hello, Kim," Jerome smiled.

"Hello," she whispered, frightened. She knew that there were *Bad Men* — and probably *women* too, but not as many of them — who were nice to children at first, so they could get them on their own and then *do nasty things* to them. Kim didn't know or understand exactly what these '*nasty things*' were, and so she feared them. She wondered if this man was one of them, the Bad Men. The thought increased her fears and her heart started racing.

"There's no need to be frightened, or afraid, of me," he said softly, almost as though reading her thoughts.

"Who are you? Where am I? Where's Linda? Where's John and Margaret?" she asked, her shocked thoughts tumbling out in a rush of questions.

Jerome laughed. "Slow down, Kim. My name's Jerome."

"That's a funny name."

He nodded and chuckled, "I suppose it is, really."

Cautiously, Kim sat up. Jerome made no move towards her, and her terror began to ebb. "I'm thirsty."

Jerome left the cave, returning seconds later with a plastic beaker full of water. Kim drank it eagerly. She looked around the cave again. "Where am I?"

Jerome discreetly moved his chair away from her and then sat, knowing from vast experience that by doing such a simple thing, Kim would conclude that she had nothing to fear from him.

Eventually, she would scream the consequences of this misjudgement again and *again*, as he, Jerome, inflicted all kinds of physical pain and sexual tortures upon her.

"I can't tell you that, Kim," he said. "It's a secret."

This puzzled her. "If it's secret, how did I get here?"

"A friend of mine brought you."

Kim frowned. She didn't understand this. "Why?" she asked.

Jerome thought about it. "Do you know what 'kidnap' means, Kim?"

She shook her head. "Not really."

"Well," Jerome explained, "we've kidnapped you. Let me put it like this. John and Margaret have something that we want. We decided to bring you here. We're going to give you back to them, if they give us what we want."

Kim considered this. "Wouldn't it have been better to buy it off them?"

Jerome laughed again. "No, Kim. We couldn't do that."

"So I have to stay here until John and Margaret give you what you want?" Kim asked him.

Jerome beamed at her. "That's it exactly. I'm going to look after you whilst you're here. I hope that you'll be a good girl and do as you're told."

Kim thought about it, her fear suddenly returning. "I'll try; but I won't do anything John and Margaret wouldn't want me to."

Jerome's smile faded slightly.

"Could I phone them to let them know I'm alright?"

"No. The man who brought you here will see them tomorrow; he'll tell them."

In the ensuing silence, Kim sighed heavily. It suddenly occurred to her that she was a prisoner here; that Jerome would not allow her out of the cave. She looked around it again. Jerome sat watching her, but saying nothing.

Kim got bored very quickly. She frowned as another thought crossed her mind. "Jerome," she asked, "what would happen to me if John and Margaret didn't give you what you want?"

"But they will," Jerome assured her.

"But what if they don't?"

Jerome moved closer to her, sat down next to her. He took her hand in his. "Kim, I'm sure John and Margaret care very deeply about you. They'll do anything to get you back. You'll see. Tomorrow you'll be back home." He squeezed her hand *gently* before moving back to his chair.

Jerome smiled inwardly. This was a part of the ritual which he enjoyed: gaining the child's trust. It was a process which he didn't want to rush, yet he had to have Kim's clothes ready for Richard.

Glancing at his watch, he estimated that Richard wouldn't be back until eleven O'clock at the earliest: *lots of time* Jerome thought. Although Kim had been unconscious for several hours, it wasn't that unlikely that the stress of being kidnapped would catch up with her, making her want to sleep. He needed to keep her mind active, but that presented him with a problem.

Kim's fears had died away. They had *not* disappeared; they were still very active subconsciously. Jerome's gentleness towards her, the way he avoided appearing to threaten her in any way had relaxed her, as far as possible in the circumstances.

She attempted to concentrate, to pull into her mind the pictures she sometimes saw, which gave her clues about what the future might hold in store. No matter how hard she tried, she could force nothing to come into focus.

Jerome glanced again at his watch, certain that something was not quite right. It was just an instinct, but it was too vague to define. He felt almost as though he was being scrutinised, although that was plainly impossible. The feeling did not disappear, nor did it grow any stronger. And it was so faint, it made him uneasy for reasons which he could not understand. He glanced at Kim; she was looking curiously at him, almost as though she knew he felt uneasy.

He wondered whether Kim could be causing it, but felt that to be unlikely. She had been living with the Brandons, he thought. Might that have a bearing? — of course not.

Kim was simply another child who would do as she was told — or suffer the consequences. She would probably suffer them anyway; he hadn't quite made up his mind.

Supreme Brother's reminder about his word being given decided Jerome. He would not beat her, break any of her bones, or subject her to anything which could be potentially life-threatening. It meant that his personal enjoyment would be vastly curtailed, but he would still be able to *touch* her, *love* her.

Blinking, he turned his thoughts to the present. Despite his resolve, he still felt peculiar. Perhaps it was fatigue. That would account for his failure to understand the nature of his unease.

He began to feel irritated. Having to check his impulses with regard to a child was a new experience for him. He thought of the pleasure now denied to him by his resolve. His irritation mounted. There was no way he was going to sit there for the rest of the morning doing nothing, he decided. The fact that he had restricted himself as to how he treated Kim fuelled his irritation; although he would *not* allow Kim to know that he was in anything but a good humour.

Kim half-smiled at him. For one brief moment, Jerome thought she understood his quandary and was laughing at him. More rational thought prevented an angry reaction. She was beginning to think that he wouldn't, after all, hurt her; was beginning to trust him.

Abruptly, Jerome decided that there was no reason to waste any more time. As his ritual was not going to achieve its logical conclusion, most of his excitement would be muted anyway. Taking longer to gain her trust was no longer imperative.

"Kim, come here," he said, softly.

Without any hesitation, she got up and moved to his side.

She looked questioningly up at him. "Kim, do you remember, earlier, I said that a friend of mine would be going to see John and Margaret?"

"Yes."

"Well, he wants to take something of yours with him to prove to them that we have you."

"What does he want?" she asked, not comprehending.

"Your clothes," Jerome replied.

Kim thought about that for several seconds. Then she understood. "He can take my cardigan," she offered, innocently.

Jerome shook his head, smiling. "No, Kim, that's not what I meant. He wants to take *all* of your clothes."

Kim's eyes widened. She looked at Jerome in total disbelief. "But...but that's rude," she complained in a voice filled with shock and embarrassment.

Kim didn't fully understand why it was wrong to take off all of her clothes in front of a stranger, but the thought really did make her cringe inside with embarrassment. And Jerome was, after all, a man. Kim knew that John and Margaret would consider doing what Jerome wanted *very* bad. They would punish her for it: they might even send her back to the Orphanage. And if that happened — Kim had never heard of a child who, once returned to the Orphanage after fostering, had *ever* been fostered again, let alone adopted.

But what might Jerome do to her if she said no? He might punish her. Perhaps he was one of the Bad Men, after all. If she said no, she guessed that Jerome would hold her down and take her clothes from her by force — and that he would *enjoy* doing it. He might *want* to have an excuse to hurt her. Kim suddenly realised that she was very afraid of Jerome, and of what he might do.

'*Perhaps*', Kim thought unhappily, '*if she explained to John and Margaret that she only did it because she was suddenly afraid of Jerome, they might* not *send her back to the*

293

Orphanage. They would probably still *punish her,'* she thought, *'but at least they never punished her* more *than she deserved.'*

"He still needs to take all your clothes to John and Margaret, Kim, rude or not. Take *everything* off."

Kim looked at Jerome in total anguish. "Can't I please keep my... my panties? She begged Jerome, much to his satisfaction and arousal.

He shook his head: "Take *all* your clothes off — now!" he insisted.

Kim retreated from Jerome slowly, never taking her eyes from him. She felt her back press against the rocky wall. She made no move to undress, couldn't, wanted time to think. Her fear began to intensify.

And then...

And then...

And then the pictures appeared in Kim's mind. She devoured the details in each set. The first set puzzled her. In the first picture, she did nothing. The next pictures were darker, so she could see no details. The rest were completely black.

The second set had her asking Jerome a question, and then....*there* was the way to gain some time.

Jerome stood and began to advance on her.

"Wait," she called: "do you play chess?"

Jerome stopped dead. "Why on Earth do you want to know that?" he asked.

Desperately, she sought the answer in the picture before it began to fade, as it surely would.

"Because....because I challenge you. Five games of chess. First to three wins."

Jerome was about to shout at her for being so obtuse, but then his curiosity got the better of him. "Why should I play you?"

She pulled the answer from the rapidly-fading picture. "If *I*

294

win, I don't have to take my clothes off." she said.

Jerome frowned. "And if *I* win?" he queried, an interested tone entering his voice.

"Then I'll do whatever you tell me to," Kim explained, *not* comprehending exactly what that meant, or what it could mean, should she lose.

Jerome almost rejected the offer out of hand, but a thought crossed his mind. This might be a big plus to his excitement. It would compensate for some of what he was missing. And, of course, Jerome could *not* be trusted to keep his word.

What Kim *didn't* know was that Jerome, apart from being a computer genius, was a brilliant chess player.

He sat again, and motioned Kim to return to her former position by his side. She did so with considerable reluctance.

"If I accept your challenge, and I win, do you *promise* you'll do *whatever* I tell you to?"

"Yes," Kim promised. "But if *I* win, do *you* promise not to make me take my clothes off?"

"Yes," Jerome replied. "Since we understand each other, I accept your challenge. Obviously, we need a chess set. I have one in my car."

Jerome was absent from the cave for around fifteen minutes. He returned bringing a table with him. He set the chess set and board down. As he turned to leave again, Kim informed him that she needed to use the toilet. He brought her a bucket, and Kim was immensely grateful that he didn't stay in the cave to watch her use it.

Jerome brought in some sandwiches and a pitcher of water. He removed the bucket.

Kim set up the pieces. Jerome returned and sat opposite her. "Help yourself to food," he said, indicating at the same time that she should choose colour. Kim took black.

Jerome used the first game to gain an understanding of the way Kim played. He was glad that he did so. He would otherwise have seriously underestimated her. Inwardly, Jerome expressed his amazement at the competence which Kim exhibited in her play. She had, he noticed, a deep, natural understanding of the way each piece complemented the others. In Jerome's opinion, the greatest of the grandmasters had all had that essential trait; the understanding of how each piece complemented *each* of the others.

Kim won the first game. The second took longer, but Kim won that, too.

"I've only got to win one more," she informed Jerome needlessly.

Jerome smiled to himself. He had, he knew, learned how deep Kim's comprehension of the game was. In time, that understanding would mature. Jerome knew that all he had to do was to play Kim on a deeper level, making his attacks more devious.

The third game was even slower, bogged down with feints, false attacks, and sound defence. Eventually, Jerome won it.

They stopped playing for over a quarter of an hour to give them each a break. Jerome asked Kim when she had become interested in playing chess.

"I don't know," she told him. "For as long as I can remember."

"You're an excellent player," he praised her, taking a sandwich. Jerome hid his smile as Kim looked down at the floor, trying to hide her blush. Even now, when complimented, Kim still felt awkward and self-conscious. Jerome's compliment, she knew, was sincere, but if anything, his praise unnerved her for reasons which she couldn't understand.

In the fourth game, Kim lost her queen early to an unseen move, Jerome castling, thereby calling check and threatening her queen as soon as she moved her king. Kim battled on, but Jerome exploited his superior position ruthlessly, winning the game.

"It's all on this one," he grinned at Kim. She smiled back at him, but felt nervous. She hadn't thought Jerome would be such a good player. She wondered if he had let her win the first two games. She couldn't be sure.

They both played more cautiously in the final game. They scrutinised every possible move before committing themselves. Kim gained an advantage, but then Jerome sprang his trap, into which Kim had fallen.

She knew that Jerome now had the initiative, and was a knight up on her, but the game wasn't over. She changed her tactics to defence, forcing Jerome to attack. Kim played very carefully now, remembering a similar game which she had played against John. The next move would tell.

Jerome moved his hand towards his knight, then pulled it away abruptly. He *stared* at Kim, stunned at what she had so nearly achieved. "An excellent plan," he observed, advancing a pawn, "but you won't get a three-fold repetition stalemate out of me."

Kim believed him. He was just too good a player.

With a sinking heart, Kim played out the rest of the game. Each time she engineered a two-fold repetition, Jerome would advance a pawn, so the stalemate law did not apply.

Jerome exploited his advantage, and Kim eventually conceded that she would be in check-mate in four moves. Then she would have to do whatever Jerome said. Suddenly, she realised that he might tell her to do things that she shouldn't do, or that John and Margaret wouldn't like her doing.

And she would have to do them, because she had *promised*.

And when she got home, she would have to tell John and Margaret about all the wrong and bad things she had done: and *how angry* they would be with her. And perhaps...*perhaps* they would decide that she was so *bad* that she deserved....

"Check-mate," Jerome said, moving his bishop. "I win, three to two." He held out his hand and Kim shook it, the way she had seen professionals do.

Jerome sat back in his chair and smiled at the crestfallen expression upon her face. Jerome almost felt sorry for her.

297

"Don't be too downhearted, Kim," he said. "Many years ago, I was a grandmaster."

"Were you?" Kim asked, awed. It was no wonder that he had beaten her. Challenging a former grandmaster to five games of chess had been utterly idiotic of her. She wondered *why* the pictures had suggested that course of action, and understood that it had been merely to delay the inevitable. Soon he would tell her to undress. And much as she hated the thought, she would have to obey him.

"Yes, I was," Jerome replied to her question. "I don't play as much as I'd like to, these days, but I must admit, I enjoyed your challenge; thank you."

"You still won," she reminded him unhappily, as he began removing all the items he had brought into the cave.

After he had cleared them away, he moved his chair so that he sat facing her. He glanced at his watch, and then put it to his ear to make sure that it was still working. It was one O'clock in the afternoon. It was incredible that five games of chess against a child should take so long.

Richard might turn up at any moment, Jerome knew, expecting to collect Kim's clothes, and Jerome didn't want Richard thinking that he was anything other than ultra-efficient and reliable.

"Kim," he said, "you *promised* me that if I won, you'd do anything that I told you to. Are you going to keep your promise?" he asked her, knowing what her answer would be, but savouring the fact that he was embarrassing her further by making her give it to him.

"I don't want to," she told him, tears in her eyes and in her voice, "but I've *got* to. I promised."

Jerome heard the tears in her voice and smiled inwardly. "Good," he said, now enjoying himself thoroughly. "Take your clothes off — *all* of them."

Kim looked at Jerome unhappily, and then nodded reluctant understanding.

She stood and began to undress, swallowing hard. She didn't look at Jerome as she began undoing her cardigan's buttons; couldn't, and yet she knew that he was watching her *every* movement. Each time she removed a garment, she felt more embarrassed, exposed and vulnerable. She could *feel* Jerome's eyes upon her, and the tears which had flooded her own eyes now began to trickle down her face.

A few minutes later, Jerome retrieved her clothes. "Good girl," he praised her, as he took the bundle of clothes out of the cave.

Kim shivered. She felt cold and very unhappy. If this was just the beginning, what other things would Jerome order her to do? Kim felt forlorn, alone and so very frightened. She'd always believed that once a promise was made, you *must* keep it. But that belief, firm as it was, had placed Kim in this impossible situation.

What if, when Jerome returned, he told her that she must do something even worse than undressing?

She couldn't imagine anything which could be worse than what he had just made her do, but what about the *Bad Men* who did nasty things to children? Surely the *nasty things* were *worse* than being made to take your clothes off?

Kim was attempting to rationalise that conundrum as Jerome returned to the cave carrying a blanket, which he handed to her. "Wrap that around yourself," he told her. "It should keep you warm."

Kim took the blanket quickly; not because it offered warmth, but because it offered protection from Jerome's penetrating *gaze*. Standing in front of him completely bared had made her feel very conscious of herself and of her nudity, and any covering was welcome.

Jerome frowned at her. This indication that Jerome was annoyed with her made Kim's heart pound within her chest. "Little girls who forget their manners may get punished," he warned her coldly. Kim's fears intensified.

"Thank you for the blanket, Jerome," Kim said hurriedly.

He smiled to himself. He had been truly surprised that Kim had kept her promise; had thought that the chess was merely a delaying tactic. Obviously not. Kim took her promises very seriously. Jerome knew that Kim would do whatever he told her to.

The knowledge thrilled him. Once Richard had collected her clothes and left, Jerome decided, he would begin giving Kim more intimate orders. His heart began to beat more quickly in anticipation.

By the time she was returned to the Brandons, there wouldn't be a vestige of innocence left about her, Jerome decided, grinning inwardly.

Kim yawned. She began to feel very tired. She glanced at the wooden planks upon which she had woken. They didn't look at all comfortable. She glanced at Jerome, but he seemed to be lost in his own thoughts. Kim was glad of that, although she didn't understand why.

Soon afterwards, the door opened and Richard entered. Jerome glanced at him and grinned.

"Thanks for having everything ready," Richard said.

"It was my pleasure, Richard."

"I'll bet. Supreme Brother asked me to check her over before I leave: just so I can honestly say she's fine."

Jerome looked at him sharply.

"No reflection upon you. Because Supreme Brother's word is being given..."

"You have to speak the exact truth. I understand."

Richard approached Kim. "Hi, I'm Richard. I just want to make sure you're okay," he said, taking her arm and feeling her wrist for her pulse.

"Are you a doctor?" Kim asked.

Richard nodded, looking into her eyes.

"Are you Jerome's friend who's going to see John and Margaret?"

Richard nodded, "Uh huh."

"Will you tell them that I'm all right?"

"Yes, I'll do that," Richard promised her, smiling. He returned to Jerome.

"What the hell have you been doing to her?" he demanded. "She seems exhausted."

"Would you believe playing chess?"

Richard wondered if this was some kind of joke. However, Jerome's face convinced him. Jerome's sexual orientation was weird, he thought. "Well, I'm afraid she needs sleep, Jerome. I'll give her a mild sedative, help her get some."

"Is that absolutely necessary?" Jerome hissed, visions of not being able to do anything to Kim crossing his mind.

"In my opinion, yes. She'll only sleep a few hours."

Jerome snorted angrily. Finally he sighed, "Do as you think best, Richard."

Richard left the cave, returning with a hypodermic and another blanket. He spread the blanket over the bed, then half-filled the hypodermic. Kim looked at the loaded hypodermic apprehensively. Like most children, she viewed the idea of having a needle — of any kind — pushed into her skin with a distinct lack of enthusiasm. "What's *that*?" she asked, nervously.

"Just something to help you sleep; don't worry, you won't feel a thing," Richard promised, swabbing her arm and administering the injection.

Kim lay upon the bed. Richard adjusted the blanket which she held around her so that it properly covered her.

Kim's vision began to blur. Then she began to feel an immensely pleasant, warm, drowsy sensation filling her body and mind. Moments later, she was asleep.

"You're certain she'll only sleep a few hours?" Jerome demanded.

"Well, maybe four or five. Not much longer."

"But it's possible the swap will take place before it wears off?"

301

"I won't lie to you, Jerome. It's possible, but unlikely."

Jerome accepted this in silence. A moment later Richard left. Jerome continued watching Kim, cursing that his pleasure had been thwarted in this way.

***

Several hours later, Kim awoke, cold and shivering. She must have uncovered herself in her sleep, she thought, pulling the blanket from around her ankles and wrapping it around herself as she sat up.

Jerome was nowhere to be seen.

She rubbed her eyes and yawned. She wished that there was something to do here, to help pass the time. Perhaps, when Jerome came back, they could play some more chess.

Jerome returned at that instant. He grinned when he saw her. Kim didn't like that grin; it reminded her of a wolf's. Jerome's eyes seemed funny too. She began to feel nervous and frightened.

He sat down, still grinning at her. "Kim, come here," he said.

As she began to obey him, he added: "...and leave the blanket there."

Kim's heart started hammering in her chest. She hesitated.

"Have you forgotten your promise already?" he demanded sharply, his eyes glinting strangely.

She shook her head. Biting her lip hard, Kim let go of the blanket, shivering as it fell to the floor. She took a half-step in Jerome's direction....

And then....

And then....

And then the pictures were in her mind again, different to those which she had seen last time. The first picture in the first set showed her dropping the blanket and going to Jerome. She scanned the rest of the pictures in that set and drew in a sudden gasp of *terror*. She saw Jerome seizing her right arm and dragging her to the bed which she had been using, and then

302

doing something really, *really nasty* to her. The next few pictures were even worse; she saw herself screaming in agony as a result of what Jerome was doing to her, and she tore her gaze away from the *nightmare* which those pictures held.

Frantically, Kim focussed on the second set of pictures. As previously, most of them were too dark to see details. Some of them were totally black. Did that mean that she would die? She wondered.

But she simply could not let Jerome do to her those things which she had seen in the other set of pictures.

Whimpering in terror, Kim did what the first picture in the second set showed her. She grabbed the blanket from the floor, covering herself as best she could, and backed away from Jerome.

He stood and slowly approached her, his face grim. Kim's terror intensified. Jerome grabbed the blanket and pulled it roughly away from her. Perhaps it was because she had not bared herself, this time, but had been stripped *violently* by another person, that Kim felt an acute sense of embarrassment, and when she saw the expression upon Jerome's face, she felt *abject* terror.

"*NO!*" Kim screamed, as he grabbed her right arm and began pulling her inexorably towards the bed. Kim struggled against him as hard as she could. The pictures had given her an idea of what Jerome would do to her if he succeeded in dragging her there; and Jerome's strength was immense compared to Kim's. Slowly, pace by reluctant pace, Kim was drawn closer and closer to the bed. Kim realised she would never manage to pull away from Jerome, and so did the only other thing that instinct dictated. She locked her mouth on Jerome's arm, and bit him as hard as she could.

Jerome bellowed in sudden pain, releasing Kim, and rubbing his arm where Kim had bit him. Small spots on his shirt turned red, and Kim realised that she had made him bleed. Relief flooded through her as she ran away from the bed, but Jerome was too quick for her, blocking the path to the

303

door so she could not escape. "You little *bitch*," he hissed at her, his quiet, soft voice now full of dark menace.

Jerome advanced on her quickly, easily recapturing her. He drew back his hand and slapped her face first with his open hand, and then backhanded. The sudden pain shot through Kim's body, and Kim knew that this was just a *tiny* sample of the pain that Jerome would inflict upon her. Refusing to give in, Kim began to struggle again.

Enraged at Kim's continued rebellion, Jerome swung around and gave her another backhanded slap across her face. A little pain might subdue her, he thought, as Kim overbalanced with the force of his blow. As she yelped in pain and struggled to regain her balance, her head struck the wall with a heavy, dull thud.

Kim collapsed to the floor, her head ringing. She rubbed where it hurt. It felt wet. She looked at her hand, and saw the blood. Kim knew it was her blood. She began to feel queasy and sick.

Jerome moved towards her, then stopped. There was something definitely *wrong*. The silence seemed to intensify: the cave became cold. He struggled to comprehend what was happening as the cave disappeared, and was replaced by the main cavern where general meetings of the Brotherhood took place.

They had been relocated, he guessed. Supreme Brother came charging into the cavern, only to stop in disbelief as he took in what was behind Jerome.

Jerome turned and saw two shapes of chaotically swirling colours: the Cult's Patron Demons. And they were plainly furious.

Jerome began to edge away from them. The Demons had not been summoned, so none of the humans were protected from their natural malevolence. The colours swirled dementedly, as the shapes changed to vaguely humanoid. Jerome tore his gaze away. Few could watch the Demons, even though they appeared translucent, without feeling nauseous.

Supreme Brother approached them cautiously, silently interrogating Jerome, who shrugged his total incomprehension.

Supreme Brother could not understand this phenomenon either. It was expressly forbidden, under the Pact, for the Demons to appear in this manner. He began to form a question, mentally, when two shrieking voices sounded in his mind, making him wince.

'*Your life is forfeit, Supreme Brother, since you have seen fit to breach the terms of our Pact.*'

Supreme Brother felt a sudden icy chill flow through him. This was a much more serious matter than he had at first thought. If what the Demons said was true they would be within their rights to kill him. Supreme Brother maintained his composure. '*How have I breached our Pact?*' he demanded, attempting to instil his thoughts with some of the anger he felt at the suggestion.

The Demons detected his anger, and the underlying sense of bafflement on the Supreme Brother's part. At first, they could not understand it. '*You have allowed one of your Brothers to harm a Baron. She is not yet of sufficient age to be legal pray, and therefore cannot be harmed: yet her blood has been spilled.*'

Confusion replaced anger in Supreme Brother's mind. '*But she is* not *a Baron. She is an orphan. Our Curse does not apply to her,*' he thought back to them, already beginning to comprehend and dread the answer.

'*Hear us, Supreme Brother,*' the Demons demanded. There was, of course, no way for him *not* to hear them. '*Your captive is a true Baron. The blood of the Barons flows through her veins. Our Curse* does *apply to her, and her blood has been spilled.*'

Supreme Brother was *devastated*. He closed his eyes briefly, then fixed his gaze upon the Cult's Patrons. Their fury was demonstrated by the terrifying speed with which the colours swirled within vague forms.

Supreme Brother now understood how the Demons could

305

appear in this manner, without being summoned. They had acted quite within the terms of the Pact. He wondered what he should do. This situation was unprecedented. Unless he acted quickly, his life was over.

'*The act was done in ignorance of her parentage. I honour our Pact and have always followed its conditions meticulously.*'

The Demons paused, as though assessing his statement. Supreme Brother felt them delve into his mind: an unpleasant experience, but not nearly as unpleasant as death at the mercy of the Cult's patrons.

Eventually they communicated with him again. '*We believe you, Supreme Brother. Your life is forfeit; yet within our Pact lies the authority to take circumstances into the reckoning. Therefore, your ignorance is spared, this time. Do you understand us?*'

'*Yes,*' Supreme Brother returned, noticing that he was trembling.

'*Very well. To ensure you cause this descendant of the Barons no further harm in breach of our Pact, we will transport her away from this place to another, in your dimension.*'

Supreme Brother could only incline his head.

The swirling, demented colours began to fade, Kim with them. Supreme Brother realised she had been looking at him with undisguised curiosity. He wondered if she had been able to understand what the Demons had decided. Normally, everyone in their presence could understand what they communicated and what others replied mentally to them.

The Demons continued to fade. This was an even bigger — and much more dangerous — fiasco than the disposal of Georgina Thompson's body. Of course, they could not, now, complete the ransom demand. And, he thought bitterly, they couldn't take advantage of Tony Baron's appearance at the rendezvous, because Supreme Brother had given his word that there would be no traps, and no tricks. He swore. The

Brandon's couldn't be aware of Kim's ancestry. Kim was definitely not Margaret's child.

Which left Tony Baron, who had been in hiding for many years. Supreme Brother nodded to himself, disgusted that he hadn't listened to his feelings of manipulation.

The thing which really annoyed him was that it was his mistake. For perhaps the first time during his reign, the Supreme Brother seriously began to doubt himself. Was he becoming old? A liability to the Society? If that were the case, he thought, he should consider nominating a successor. First Margaret Brandon, he thought, motioning Jerome to follow him, then Kim Logan. Why was it that recently, when he thought he had a strangle-hold on the Baron family, events conspired to *cheat* him? There was, surely, more to this than he understood.

Jerome told him everything which had occurred between himself and Kim. Supreme Brother listened, not blaming Jerome for his own ignorance. As Jerome left him, Supreme Brother wondered how they should proceed.

What a shambles. He rubbed his temples to relieve the tension which he felt. He was tired and *longed* for rest. This was, he decided, one of the blackest days ever, in the entire history of the Brotherhood.

***

Kim opened her eyes. She felt dizzy. She sat up, taking in the grass all around her. It seemed to go on as far as she could see.

She shivered, feeling *very* cold. She looked for something which she could use to cover herself, but saw nothing. A distant sound attracted her attention. Looking in that direction, she saw a car, moving from her right to her left.

She didn't understand how she had arrived here; she was *more* than glad that Jerome wasn't in sight. She shivered again. She needed to get help, she knew. Her teeth chattered. She got up slowly and painfully. Her cheeks still stung from Jerome's blows. Her right cheek felt bruised and swollen.

She began to make her way towards where she had seen the car.

Fifteen minutes later, she reached a low stone wall which bordered the road. Very conscious of her lack of clothes, Kim walked alongside the wall, alert for the sound of another car.

But would the people in the car help or hurt her? She bit her lip. After her experience with Jerome, Kim didn't like the idea of trusting strangers.

A car came into view. Kim ducked down, now invisible behind the wall. The car had been driven by a man. Kim hadn't wanted to let the man see her. As the car disappeared, Kim stood and continued walking.

Some twenty minutes later, Kim saw something which made her heart beat faster: a public telephone and call-box.

Kim's first thought was to phone John and Margaret, but she had no money, and didn't know about transfer charge calls. She reached the phone, wondering what to do.

She wasn't sure if this was an emergency or not, but she was too cold and miserable to care whether or not she got told off for it. She lifted the phone and dialled 999.

When asked which service she required, Kim said, "Police," hesitantly.

As she was connected, a man's voice with an unusual accent said, "Police: how may I help you?"

Kim took a deep breath. Her words came out in a rush: "My name's Kim: Kim Logan. I've been kidnapped and I'm cold and I want to go *home*."

As the strangely-accented voice asked her questions, told her to stay inside the call-box, attempted to reassure her that help was on its way, and that she would *soon* be home again, Kim began to cry.

Chapter Thirteen: *Reunions*

John and Tony had barely left the flat when the phone rang. Margaret answered it, her mind occupied by what Tony was doing for them. For Kim, she amended silently.

D. S. Bradley's voice sounded excited. When he told her why he had called, Margaret was certain that she must be hallucinating. She made him repeat himself and then, asking him not to hang up, she ran after John and Tony.

She caught up with them as they were about to get into John's car. Breathlessly, she told them what D. S. Bradley had said. Both of them looked at her in open disbelief. Laughing, crying, Margaret assured them that Kim had been found, that she was safe.

The three of them returned to the flat. John picked up the phone, Margaret hovering anxiously at his shoulder. A few moments later John hung up. He turned to Tony.

"It's true. Kim called the police from somewhere just outside Leeds. The Leeds police are driving her to our local station. They're getting a doctor to examine her, then they'll interview her if she is up to it. Afterwards, we can bring her home." To Margaret he added, "Do you want to go and wait for her, or shall I?"

Margaret shook her head. "I'm shaking too much to be able to drive. Apart from that, police stations make me nervous. I'll stay here. Linda might want something," she added, glancing meaningfully towards Tony.

John understood that Margaret still didn't trust Tony, and was uneasy about allowing him the responsibility of looking after Linda in their absence. Equally, Linda had never met Tony, and it would be something of a shock for her should she wake up to find her parents gone, and her welfare entrusted to someone she had never met before.

"I'll be back as soon as I can," John said, hurriedly kissing her and then leaving.

Left alone with Tony, Margaret thought he might begin to talk to her, given the inexplicable fact of Kim's escape from the Cult, but he didn't seem so inclined. However, Margaret's relief could not be subdued. She sat in a chair, allowing pleasurable sensations to flood through her body. A tingling feeling, which she associated with extreme happiness seemed to course through her limbs and inner being. Tears of joy ran down her face.

Tony sat opposite her, watching these emotions coursing over her face one after another, but moodily eyeing her.

Margaret found his lack of appreciation of the fact that Kim had escaped the Cultists *hugely* irritating. "Aren't you happy that Kim is safe?" she demanded

Tony glared at her without replying. Eventually he retrieved the grimoire and returned to perusing it, completely ignoring Margaret's efforts at conversation, which seemed only to irritate him.

"How did it happen? How did she manage to escape?" Margaret mused aloud for the twentieth time, not really expecting a reply from Tony, but posing the question nevertheless.

Tony sighed a heavy sigh, favouring Margaret with an annoyed glance before continuing to read. In fact, Tony was asking himself much the same question, but from a completely different point of view than Margaret.

For Kim to have escaped from the Cult implied that she was either one of the most powerful occultists ever born, or that the Cult's security measures had failed somewhat spectacularly. Tony didn't for a moment believe either of these scenarios, and found himself completely baffled by the fact of Kim's escape — not that he intended giving Margaret the satisfaction of knowing that Kim's escape had seriously wrong-footed him.

"Do you know if anyone else has ever escaped from them since they re-formed?"

Tony bit his lip angrily. He felt a trace of blood on his

310

tongue. His glare was harsh and unforgiving: "Would it be even *remotely* possible for you to keep quiet?" he snapped at her.

Margaret felt a twinge of anger at him, but her exuberance at Kim's safety refused to allow it to develop. She bit down her urge to talk, and regarded Tony as he read. She wondered how long it would be before John returned with Kim. She smiled at the thought. Her smile disappeared as she thought of Linda. Margaret was still determined to punish Linda thoroughly for her disobedience. But for the hand of Fate intervening, Tony would by now be well on his way to surrender himself to the Cult's representatives, and Margaret knew that had that situation been allowed to come about, no one would ever have seen Tony Baron alive again.

After his part in the near-annihilation of the Cult many years ago, Margaret knew that the Cultists would have ensured that his death was a *particularly* brutal and violent one.

And even though Margaret now loathed Tony and what he had become, she remembered a time when her feelings towards him were very different. Back then he had been so different; how time had warped and changed him from the man she had thought she knew.

And yet, because of Linda's disobedience, Tony's life had almost come to an end. Margaret wasn't sure what she was going to tell Linda about this episode, but somehow she had to impress upon Linda that there could have been serious consequences as the result of her disobedience. That said, Margaret knew she had to avoid punishing Linda for things about which she could have had no understanding.

Linda had been told nothing about the Cult; John and Margaret had, until recently, both believed the Cult destroyed, and the Curse therefore at an end. No reason, then, to frighten Linda with horror stories about fiendish and cruel Cultists.

But Linda's disobedience had resulted, unfortunately, in Kim's abduction. Linda *had* to be told that, although she had surely deduced it for herself. Margaret needed to make Linda

311

understand exactly *why* such disobedience was *always* a bad idea. She *still* hadn't decided upon the severity of Linda's punishment. Perhaps she would ask John's opinions later, when he returned.

Linda needed to...

Her eyes focussed more strongly upon Tony as he stiffened and stopped reading, his gaze now focussed upon infinity. At first she feared that another Cultist was near, but Tony didn't seem at all concerned about that possibility. He seemed fascinated by what he was reading. His gaze returned to the page before him. Margaret didn't interrupt him; knew that if she did he would be angry at her. She remained silent.

Eventually Tony stopped reading. He looked up from the grimoire, staring into space, oblivious of his surroundings. Frowning deeply, he seemed to return to reality, starting nervously. Returning Margaret's gaze he stood and moved to a cabinet at one side of the room. He stared long and hard at the photographs which it contained.

Abruptly, he retrieved the grimoire and headed towards the door. "I've got to go," he mumbled over his shoulder to Margaret, almost as an afterthought.

Margaret didn't reply. She knew that Tony would not hear any response which she might make. Despite the good news about Kim, he seemed to be weighed down by a tremendous burden which, embittered as he was, he would not share. Their problems with the Cult had never before, when she had first known him, seemed to affect him to the same degree; Margaret wondered what could be causing this preoccupation.

She heard the door close and took a deep breath, suddenly feeling free to relax. Tony's presence, she realised, inhibited her in ways which were strange. Perhaps it was his bitterness, his cynicism.

Long ago, it seemed almost as if it might have been in another lifetime, Tony had been so very different. Margaret thought about the way he used to break into a ready smile even when things seemed to be against them. She remembered how he used to be so loving and gentle towards her, at a time when her own emotions were so tangled and confused that she hadn't known how to respond to him.

And when she had finally untangled her own emotions and realised that she loved him, it had been too late. He was already following a guilt-ridden path which, by his own admission, had almost led to his own destruction.

Margaret sighed, understanding that there was nothing to be gained by such reminiscences.

Lighting a cigarette, she wondered again how Kim had managed to escape from the Cult. It was not something easily managed, she knew. Her mind could not understand it. There were simply too many things which she did not know. She glanced at her watch, wondering how long John could possibly have to wait for Kim.

Without her being aware of it, her eyes closed. The emotional stress which she had been under finally took its toll. She began to dream about her tortures at the Cult's hands. They were flogging her again, burning her fingers, restraining her…

She jerked upright with an inarticulate shout. Her cigarette had burned down and was scorching her fingers. Angry with herself, she crushed the cigarette into an ashtray. Taking the hint which her body had given, she lay upon the sofa. Seconds later, she was asleep.

***

Tony returned to the bedsitter which he had rented. He lay upon the floor, his head propped up by his hand. He pulled a notebook close to himself as he read through the final pages of the grimoire. Those pages seemed to be devoted to Anton's understanding of the Cult and its workings; however, it also talked of *other* things…

He began copying the information:

'*It is, therefore, quite obvious,*' he read, reproducing it faithfully in his notebook, '*that in the future, the Brothers will*

313

overwhelm and destroy my family. Those who are yet to be born cannot hope to withstand my eternal enemies. Even I, with my vast knowledge and understanding of the Art comprehend that I do not possess the power to destroy them.

'Yet, I must do all possible to safeguard future generations of my family, until the far-off day when our success may be guaranteed. I, myself, intend to participate in that destruction; however, it would be imprudent to commit the details to paper. I intend that only males of my seed shall read this — yet I may not overlook the possibility of treachery.

'Let me, then, turn to the terms of the Curse upon us. Essentially, it is that we are doomed to death. However, there are certain conditions attached to the Curse which are important.

'First, our eternal enemies must bring about our deaths through the occult arts. Therefore, they may not to resort to direct murder. We need not fear a knife in the back, poisoning, etc. as this would break the terms of the Curse. They must utilise their knowledge upon us, usually on an individual level, and that makes it a slow process.

'Second, they may not harm a female Baron if she is known to be pregnant. This is not a very sure form of protection, but for the term of her pregnancy, the woman is safe. It is of no consequence if she is married or not.

'It occurs to me that if the female heirs of my seed continually claimed pregnancy, our eternal enemies would be confounded until they had concrete proof to the contrary.'

Despite himself, Tony laughed aloud at the idea of the Cult having to prove a Baron's claims to pregnancy to be false. He returned his attention to the grimoire.

'Third, under no circumstances may our eternal enemies harm a child of my seed before it has lived twenty years. Hence, all children are safe from the time of conception until their twenty-first year. It makes sense to me that we should, as far as possible, take advantage of this immunity.'

Tony looked up, thinking intently. He had been very

314

puzzled by Kim's escape from the Cult. People simply didn't escape the Cult in any condition except dead. So how had she managed it?

His eyes caught the passage he had just read. Startled, he began to consider the thought which his mind had generated.

If Kim was of the Baron bloodline, it would, he thought, explain her escape. But how could she be? She wasn't Margaret's child, and that left only him.

Him.

Tony jumped to his feet, his heart thudding. Slowly, blood drained from his face. He thought back to the time when his days had been filled by depression, despair and alcohol. He remembered the prostitute he had visited on numerous occasions — until the night he had been deeply shocked by certain events. He had never given any thought to contraception; couldn't even claim that he had assumed that she would have taken the necessary measures.

He tried to remember her name. Sheila or Sharon; something like that. He remembered her surname easily, since it was the same as Kim's. *Coincidence?* Tony doubted it. Which meant that Kim was his....

Sandra! That was her name. All Tony needed was confirmation of Kim's mother's name and he would be certain.

Although he was certain already.

He lay upon the floor again, considering. A child: *his* child. His *daughter*. Tony banished the thought. He felt no warm glow, no surge of parental affection. He was annoyed at this turn of events. There was no way he wanted the responsibility which a child represented.

He smiled suddenly. John and Margaret wanted that responsibility; they could have it, as far as he was concerned. There was no need to tell anyone what he had deduced, for the time being. After all, *some* secrets were best left undiscovered.

Content with that, he returned his attention once more to the grimoire.

'A question that must be asked is: 'what constitutes harm?'
If one of our enemies were to jump out of hiding and shock a
child, would that be harm? Or if this Brother were to strike the
child, would that be harm?

'The answer is no in each case. There are two criteria by
which such acts may be measured. The first is could the harm
inflicted have been life-threatening? The second, has it caused
blood to be spilled?

'The latter seems easy to apply; although the former seems
vague to the point where nobody understands fully how it may
be applied. So our eternal enemies will not risk attacking
children of my line.

'These constraints apart, it seems to my mind that future
generations will be at a severe disadvantage. I mentioned
earlier that it is my will to be a part of the destruction of my
enemies; yet there is more which I will do.

'I will contrive a short prophecy. Within it, I will generate
an awareness; a life, if you will. The true meaning of this verse
will remain secure and obscure until the time and
circumstances are correct for our enemies' ultimate
destruction.

'Within certain limits, which I will not divulge, it will
nudge events along the course which will lead most quickly to
its fulfilment. It will be a law unto itself, even to the point of
sacrificing some of the Baron line, in order to bring about the
destruction of my eternal enemies. The prophecy will know no
rest until the day of its fulfilment. Then, on that day, it too will
die.

'The future may judge me and my actions as cavalier and
arrogant. I freely admit that they are. I shudder that what I
will do will cause anguish and pain to some of my offspring,
but I justify myself thus: until our eternal enemies are
annihilated, extirpated, none may be truly happy. We are at
war. We fight for our very existence.'

Tony turned the page, not particularly surprised that he had
reached the end of the grimoire. He concentrated, digesting

what the last few paragraphs might mean.

He wondered why Anton had not reproduced the verse in the grimoire; obviously he had not felt it necessary. Tony ran the prophecy as it had originally been presented to him, through his mind.

***

When the flesh of my flesh again be united, then
Shall my kin do battle with my eternal enemies;
The days of the Brotherhood shall at last be
Numbered — my offspring, even though it mean their
Death, shall enable my victory.

***

He thought, then, of John's 'unscrambled' version.

***

When my kin do battle with my eternal enemies
Then shall the flesh of my flesh again be united
Though it mean their death, the days of the
Brotherhood at last shall be numbered — even my
Offspring shall enable my victory.

***

Abruptly, the pieces of the puzzle came together in Tony's mind. As the prophecy was a *living* entity in its own right, it was multifaceted. Hidden meanings and red herrings for those who tried to make sense of it.

Hayter had led the last battle, sacrificing himself to allow Anton Baron to participate in the beginning of the Cult's destruction, uniting the flesh of Anton's Flesh. At that point, the Brotherhood's days became numbered.

Tony referred back to the grimoire, and the answer became plain to him. He closed the book quietly and lay, staring into space, for a long time.

***

D. I. Davies left the interview room. To D. S. Bradley, Kim had insisted that she couldn't remember anything about her ordeal or her abductors. The doctor who had examined her had agreed that her head injury could have induced amnesia.

However, when *he* had spoken to her, she told him *many* things. Before she was half-finished, he wished that she had, truly, lost her memory. Everything she told him agreed with what John Brandon had told him.

When she had finished he asked her many questions, attempting to trip her, so he would know that she had been lying. *'Perhaps Brandon had told her his story at some earlier time,'* he thought.

But Kim *didn't* contradict herself. D. I. Davies knew that she couldn't be telling him the truth.

However, his *gut* told him that she was being perfectly honest with him. It couldn't be true, his mind asserted; but D. I. Davies had learned to trust his instincts.

Confused, baffled, he didn't know *what* to think. He saw John Brandon talking to D. S. Bradley. He turned away. He couldn't face John Brandon at that moment. He needed to do a *lot* of thinking.

Reporting himself feeling very ill, D. I. Davies went home.

***

Margaret woke as John softly touched her shoulder.

"This young lady has missed you," he told her.

Margaret caught sight of Kim.

John grinned as Margaret enveloped Kim in her arms, hugging and kissing her. He left the two of them alone for several minutes.

When he returned, Kim was sitting next to Margaret. Margaret asked about the bandage around Kim's head; she was relieved when he told her that the wound was only superficial. The bruising on her face wasn't serious, and would subside in a couple of days.

Once the initial excitement of Kim's return had receded somewhat, Margaret attempted to steer the conversation around to Kim's ordeal. However, Kim seemed less than inclined to be informative.

318

During a few moments when Kim had gone to the bathroom, John said to Margaret: "She's *not* been sexually assaulted — or physically, apart from the wound on her head, and the bruising."

"Has she told you *anything* about what they did to her? Or how she got away?"

John shook his head. "Give her a chance — she's only been back five minutes."

Margaret suddenly grinned at him, nodding understanding of his point.

Kim returned to the living-room, a resigned expression upon her face.

"*John*," she said quietly, "can I *please* talk to you .... alone?" she asked, glancing apologetically at Margaret, who hid her sudden hurt as well she could.

John took her to the bedroom which she shared with Linda, who lay in bed asleep — still being punished by being confined to bed until Margaret decided upon a suitable punishment for her disobedience — then wondered whether their voices might wake her. He took Kim into his and Margaret's bedroom.

He sat upon the bed and motioned Kim to sit next to him. She did. John slipped his arm comfortingly around her shoulders. But Kim slipped out of his comforting embrace and moved herself a few inches further away from him, attempting to prepare herself for the emotional — and if she was lucky, physical — pain to come after she made her confessions to him. He waited for her to speak, wondering whether she wanted to talk about the Cult, or about something else.

"I've got to tell you some things, John," Kim said tentatively, almost stopping on that single sentence.

John smiled down at her reassuringly as she glanced up at him, almost as though she was trying to gauge his mood. His smile seemed a good sign, she thought, but how quickly would that change when he heard of *all* the bad things she had done, which she shouldn't have done, whilst under Jerome's care?

"I... I did some *very* bad things whilst I was kidnapped," she admitted, her voice so soft that John could only just hear her. "I...I..." she continued, miserably, obviously on the verge of bursting into tears. John completely misunderstood why Kim was so afraid.

"Kim," he interrupted, "you're safe now, and..." His voice trailed off as she looked up at him. She frowned, and John understood that Kim was finding it extremely difficult to talk to him, and that his interruption was only making it more difficult for her. "I'm sorry, Kim. I won't interrupt you again: what d'you want to tell me?" he asked her, gently.

Almost in a whisper, Kim told him about Jerome, his wanting her to take her clothes off; about losing the chess games. She told him that she knew he and Margaret would be furious at her for taking her clothes off: told him that she had *had* to break her promise to Jerome, another Bad Thing. She told him she had been disobedient, had not done as she was told; and about biting Jerome so hard that she had made him bleed, surely a *Very Bad Thing*. She said nothing to qualify her confessions, such as the fear which Jerome had inspired within her, or her knowledge of the perverted things which Jerome *would* have done to her had she not acted as she had.

As she finished speaking, Kim stood nervously. She waited anxiously for John to speak, certain that he would be *furious* with her, that he would shout at her, and then inflict some *severe* punishment upon her. Kim didn't care what he did to her nor *how severely* he did it, so long as he didn't send her back to the Orphanage.

John smiled gently at her, and shook his head ever so slightly. Frowning, feeling utterly confused, Kim wondered why John didn't *seem* angry.

He motioned her to sit again.

Kim remained standing, obviously confused, afraid and unhappy. "But I thought you'd *punish* me. I thought... I *thought* you'd spank me."

John guided Kim back to her former position, sitting next to him. Placing both his hands upon her shoulders, he shook his head. "*No, Kim,*" he attempted to reassure her. However his attempted reassurance only served to confirm Kim's darkest nightmares.

Tears filled her eyes. If John wasn't going to spank her, or punish her in some other way, then surely it meant that she would be sent back to the Orphanage, after all.

Seeing the unshed tears, John *suddenly* understood that there was more to this situation than was at first apparent. Softly, he asked Kim to tell him what it was that was so terrifying her.

As the tears began to roll down her face, Kim haltingly told him of her fears whilst in the Cult's hands. Dominating them, out of all proportion, was her fear of being sent back to the Orphanage as punishment for what she thought of as being deliberately naughty. Her disobedience, lying, not keeping her promises, hurting Jerome, were just the things she was guilty of during her kidnapping ordeal — there were many more things which flashed across her mind: but what she had admitted to was surely *more* than sufficient for John to realise that she didn't deserve to be a part of his and Margaret's family, or to be both sister and friend to Linda.

As she finished, John sighed and *hugged* her tightly. Given her background, it wasn't surprising that Kim should be so intensely anxious and apprehensive. She was so forlorn and insecure and frightened. Tentatively, she put her arms around him, hugging him in return.

Releasing her, John gently and lightly ran his finger down her bruised cheek. "Kim," he said, after a moment's pause, "when you were kidnapped, the *most* important thing was not to do anything which might have made those men hurt you. The normal rules of right and wrong didn't apply any more. If you hadn't done all of those things, they might have seriously harmed you. They might even have killed you.

"What you did wasn't naughty; you did what you had to do

to stop them from seriously hurting you. In that situation, the things that you did weren't bad, and you don't need, or *deserve*, to be punished."

Kim's eyes stared at him in amazed disbelief, as though seeking confirmation of what John had just said to her. Smiling suddenly, she hugged him again, with all her strength. John held her close to him, carefully deciding what else he should say to reassure her.

"I haven't finished, Kim," he said. Kim looked up at him, relaxing her hold only slightly. Seriously, John continued, "I love you, Kim; as much as I love Linda. You're a part of our family, now. When we asked you to come and live with us, we didn't mean just until you were naughty. If you are naughty, you'll be punished appropriately. But," he emphasised the words, "I want you to understand, you are never, *ever*, going to be sent back to the Orphanage. You're *here* to stay."

Kim moved to sit on John's knee. He wrapped his arms around her. He felt her shaking as she cried out her relief. Whilst her head was pressed tightly against his chest, John heard Kim whisper: '*I love you*, John.'

Unsure if he was supposed to have heard her, John simply continued stroking Kim's hair, knowing that she was drawing immense reassurance from his holding her.

Eventually, as Kim's trembling subsided, and she slowly relaxed, he talked softly, comfortingly, to her. Stroking her hair, he murmured: "Would you like to tell Margaret all that you just told me?"

Kim nodded, now in a much happier frame of mind.

Margaret was even more gentle with Kim then John been. She listened to Kim's account without once interrupting. Her hand held Kim's all the while. Throughout her account, Kim's eyes were downcast. Margaret thought about telling Kim something about her own experiences as a 'guest' of the Cult's. Perhaps then, Kim might feel more willing and able to talk freely about her experiences. Margaret remembered well the 'hospitality' the Cultists had given her. Margaret found that

322

she wanted Kim to know a little of her experiences; thought that it might help Kim if she knew that Margaret had been through some of the terrors and humiliations of being held by the Cult.

On impulse, Margaret said softly, "I understand what it must have been like for you, Kim. You see, the *same* men kidnapped me once. And they hurt me very badly."

Kim looked at her, startled. "What did they do to *you*?" she asked breathlessly. "Did they make you take *your* clothes off, too?"

Margaret nodded. "Among other things. They beat me, and used cigarettes to burn me... — you *don't* want to know the details. Perhaps I'll tell you when you're older. What I'm trying to tell you, Kim, is that I know what it must have been like."

Kim bit her lip, wanting to ask Margaret to tell her more, but somehow afraid that she might not like the answers. Shortly afterwards they returned to the living-room.

Later, Margaret insisted on allowing Kim to sleep with them. John felt vaguely uneasy about the idea, but had to admit that it would give Kim a sense of security which she needed.

He woke early in the morning: 3:47 am. He sat up, glancing in the dim light at Margaret. Kim wasn't lying next to her. John wasn't surprised. He got out of bed and made his way to the children's bedroom, putting on his dressing-gown as he went. Linda muttered and turned over as he opened the door. Kim was not there.

John moved quietly to his studio. The door was *ajar*, the light on. He eased the door open slowly, moving into the room until he could observe Kim.

She stood before the portrait of George Hayter. It seemed to John that she was staring at it in rapt attention. He remembered his reaction the last time she had entered his studio.

"Yes, *George*," he heard Kim say quietly, nodding her

head.

John stared at her, and then at the portrait. It moved. John rubbed his eyes in disbelief. He saw the animate portrait of George Hayter: saw the lips moving, although he could hear *no* words.

"I *will*, George," Kim murmured.

The portrait glanced at him. John blinked. When his eyes opened again, Kim had gone, the portrait was merely that, the lights were off, the door closed. John couldn't understand what he had or hadn't seen, whether he had hallucinated or not. He wondered what time it was.

He returned to bed. Kim lay next to Margaret, sleeping peacefully. John sighed as he glanced at the clock. Somehow, he *wasn't* surprised to see that it read 3:47 am. John got back into bed, but sleep did *not* come easily to him. He tried, in vain, to make sense out of the senseless.

Tony did not reappear until late the next day. He looked around nervously. "Have you put the kids to bed?" he asked.

John nodded; Tony sat. Taking a deep breath he asked, "How's Kim?"

"Fine, considering what she's been through. They didn't *really* harm her. D. S. Bradley tried questioning her again, but she insists that she can't remember anything. I know differently. She's very vague on how she escaped. Maybe she *honestly* can't remember."

Tony looked at Margaret, and then back at John. "The grimoire gave me all the answers. Told me how to destroy the Cult once and for all."

"How?" Margaret demanded quickly.

"The answers were there all the time. Anton's prophesy is alive. Not in the normal sense of the word, but it's sentient enough to be able to manipulate events — you, me. Have you done anything unusual recently and then wondered why? Nine times out of ten I'll bet it was the prophesy working through you. Anton ensured that the true solution was only attainable when circumstances were right for the Cult's destruction. They are right now.

"But," Tony cautioned, "you aren't going to like it."

"Go on," John encouraged him.

"We cannot defeat the Cult. They are simply too powerful. Our defeat is a certainty in all-out battle. We must use guile and cunning. We must make them defeat themselves."

John and Margaret glanced at each other. "And *how* do we do that?"

"Anton says that if the Cult breaks the terms of their Pact, by, say, the Supreme Brother *not* electing a successor, the Cult would die. Later, he says that if the Cult breaks the terms of their Curse, their Patron Demons would turn on them.

"So, we have manipulate them into breaking the terms of their Curse."

"How?" Margaret's voice sounded impatient.

"They may *not* harm a Baron who is under twenty years," Tony told her, his eyes locked on hers.

It took several minutes before Margaret fully understood what Tony was suggesting. "You can't mean..." her voice faltered as she comprehended the enormity of what he was saying.

"Yes," he agreed. "You must attack them through Linda. If she is harmed by them, we win."

"And if they kill her?" John protested, aghast.

"I said you wouldn't like it. There are no guarantees. But we can win. It's not certain, but nothing ever is. If you are willing to do it, I'll create a diversion by attacking them from another place simultaneously."

Margaret shook her head. "It's Linda's *life* you're talking about so casually. She doesn't even *know* about the Cult."

Tony shrugged. "So? We destroy them or they destroy us — or you, at least. This is what everything has been leading up to; the last chapter in the saga."

"We can't risk it," Margaret insisted.

325

Tony bit his lip.

Abruptly, John said, "I don't know, Margaret. If we *don't* take the risk, Linda will have to go through the greater part of her life looking over her shoulder. I think George would want us to try."

"Don't use George to...to *blackmail* me," Margaret snapped back at him. "You don't know what he would have wanted."

The room became very still; tranquil almost. Margaret and Tony glanced at each other in surprise.

The door to the living-room opened and Kim entered. She glanced around the room, her gaze resting briefly upon each of them. Her eyes seemed distant, somehow abstracted.

Each of them understood, once the gaze had met their own, that although it was Kim who stood in front of them, the personality behind that gaze was *not* Kim's.

Kim moved to stand in front of Margaret. When she spoke Margaret drew in a sharp breath. The voice she heard belonged to George Hayter. "You never could listen to sense, Margaret," Hayter's voice snapped at her. "When I told you it could be dangerous outside my mansion you took the first opportunity that presented itself to put my words to the test. *Listen to Tony.* Do as he tells you."

"*George*?" Margaret whispered, incredulously.

"*Do as Tony says.* You must destroy them. Succeed where I failed. I *cannot* aid you."

"But, George, Linda might be killed."

"Margaret," Hayter's voice sharpened irritably, a typical Hayter reaction. "If you *don't* do as I say, Linda will grow up to regret it. I *dare* say no more. *Do as Tony says.*"

Margaret opened her mouth to reply, but found no words would come. Margaret noticed Kim's eyes slowly becoming less and less abstracted, until they had returned to normal.

"Kim?" John asked.

"George is *angry* at you, Margaret," she said. "And he told me that I've *got to go* with Tony and to do what he tells me to."

Into the silence which followed Kim's statement, Tony asked: "Well?"

"I don't know," Margaret replied with deep anguish. "George was never one for explaining himself — I just don't know."

"He said Linda will regret it if we do nothing," John observed. "I think that we'll regret it, too."

Margaret stood and left the room. John followed her. Tony glanced at Kim. If she was confused by these events she didn't let it show. She sat next to him.

Shortly afterwards, Margaret and John returned. At Tony's questioning glance, Margaret nodded. "What do we do?"

"The Cult will meet early tomorrow. You launch an attack using Linda as a channel. At the same time, from a different location, I'll attack as well. The Cult will defend itself before they realise what is happening. Can you manage to attack if I give you the location of the meeting?"

Margaret considered: "Yes," she said, finally. "But *why* does Kim have to go with *you*?"

"Probably so she'll be safe. One less thing to distract you," Tony replied smoothly.

Margaret didn't look convinced.

"We attack at four-thirty exactly." He took a map from his pocket: "This is where they will meet. There's a photograph, if that will help you visualise the place."

Margaret shook her head. "I'll manage," she told him.

"Is there anything else you want to know before I leave?" he asked.

"Yes," John cut in. "Are you certain that this will work?"

"I hope so," he replied, nervously. He looked at Kim. "You go and get dressed, and then we'll go for a ride."

Kim returned his glance gravely before leaving the room.

"How do you know so much about the Cult?" Margaret

327

asked.

Tony *glanced* at Margaret, and then turned contemptuously away from her. John took a deep breath and then repeated Margaret's question.

Addressing himself to John, Tony actually grinned. "I had many years to track them, and I was *very* careful. They are in confusion at the moment over Kim's escape. That's in our favour. If all goes well, I'll be back at around seven O'clock."

"Good luck, Tony," John said as Kim reappeared and Tony stood.

"I don't need it. I *know* we're doing the right thing."

Letting Kim precede him, Tony left the flat.

Chapter Fourteen: *Possessions*

Neither Tony nor Kim spoke as he drove. Tony was surprised that *he* had made a point of pairing him with Kim, although that surprise was short-lived. He had deduced almost immediately what he was supposed to do. He glanced at Kim, who was staring through the window. He felt uncomfortable that, despite his earlier resolution, when he had concluded that Kim was his daughter, he had been forced into a situation where he was responsible for her welfare. It made him feel mildly uneasy that John and Margaret had trusted him to the point of allowing Kim into his protection.

Although he hated them passionately, he took his new-found responsibility remarkably seriously. He glanced at Kim again. She caught his glance and smiled at him. Tony's heart thudded suddenly. Kim was his daughter.

His child. He felt his heart swell in pride as he thought of her bravery, her abilities....

He gripped the steering-wheel more tightly, at the same time clamping down on the sudden surge of warmth which coursed through him.

He parked the car. As they walked towards his bedsitter, Kim slipped her hand into his. Tony began to pull his hand away, but Kim's small palm felt so right there. Forcing a smile through his confusion, he squeezed her hand.

Inside the bedsitter, Kim looked around with undisguised curiosity. "Haven't you got any chairs or furniture?" she asked, obviously surprised at the room's starkness.

Tony glanced around the bare room, perhaps for the first time taking in its emptiness. "No," he replied, "I don't need things like that."

Accepting his answer, Kim sat upon the floor. Tony sat next to her. How could he explain what he had to do in terms simple enough for her to understand?

"Kim," he tried, "do you know why I've brought you

here?"

"Oh, yes," she replied simply. Seeing his smile of relief, she added: "Because *George* said to."

Tony's smile disappeared and he shook his head. He tried to think of what to say to her. "Do you know what I'm going to do?" he asked.

"Not really. Are you going to tell me?" Kim asked him, inquisitively.

Tony nodded, suddenly feeling exasperated. "Kim, the people who kidnapped you have done similar things before. They've been trying to kill us: me, Margaret, and John, for a long time. In fact," Tony found himself saying before he fully realised it, "In fact, they killed my parents several years ago," Tony admitted to Kim, remembering suddenly the pain of loss.

Kim's mouth dropped open in shock at this admission. She moved over to Tony and hugged him. "That's so sad, Tony," Kim averred softly. After a moment's thought she added: "But at least you knew your parents; you remember them. They cared for you and they loved you.

"My mother died when I was born," Kim continued, softly, sadly. "No one knows who my father was. If he knew about me, I don't think he can have loved me," she said, suddenly looking into Tony's eyes. "I'm sure that he didn't want me," she added pathetically, her expression becoming sad and forlorn. "Sometimes, Tony," Kim continued, "I wonder if I did something to make him *hate* me."

Tony glanced quickly down at Kim, stung by her words, and the sad expression upon her face. "I'm sure that your father doesn't hate you," he tried to reassure her.

"Then why would he be happy to leave me in the Orphanage? No one loved me there," Kim answered him with simple, inescapable logic. "Why would any parent leave their child all alone there, Tony? Unless they hated her — hated *me*," she amended guiltily.

"Perhaps he didn't know you'd been born," Tony

suggested, more truthfully than Kim could ever have realised.

"My mother was...." Kim began, and then faltered.

"Was what, Kim?" Tony asked, without thinking, struggling with this entire conversation.

"She was a prostitute," Kim whispered softly, tearfully. "She'd go with anyone as long as he could pay her."

Tony was shocked that Kim knew this. He wondered angrily how she had ever managed to find out this piece of information.

"You know, Tony," Kim continued," if she hadn't died, I'd have been taken away from her, so I'd still have ended up in the Orphanage, and no one loved me, there."

Kim began to cry softly.

Tony turned his face away from her. For a moment, he struggled to keep his composure. "Kim, we should talk about this another time," Tony insisted, turning back to face Kim and hugging her tightly. "Right now, we have serious things to prepare for," Tony insisted.

Kim looked up at Tony, wiping her tears from her cheeks. She remembered that *George* had said she must do whatever Tony told her.

"As I was saying, Kim, the people who kidnapped you have hurt and killed hundreds - maybe thousands of people over the years. More recently, they have tried to hurt Margaret and me and John, and of course they kidnapped you. These people are *unusual*, Kim. They have some... *powers*... that are very strange. They can do things that other people can't."

"Like when I see the pictures and know things before they happen?"

"Yes," Tony agreed, "things like that. Except they use their powers to hurt people. But Margaret and I have the same kind of abilities. We're both going to try and fight back against these people. Margaret's going to need Linda's help, and I'm going to need yours. Kim, will you help me?"

Kim thought about it for a moment: "What do I have to

331

do?" she asked slowly. "I don't have to take my clothes off again, do I?" she asked, nervously.

Tony laughed, despite his own nervousness. "No; nothing like that. All you have to do is to relax, and let me in there," he said, tapping her head gently.

"Like *George* does, sometimes?" Kim asked him.

Tony clenched his teeth. He had forgotten about that. He needn't have attempted such a difficult simplification of circumstance. "Yes, similar. And after I've attacked those men, you'll hardly know I was inside your mind at all."

Kim frowned at him. "You won't *hurt* me, will you?" she asked, timidly.

"No, Kim. I'd never hurt you — I'll do everything I can to protect you," Tony assured her, realising suddenly just how absolute his conviction was on that issue. "But you must understand that attacking these people is a very dangerous thing to do. They'll try and fight back."

Kim bit her lip. "It's going to be the same for Linda, isn't it?" she asked, suddenly displaying a shrewd grasp of the situation, which amazed Tony.

He shook his head: "No; it'll be more frightening for Linda because she doesn't know anything about this; these powers, these people, why we are fighting them. I don't think that Margaret will find it an easy thing to explain, either."

Kim remembered waking up after Richard had injected her to make her sleep. She remembered when the pictures had appeared for the second time. She remembered looking at them, and seeing the things that Jerome had *wanted* to do to her. The memory made her feel both terrified and angry. She wanted to fight back, too.

"Yes, Tony, I'll help you," she said.

Tony smiled at her. "Thank you, Kim. I couldn't do this without you."

He kissed her forehead softly. He had not doubted that she would come to this decision. After all, she *was* his daughter.

332

***

The Supreme Brother paced from one side of his chamber to the other. His body radiated naked fury. Even Richard — were he still in Britain — or Jerome would have hesitated to intrude upon their leader in his present mood

Richard had, before the whole assembly, received his reward for the capture of Kim Logan, and had, immediately afterwards, left for America on a somewhat delicate mission.

But neither Richard, nor Jerome, would have been able to remember the last time that their leader had been so dangerously angry. Several Brothers were already suffering the effects of irritating him. Sister Margaret understood beyond all doubt — had their ever been any — that she meant nothing to the Supreme Brother. Her innocent interruption had been greeted with a roar of insane wrath and a violent assault at Supreme Brother's hands. He drove her from his presence and continued his pacing and his frenetic thoughts.

The fiasco of Kim Logan's escape had, he knew, undermined his position within the society. The irony of the Patron Demons working against him had not been lost upon the Brotherhood. Some felt — although it would have been at least imprudent to voice the suggestion — that it sent clear signals regarding Supreme Brother's competence.

He could not resign his position: *death* was the only acceptable form of resignation.

Supreme Brother continued his menacing paces. He was confused as never before. On other occasions he had little difficulty in seeing the way forward. However at present his mind was divided, one part urging him to admit that he had lost his touch, had become a serious liability to his Brothers. Another part of his mind wrestled with recent events, rationalising them, assuring him that there were forces at work of which he had no knowledge.

He had acted as logic dictated, that part of his mind asserted, taking into account all the information which he had available. Analysing events again, the Supreme Brother knew

333

that he could have acted in no other way.

Nor could he fault Jerome. Any of them might have struck Kim had she proved recalcitrant. Any of them might have spilled her blood. And, it seemed, *neither* the Brandons nor Tony Baron had known that she was of the Baron line.

Had he known, Supreme Brother was certain he would have been able to utilise the information. Now, surely, the Cult's enemies would *deduce* how Kim had escaped. The act was so unusual that it would fascinate them until they did understand it.

Furious, he thought upon the many instances when he felt that he, and in effect the Brotherhood, was being manipulated and toyed with. Automatically, Supreme Brother thought of Margaret's escape, comparing it to Kim's and pulled out of the comparison some interesting — and disturbing — thoughts.

Given the circuitous route of the Baron line, Supreme Brother had questioned the coincidence of the last of the American Barons — as Margaret had then been — having, with no knowledge of her ancestry, allied herself with Hayter and Baron.

He had felt that it was too far-fetched to be coincidence: and now, the Brandons had fostered an 'orphan' who just happened to be Tony Baron's daughter?

The bounds of credulity was surely being stretched too far. One such occurrence he could — but only just — rationalise as the whim of fate; but two such occurrences?

The Supreme Brother sat, his pent-up energy radiating from him as though he might suddenly explode into action.

Each time, events had conspired to the detriment of the Society, almost as though... He cursed aloud as the thought entered his mind. Almost as though that were the object of the exercise. And only one person could conceivably be behind it: *Anton Baron*.

Supreme Brother thought about the near annihilation of his Society. What had Anton Baron boasted? '*Your failure to*

334

suspect my intentions, to allow them to come to fruition, demonstrates my brilliance and your *ineptitude.'*

Yet Anton Baron had failed to destroy them. Had he miscalculated? That made no sense — not for a master occultist, as he had been. Which meant that Anton knew he would not be successful at that time. So why expose himself to his enemies?

Supreme Brother cursed again. The answer was absurdly simple. To make the Society, — him, the Supreme Brother, — certain that Anton had failed; to make the Supreme Brother believe that he had nothing more to fear from him. And that had made him centre his attention upon the survivors of the battle who were of the Baron bloodline. It had made him ignore his feelings of manipulation.

He sat bolt upright, his fury redoubled as a part of the jigsaw fell into place. Anton Baron had gambled that Supreme Brother would not consider such a simple solution. He had out-bluffed the Supreme Brother — something not easily achieved.

Somehow, he had set forces in motion to pervert events towards an obvious conclusion; the destruction of the Society.

Considered in this light, Margaret's escape and the fact of Kim's parentage made sense. On each occasion, he had felt that sense of not being in control, which must have meant the forces which Anton had set at work were actively slanting events in the Barons' favour.

Further, that must mean...

A hesitant movement caught his eye; his train of thought fled. Supreme Brother focussed upon Sister Margaret. She regarded him fearfully. When he said nothing, she moved cautiously forward, one hand pressed to her body just below her breast.

Supreme Brother assessed the damage he had earlier done to her. One eye swollen and virtually closed, numerous bruises upon her arms and legs. Perhaps a couple of cracked ribs. At least, he thought, it was a useful reminder to her of her actual

335

standing within the Society.

In a quiet, subdued voice, she informed him that the Brothers and Sisters had begun to arrive for the scheduled meeting. Supreme Brother nodded, told her to ask Jerome to join him, then waved his hand dismissively at her.

As she left, Supreme Brother attempted to regain his train of thought.

If events were being affected, it implied that Kim's capture and escape took on a new — and very serious — significance. But what might that be? As the answer came to him Supreme Brother began pacing again. Obvious: it was an attempt to destroy the Society by destroying him, the Supreme Brother. And it had almost succeeded.

Biting his lip, he realised exactly how close the Barons had come to assassinating him and destroying the whole Brotherhood. The cunning with which Anton Baron had laid his plans staggered Supreme Brother's imagination.

He whirled around angrily as he heard footsteps. Brother Jerome met his gaze, not seeming in the least intimidated. He sat.

Supreme Brother continued pacing for several minutes before sitting opposite Jerome. He asked only that Jerome listen, and then outlined the deductions which he had made.

Supreme Brother noticed Jerome's eyes darkening in anger as he, too appreciated the danger which this insidious plot represented. As Supreme Brother finished speaking, Jerome frowned, thinking deeply. Eventually he asked if Supreme Brother had thought of a way to neutralise the danger.

Standing, pacing again, Supreme Brother shook his head, qualifying the negative by saying that before those forces of Anton Baron's could be neutralised, they had to be comprehended. He was certain, he assured Jerome, that the Brandons did not understand them; however he could not be sure about Tony Baron.

Elaborating, he told Jerome that if Baron didn't understand

these forces which his ancestor had brought into play, then that information would be almost impossible to uncover.

Yet, if Tony Baron did have an understanding of them, would he break under torture and give them that information? Supreme Brother wasn't sure that he would.

Jerome retaliated that nobody — not even Margaret Brandon — had ever withstood the Cult's methods of persuasion.

Managing an icy smile, Supreme Brother nodded, pointing out that the only difficulty lay in capturing Baron. His smile faded as Jerome's expression soured. They had always planned such actions carefully beforehand, he emphasised, especially in the light of Supreme Brother's deductions.

Supreme Brother's face wore a calculating expression. "No, Jerome," he snapped. "If my instincts still serve me, the more we plan, the more time we give Anton Baron's forces to manipulate events. In the past, that has been our undoing. Whatever power Anton Baron has unleashed must require time to calculate the probable effects of a specific action through time. I become convinced that acting quickly will circumvent Anton Baron's machinations."

Jerome thought for long moments. At last he asked Supreme Brother whether he had considered that Anton's forces might exist with the ability to suspend time. If that was so, he argued, then those powers would seem to act instantaneously, whether they planned their actions to the minutest detail or not.

Supreme Brother excepted the validity of Jerome's point. However, he countered by insisting that the only way to find out which of them was correct was by attempting a sudden strike at Tony Baron, at all times being alert for any feelings or sensations of unease or manipulation.

"It is a dangerous and bold course you propose, Supreme Brother."

Supreme Brother nodded. "True: but to do nothing might be even more dangerous to us."

337

Thoughtfully, Jerome agreed.

***

Alone once more, Supreme Brother pondered his resolution. Could this be another of Anton Baron's manipulations? He dared not allow his thoughts to run along those lines, or he would never be able to take any decision without wondering if it was, truly, his own.

He grinned mirthlessly.

He attempted to understand what his enemies might try next. The Brandons he dismissed easily. They would be too relieved at Kim's escape to think of attempting anything against the Cult.

Tony Baron, however, was more of an unknown quantity, having re-emerged only recently. In that respect, he was similar to Hayter. Supreme Brother frowned at a sense of déjà vu. That being so, Tony Baron presented more of a threat, at the present, than the Brandons.

Supreme Brother's icy grin stretched wider. This could be the turning-point; the key which he had laboured long years to locate and possess.

Sister Margaret entered cautiously. Only when Supreme Brother nodded permission did she speak. "Supreme Brother, all are assembled."

"Very well."

***

As his gaze travelled around the assembly, Supreme Brother wondered at, and understood exactly, how deeply Kim's escape had affected his followers. He could not allow this situation to go unchecked. It severely weakened the Cult.

"Brothers, Sisters," he grated in his rasping tone, "you may have heard of Kim Logan's escape, aided by our Patrons. Some of you feel that I am responsible, that I am no longer capable of executing the duties of my position. Let any who so think speak now."

Again his gaze swept around the assembly. No one hurried

to take up his invitation.

"Good: any of you who wishes to challenge my position may do so — but I warn you not to expect me to show mercy.

"It is true that Kim Logan has escaped, and that our Patrons aided her." His voice building in volume, he continued: "But that was done to protect us all. Kim Logan is of the Baron bloodline — something of which none of us were aware."

He allowed the information time to sink in, noting a subtle shift in the atmosphere. Gauging his timing perfectly, he resumed, "This was an attack upon us by *Anton Baron*, who hoped we would be fooled into forcing our Patrons to destroy us.

"Brothers, I am not such a fool. That is why I agreed with our Patrons' plan to aid Kim Logan's escape."

The assembly attended to Supreme Brother's every word. Spontaneously, Brothers rose to their feet, cheering their leader, who smiled his frigid smile.

"Brothers, you exhilarate me," he protested, allowing none of that emotion to enter his voice.

As the ovation died down, Supreme Brother knew he had recovered their confidence. As he called upon a Third Circle Brother to make his report, Supreme Brother reflected that he had never been in any doubt regarding his position.

***

Tony took a deep breath. He couldn't understand why he was doing this. Not after the pains to which he had gone to ensure that John and Margaret knew he wouldn't help, nor shed a tear at their defeat.

It made no sense to him.

That *George* had ordered it put the whole thing into a different perspective — even though Tony had decided upon this course before that intervention.

His mind suggested that he was doing it for the love of his daughter. Tony dismissed the idea, amused by it. He cared for nothing and for nobody.

He glanced at his watch, and then at Kim. She lay upon the floor, one arm crooked under her head as a pillow. Tony wasn't sure whether or not she was asleep.

He called her name softly. Her eyes opened. Yawning, she sat up and regarded him. She asked if it was time yet.

Tony nodded, moving to sit in front of her. He asked if she was frightened. Kim half-smiled and shook her head.

"What do you want me to do, Tony?" she asked.

"Just close your eyes, relax and listen to my voice," Tony said gently.

Kim did as he said. She listened to Tony's voice, and at his gentle insistence, she began to feel pleasantly drowsy, and then gradually she drifted deeper and deeper into relaxation. She was vaguely aware that Tony had moved and now sat behind her. From a vast distance she felt his hands lightly touch her shoulders, his thumbs resting gently against the upper vertebrae of her neck.

Almost immediately she began to feel Tony's presence in her mind. Mentally, she pulled herself away from his awareness. Calmly, she understood that, although Tony had said he wouldn't hurt her, he could do so accidentally. He didn't seem to know how to be gentle, like *George*; perhaps he just wasn't used to it.

Confined deep within her own consciousness, deeply relaxed, as though another mind interloping was an everyday occurrence, Kim gave the equivalent of a smile. It wouldn't last very long. Becoming curious, she focussed upon what Tony's mind was doing.

Tony marvelled at how *easy* the whole operation had been. Kim had responded superbly to his hypnotic suggestion. Sitting behind her, he placed his hands upon her shoulders. Regulating his breathing, Tony visualised his body, Kim, his arms, Kim, his hands, Kim. As carefully as he could, he began forcing his awareness, his consciousness, into Kim's body. He became aware of her mind retreating from his. As his consciousness completed its transition from his body to Kim's,

340

Tony realised with some surprise — and a little embarrassment — that he had access to all of Kim's memories. He scanned her recollection of her time with the Cult without fully realising that he was trespassing, that these memories were private and not his to sift through.

It took an effort to wrench his mind away from Kim's memories, partly because they fascinated him, partly because under the peculiar circumstances it was difficult not to share her memories.

Cautiously, he opened his eyes — *Kim's* eyes. It was eerie to feel the sensations of a ten-year-old child. Turning around slowly, he viewed his own body through Kim's eyes. He checked the pulse; slow and regular.

It occurred to Tony just how vulnerable his body was now. If it was to die, he would be trapped within Kim's body. As he glanced at Kim's skirt, the thought made him laugh. A transsexual paradise. He chuckled and started at the girlish giggle which resulted.

He retrieved his watch and fastened it upon Kim's wrist. A quarter of an hour before the agreed time. Absently, he began perusing Kim's memories again, whilst a more active part of his mind formulated plans, revised methods of attack and defence.

Tony began feeling uneasy. He concentrated, visualising the Brandons' flat. Moments later, he could see into it, into the studio. Margaret's body lay upon a camp bed. Linda sat upon a chair next to it. '*Typical*', he thought, '*that that* bitch *would think of erecting a bed so that her body didn't suffer* any *discomfort*'.

Linda's head swivelled in his direction. She almost seemed to see him, although Tony doubted that she actually did.

"We're ready, Tony," Linda whispered.

Tony opened his eyes — *Kim's* eyes — again. He glanced around, and then at his watch. Another seven minutes to go.

'*Tony*?' Kim's mind enquired, '*Why do you think*

Margaret's a bitch?'

Alarmed, perplexed, he returned, "It's a long story. Please, Kim, don't interrupted me again." Guardedly, he understood that he would have to temper his thoughts somewhat.

He considered checking the location of the Cultists' meeting, but feared he might give prior warning of what was planned, or alert them in some other way. He thought — briefly — of the last time he had attacked the Cult. The circumstances had been vastly different, yet the ultimate aim the same. He couldn't remember if he had felt more nervous, that time.

He checked the time again and grinned.

Sixty seconds.

He began to visualise the meeting-place.

Thirty seconds.

Tony concentrated, drawing in every scrap of his will to instil his attack with the maximum *venom* and *ferocity*.

Ten seconds.

Concentrating so intently, his feelings of nervousness had gone. Every emotion which might have been a distraction ruthlessly shut away from his awareness. He was filled with a sudden burning, all-consuming desire to strike a blow against the Cult for all they had done to him, for what they had made of him, for what they had forced him to become. His self-loathing suddenly erupted into his consciousness, feeding his anger and thirst for vengeance — not just for himself, but to atone in some measure for his failure of Hayter.

With a crashing, splintering roar, the door to the bedsitter burst open. The sudden noise shattered Tony's preparations. Starting he gazed in the door's direction. A man stood there. Drawing upon Kim's memories, Tony recognised Brother Jerome. Quickly, Tony calculated: he understood, a fraction later, that by the time he managed to transfer his consciousness back into his own body he might well find that Jerome had destroyed it, trapping him in Kim's mind. Rooted to the spot,

Tony could feel Kim's heart hammering. Her mind squealed and screamed in *terror* at the appearance of Brother Jerome. Kim's memories of her time spent as Jerome's guest flashed through Tony's mind. He felt the horror, terror, helplessness, despair, embarrassment, degradation and humiliation which Kim had felt at various points of the time she had been forced to stay with Jerome. He felt her emotions keenly as he learned how she had had to submit to the depravities which Jerome's warped and perverted mind had decreed for her.

These experiences, these *emotions*, hit Tony's mind like a battering-ram, and made him more aware than anyone else could be, of the intensity, savagery, and *depravities* to which Kim had been exposed.

Realising that he must impose order on his chaotically whirling thoughts, lest Jerome kill his body, and trap his consciousness inside Kim's mind for the rest of her life, Tony purged his mind of the confusion, anxiety, anger and rage which exposure to the full horror of what Kim had been forced to endure generated within his whole mind: Tony struggled to contain the panic which he felt.

***

Margaret visualised the Cult's meeting-place. Allowing her emotions no opportunity to express themselves, lest they distract her, she superimposed upon the picture an intense wave of energy flowing rapidly from her to the Cult, to the Supreme Brother.

Almost instantly she felt, as she had many years before, her intangible will coalesce, felt the wave of energy discharge through her, and thus through Linda, speeding unerringly to its destination.

She spared no time to assess what damage, if any, she had achieved; she expected the Cult's retaliation almost immediately. Linda's body was not protected from the Cult's response. Margaret was ready to shield Linda at a second's notice.

Rather than try to explain everything about the Cult, their

343

Curse, Anton Baron, and all the rest to Linda, Margaret had taken the somewhat easier option of hypnotising her daughter before very gently easing her consciousness into Linda's mind. Although deeply hypnotised, and in a *very* deep sleep, her subconscious mind was still alert, and taking account of what was happening. Whether any of these subconscious memories would ever surface in Linda's mind, Margaret didn't know, and prayed that they *never* would.

She bombarded the Cult with salvo after salvo of intense energy, attempting to instil each assault with barbaric viciousness.

After several minutes Margaret paused, suddenly confused. Not only had the Cult not responded, but Tony, who had said he would create a diversion, had done nothing.

Panting, sweat running down her face, Margaret's anger erupted at Tony. No doubt he had had second thoughts, and decided that he didn't, after all, want to face the Cult in all-out combat. In that case, what had he done with Kim?

Margaret realised that Tony had tricked her into launching this attack, and had left her alone. Damn him to hell. She had felt so certain that he had meant to do as he had promised.

Gritting her teeth, Margaret returned her concentration to the meeting-place and renewed her bombardment with an intensity which stunned her, born of desperation and fear, and utter fury at Tony.

***

Supreme Brother nodded as Brother John completed his report. He enquired if any other had matters to report, and sat as a Brother rose and began talking about the problems inherent in smuggling arms into Britain.

Supreme Brother's mind wandered uncharacteristically. He could always have the report reiterated in private. He wondered whether Jerome had reached Tony Baron yet. He had become somewhat lax about keeping his location secret, over the last few days.

344

If Jerome succeeded, Supreme Brother knew that, once more, he would gain an advantage over his enemies the Barons. Jerome must succeed. He had *never* failed Supreme Brother in all their years of association.

The Brother concluded his report. Supreme Brother nodded and stood once more. He opened his mouth to call upon the next Brother.

An eruption of savage, raw energy struck him. Supreme Brother's face registered his amazement as he overbalanced backwards under this onslaught.

Several of the Brothers vaulted onto the dais to assist him, although he was already getting to his feet. Supreme Brother swept his gaze rapidly around the assembled Brothers, all now standing. Supreme Brother's face went white. One of the Brothers swatted his ceremonial robes, which had begun to smoulder.

Regaining his wits, Supreme Brother shouted, "BROTHERS, neutralise or deflect any further attacks upon us: NOW," he yelled, as a second pulse of energy slammed into him. It has less effect since he had had time to prepare for it.

Quickly, but not as quickly as he would have liked, the Brothers began to do their leader's bidding. Slowly, painfully, gritting his teeth, Supreme Brother regained his chair and sat heavily.

His body burned and smarted. Angrily, he blocked the pain from his mind, analysing the source of the attack, although he already knew what he would discover.

Margaret Brandon: the *bitch*. He had underestimated her — again!

His first instinct was to order a blistering counter-attack, but something made him pause. It was strange, this attack; almost as though *two* people were attacking...

Cautiously, he located the source of the attack — and understood what Margaret was doing. No doubt Margaret's body was close by, but he could not risk accidentally harming the child. Supreme Brother swore.

"Do not be tempted to retaliate, Brothers. This is yet another trap. Do NOT retaliate."

Supreme Brother glanced around, furious at this impasse. His two most trusted lieutenants were absent; Jerome to deal with Tony Baron, Richard on a mission to the American Society.

Margaret Brandon could not keep up this barrage all morning, he realised. She would become exhausted sooner or later. Once she broke the link with her daughter she *must* be destroyed. He had no option, he knew. This attack forced his hand.

***

Tony saw Jerome's eyes widen in surprise. He stared *hard* at Kim, and then at Tony's unconscious form. Jerome seemed to understand what this meant. He moved purposefully to Tony's body. He grinned at Kim as he placed his hands around Tony's throat and began to apply pressure.

The action woke Tony's mind from its paralysis. Cold fear drove him to act. Expanding his control over Kim, Tony *made* her run over to Jerome and pummel him with her fists.

The blows were ineffectual. Tony cursed the limitations of a 10-year-old child's body. Fearing that it might already be too late, Tony did the only thing he could think of. Kim's hands reached between Jerome's legs, grabbed his testicles and then she clenched her hands as tightly as possible.

Jerome bellowed and swung around, his fist arcing towards Kim's face. At the last possible instant he yanked his arm back, suddenly appreciating the danger which he faced. His fist grazed Kim's nose with the merest of touches.

He took an awkward half-pace back, snarling his frustration, pain and anger.

Tony/Kim grinned at Jerome. "*What's* wrong?" Tony taunted him. "Don't you like Kim emulating you? Don't you want to *beat* her or *strip* her *naked* anymore? Don't you want to..." he fought for words, aware that Kim's mind was cringing in the knowledge that Tony *had* accessed her memories and knew of *all* the humiliating things which Jerome had done to her. He could feel her terror, which came at him in wave after wave. He attempted to radiate reassurance to her as he continued: "... to *rape* her? Or would you *prefer* to *sodomise* her? Are you totally impotent when you don't have a child to *defile*, to *degrade*, to *humiliate*, to *murder*?"

Jerome glanced at Tony's body. Quickly, Kim was between him and it. "You're just a perverted psychopath, Jerome. Does it make you feel strong and *masculine* to degrade and defile children? Is that a measure of how *inadequate* you feel? Or of how inadequate you really are?" Tony goaded him.

Suddenly enraged beyond endurance, saliva dribbling from his mouth and falling from his chin, Jerome shoved Kim's body away roughly. She fell.

As Kim got to her feet, she saw Jerome had resumed his attack upon Tony's body. Something within Tony's mind snapped. Savagely, he drew in his will and discharged a thunderous explosion of energy which slammed into and engulfed Jerome.

As though in a dream, Tony heard Jerome *screaming*; he could smell ozone. '*How*?' he demanded of himself. How had he managed to summon and direct such a *massively* destructive force?

The force he had just summoned, directed and discharged in a matter of seconds was more powerful that anything he had ever known, with only *one* exception. But that made no *sense* whatever....

Relegating the question, he regarded Jerome.

He lay either unconscious or dead. Ignoring him, he hurriedly checked his *own* body. The pulse was fast. Bruises were appearing around the neck. Tony laughed in relief. Ludicrously, he wondered if he had had to attempt resuscitation, would he had been the first person *ever* to give *himself* mouth-to-mouth?

Batting down his hysterical laughter, he returned his attention to Jerome.

Kim's fingers felt for a pulse, found none. Jerome was undoubtedly dead. Tony regarded the rictus of agony upon the dead face. Poetic justice he thought, that one who had wallowed in the suffering and torture of others should have died in pain. Kim's mind was very quiet, in total and absolute shock that Tony had killed Jerome.

With an effort, he returned his thoughts to what he was supposed to be doing. He glanced at his watch.

Scarcely ten minutes had passed since Jerome's appearance; but he was still ten minutes late in aiding Margaret. Imposing some order upon his mind, Tony focussed his attention upon the meeting-place.

Margaret had gone ahead with the attack, he understood almost immediately. The Cult seemed happy enough to absorb her assaults without any direct retaliation, allowing her to wear herself down, he assumed.

As Anton had said, the Supreme Brother possessed a deep cunning and deviousness. Tony assessed his chances of altering the current situation as virtually zero if he followed his original plan. The Cult would simply absorb whatever he sent at them. He would lose his element of surprise and exhaust himself for no good reason.

He wished that he had Anton's Ritual of Destruction to follow, but knew that, this time, circumstances were different. Anton could not help them again.

Taking a deep breath, Tony wondered *desperately* what he could do which would be such an insult to the Cult as to lure them to act against him.

Kim's mind began to recover from the shock of Jerome's death. Her mind now radiated terror at the fact that Tony had *killed* Jerome and that she was standing just feet away from his corpse. Kim was equally paralysed with fear at the notion that

348

she might be blamed for killing Jerome.

Tony took the time to reassure Kim that she had no reason to be scared, that he would take care of everything, and *especially* that she wouldn't be blamed for anything which happened.

He regarded Jerome's corpse again.

And again.

A slow smile crossed Kim's face.

***

"Supreme Brother, the attacks are losing frequency and intensity."

The Supreme Brother nodded, smiling slightly. He had completely recovered his composure — outwardly — in the last few minutes. However, inwardly he seethed with barely-controlled fury. "Very well, relax our defence accordingly."

The Brother inclined his head and moved away.

Supreme Brother looked around the assembly again. True, his Brothers had been slow to react, initially, but that was simply inexperience. Now Margaret Brandon was tiring. Not really surprisingly. What, he wondered, had possessed her to believe that he would fall for her *infantile* ploy?

He mused upon this, gaining no clear insight.

"Supreme Brother," a voice shouted, as he himself became aware of the different form of activity near him. He spun around.

Brother Jerome materialised less than two metres from him. "Jerome?" he queried hurrying to the inert form.

Supreme Brother stared at Jerome's face for a long moment. His features softened to an extent which would have surprised Richard, had he been there.

"*Jerome,*" Supreme Brother whispered, falling to his knees. He reached out two fingers and felt Jerome's neck for a pulse. His features suddenly snapped back into their *frigid* mask. He stood slowly, insane hatred filling his eyes.

Not only had Tony Baron killed — *murdered* — one of his

most faithful followers, he had calmly relocated the corpse *here* to demonstrate how much he was gloating over this victory. The thought consumed the Supreme Brother.

Bellowing his rage, he attempted to assess the point from which Jerome had been relocated. He was aided as a Brother called out, "A second attack, from a different location."

No sooner had Supreme Brother located the source of the *new* attack than understood it was Tony Baron himself, attempting to press home the advantage which he had created.

A murderous grimace crossed Supreme Brother's face as he launched a single eruption of unbelievable *power* and savagery at Tony Baron, drawing upon the Patron Demons' *augmentation* of his own capabilities.

He felt the explosion rip away a defensive barrier, which deflected most of the energy, and briefly engulfed Tony Baron, whom the barrier had been protecting.

He sensed that Baron had either lost consciousness, or was too *dazed* to react.

Laughing openly, the Supreme Brother prepared to release a second attack, which would send Tony Baron into oblivion.

***

As he relocated Jerome's corpse, Tony resisted the urge to attempt to gain some insight into how the Cult reacted. He was quite certain that the reaction would come his way *very* soon.

He concentrated, protecting Kim's body from the forthcoming assault. He could feel Kim's mind watching him, terrified by the act which he had committed, and petrified that he might not be able to keep her safe, as he had promised he would.

Remembering what *George* had said years before, Tony began to visualise Kim's body surrounded by a *circle* of energy. The process could not be rushed, and he was very aware that the Cult's response could come at any second.

He completed visualising the first circle, and began to construct a second, when the vitriolic assault crashed into his

350

barrier, tearing it away. Like some out-of-control volcano, the energy erupted into Kim's body, burning her.

Tony screamed, and heard Kim's piercing shriek of pain, feeling her whole body burning. Kim's mind joined Tony's, screaming in *terror*. Only dimly now did Tony hear Kim's voice. The attack dissipated. Tony felt Kim's body fall to the floor. He struggled desperately to remain conscious. If no blood had been spilled, and the attack not categorised as life-threatening, Tony understood that he would have failed *everyone* — again.

He waited for the second attack, which, he knew, would also be the last.

***

Supreme Brother unleashed a vicious second attack. He stood stock still as *nothing* happened. Something was extremely wrong.

The other Brothers — and Sisters — sensed it, too. They glanced uncertainly at each other, and then at their leader. The animation faded from his eyes. Suddenly, he *understood; comprehended.*

He made his way to the chair upon the dais and slumped heavily onto it, the action of a defeated man. How could he have allowed himself to be outmanoeuvred so easily? Why hadn't he realised that Baron was attacking through the girl?

He glanced in their direction as two swirling, shapeless entities slowly materialised. The temperature dropped rapidly. The assembly watched in utter *silence*.

"Supreme Brother, your life — and the lives of all *assembled here — are forfeit.* Again *you have threatened the life of the Baron who is* not *legal prey. There can be no claim of ignorance, this time."*

Supreme Brother took in a deep breath and then inclined his head slowly, knowing that he had lost; that his life, and the lives of all those with him, were at an end. Calmly, almost serenely, the Supreme Brother gave himself up to his Patrons, to whom he had devoted — and dedicated — his life.

Less than five minutes later, the Supreme Brother, and the whole assembly, lay dead in their meeting-place.

Chapter Fifteen: *Evasions*

John and Margaret sat in the living-room, talking quietly. Five days had passed since the Cult's destruction. True to his word, Tony had returned Kim to them, although he had hurried away before either John or Margaret could ask him any questions. He had not contacted them since then, but both felt that he would before long.

"This time, I know they are all dead. I... I saw them die. Even though I hated each and every one of them, it was horrible. I thought it would be something I could cheer about. But it wasn't. I couldn't find anything enjoyable about it. It was appalling."

John bit his lip. "I'll bet it was. There are so many things about all this that neither of us understand. I've tried asking Kim about *what* she remembers, but she doesn't want to discuss it with me. Whatever it was she saw has scared her pretty badly."

Margaret sighed: "Linda doesn't remember anything at all. Definitely a good thing. She could have seen the same things that I did."

John shrugged, "I wonder what D. I. Davies will make of it when the bodies are found?"

She laughed. "No doubt he'll be back here to ask more questions, and he won't believe the answers. I doubt we'll ever convince him — we'll do well if he decides to keep an open mind about it all."

"If he *did* believe us, he'd probably have nightmares about it. The very idea that crimes could be committed and no traces left would give him heart-failure."

"You know, John, I still don't understand what Tony did to make them attack him. I couldn't draw them out."

John threw open his hands. "If we ever see him again, we can ask him."

He stood to answer the door, and returned moments later

with Tony following him. Tony glanced around the room nervously before sitting down.

"We were just talking about you, Tony." Margaret informed him warmly.

Tony favoured her with a quick glance, irritation written all over his face. "I don't want you two have *any* misunderstandings," he said, in a tone which betrayed his loathing. "I've told you that I despise you both, and I do. I've told you that I'd only help for Kim's sake, and that's what I did. *I* didn't change. Nothing's happened to make me change. I haven't gone soft. My feelings for you two are exactly the same now as they were before."

He stopped talking abruptly, turning his gaze away from them to the floor. John glanced at Margaret, sighing heavily.

"Tony," he said, "I understand what you're saying, but why are you saying it? After all we've been through, can't we start again? For God's sake Tony, something like this should bind us together."

Tony was silent for several minutes, then, slowly, he shook his head. "No, John, I don't think so."

"Tony," Margaret interjected into the ensuring silence, "there are some things that I don't understand. Why didn't you attack at the same time as me? Why didn't you create the diversion at the time we agreed? How did you make the Cult attack you? Why did you run away as soon as you brought Kim back? Why did you…?"

"Can women *NEVER* accept something for what it *is*?" Tony shouted back, angrily. "Do you have to know every little detail?" He glared at John. "You know, I actually feel sorry for you. You've got to live with her, day in, day out. Perhaps if you were to *beat* her occasionally, she might learn to keep her mouth shut."

Margaret contained herself as best she could.

John grinned, "I'll *think* about it," he offered.

Margaret glared warningly at him.

Silence returned.

"So, Tony, why are you here? What do you want? You've got the grimoire; I thought that was all you cared about," John observed.

Tony seemed suddenly uncomfortable, "You're right," he admitted. "I came here because I want something. I'll come to that. Give me time. I don't find asking *you* for favours easy."

Margaret looked at him in surprise. John's expression became guarded.

They waited.

Tony took the grimoire from his pocket. He flicked casually through it. "I want you to take care of this: very good care. It's probably the most valuable treatise ever written." He tossed the book towards John.

"But this meant so much to you," John protested, as he caught it.

Tony nodded agreement. "I've copied the relevant sections. I can't keep it with me, it would cause problems. But it must *not* pass out of the possession of the *Baron* line. Linda might have a son, one day. For that matter," he glanced slyly at Margaret, "*she* might have one."

Margaret didn't seem keen about the idea.

"I've another reason for being here; to say goodbye to you. Sounds weird after telling you how I feel about you both, but there it is. Neither of you will ever see me again. At least, it's very unlikely."

"Where are you going?" John asked, "Europe? America?"

"France," Tony said.

"That's not so far," John remarked.

Smiling suddenly, as though warming to his subject, Tony explained: "No, John. France in the reign of Louis XIV. I'm going to relocate through time. Perhaps I'll find peace and tranquillity; maybe even a woman or two who *doesn't* nag."

"Woman or two?" John asked in a surprised tone of voice. Frowning, he added, "But what of causing a paradox? If you

355

did manage the relocation, and started another offshoot of the Baron line..."

Tony laughed. "No chance of that. I'll manage the relocation. Anton detailed the Ritual. It's too exciting an opportunity to miss."

"Are you certain it can be done?"

Tony hesitated, and then for the *briefest* instant, Margaret caught sight of the *old* Tony Baron grin: "If it can't, I'll be the first to know," he said.

"So, what's the favour that you want?" John persisted.

Tony made his way to the cabinet. He opened the glass door and removed a photo of Kim. "I want *this*," he said simply.

Margaret's eyes narrowed. "Why? Tony, I just don't trust you. You're hiding something. How do I know that you don't want it for some underhand purpose? You've done nothing to make either of us trust you. You promise to attack at a specific time and then leave everything to me. God alone knows what happened to Kim whilst she was with *you* - she *still* won't talk about it."

"*Margaret*," Tony appealed, the *first* time since his reappearance that he had called her by name, "this is what I meant earlier when I asked why you needed *every* little detail. If I promise you that I haven't an ulterior motive, isn't *that* enough?"

Margaret thought about it. "No!" she said, finally.

Tony let out a deep breath. "It cuts both ways," he said, gazing at both of them in turn. "You won't see *me* again, *I* won't see you. I won't see *Kim*."

He took a deep, shuddering breath. "And Kim will never have an opportunity to *know* me. You see, I'm her *father*."

As their faces reflected their incredulity, he hurried on: "That's how she escaped from the Cult. They made her bleed, and the Patron Demons relocated her away. We two were the last of the Barons. Kim isn't your daughter Margaret, she's

356

mine. Her mother was a prostitute I slept with, years ago.

"I didn't want to like her, I didn't want to attack through her, but *George* had other ideas. In the few hours I spent with her, she got to me. Do you *really* think I'm capable of harming my own *daughter?*"

John and Margaret regarded him speechlessly. Taking their silence for assent, Tony slipped the photograph into his pocket.

He turned away from them. "One other thing," he added, his back *still* to them. "Don't tell her that *I'm* her father. Not yet. Not until she's old enough to understand that I *didn't* leave her because I don't care about her. I only realised that she *was* my daughter the night she escaped the Cult.

"And I'm not leaving her now because I hate her, or don't care what happens to her. It's all happened too quickly. I'm not capable of looking after her; I've been alone *too* long to change.

"I'm leaving because I know you can provide her with the love and care she'll *need*. It's hardly a job for a cynical, bitter *sod* like me."

He seemed to want to say more, but no more words came. He turned and made his way to the front door.

"Tony," Margaret called after him, "you don't have to *keep* running away."

He hesitated for a *long* time at the door.

"Goodbye," he called suddenly. The door slammed after him.

From the window, they watched Tony cross the road. A few seconds later, he disappeared from view.

"There he goes," John whispered. "We carry on, knowing that the saga is *finished*."

"Do you think he'll *ever* find what he's looking for?"

John nodded slowly. "You know, Margaret, I believe he will," he replied quietly.

***

As Tony Baron crossed the road and turned away from the

Brandons' flat, he *cursed* the strong wind, which caused tears to roll steadily down his face.

The End